The Blind Man's Garden

The
Blind Man's
Garden

NADEEM ASLAM

Alfred A. Knopf · New York · 2013

THIS IS A BORZOI BOOK
PUBLISHED BY ALFRED A. KNOPF

Knopf, Borzoi Books, and the colophon are
registered trademarks of Random House, Inc.

Library of Congress Cataloging-in-Publication Data
Aslam, Nadeem.
The Blind Man's Garden / Nadeem Aslam.
pages cm — (First Edition.)
"THIS IS A BORZOI BOOK."
includes bibliographical references.
ISBN 978-0-307-96171-6
1. Pakistanis—Afghanistan—Fiction.
2. Pakistan—Fiction.
3. Afghanistan—Fiction. I. Title.
PR9540.9.A83B55 2013
823'.914—dc23   2012041083

Jacket photograph © Marc Atkins/panoptik.net
Jacket design by Abby Weintraub

Manufactured in the United States of America
First United States Edition

For Sadia and Nasir

CONTENTS

I

Footnotes to Defeat

But a man's life blood
is dark and mortal.
Once it wets the earth
what song can sing it back?

—*Aeschylus*

1

History is the third parent.

As Rohan makes his way through the garden, not long after night-fall, a memory comes to him from his son Jeo's childhood, a memory that slows him and eventually brings him to a standstill. Ahead of him candles are burning in various places at the house because there is no electricity. Wounds are said to emit light under certain conditions—touch them and the brightness will stay on the hands—and as the candles burn Rohan thinks of each flame as an injury somewhere in his house.

One evening as he was being told a story by Rohan, a troubled expression had appeared on Jeo's face. Rohan had stopped speaking and gone up to him and lifted him into his arms, feeling the tremors in the small body. From dusk onwards, the boy tried to reassure himself that he would continue to exist after falling asleep, that he would emerge again into light on the other side. But that evening it was something else. After a few minutes, he revealed that his distress was caused by the appearance of the villain in the story he was being told. Rohan had given a small laugh to comfort him and asked,

"But have you ever heard a story in which the evil person triumphs at the end?"

The boy thought for a while before replying.

"No," he said, "but before they lose, they harm the good people. That is what I am afraid of."

2

Rohan looks out of the window, his glance resting on the tree that was planted by his wife. It is now twenty years since she died, four days after she gave birth to Jeo. The scent of the tree's flowers can stop conversation. Rohan knows no purer source of melancholy. A small section of it moves in the cold wind—a handful of foliage on a small branch, something a soldier might snap off before battle and attach to his helmet as camouflage.

He looks towards the clock. In a few hours he and Jeo will depart on a long journey, taking the overnight train to the city of Peshawar. It's October. The United States was attacked last month, a day of fire visited on its cities. And as a consequence Western armies have invaded Afghanistan. "The Battle of the World Trade Center and the Pentagon" is what some people here in Pakistan have named September's terrorist attacks. The logic is that there are no innocent people in a guilty nation. And similarly, these weeks later, it is the buildings, orchards and hills of Afghanistan that are being torn apart by bombs and fire-shells. The wounded and injured are being brought out to Peshawar—and Jeo wishes to go to the border city and help tend to them. Father and son will be there early tomorrow morning, after a ten-hour journey through the night.

The glass pane in the window carries Rohan's reflection—the deep brown iris in each eye, the colourless beard given a faint brilliance by the candle. The face that is a record of time's weight on the soul.

He walks out into the garden where the first few lines of moonlight are picking out leaves and bowers. He takes a lantern from an alcove.

Standing under the silk-cotton tree he raises the lantern into the air, looking up into the great crown. The tallest trees in the garden are ten times the height of a man and even with his arm at full stretch Rohan cannot extend the light beyond the nearest layer of foliage. He is unable to see any of the bird snares—the network of thin steel wires hidden deep inside the canopies, knots that will come alive and tighten just enough to hold a wing or neck in delicate, harmless captivity.

Or so the stranger had claimed. The man had appeared at the house late in the morning today and asked to put up the snares. A large rectangular cage was attached to the back of his rusting bicycle. He explained that he rode through town with the cage full of birds and people paid him to release one or more of them, the act of compassion gaining the customer forgiveness for some of his sins.

"I am known as 'the bird pardoner,'" he said. "The freed bird says a prayer on behalf of the one who has bought its freedom. And God never ignores the prayers of the weak."

Rohan had remarked to himself that the cage was large enough to contain a man.

To him the stranger's idea had seemed anything but simple, its reasoning flawed. If a bird will say a prayer for the person who has bought its freedom, wouldn't it call down retribution on the one who trapped and imprisoned it? And on the one who facilitated the entrapment? He had wished to reflect on the subject and had asked the man to return at a later time. But when he woke from his afternoon nap he discovered that the bird pardoner had taken their perfunctory exchange to be an agreement. While Rohan slept, he visited the house again and set up countless snares, claiming to Jeo that he had Rohan's consent.

"He told me he'll be back early tomorrow morning to collect the birds," Jeo said.

Rohan looks up into the wide-armed trees as he moves from place to place within the garden, the thousands of sleeping leaves that surround his house. The wind lifts now and then but otherwise there is silence and stillness, a perfect hush in the night air. He is certain that many of the snares have already been activated and he cannot help but imagine the fright and suffering of the captured birds, who swerve and whistle delicately in the branches throughout the day, looking as though their outlines and markings are drawn with a finer nib than their surroundings, more sharply focused. Now he almost senses the eyes extinguishing two by two.

The bigger the sin, the rarer and more expensive the bird that is needed to erase it. Is that how the bird pardoner conducts his business? A sparrow for a small deception, but a paradise flycatcher and a monal pheasant for allowing a doubt about His existence to enter the mind.

He places his hand on a tree's bark, as if transmitting forbearance and spirit up into the creatures. He was the founder and headmaster of a school, and his affection for this tree lies in its links with scholarship. Writing tablets have been made from its wood since antiquity, a use reflected in its Latin name. *Alstonia scholaris.*

Carrying his lantern he begins to walk back to the house that stands at the very centre of the garden. Before building it he had visited the cities of Mecca, Baghdad, Cordoba, Cairo, Delhi and Istanbul, the six locations of Islam's earlier magnificence and possibility. From each he brought back a handful of dust and he scattered it in an arc in the air, watching as belief, virtue, truth and judgement slipped from his hand and settled softly on the ground. That purifying line, in the shape of a crescent or a scythe, was where he had dug the foundations.

In the nineteenth century, Rohan's great-grandfather had bred horses on this stretch of land, his animals known for their wiriness and nimble strength, the ability to go over the stoniest ground without shoes. During the Mutiny against the British in July 1857 a band of men had visited the horse breeder, the day of the eclipse, and in the seventeen minutes of half-darkness the Mutineers spoke about cause and nation, aiming these words like arrows against the Empire's armoured might. Britain was the planet's supreme power at the time and nothing less than the fate of the world hung in the balance. They needed his help but he told them there were no horses for him to give. The Norfolk Trotter and the Arab stallions, the Dhanni, Tallagang and Kathiawar mares—they had been sent to a remote location to escape the Ludhiana Fever sweeping the district.

As the rebels turned to leave, the ground splintered slowly before them and a crack grew and became a star-shaped fracture. A small sphere of blackest glass materialised at the centre of the star. Then they realised that it was in fact an eye, an ancient glare directed up at them through the grains of earth. A phantom. A chimera. One more instant and the entire head of the horse had emerged from the ground, the large-muscled neck giving a thrust and spraying soil into the eclipse-darkened air. The hooves found whatever purchase they needed and the rest of the grunting animal unearthed itself, the mighty rib cage and the great, potent haunches. Flesh tearing itself away from the living planet.

The ground exploded. A dozen horses, then almost two dozen, their diverse screams filling the air after the hours spent in the dark. An eruption of furious souls from below. The thrown earth and the shrieking of freed jaws and the terror of men during the daylight darkness.

Rohan's great-grandfather had been informed the day before that Mutineers being hunted by the British would attempt to appropriate his animals. Over several hours he and his nine sons had prepared a trough deeper than their tallest stallion and had then led all twenty-five of their horses to it, their black, white, tobiano and roan colours shining in the oblique rays of the setting sun.

The horses were loved and they trusted the masters when they were blindfolded and led into the pit, but they reacted when the men began to pour earth onto them, beating their hooves against the ground as the level of soil rose higher along the legs. Stripes of white salt-froth slid down each body and in low voices the men spoke the phrases or words each animal was known to like. To comfort them if possible. But they continued with the work steadily and with determination all night as the stars appeared and hung above them like a glass forest, and later when a storm approached and the night became wild with electricity, the sky looking as though there was war and rebellion in heaven too, because not a single one of the horses would be allowed to fall into the hands of the Mutineers, who Rohan's great-grandfather was convinced were misguided, his loyalty aligned with the British.

With only the horses' necks remaining visible, the men leapt down into the trench and packed the earth with their feet, running among the twenty-five heads growing out of the earth as specks of soft blue fire came down from the lightning-filled sky to rest in the manes and in the men's own beards and hair.

Allah had said to the South Wind, "Become!" and the Arabian horse was created.

The thought of clemency entering their hearts at last, the ten men went down the rows and placed a large basket upside-down over each head, a hood of woven grass fibres and reeds and palm fronds, a pocket of air for the animal to continue breathing. Then they climbed out and began the final throwing on of the soil, making sure not to cover the baskets entirely, leaving a thumbprint-sized entrance in each for air to slide in. There was nothing but a faint ground-shudder of hooves from within the earth as the horizon became marked with a brilliant red line behind the men and the sun rose and they began to wait for the arrival of the Mutineers, conscious suddenly of their weight on the ground.

Insects are being attracted by the lantern in Rohan's hand as he walks back to the house, moths that look like shavings from a pencil sharpener, and moths that are so outsized and intensely pigmented they can be mistaken for butterflies.

There is a black feather on the path ahead of him, dropped by a struggling bird overhead.

The Mutiny was eventually put down across the land and one thousand years of Islamic rule came to an end in India, Britain assuming complete possession. A Muslim land was lost to nonbelievers and Rohan's ancestors played a part in it.

This was the century-old taint that Rohan had tried to remove by spreading the soils of Allah's six beloved cities here. Mecca. Baghdad. Cordoba. Cairo. Delhi. Istanbul. Scattering them broadly in the shape of the trench in which the horses were interred, the cleft out of which they had resurrected themselves.

3

The boundary wall of the house is draped in poet's jasmine, Pakistan's national flower. Jeo walks along it and enters the room that had been his mother's study. He places the burning candle on the desk, its surface covered with ink stains from her fountain pen. The leaf of the calendar hasn't been changed since her death, the month he was born.

He opens a large book of maps, its pages and his own breath the only sounds in the room. He has lied about going to Peshawar. Wishing to be where he is most needed—to be as close as possible to the carnage of this war—he has arranged in secret to cross over into Afghanistan from Peshawar.

Leaning close to the maps in the frail light, he looks at the geography of the North-West Frontier Province, to where he will be journeying with his father tonight. His eyes move from place to place. Here is the mountain ridge named Pir Sar that Alexander laid siege to in 326 BC—a redoubt so formidable that Heracles himself, son of Zeus, was said to have found it impregnable. And in 1221, Genghis Khan had pursued the last Muslim prince of Central Asia to this place just south of Peshawar. And here is Pushkalavati, visited regularly by Chinese pilgrims during the fifth, sixth and seventh centuries, because the Buddha had made an alms offering of his eyes here.

That he will cross the boundary into Afghanistan is a secret not just from his father. Jeo hasn't disclosed his intentions to his wife of twelve months either, or to his sister and brother-in-law, sparing them all the unnecessary fear. Rohan will go with him tonight to Peshawar and return home the day after tomorrow, by which time Jeo will already be in Afghanistan.

As a child he would fall asleep listening to the stories being told by his father and he would dream of martyrs. He would see them where they lay with their souls just emerging from their bodies assisted subtly by angels and other winged beings, the sun and the clouds red and the birds appearing bloodstained as they flew. And in the dream he would know that they had fought with a fearsome will and a fearsome strength, both of which were not forged by war but revealed by it, placed in their souls long before birth, and as he slept Jeo knew that they were all him, that they were the men he was before he was this man, the ghostly thousands stretching back through the generations and as he slept they imparted things to him not just of life and death but of eternal life and death.

From the book he carefully tears out several maps, and in this light Afghanistan's mountains and hills and restlessly branching corridors of rock appear as though the pages are crumpled up, and there is a momentary wish in him to smooth them down. Laser-guided bombs are falling onto the pages in his hands, missiles summoned from the Arabian Sea, from American warships that are as long as the Empire State Building is tall.

He emerges from the room and crosses the garden, releasing movements and shadows in every direction as he brushes against foliage, looking upwards. Once a bird has become trapped in the initial knot, a series of further knots will be activated instantly, to hold the entire body in place, to stop it from thrashing and harming itself.

On the veranda he transfers the maps to his travel bag. There is lamplight in the window of the room he shares with his wife Naheed, the glide of her shadow across a wall. The light is amber like the colour of her eyes and his mind evokes the dark Niagara of her hair and the weight of her hand on his chest during the night. Desire appears in him yet again today, a wish for her to be within arm's reach, knowing he will not see her for some time after tonight. He crosses the black hallway and enters the room and she turns towards him.

Mikal is coming with him to Afghanistan. It was a chance encounter last week, when Jeo rode his motorcycle out of the house and went towards the other side of the city, along the Grand Trunk Road. There he formally presented himself at the headquarters of the organisation that is sending men into Afghanistan. They need doctors and—although Jeo is only in the third year at medical school, his education anything but complete—they were delighted at his offer of help. The organisation is a charity and includes a madrasa, providing literacy to the children of the poor—twenty rooms, each of them alive with voices murmuring like a honeycomb of warning and praise—and he was on his way out when he saw the figure emerging from a nearby door. The face that held a look of unbreakable isolation.

"Mikal."

If love was the result of having caught a glimpse of another's loneliness, then he had loved Mikal since they were both ten years old.

Mikal looked up and Jeo went forward and they placed their arms around each other.

"What are you doing here?" Jeo asked when they separated. Mikal embraced him again. "I was delivering some guns I mended for them," he said eventually, speaking as always with a gravity to his words, a minute shifting of those eyebrows that joined in the middle. "I work at a gun shop."

Around them the madrasa was noisy with the voices of children who, knowing little but life's deprivations, prayed the way they ate, with a deep hunger.

Jeo did not hesitate in telling Mikal about Afghanistan. This almost-brother. This blood-love in everything but name. Mikal was ten years old when he and his older brother came to live at Jeo's house, Mikal carrying a book of constellations under one arm, the large pages full of heroes and beasts caught in diamond-studded nets. The puppy he held in the crook of the other elbow would have to be given away within two months when it became apparent that it was a wolf. Mikal and Jeo were the same age and had soon become inseparable, a dedication in Jeo for Mikal's watchfulness and self-containment, the grace that shaped his every move, though it was interrupted by short spells when something would madden in him and he would refuse to be found.

"You are going to Afghanistan?" Mikal said when Jeo finished speaking.

"Just for a month. Later I might go for a longer period."

"What about your studies?"

"I'll catch up." Rohan had taken Jeo to watch his first surgical operation at the age of twelve, and he knew at thirteen some of the things that were taught to his first-year class at medical school.

As the motorcycle sped through the traffic—he was taking Mikal to the gun shop—he said over his shoulder, "You still haven't told me why you completely disappeared last year. Missing my wedding. And nothing but a short visit to the house since then. I wonder if you even remember my wife's name."

"I didn't know you were getting married," Mikal said.

Mikal's parents had been Communists, and his father was arrested around the time Mikal was born, never to be seen again. It was the mother's death a decade later that led to Rohan taking in Mikal and his brother. People fallen on hard times would come and ask Mikal to say a prayer for them, because orphaned children were among those beings whose prayers Allah was said never to ignore.

At the gun shop, AK-47s were stacked six high on the shelves. If genuine, these rifles would cost eighty thousand rupees each, but these were replicas at a quarter of the price. The day after the West invaded Afghanistan, a "piety discount" was introduced for those who wished to buy the weapon to go to the jihad. There were reproductions of older guns too, of rifles to be found in the armouries of the Tower of London, .30 calibre Chinese pistols, Argentinian Ballester-Molinas. On the wall was a large photograph of a flock of eagles that had been trained to fight in human wars, the wings outspread at a slant like living book-rests—a dream from the land's past.

The proprietor gave Mikal instructions regarding various repairs and left to answer the muezzin's call. The trigger was stiff on a shotgun and the owner of a revolver wished it to make a louder sound when fired. Prising off the forearm, Mikal unbreeched the shotgun and lifted away the barrel. "So. Afghanistan," he said.

"You are the only person I have told."

"What if something happens to you?"

"Will you come to the house before I leave?" The ties between them had strengthened—Jeo's sister was now married to Mikal's brother.

"Jeo. Something could happen to you out there. You could be killed, or come back without your sanity, your limbs, or your eyes."

"What if everyone began to think that way?"

Mikal's glance remained on him and then he returned to his work. Jeo could sense the careful mind addressing the task. Anything mechanical, Mikal had to know its secrets. Once he almost stole a helicopter. "They should never have left the keys in," he said. "But I thought better when I saw the number of gears." By the age of fourteen he had driven a bulldozer, various cars, a boat.

"You used to make toys," Jeo said.

Mikal leaned back on his stool and, without looking, opened the cupboard behind him and took out a small windup truck. He turned its key several times and placed it on the glass counter. Jeo held the palm of his hand beyond the edge for it to arrive and fall onto.

"Keep it. It's yours." Mikal slid the key towards him along the counter. "What if I said I'd come with you?"

"I don't need to be looked after."

Mikal had thumbed open the gate of the revolver and put the hammer at half cock but now he paused and looked up. "I didn't mean that." He turned the cylinder and ejected the round from the chamber with the ejector rod.

He lit a Gold Flake and said with a grin, "I smoke five a day. My five prayers."

Jeo was forced to smile. "You're going to Hell." Then he said, "Are you serious about coming with me?"

"Yes. I'll go back later today and give them my name."

"What will you do there?"

"I'll carry the wounded to you from the battlefield." And after a while without looking at him he added,

"And I do remember her name, Jeo. Her name and the fact that she is descended from the Prophet."

Naheed lifts Jeo's arm from around her waist. He'll leave with Rohan to catch the train for Peshawar in just under two hours but for now he has closed his eyes in shallow sleep. She buttons the neck of her tunic and is walking away from the bed when a small jolt makes her look back. He is lying on her veil. Moving closer through the candlelit air she sees that he has in fact tied a corner of it to the index finger of his right hand. She releases the knot and her glass bangles rattle as she gently slaps his bare shoulder. He smiles with eyes still closed, the inch-long dimple materialising in each cheek. He had stunned her one day by saying, "I'd like to die watching you."

She looks out of the window, past the low rosewood bough from which a sheep is hung every year to be disembowelled and skinned just minutes from its last conscious moments, to mark the Sacrifice of Abraham. It is bought fully grown a few days earlier but ideally should be raised from a lamb, given love, and then killed. She turns to see him gazing at her. Rising on one elbow he picks up the toy truck from the stack of books on the bedside table. It comes towards her between the clothes he had shed on the floor earlier and goes past and is soon out of sight under the armchair, the sound of its tin gears vanishing suddenly where it must have met the wall.

"Mikal gave me that toy," he says, lying down again.

She collects his clothes and places them at the foot of the bed. She had made this shirt for him—in great secrecy, not revealing to anyone how it is possible that not a single seam or stitch can be discovered upon it.

She takes a lamp from a ledge in the hallway and steps out into the cold darkness. Looking up into the trees. After Rohan and Jeo leave for Peshawar tonight, she will walk to her mother's place a few streets away, but she will return early tomorrow morning to wait for the bird pardoner. Rohan has instructed for all ensnared birds to be set free. "And he must take down the wires. I do not recall giving him permission." She raises her arm and the light from the lamp breaks up into sharp glints on several high wires above her.

She wonders where Mikal is at this moment. In some respects, grief for the lost and missing is worse than grief for the dead, and sometimes just for a fraction of a second its intensity makes her wish Mikal would cease to exist, so she wouldn't have to wonder if she will ever see him again.

"Let's just leave," he had said to her a week before she was to marry Jeo. He had pointed into the night. "Let's just disappear out there somewhere." She had been shocked by the suggestion, but had then agreed, suddenly fierce in her determination.

But on the agreed hour, he hadn't come for her.

She moves along one of the many red paths that wander in the garden.

The crescent-shaped house was the original building of Ardent Spirit, the school Rohan and his wife Sofia had founded. When the number of pupils outgrew it, a new building was constructed on the other side of the river that flows behind the house. This building then became Rohan and Sofia's home.

Decades ago when they formed the idea of Ardent Spirit, Rohan had used matchsticks to explain the layout to Sofia.

It is divided into six pairs of rooms, arranged in an elegant curve, a screened corridor linking them all. Each pair of rooms is named after one of those six centres of Islam's bygone brilliance.

Mecca House is situated amid Arabian date palms that release their fruit onto the roof throughout summer, the dates that are like sweet chewable leather in the mouth. A tablet carrying the name is affixed beside the entrance, reading, *It was in order to determine the exact direction of Mecca that Muslims had developed an interest in geometry and mathematics, and had eventually invented trigonometry.* The words were intended to remind the children of their legacy, Islam's long inheritance of knowledge and achievement.

The calligraphy is in Sofia's hand and its grace makes the reader aware of, and even feel responsible for, the soul of the calligrapher.

Climbing roses curtain Baghdad House, spreading on the walls in lean assessing tendrils, and the undone petals lie on the tiles to return loaned light deep into the evening. The children were informed that in Baghdad there was a "House of Wisdom" as early as the year 830.

Spanish almond trees and carnations grow around Cordoba House. According to the tablet outside it, the flower the king of djinns presented to Solomon, to give to the Queen of Sheba, was a carnation. She would wear it in her hair. The tablet records that the Muslims of Spain had manufactured the first paper in Europe around 1150, and also that in 1221 the Holy Roman Emperor Frederick II had declared all official documents written on paper to be invalid—paper having become associated in Europe with Muslims.

Egyptian blue lotuses stand in crystal-tight arrays in a triangular pool before Cairo House, the blossoms closing at night and sinking underwater to re-emerge in the morning. Cairo, where the "House of Science" was created in 995 and where the Fatimid palace library had comprised forty rooms, its collections including eighteen thousand manuscripts on the "Sciences of the Ancients" alone, the staff comprising mathematicians, astronomers, physicians, grammarians, lexicographers, copyists and readers of the Koran.

Beside that, sheltered by a century-wide banyan, are the two rooms named after Delhi, and next to that is Ottoman House. According to Mikal's book of constellations, in the sixteenth century the clergymen had convinced Sultan Murat III to destroy Istanbul's first ever observatory, telling him that the lenses were peering too far into the secrets of Allah's heavens in the name of progress and science, and would result in divine wrath being visited on his kingdom.

Mikal.

One afternoon just over two months into the marriage, Jeo brought him home, thinking they were meeting for the first time.

She heard him whisper something when Jeo briefly stepped out of the room. He was sitting on the edge of the chair, looking down at the floor. She still had the letters he had written to her in the months before she learned she was to marry Jeo. Several times she had taken them to the river but had failed to relinquish them.

He looked at her and said, more clearly, "I couldn't betray him. He is a brother to me."

She remembers nodding. Concentrating on remaining composed.

They were both silent and eventually, listening out for Jeo's return to the room, she had said, "Nothing can be done now."

"Yes." He had to attempt the word twice and it came out unshapely as though a bone was broken somewhere inside it.

He stood up. "Tell Jeo I had to go."

"It might make things easier for me if I don't see you. I must learn to love him, none of this is his fault."

"I won't come again. I'll try to leave the city."

It was the sixty-sixth day of her marriage and the last time she saw him.

She looks up at the sky. He said Orion was shaped like the cow's hide from which he was born nine months after it was urinated on by Zeus, Hermes and Poseidon. He told her that some Arab astronomers saw a woman's hand dyed with patterns of henna in the constellations Cassiopeia and Perseus, while others said it was the hand of Fatima stained with drops of blood—Fatima, the daughter of Muhammad, Naheed's ancestor.

She hears the two-note call of a bird and, bending into a tunnel of foliage, sets out to search for it, the moonlight pale as watered ink. She stops beside the citrus tree whose branches filled entirely with white flowers Sofia had mistaken for an angel as she lay dying. From their faultless portraits painted by Sofia, Naheed can recognise almost all the trees and plants in this garden, the seedpods and leaves and the berries dense with sugar.

She had also made pictures of living things but Rohan had burned them during her last hours, fearing she would be judged for disobeying Allah, who forbade such images lest they lead to idolatry. The black smoke of the fire had sidled up to her deathbed. The sketch of a bull's skull and that of a fossil from the Bannu hills were destroyed too—these creatures were already dead when she drew them, but they had lived once, and he wished to eradicate all doubt to ensure her salvation. He asked her to tell him where the rest of the paintings and drawings were, to tell him the address of the friend for whose home she had designed several murals. In his fear he had cleansed the house of every other image too, every photograph and picture, even those not created by her.

And then a decade after her death, he saw her looking in his direction through a high window. It was the last day of Ramadan: a group of distinguished citizens had been invited to climb the minaret of the Friday mosque in the city centre, to view the new month's crescent moon. As the binoculars passed over the city he recognised her eyes among the rooftops, the face turned three-quarters towards him, the pattern of her aquamarine tunic. It took him some time to bring her back into the glass and the distance between them was in miles—too many streets and at least three bazaars. Beside her was a giant bearded head, and in her hands she held several flower bulbs with lilies sprouting out of them, and curled up inside each bulb was a very young human infant, perhaps a foetus.

Rohan hadn't known that she had included her own portrait in the mural for the eight walls and two ceilings of her friend's home, the coloured skin of the rooms. Rohan would set out across the city to locate them, systematically entering the narrow lanes and alleyways, arriving at his destination several weeks later. "I have permission to speak about one of the eight angels that hold up Allah's throne," the Prophet had said. "So large is he that the distance between his earlobe and shoulder will require a journey of seven hundred years." And the giant head next to Sofia's portrait belonged to one of the eight angels.

Naheed takes a gulp of air and extinguishes the lamp, standing perfectly still in the night, the smoke withering around her.

She listens, determined to locate the trapped bird that had called out from within the madness of suffering. But there is only silence now, not even a halting fragment. *Ali! Ali! A dervish, having renounced dealings with all words except that one, never utters another, in any circumstance . . .* The sentence enters her mind from a book she had been looking at earlier. Her gaze is drifting across the sky where the moon sits in a great cold ring as she recalls more and more words. *Only one thing matters, only one word. If we speak, it is because we have not found that thing, nor shall find it.*

Mikal has never stopped being surprised at how heavy a bullet is, given its size.

He is in the high room he rents in an alley winding off the Grand Trunk Road. The first time he dreamed of Jeo dying, he woke up to find the air of this room full of his frightened shouts. It was just before the wedding, and the nightmares had continued over the following months.

He takes a bag of bullets and various other items from the cupboard and places them in a canvas rucksack, getting ready to catch the same overnight train as Jeo and Rohan. A Monday evening during a world war. He is wearing a navy-blue sweater and over it the black jacket of a Western suit, and in a holster under the sweater is the M9 Beretta handgun.

His parents had lived in this apartment, and he himself had lived here until the age of ten. Almost two months after his mother's death he had opened the door to a dignified and imposing stranger who wore a *sherwani* frock coat and a Jinnah cap. Mikal remembers him saying that he had come to look at the pictures on the walls, remembers staring at the man wordlessly and then stepping back to allow him in. The stranger was transfixed by one painted woman in particular, the face situated between a high wall of books and a chair. He stood before her as though he wished to memorise her. And then his clothes rustled as he lowered himself into the chair and gently began to question Mikal, asking his name, asking him where the adults were. Mikal, who hadn't spoken since the funeral, told him that he and his eighteen-year-old brother were living there by themselves.

"Mikal, my name is Rohan," the man said. "I am here to take you and your brother home with me." He pointed to the woman on the wall. "She sent me."

Mikal looks at his wristwatch. He heard the word "death" thirteen times in the half hour he spent at the charity headquarters when he went to sign up, and ever since then he has felt himself move closer and closer to the unknown. According to a newspaper a brick from the pulverised home of Mullah Omar has been flown to the United States as a war trophy for the White House. And, according to another, on 19 September a CIA paramilitary officer was told by his chief at Langley, Virginia, "I want bin Laden's head shipped in a box filled with dry ice. I want to show it to the President. I promised him I would do that."

A candle flickers in an alcove near him as he stands at the window. There is no wind and it is dark and the constellations are burning with a frozen fire, dripping fragile light onto Heer, his city. He scans the high view before him to see which other areas of Heer are without electricity tonight. His city within his fraught and poor nation, here in the Third World. He looks into the far distance to the right of him, towards

Rohan's neighbourhood. A memory comes to him of the day he was singing and she had lifted his hands and put them on her ears, one on each side, holding them tightly in place. She stood listening to the song that travelled into her through his arms instead of through air, flowing down his bone, blood and muscle. There was nothing between her and the song but him and it would become a ritual between two lovers, a custom to be repeated and a game of wonder.

Switching on the transistor radio, he lies down on the sheetless mattress on the cement floor and listens to the news, his eyes closed. The Taliban are still in power in Afghanistan but the Americans have sent in Special Forces soldiers—guerrilla warriors who are building alliances among the local population and orchestrating rebellion. And all the while the air and the sky are being traversed by jets and bombs weighing tens of thousands of pounds. And that is where Jeo wants to go.

"Are you sure about this?" Mikal had asked him when he came to see him here earlier today.

"Yes."

"Did you hear how the Taliban are putting inexperienced Pakistani boys on the frontlines, where they are getting slaughtered?"

"The organisation I am dealing with has nothing to do with combat. We are not going there to fight."

Mikal had nodded and said, "All right."

Now he looks at the wristwatch again. Shouldering his rucksack, he pinches off the candle without looking and after locking the door he climbs down the stairs and goes out into the dark street. Remembering too late about the radio, but not turning back. Thinking of it filling the room with song and news until the batteries die.

Any minute now the rickshaw will arrive to take them to the train station. Rohan listens for the driver's horn as he enters Sofia's room and discovers two large books of maps lying open on the table, their colours brilliant even in this light. And even in this light he notices that a number of pages have been torn out of them. He wonders when it had happened.

He touches the colours, almost in farewell. He is sixty years old and his eyes have been deteriorating for almost two decades now. Five more years of looking is what remains, at most. After that illumination will slip into mystery. He must bathe his eyes in belladonna and honey thinned in dew and must avoid light beyond a certain strength, but even now there are durations, each lasting several moments, when a shadow can appear white to him, or the entire sky green, his hands black as coal. There are small indigo shapes like landmasses across his vision. Or suddenly there is a golden absence of everything, a luminous annihilation he perceives even with his eyelids shut.

He has come in here to select something he might wish to read during the journey. This is Baghdad House, wrapped thickly in the rose of Iraq, the two rooms made into one for Sofia. He carries the atlases to the other side of the long interior. Two hundred boxes filled with books had arrived at the house the previous week. The truck driver who brought them produced a letter addressed to Rohan and Sofia. One of their former students—from the earliest days of Ardent Spirit—had recently passed away. He had written the letter shortly before dying and in it he said that the couple had instilled a keen love of learning in him, that he had gone on to collect thousands of books over the course of his life. And these he was bequeathing to Ardent Spirit, remembering how impoverished the school library had been in those days. Twenty of the boxes were placed here in Sofia's room and the rest distributed elsewhere in the house, a corridor suddenly narrowing to half its size.

Rohan places the atlases in one of the boxes. He is accompanying Jeo to Peshawar because he wishes to visit his dead pupil's family there, to express his gratitude for the gift and say a prayer at the grave.

He briefly opens *The Epic of Gilgamesh* and then *The Charterhouse of Parma* and *Taoos Chaman ki Mynah,* and then looks into a book of history while the candle burns in his other hand.

After Granada fell in 1492 two hundred thousand Muslims were forcibly converted to Christianity. The Inquisition had corpses dug up to make sure they had not been buried facing Mecca, and women were forbidden from veiling themselves . . .

He hears the rickshaw driver's horn at the gate. As he secures the windows he looks towards the river where egrets and herons must be settling for the night in the tall reeds and cattails. The new building of Ardent Spirit, situated on the other side of the green, barely moving water, is concrete, glass and steel, but still divided into six Houses. Five years ago Rohan was forced out, the place taken over by a former student who could no longer tolerate Rohan's criticism of what the children were being taught.

He emerges and bolts the door to Baghdad House. He is immensely proud of Jeo's desire to go to Peshawar and be of help. He knows that had he been a young man himself he would not have stopped at Peshawar: he doesn't know how he would have resisted entering Afghanistan. And not just for help and aid—he would have fought and defended with his arms. And, yes, had he been present in the United States of America back in September, he would have done all he could to save the blameless from dying in those attacked cities, partaken in their calamity.

How not to ask for help these days—from others, from God—when it seems that one is surrounded by the destruction of the very idea of man?

He mouths verses of the Koran as he walks towards Jeo's room. It is possible to think of fragrance existing before flower was created to contain it, and so it is that God created the world to reveal Himself, to reveal Mercy.

Once or twice a year, perhaps three times, a woman visits the garden, her face ancient, the eyes calm but not passive as she approaches the rosewood tree and begins to pick and examine each fallen leaf. Whether she is in full possession of her mental faculties, no one is sure. Perhaps she is sane and just pretending madness for self-protection. Many decades ago—long before the house was built, when this place was just an expanse of wild growth—she had discovered the name of God on a rosewood leaf, the green veins curving into sacred calligraphy. She picks each small leaf now, hoping for the repetition of the miracle, holding it in her palms in a gesture identical to prayer. The life of the house continues around her and occasionally she watches them, following the most ordinary human acts with an attention reserved by others for much greater events. If it is autumn she has to remain in the garden for hours, following the surge and pull of the wind as it takes the dropped foliage to all corners. Afterwards, as the dusk begins to darken the air, they sit together, she and the tree, until only the tree remains.

What need her search fulfils in her is not known. Perhaps healing had existed before wounds and bodies were created to be its recipient.

4

When a coin is minted, the devil kisses it.

Major Kyra stands on the roof of Ardent Spirit with the hound beside him. A saluki is said to have watched over the Prophet while he was at prayer, so there is a certain fondness towards this breed of dog in Islam.

He paces the long crescent-shaped roof with his military gait, the tips of his fingers touching the saluki's fur, wet from the long grasses and reeds of the riverbank, and the Ardent Spirit flag shifts in the darkness. High above him in the night's silence he hears clearly a flight of cranes migrating from Central Asia to the deserts of Pakistan, the creaking of wings and a series of thin trembling calls.

Time and again he looks towards the school's old building, the intermittent points of candlelight in the windows. It is home now to the founder, Rohan. Following his wife's death twenty years ago Rohan had signed the school over to a former student, Ahmed, because money carried the devil's taint, because he wished to erase from his life the entanglements of wealth and assets and possessions. Staying on at the school only as the salaried headmaster.

Ahmed died in Afghanistan ten days ago and, as his brother, Major Kyra has inherited Ardent Spirit.

The hound watches the moon as if surprised by it. The mist rises from the river in long winding sheets, appearing chalky above the black reeds. Ahmed was known as Ahmed the Moth, acquiring the name at the age of five at his childhood mosque in Abbottabad. There one day he was told that the bag thrown onto the fire contained money and toys and he had watched it burn, but when he was told that the bag was in fact full of Koranic pages, Ahmed had burnt his hands trying to retrieve it, carrying the scars and the name into adulthood.

Last year during a visit to Ardent Spirit, Major Kyra witnessed a number of small boys emerging from classrooms with bandaged hands. They had been imitating Ahmed the Moth as part of their education.

He knows Rohan's son Jeo and foster son Mikal are on their way to Afghanistan tonight. And he has been given guarantees that they will not return. At least not alive.

Kyra has not slept for almost seventy-two hours. He resigned from the army the day before yesterday, unable to accept the alliance that the Pakistani government has formed with the United States and the West, helping these empires as they annihilate Afghanistan.

Nine-Eleven. Everything about it is a lie, he is beginning to believe. A conspiracy. Flying large aircraft at low altitudes in an urban sky is not a simple thing. There had to be somebody manipulating air traffic control. There had to be somebody who switched off the warning system for the Pentagon. From what he has read and heard it seems that the air force did not scramble for more than an hour. Kyra is a military man so he knows about such basic things. It was all staged, to invent an excuse to begin invading Muslim lands one by one.

He looks towards the arch above Ardent Spirit's front gate. It was removed from the entrance of the original building and brought here when the school changed premises. When Rohan and his wife founded it, the arch had read *Education is the basis of law and order.* Soon the word *Islamic* was added before *Education,* by Rohan himself, apparently against his wife's wishes. Over the years it has been amended further, going from *Islamic education is the basis of law and order* to *Islam is the basis of law* and then to *Islam is the purpose of life,* while these days it says *Islam is the purpose of life and death.*

Under Ahmed the Moth, Ardent Spirit had developed links with Pakistan's intelligence agency, the ISI. Pupils were selected to be trained in combat at jihadi camps run by the ISI, and ultimately sent to carry out covert operations in Kashmir. It was the reason for Rohan's clashes with Ahmed, the reason why Rohan was eventually forced out five years ago.

But with Ahmed dead the immediate link with the intelligence agency has been severed. Kyra could have maintained the connection but he feels nothing but revulsion at the army and the ISI, for abandoning Afghanistan. The Ardent Spirit pupils now belong to him alone and through them he'll set his plans in motion, moulding them to be warrior saints, brilliant in deceit against the West and its sympathisers here at home.

We are not men of hate, but we must be men of justice.

When he arrived to assume control of the school yesterday the older pupils were preparing to depart for the fight in Afghanistan, many in tears at the news of the destruction and slaughter. One million new refugees have entered Pakistan and eight million will require aid. Some of the teachers and the older children were telling stories of rescue and heroism from Islam's past, of populations in distress saved by pious gallants, and the listeners, becoming impassioned, were letting out cries of "Fear not! Help is on its way from Heer!" Hoping to be heard across thousands of years.

In a quarter to the east of the city there is a charity and madrasa which was operated by Ahmed the Moth but is owned by the ISI. The charity is a facade: boys and young men are transformed into jihadi warriors behind it. And yesterday he was brought a stack of papers by one of the people there—Kyra had wished to understand in detail how Ahmed had managed his day-to-day affairs.

The man had selected a sheet covered with names and handed it to him. "The name at the top of the third column."

To Kyra the name Jeo hadn't meant anything, but a sound of surprise escaped his mouth when he saw "Rohan" written in the box provided for *Father's Name.*

"He wants to go to a medical centre near one of the battlefields in Afghanistan," the man said, "without telling his family."

Kyra had stared at the paper. "Why is he joined with a red line to this other name further down? Mikal."

"That is Rohan's foster son. A mud-child and drifter. A disappearer.

I have thought about telling Rohan. I am wondering whether we do not owe him that much because of his former links with Ardent Spirit."

Kyra's fury had surprised even him. The lack of sleep. The manner of his brother's death less than two weeks ago. "This is not the time to be tempted by sympathy and forgiveness," he said.

"Let me say this as plainly as possible. I would like this boy to be sent to the very heart of the war, or bring one of the battles to where he is. Do this in Ahmed's memory. You owe him before you owe Rohan. Do you know where precisely he is going?"

"Of course. We are the ones who are sending him. We not only know the location, we more or less know the route he will take."

"Then do it."

A bomb had exploded in a market in Kashmir, killing bystanders as well as two Indian soldiers. Simultaneously, in another part of Kashmir, a device went off ahead of time and killed the boy who was planting it. When both of these incidents were traced back to Ardent Spirit, Rohan had confronted Ahmed, and Ahmed had let Rohan know that he had long had doubts about the soundness of his faith.

"You promised me again and again that nothing to do with jihad would occur at this school," Rohan said. "You gave me your word."

"I gave it to an infidel."

"It was your word."

"It's who you give it to."

And then Rohan had proceeded to sicken and enrage everyone by saying that he was glad the second boy had died while installing the explosive device, pleased and thankful that he had been spared the act of killing his fellow men. "Allah took pity on the misguided child before he could shed innocent blood."

It was then that he was forced out of Ardent Spirit.

Major Kyra—he must learn to think of himself as just Kyra—descends the stairs into Baghdad House, the saluki bounding ahead of him and turning from the lowest step to climb back all in one smooth motion. As he lights a lamp he catches a glimpse of himself in a windowpane, the face scarred by an explosion during the war with India two years ago.

He thinks of the train carrying Rohan and the two boys to Peshawar at this very moment, and opening the Koran he begins to read. *By the charging stallions of war, snorting! Which strike sparks with their hooves, as they gallop to the raid at dawn, and with a trail of dust penetrate and split apart a massed army! Verily, man is ungrateful to his Lord. To this he himself shall bear witness . . .*

5

Three hours into the train journey Mikal gets out of his seat. Jeo has given him the number of the cabin he and Rohan have reserved for themselves. Four carriages along from where he is. The other passengers don't stir as he moves down the aisles, the noise of the train unable to disturb them behind the thick door of sleep.

Jeo undoes the latch and comes out on his first knock, a tenderness in Mikal on catching a glimpse of Rohan's sleeping form, thin and frail under a blanket on the lower bunk. Rohan doesn't know about Mikal coming to Peshawar. They haven't told him to keep away needless questions, fearing something in an answer might lead to suspicion.

Jeo has the maps with him. Going down the long narrow passage-way, they sit side by side against the Formica-lined carriage wall and examine them with a torch, the night sliding by in the window above their heads. The bright circle of torchlight moves on the terrain making it look as though the sun has drawn very close to the earth, as the Koran says it will on Judgement Day, the height of a spear and a half. Mikal reads the English words on the maps extremely slowly, syllable by syllable. Sometimes letter by letter. The language was the greatest difficulty of his school days. Let alone read, write or speak it, he couldn't remember some of the alphabet the last time he tried.

"I worked with a group of men panning for gold up there last year," he says, pointing to a mountain.

"There is gold in the mountains of Pakistan?"

"In places. And when I was here, this slope, the snow was so heavy on the peaks it drove the wolves down into the village."

"When we come back from Afghanistan we'll go. Have you brought a gun with you, Mikal?"

"It can be so quiet up there you can hear the snowflakes land. I'll take you."

"Naheed will love it."

Mikal stands up and turns to face the window, looking out as the train passes through a station with the bone-coloured lights of houses scattered in the far distance, and the moon like a single luminous music note in the wires beside the tracks, its reflection being creased by the flow of the water in a flat braided river, and the nighthawks are hunting high among the stars.

"Around here is where we'll be." Jeo too has risen to his feet and is pointing to an area on the map just inside Afghanistan. The territory of clans and tribes. Where along with jewellery and land, children inherit missiles.

"It looks like a web made out of rock." Mikal holds the map at arm's length.

Jeo smiles. "If I get lost you'll find me." Mikal knows the names and locations of all fifty-seven navigational stars.

They look out at the darkness.

"What were you doing up in the mountains?"

"Sometimes when I sang, I almost knew. For about half a second, but then it would be gone."

"Your singing told you what you were searching for?"

"Sometimes. Mostly I kept saying to myself, 'You'll know it when you see it.' But I didn't."

Jeo folds the map into a square and takes another from the sheaf and opens it. "You didn't see it, or you saw it but didn't realise that that was what you were searching for?"

"Isn't it the same thing?"

"This is giving me a headache."

"Me too."

Jeo returns to the map. "They are saying the war won't be quick. If Kabul falls, it won't be for at least a year or eighteen months. I don't think the real fighting will start until the spring thaw next year. Western soldiers will just sit on the hills and mountains, eating boiled goat and keeping their heads down around dung fires, battered by winter blizzards." He looks at his watch. "I think I should get back in there soon, Father might wake up."

"I'll come to your hospital late in the morning. Leave the maps with me until then."

"We'll have to visit a bazaar quickly to buy a satellite phone, so I can call home from Afghanistan and pretend I am calling from Peshawar."

Jeo turns to go and he, with a small touch under his arm where the Beretta sits in the holster, says, "Jeo, yes I do have one."

After Jeo leaves he lights a cigarette and smokes it, exhaling out of the window. He picks the lock of a cabin in the adjoining carriage and slides in, moving through its pitch-dark interior, guiding himself with his hands held out like a blind man, towards the mass of plastic lilies he had glimpsed being taken into the cabin earlier in the evening. Two stations along, the son of a feudal lord is getting married and the family has been visiting nearby towns to buy flowers. If they had been real Mikal would have moved by scent. Musk, cinnamon, river-mud, ether, blood, monsoon moss. They grow in Rohan's garden and he takes out one flower from each bundle and returns to the window in the corridor, holding the white cluster of them against his body—an obligatory tithe. Out there is the cyclorama of night and each time the train passes a shanty or a hut he throws one of the large white blooms in its direction, whipping his head to look back as it arrives and sticks in the rotting thatched roof or in the jute sack and cardboard that serve as a wall.

He comes back to his seat and closes his eyes. The afternoon he approached Naheed for the first time—to hand her the first ever letter— she had been waiting for a rickshaw in the shade of a tree. And he had entered that shade, a pattern of leaf-shadow covering them both, but had then stepped back into open sunlight and had even turned the peak of his baseball cap backwards, bringing his features in full view.

The train tracks curve under him and there is a swing of gravity in the blood.

One day—after they had been exchanging letters and meeting in secret for six weeks—she mentioned the beauty of a neighbourhood boy and then quickly offered something like an apology, in case his pride was injured. But he had just shrugged.

"But then I am sure you look at other girls," she said.

He had shaken his head.

"That means you love me more than I love you."

"I know."

The revelation seemed to strike her almost with a physical force. "And it is not a problem?"

"No. I am grateful that you love someone like me at all."

She said that it was after that conversation that she had fallen in love with him completely.

He opens his eyes and looks into the darkness, pulling his jacket around him tighter against the cold.

What *was* he doing in the mountains? By the age of thirteen he had begun to play truant, sneaking on to any bus out of Heer that he could, ending up halfway to Karachi or at the base of K2, wandering with a band of itinerant singers in Southern Punjab and climbing into cinema halls through the roofs, surviving in the Baluchi desert by drinking water from wells dug by smugglers.

Rohan would implore him to say what was wrong, what might be done to make him remain at home, and he followed Mikal one morning when he was fifteen years old and discovered that he had found work as a car mechanic. He would not reveal why he needed the money, where he spent some of his nights, and everyone feared the possibility of heroin or the jihad in Kashmir.

The money was of course for the room he was renting, the high room with the pictures on the walls, with doves and wood pigeons as his immediate companions, in the dilapidated century-old neighbourhood where more than half the lanes had dead ends. Avoided by outsiders because it was where domestic servants and day labourers had their homes, eunuchs and wedding entertainers, beggars and ragpickers, and by implication thieves and prostitutes and other criminals.

"What is the meaning of this?" his brother Basie asked, having tracked him down to the room one day.

"I don't know," Mikal remembers saying, the eyes stinging suddenly. He had hidden his face and begun to weep in the manner of very young children and infants—humans before they have learned language.

Basie came forward and collected him in his arms. That room was where both Basie and Mikal were born, where the Communist comrades of their father and mother had come for meetings, and from where the father was taken away by the agents of the government aligned with the United States, the enemy of Communism.

As he dreamed of a revolution, their father had seen no need to make provision for the family, allaying their mother's and his own occasional doubts by saying, "We don't need to worry about the future of these two. By the time they are adults, life's basic necessities will be free for everyone. There will be no personal wealth and these boys will be equals among equals. Let's concentrate on bringing about that state of affairs."

Mikal more or less moved out of Rohan's house at seventeen and began to live in the room, the others coming to visit him as much as possible. Being eight years older than Mikal, Basie had deeper and more vivid memories of their mother, while Mikal hadn't known their father at all.

Basie would lie on the mattress and talk endlessly, sometimes drinking from a bottle of Murree's whisky he'd bring with him, bought from one of the clandestine bars in Heer where there were locked cages for female drinkers, to prevent them from being sexually assaulted by the inebriated male clientele, as well as to stop the drunk women from killing every man in sight. According to Basie, his smart brother, full of gregariousness and laughter most of the time, with a good-natured swear word in every fifteenth sentence.

"I think he's alive," Mikal said to Basie once when the bottle of Murree's was nearly empty.

"No. He was tortured to death, most probably in the dungeons of Lahore Fort." Basie opened his eyes. "Is that what this is about? You wanted to come back here to wait for him."

"I don't know."

Basie would go back to Rohan's house—having failed yet again to persuade him to return with him, or he would stay with Mikal for days at a time.

Terrified of darkness Mikal never switched off the lights when he slept, and each week he put into a box the money he earned, not knowing what to do with it beyond the few essential needs, holding the meaningless pile of it in his hands one day and looking around at the walls of the empty room. He had placed it in a bowl in the middle of the floor and set it on fire, reducing it all to ash.

He saw her near Rohan's house when he was eighteen, the girl with the serene yellow gaze. He noticed her more and more after that and she was too beautiful for him to think about without suffering, but then one afternoon she had held his gaze. The smile was brief. Nothing when seen, everything when contemplated.

Something in the train's motion as it moves through the night awakens Rohan and he turns on the small light above his head. Jeo is asleep on the upper bunk—the light shines down at Rohan from directly beneath the boy's chest.

Sometimes he feared he was distant from Jeo in his childhood, the boy's existence a trial for him, a constant reminder of his loss, and he remembers asking him one day, "Do you know I love you?" Jeo must have been about four years old and he had dismayed Rohan by shaking his head.

"You don't?"

"No." Then the child began to look carefully at his face, even raising his hands to touch the features. "How do you know if someone loves you?"

He thought it might be an observable mark or seal. Something he had missed.

Jeo's arm is hanging out beyond the edge of the bunk and swaying in the air, and Rohan turns the hand gently to look at the wristwatch. It's almost 4 a.m. Rohan should get up and read a chapter of the Koran for the repose of Sofia's soul.

With a solemn effort he sits up and runs his hands over his face and beard. The sun will rise at six, and the predawn prayers can be said at any time from five onwards.

He stands beside the sleeping Jeo and sees how beautiful he is, how young.

One of his feet has emerged from the blanket and Rohan begins to rearrange the folds to cover it, unable to bear how vulnerable and naked to the world it looks. There is a small rust-brown mole halfway along the arch and it is something he didn't know about his son. The mystery of another human being. The places these feet have trod and will tread, of which the father will have no knowledge. He leans forward and places a kiss on his grown-up son's face.

In the bathroom he performs the ritual ablutions and comes out and begins to read the Koran, asking Allah to look after her in her death, just as He is looking after him and his children in their lives. To forgive her. The subject of the Koran is mankind, and for him the verse that induces most fear is in the chapter entitled *Man*. In itself it is somewhat beautiful, speaking of the rewards awaiting the faithful and the steadfast in Afterlife, but when he had quoted it to Sofia in her dying moments she had corrected a small mistake of his. It was evidence that she knew intimately and precisely what she was rejecting. And there lies the source of his terror for her soul. Sofia had died an unbeliever, an apostate.

Until the time she is resurrected on Judgement Day, she will be subjected to torments, the consequences of her rejection of God. After the world ends she will be cast into Hell. In her last hours he had tried desperately to make her repent. It was a gradual and unsudden thing, her loss of faith, growing slowly around them like a plant, its rings widening.

Apostasy was punishable by death in Pakistani law so it had to remain a secret after she revealed it to him.

"I will continue to pretend for the sake of appearances and for our safety. But I have to share with you the fact that I am no longer a believer."

He invited distinguished clerics and holy women to the house to help her see again the beauty of belief. In his mind he accused her of misrepresenting herself to him before marriage, because he would never have chosen someone with such monstrous doubts. The marriage was in all likelihood null—a Muslim could not remain married to an unbeliever—but he also kept reassuring himself that her condition was reversible, waiting for God to make His presence felt to her once more.

After the first child the doctors had warned her against having another but he was somewhat glad when Jeo was conceived, thinking the marvel of a new life would renew her soul.

He reads the Holy Book, trying not to think of how her beautiful body is receiving injuries inside the ground at this very moment, a toy for Allah's demons. Tortures known as *Kabar ka Aazab.* She is alive down there, fully sensate and conscious, the underworld from where no smoke or cry escapes. A person is brought to life immediately after the grave is closed up and is even said to clearly hear the receding footsteps of the men who had come to bury him.

After her death he gave away Ardent Spirit to Ahmed the Moth, wishing to concentrate on the alleviation of her death-suffering, fully able to imagine her calling out in pain from beneath his feet. There was little time for Jeo and Yasmin, the eight-year-old daughter. He would leave to meet with scholars and seek rare books, pursuing doctrines, commentaries and records of controversies, searching for anything that might absolve her of her sin, coming back from some journeys more shaken than when he had left, at peace from some others.

While he was preoccupied with this, Ahmed the Moth distorted his vision beyond recognition and adapted Ardent Spirit's crescent-shaped layout to his own ends. A green flag was designed with six flames arranged in a curve at its centre, each flame rising out of a pair of crossed swords. It flies on the roof of Ardent Spirit every day, and the boys wear green turbans which, when unwound, reveal the same six swords-and-flames on them. The six centres of vanished glory, whose loss is to be avenged with blade and fire.

In the small bathroom Rohan washes the tears off his face and performs his ablutions again. When the apostate dies the spot of earth which is to be his grave cries out in vehemence and pain, unwilling to receive him. As she breathed her last breaths he had kept asking her quietly, "Tell me what you see," because in a minute, in ten minutes, everything would have become irreversible, because it is too late to repent once the dying eyes begin to glimpse the Angel of Death.

But after two decades of thought he does sometimes suspect that his conduct had resembled sin, the sin of pride. Had he really decided that Allah lacked compassion, even for an apostate? Yes, he sometimes fears that his grief at her death—and before that at her doubts and renunciation—had driven him to something resembling an offence. How can he know for certain that the area of earth that became her grave hadn't rejoiced at her death, "adorning itself like a bride, exulting in having to embrace her soon," as the books of spiritual devotion say about the virtuous?

She had founded the school with him and had taught there but disagreements had emerged very soon and she had finally stopped teaching when he expelled a pupil whose mother was revealed to be a prostitute.

He raises the louvred blinds and looks out at the train tracks and the Grand Trunk Road running along them. Eternity suspended over human time, the stars are shining above the world like grains of light, this world that she had loved and called the only Paradise she needed. Preparing himself for blindness he commits everything to memory as she committed everything to paper, painting the garden's flowers and birds onto his mind, and for several years after she was gone the garden looked as though something important had befallen it. The limes and the acacia trees seemed to mourn her, the rosewood and the Persian lilacs, the peepal and the corals, and all their different fruits, berries and spores, the seeds tough as cricket balls, or light enough to remain afloat for half an hour. Inside the earth the roots mourned her even without having seen her, and the white teak whose bark came off in plates the size of footprints, the lemon tree that produced twenty-five baskets of fruit each year. He was sure that all of them, as well as the lightning-fast lizards of the garden, were mourning her with him, and the stiffly rustling dragonflies and the blue-winged carpenter bees and the black chains of the ants and the tough-carapaced beetles and the various snails. In grief he had whispered her name as he walked the red paths set loose in the garden, and the word had gone among the glistening black brilliance of the crows and the butterflies floating in the sunlight—the Himalayan Pierrot, the Chitrali Satyr, the blue tigers and the common leopard and the swallowtails and the peacocks. She had loved them and the world in which they existed, saying, "God is just a name for our wonder." There was no soul, only consciousness. No divine plan, only nature, and we were simply among the innumerable results of its randomness. Saying, "I will miss this because this is all there is," her last words, and then she had slipped out of his life, consigning him to decades of apprehension on her behalf, because he knew that the soul existed, and not only that, it was accountable to Allah and His providential rage. Unlike her he knew that the dead were not beyond harm.

6

Arriving in Peshawar, Rohan accompanies Jeo to the hospital where the boy is to spend the next month. Afterwards, the early morning sunlight flooding the roads, he takes a rickshaw towards his former pupil's house, to thank the family for the books. It's much colder here in the mountains, 1,600 feet above sea level, and he buttons his coat to the neck and turns up the collar. Out there are mountains higher than the Alps placed onto the Pyrenees. Glaciers that Tamerlane's soldiers had had to crawl over on hands and knees in 1398.

It is appropriate in some ways that the books had arrived in a truck painted brilliantly with mythological creatures, with saints and figures of legend, birds and garlands of flowers. The rickshaw is decorated similarly, and as it moves deeper into the city it encounters a crowd of demonstrators, the roads suddenly filled with men of all ages, holding placards and banners. A display of support for victims of the war in Afghanistan. As the rally grows the rickshaw-wallah has to reduce his speed, and soon enough they can neither move back nor go forwards, and so Rohan gets out and begins to walk with the crowd flowing like a river through the bazaars and streets, the sun falling through the noise and the raised placards. "Why didn't three thousand Jews turn up for work at the World Trade Center on 11 September . . ." someone is asking, while another says, "The West wants to take over Pakistan's nuclear weapons . . ."

Eventually he decides to turn around and make his way back to the hospital, to be with Jeo until the rally is over.

It's past noon when he arrives at the hospital. No one can tell him where he might find Jeo and he walks around the maze of corridors, the wards chaotic because the rally has turned violent out there, resulting in injuries and fatalities, the police opening fire. Parts of the city are an inferno and soon there are flames in the vicinity of the hospital too. He asks for the doctor to whom he had entrusted Jeo and is told to go to an upper level. A canister of tear gas enters through a window and explodes in the staircase, enveloping him in a bitter choking fog. He finds himself trembling with consternation and foreboding, his eyes streaming. Outside slogans are being shouted, about ancient history as well as this week's news, the people of today as distressed about things that happened a thousand years ago as the people who had lived through them. Perhaps more. But with a caustic half smile a nurse shakes her head and says into the air of the room, "Would someone tell the marchers that visas to Western countries are being given away in the next street. That'll disperse them."

He turns into a corridor with a handkerchief on the lower half of his face. The doctor is examining an English journalist who is bleeding from the head and has a broken arm, the enraged crowd having set upon him. He is weak but keeps saying he holds no grudge, that if he were someone from these lands he too would be unable to stop himself from venting his anger at the first Western person he saw.

When the doctor is free for a few moments Rohan reaches forward and asks him about Jeo and is told that Jeo and his companion Mikal left three hours ago. Jeo had told one of the nurses that they were on their way to the battlefields of Afghanistan, had asked what essential medicines might be needed over there.

"Mikal?" Rohan asks. He points to the area between his eyebrows. The doctor nods. "Yes, that's him."

Feeling inadequate and too old for the emergency, he moves towards the nearest phone and dials the number for Mikal's brother Basie in Heer, to ask him for advice, to tell him to come to Peshawar immediately. They must follow the two boys into the conflict and bring them back. With each minute they are moving deeper and deeper towards the war, into the crosshairs of history.

It's mayhem in Afghanistan. The Taliban are ruling with an iron fist, punishing traitors, informers, spies and those inciting rebellion. But the people are rising up, encouraged by America's covert help—the Special Forces soldiers are moving on horseback from village to village, between towns and cities, dressed in shalwar kameez and shawls and woollen caps, emboldening, bribing and arming the population. Ahmed the Moth died there ten days ago while visiting his Taliban friends. A group of ordinary citizens had grabbed hold of him and a Taliban soldier on the street corner and forced them to the ground. Every ounce of rage—every rape, every disappearance, every public execution, every hand amputated during the past seven years of the Taliban regime, every twelve-year-old boy pressed into battle by them, every ten-year-old girl forcibly married to a mullah eight times her age, every man lashed, every woman beaten, every limb broken—was poured into the two men by fist, club, stick, foot and stone, and when they finished and dispersed nothing remained of the pair. It was as if they had been eaten.

7

The door has opened and both of them have entered the future. Jeo sits in the back of the van with Mikal as they are driven through the shadowland of hill and plateau, the use of headlights kept to a minimum so that at times there is no knowing what lies a mere five seconds into the darkness. Later in the night lightning appears overhead and illuminates not only the earth and the clouds but also the place in the mind where the line of fear crosses the thoughts, and the ground glows blue for a few seconds with a crystal immediacy, vistas opening up as in a vision, with black shapes looming in them, shadows perhaps, perhaps creatures who can be fought only with the weapons forged by the spirit, not the flesh, and then as the night deepens the stars come out and wheel overhead, smearing the sky with ancient phosphorescence.

There are ten men and there is silence between them. A few, including Mikal, are in deep sleep. Occasionally, without realising it, one of the waking men begins to read aloud the verses of the Koran he must be reading in his heart and the voice materialises in the darkness and after a few moments is gone.

Jeo reaches into Mikal's bag. His fingers touch the very cold metal of the handgun's spare bullets. Switching on his small flashlight, he sees that interspersed with the maps he has taken out there are letters, and he smiles immediately, feeling as though he's sixteen years old once again, when all the girls were in love with Mikal. He separates the letters carefully and places them back in the bag just as the vehicle enters an expanse strewn with bright yellow packets of food air-dropped by Americans. The packs crunch and explode softly as the tyres go over them, and he pulls out the letters again. A name had caught his eye at the end of the text in one, and now he sees that it is there on another. And another. Suddenly his skin is burning because the handwriting in all of them is identical, and it is hers. It's almost as though Naheed's face appears behind the sentences, the eyes looking just past his shoulder.

Mikal stirs at the noise from outside and Jeo drops everything back into the bag and quickly zips it up. It could be another Naheed. *Has* he recognised her handwriting?

He needs to look at the letters again. He thinks of the night early in the marriage when he had come out of sleep to discover her weeping in the darkness. Months later in the garden he would hold her and she would be smiling and suddenly her eyes would fill up. Was she sorrowful at having forgotten Mikal for a few instants? Feeling blameworthy for *not* loving Jeo?

To look into her eyes was to realise that eyes were part of the brain. Thoughts were visible through and in them. Was he mistaken?

The driver has a handheld Motorola radio with which he is communicating with the other two vans in their convoy. Jeo and Mikal have been told that they can expect to arrive at the medical centre at noon the next day. The other eight men in the truck will go elsewhere.

There are cries of jackals in the distance.

"Are you all right?" Mikal says, draping his arm along Jeo's back.

"Yes."

She is the miracle in his life, granted to him suddenly last year, he who had resigned himself to loneliness, his studies being his primary horizon, knowing he wouldn't experience certain aspects of life until he married after completing his education in his mid-twenties. He closes his eyes, and when he opens them his wristwatch tells him he has slept for two hours. It is still dark but the vehicle has halted on an elevated ridge and the driver has stepped outside, looking around with a flashlight. Jeo thinks of his father. At this hour he would be awake and saying prayers for his mother.

"We are lost," Mikal says, pointing to the stars. "I told him an hour ago but he wouldn't listen. We haven't been going in the right direction for some time." He gets out of the van with his bag over his shoulder and

Jeo watches him talk to the driver, gesturing at the sky and at the maps. Jeo goes out to join them as do the others, each wrapped in a blanket against the cold air, their several flashlights revealing that they are in the remains of a very extensive iron foundry, the surface of the hills for many hundreds of yards covered with the ruins of ancient furnaces made of soapstone, indestructible in the fire, for the smelting of iron ore. Relics of the departed Buddhist races of these lands. The ground strewn with small cubes of iron pyrites. And as they stand there surrounded by the strange earth and the strange sky, Jeo hears what he has never heard before, the awful crump of tank shells, explosions and gunfire in the far distance.

"Do you hear it?"

"Yes," Mikal replies.

"It's a battle, isn't it?"

"Yes."

"It's the world," one of the other men says. "The world sounds like this all the time, we just don't hear it. Then sometimes in some places we do."

There is a string of massive impacts and suddenly he is unable to glance at a spot of earth without imagining pieces of metal speeding towards it, large and small and of all shapes. The moon has long since disappeared but the stars are so many that they are still casting shadows within the roofless ruin, and now everything has fallen silent and from very high overhead he hears the slender calls of birds moving eastwards in faint calligraphy-like lines and strokes, thousands of them amid all the smouldering silver.

"Before we go, we need to refill our water bottles," the driver says. He points to Mikal and Jeo. "We passed a spring a few minutes back. Take the empty bottles from the truck and fill them. Follow the tracks the jeep made in the dust and you will avoid the land mines."

"I'll go on my own," says Mikal.

"No, take your friend. We'll wait here for you."

"I said I'll go alone," Mikal says, with surprising firmness in the voice. "I want Jeo to stay here with you."

The driver walks up to him and grabs him by the lapels with his large thick-wristed hands, Mikal almost losing his balance. They both stand glaring at each other in silent opposition and then just as suddenly the man releases him. "Do as you are told."

Jeo takes Mikal's sleeve in a light grip. "I'll come with you."

They take the two gallon bottles and walk back along the tyre marks through the pebbles and fragments of quartz, primitive limestone and mica, but fail to locate the spring. Just as they are about to abandon the search, however, the sound of falling water reaches them from the other side of a gorge, accessed through clay slates and traprock. They climb down into another geological age and walk towards the water through the scar of a dried riverbed, dwarfed between boulders lying where they had fallen ten thousand years ago.

"Make sure you fill it to the very top," Mikal says as Jeo holds one of the bottles under the vertical trickle of water falling from a hill spur, a rope of thin silk that breaks at the merest contact. "You'd hear it sloshing a mile off otherwise."

His feet sunk in muddy earth, Jeo is tightening the cap back on when he becomes aware of a figure in black sitting on the ground just ten yards away. The man is perfectly motionless with his back to them, but there is no prayer mat under him and he is facing in the wrong direction, otherwise Jeo would have thought of him as someone at prayer.

Keeping the flashlight trained on his back they slowly walk towards him. The small stones that cover the ground shine in the beam of light as if wrapped in foil. They approach through all that moon debris and Mikal clears his throat to alert the stranger. They walk to his front and see that a piece of cardboard is held in place on his chest by the broken-off tip of a spear, driven into him between the fifth and sixth ribs.

Jeo withdraws the spear and blood jets out of the wound onto the lap.

"I thought the dead didn't bleed," Mikal says, taking a step backwards.

"They don't. The right side of the heart holds liquid blood after death—the spear must have punctured it."

He hands the freed cardboard sign to Mikal, who knows Pashto.

"It says, *This is what happens to those who betray Allah's beloved Taliban.*"

Mikal runs the torch into the darkness around them, along the strata of the hills aligned northwest to southwest. "We should go." Jeo takes off his blanket and covers the dead man with it and stands up. "We'll say a prayer for him later."

They get back with the water to find that the three vans have driven off. On the dusty ground—that sends up a puff at the lightest step—the imprints of the tyres stretch away into the darkness, and they stand wordlessly beside each other for some minutes.

"All my things were in the truck," Jeo says. "The satellite phone, the bag of medical supplies, my clothes."

Mikal still has his rucksack strapped to his back and he is looking up at the stars, examining their positions. And all the while, over the ridge, the battles are continuing.

"Something happened and they had to drive off in a hurry. They'll come back for us."

"They are not coming back."

Jeo looks at Mikal. "What do you mean?"

"They wanted to leave us here, that's why they insisted you go with me." He looks into the darkness while he speaks as if addressing the night. "I think we've been exchanged for weapons. Or were we sold for money? The Taliban need soldiers, reinforcements, and I think we are two of them."

"You were talking about this back in Heer. You are wrong."

"I think we should get as far away from here as possible. Someone is coming to pick us up and take us to a battlefield."

"You want to walk out into the night? Are you trying to get me killed?"

"What?"

"Are you trying to get me killed?"

Jeo grabs the torch from him and looks into the darkness with its raw glare and then at his face. "Why are you really here? Why did you decide to come with me suddenly?"

"Have you lost your mind?"

Jeo moves forward and puts his hand on the rucksack. "Give me the maps."

Mikal steps away from him, whipping around. "Let me get them," he says. Taking the bag off and plunging his hands in there with his back to Jeo. Jeo spends his week at the medical school in Lahore and comes home at the weekend—do Mikal and Naheed meet in his absence?

"They know I am not a fighter," Jeo says quietly as Mikal hands him the maps.

"They'll make you fight, Jeo. They've *paid* for you. We have to get away from here as fast as we can."

In the darkness thirty minutes away they find a cave and they send in the beam of light ahead of them, onto the curved walls of rock in which sharply polished pieces of a mineral are embedded, reflecting their eyes and fragments of their faces all the way up to the ceiling—a stirring awake of deep yellow and deep red wherever the torchlight lands. There is a powerfully heightened sense that the two of them have been imprisoned in the mountain and are now moving around inside it.

Jeo gathers an armful of dusty wood and Mikal collects the dried-up swallow droppings from the back of the cave. Taking the spark-mechanism of a dead cigarette lighter from his pocket, he starts a fire and they rub their hands before the flames, run them up and down on their clothing to gather the soaked heat while their reflections look at them from the other side of the mountain.

"Mikal, we have to go back and bury the dead man."

"I know."

To look for more wood Jeo stands up and walks over to the high piles of rocks that lead to the depths of the cave and there he finds an electricity generator and a cardboard box filled with glass lightbulbs. When he returns carrying the box, Mikal is surrounded by a group of armed men, dressed in black like beings provoked out of the absolute darkness. One of them motions with the gun for Jeo to join Mikal.

"What is that in your hands?"

"I just found these. I don't know what they are."

One of the men examines the contents of the box while the others watch Jeo and Mikal with slow movements of their eyes.

"Are you trying to send signals to the Americans?"

One of the men says that he had recently seen a string of electric lightbulbs laid out on a plateau on the outskirts of his village, hooked to a gas-powered generator. The bulbs lay glowing on the ground and then a helicopter had landed, guided by them, and several white men had emerged, wearing jeans and carrying computers and guns and heavy black canvas bags. They had gone away with the warlord who controlled the village—a Taliban loyal who is now with the Americans. The black canvas bags were no doubt full of dollars with which he was bought.

"We have nothing to do with any Americans," Mikal says.

Jeo could have shown them his medical supplies but they are in the van. He tells them that he is training to be a doctor and is here to help his Afghan brothers and sisters.

"So which of you is Jeo and which Mikal?" one of the men asks, looking at them carefully. "We were told one of you knows the language of stars."

"How do you know our names?"

"We met the convoy you were with. Now you will travel with us." Half the light from the coloured mirrors scattered on the cave wall has been obscured by the black the men are wearing.

Outside there is a glowing shiver of the unrisen sun in the darkness to the east and the morning star has climbed higher. Trucks are parked among the boulders and their occupants get out and embrace Jeo and Mikal, calling them "brothers." Everyone says the predawn prayers with their faces turned to the dense blackness in the west.

A long fan of light comes from the sky when the sun rises and they get into a truck and the convoy moves onwards. The metal roof is perforated with a line of evenly spaced bullet holes, where one of the boys had madly opened fire at an American helicopter overhead, unable to contain his rage.

"How old are you?" Mikal asks the boy next to him.

"Sixteen."

Mikal reaches out and feels his throat for the Adam's apple.

"You are twelve. Thirteen at most."

. . .

Full of courage and sense of duty, the new boys are fighters and veterans of various jihad training camps. They have a feeling of relief and a subdued stimulation in them at the prospect of holy combat drawing near, their clothes marbled with sweat and dust, their shoes in disrepair, their skins deeply weathered. They talk earnestly about the Crusades and jihad, of legendary weapons and famed warriors, and they are from all parts of Pakistan and the wider Muslim world, Egyptians, Algerians, Saudi Arabians and Yemenis, between the ages of sixteen and twenty-five, recruited through a fatwa issued by the Saudi cleric Sheikh al-Uqla, a fatwa praising the Taliban for creating the only country in the world where there are no man-made laws. There are Uzbeks and Chechens also and a group from northern England, several of them with turbans wound around baseball caps so they are easy to remove. Among them though there is one Pakistani who just wants to catch an American soldier and collect the bounty being offered by Osama bin Laden, one hundred thousand dollars per soldier, more than a million rupees.

Interrupting the journey only to say the noon and afternoon prayers, they travel all day and in the evening they arrive at a mud-built village on the lower slope of a hill. The fort at the top is the area's Taliban headquarters and they drive through the village towards it, the speed reduced due to the narrowness of the streets, men and women withdrawing to either side on seeing the Taliban vehicle, hugging the walls with eyes lowered. The doors and windows of many houses have had splinters torn out of the wood by bullets and in one place a number of people have been lined up and shot in recent days, their blood remaining in bursts on the walls. One of these is at the height of a child's head.

A grey dog yaps at the truck and a Taliban soldier jumps down and delivers it an expertly placed kick under the jaw and then, when it recovers and snarls back, shoots it dead with his AK-47, the truck coming to a sudden stop and the driver leaning his head out of his window to assess the situation. He tells the soldier to get back in but just then a small metallic sound issues from the burka of one of the women standing against a wall—a bangle or an earring. An item of *audible* jewellery. The driver reaches under his seat and takes out a leather whip with dozens of coins stitched along its length. He gets out with the two-yard-long instrument and, enraged, demands to know who it is that is wearing the loud jewellery, attracting the men of faith by her wiles.

"Who is it?"

The women huddle together and the driver whips this mass of dirty blue fabrics several times, running around to aim at whoever cries out, while with the stock of his AK-47 the other soldier tears open the head of the man who dares to intervene.

"Are you a Muslim or aren't you? Does Allah forbid women from such things or doesn't He?"

The fighters in the truck view the punishment with a sense of justice on their faces and one of them beseeches Allah to prevent everyone from sinning.

Mikal touches Jeo's sleeve. "To your left." His lips barely move. Jeo glances in that direction but is not sure what he is looking for.

"Did you see him?" Mikal whispers. Jeo shakes his head.

Mikal looks quickly. "He's gone."

"Who?"

"An American."

The white man was in an upper-storey window on the other side of the street. It was a fleeting glimpse, and suddenly the air had become much colder for Mikal. They are here. *They are organising an attack on the Taliban headquarters—the place where he and Jeo are being taken.*

As they move on towards the fort, another thin dog appears and follows them for a distance and then stands watching them. There are tank tracks in the dust leading out of the fort's tall arched gate. The truck goes through it and stops before a complex of buildings inside, the gate closing behind them, and they climb out stiff-limbed.

Jeo is taken away immediately to tend to a group of injured Taliban soldiers. His eyes hot from fatigue, Mikal assesses the boundary wall—it is at least thirty feet high and twenty feet thick, and along the parapet there are holes for guns, wide enough to accommodate the swing of a barrel.

He doesn't see Jeo until everyone gathers for the night prayer at the fort's mosque.

"There are just over a hundred and twenty men here," Mikal tells him. "There were many hundreds until two days ago but they have gone to reinforce an important battle a few villages away, taking tanks and armoured vehicles."

"Tell me about the American."

"This place will be attacked."

"I heard a few al-Qaeda members were here," Jeo says. "But they disappeared very soon after 11 September."

"We could try to steal a truck."

The fort is—it must be—the most hated and feared place in the region. The people in the village will show no mercy when they come in with American reinforcement and weaponry.

"In the morning I will ask them for a gun and I want you to learn how to fire it."

"No."

"Jeo. I am not going to shoot anyone either if I can help it. I just want you to memorise how the gun works and keep it with you."

"When the attackers see a gun in my hand they'll think I am the enemy."

"They are not going to be that discerning. You saw how these Taliban treat them. They will not leave even a sparrow alive in this place."

Mikal awakens with the sense that someone is looking at him through the darkness. They are sharing the sleeping quarters with a group of young men, the mattresses greasy and infested. A hand has brushed his face, perhaps a fingernail has come into contact with a metal button on his coat. He was using his rucksack as a pillow and now realises that it is missing. He puts his hand into his pocket and brings out the flashlight. Muffling its light by cupping a palm over the glass, he raises it in the air, a glowing stone in his hand. Sending a spray of light over the sleeping bodies. Jeo isn't in the room.

He steps out into the night, being tracked by the moon as he walks across the vast courtyard, keeping the flashlight's beam turned to the ground as much as possible. The area enclosed by the fort walls is the size of a neighbourhood—there are stables, plots of corn and wheat, and there is a stream and a rose garden. "Jeo?" he whispers repeatedly. He tries the door handles of the trucks parked near the gate but all of them are locked, the metal freezing to his fingertips. One stable is filled to the rafters with weaponry—grenades, rockets and firearms, crates of ammunition, anything made for killing, even Lee Enfield rifles with dates stamped on the bayonets—1913—from the time that the British were contesting the area. He washes his face from the stream to remain focused. Walking back through the rose garden he finds a letter torn in half—written a year ago by a woman in the village below, addressed to the United Nations, saying she's a teacher and is in Hell, *it is my 197th letter over the past five years, please help us . . .* He looks up into the darkness above the world and orients himself by locating Cassiopeia in the north and the two fused diamonds of Orion to the west, staring as if the secret design of the world will be revealed to him. To the east is the planet Venus.

"Jeo?"

The Angel of Death is said to have no ears, to stop him from hearing anyone's pleas.

"Yes."

Mikal locates him with the light. "Do you have my bag?"

"No. I thought you went away with it somewhere."

"It's gone."

"You are an accursed liar." The voice comes out of the black air. Two men with Kalashnikovs appear before them. "What are you doing out here?" The words issue on gleaming vapour.

"We couldn't sleep."

The men come forward. They are in Pakistani dress but one of them is clearly an Uzbek. He says to Mikal, in Punjabi, "We asked you if you had any maps and you said you didn't. We found them in your bag just now."

"They are his, not mine. You asked me not him."

"I gave them to him for safekeeping," Jeo says.

"Do you—either of you—have any money?"

"Just a small amount to get by."

"No dollars?"

"No. No dollars."

"You are an accursed liar."

The other says, "What are you doing out here in the middle of the night? If you were in our place wouldn't you think you were spying for the Americans?"

"We just came out here to talk. We did not want to disturb the sleepers."

"Why are you looking up? Are you expecting American planes? Why didn't you want us to have the maps? Your brothers and sisters are being murdered all across Afghanistan as we speak and you are too selfish to help."

"That is not true," Jeo says. "We are here because we want to help."

"Selfish people like you are the reason Islam is in the state it is."

"Just give me one map and you can keep the rest."

"People who don't want to make sacrifices," the Uzbek says contemptuously. "Now go back in and don't come back out again."

They return to their mattresses, not stirring until just before dawn when in the bitter cold everyone walks to the mosque to say their prayers, and as the sun rises the fighters begin their exercises with cries of "God is great!" at every exertion, firing bullets into telephone directories of Pakistani cities soaked in water, proof that the Taliban were supported and funded by the Pakistani government and military, and then, exactly what Mikal has been expecting, the Taliban announce that an informer from the village has just sent news of an imminent attack on the fort.

Evacuating is an impossibility since the paths out of the fort have been blocked. Out there is the gathering of half a dozen villages from the surrounding area, a flash of bayonets in an unbroken circle around the base of the hill.

There is a day moon composed of white ash in the sky.

Mikal feels the whole mass of the war bearing down on them with nothing but their bodies and selves to hold it at bay. He needs the spare bullets for his Beretta and must look for his rucksack, asking around and almost breaking into a run as he moves from location to location. The fort was used in the 1980s by Soviet soldiers to torture and imprison the population, and there is graffiti in Russian on several walls. Someone told Mikal yesterday that there is a skeleton chained to the wall in an underground chamber, making him think of his father in Lahore Fort.

"Your friend Jeo was also asking about the rucksack just now," one man tells him, opening the door to the arsenal Mikal saw last night— the weapons are soon piled up under a mulberry tree, clusters of them dragged zigzagging across the dust so that they leave a wide trail. He stands still for a few moments, looking at it, trying to bring clarity into his mind. And then as he hurries forward he remembers following the adder-like trace that a holy man had left in the streets—a fakir, a travel-ler. Mikal was about eight years old and he had overheard someone say that the holy man had a certain resemblance to his father, with his head of a sad and wise lion. As penitence for a grave transgression in the past, the mendicant wandered around Pakistan with massive lengths of chain wound about his body, dripping in loops from his neck and wrists, and trailing behind him from his ankles, and Mikal had set out to look for him, following the trail of him for miles, but unable to find him. It was the first time he had strayed from home, Basie and his mother frantic in the painted rooms.

"Half these boys are not soldiers," Mikal says to a Taliban leader. "They'd be better off lying low."

"They will be better off but not our cause," the man says. "Everyone has to fight." And he adds with finality, "Allah has plans that include this."

His mind fails to locate intimations of a higher order behind any aspect of this place, a site all the more crude for its distance from the real world, a cold and barren frontierland of life.

From the weapons under the mulberry tree—the sun has broken

the chill of the various metals and a butterfly has appeared to collect warmth from a trigger guard—he picks up two Chinese Type 56 SMGs and begins to look for Jeo. The mulberry leaves—with their outlines composed of many sudden curves—have always made him want to draw them. No wonder Jeo's mother couldn't resist making paintings of them.

In the sleeping quarters he places one of the guns on the floor and examines the other, looking up when Jeo appears in the doorway.

"Pick it up," he points at the SMG at his feet. "I'll make sure you don't have to use it. I'll do whatever I can. But if there is no alternative I want you to know what to do."

He can hear boys shouting "Allah is great!" out there.

Jeo remains where he is, staring at him from the door. There is a paper in his left hand, half crumpled up in the fist.

Mikal walks towards him with the SMG held out. "You must try to shoot a gunman under the nose. The bullet will go through and sever the brainstem so the hand will be paralysed and won't pull the trigger, not even in reflex." Working together they had built a computer when they were twelve years old. He closes Jeo's fingers around the gun. "Keep your right hand here . . ."

A drop of water falls onto his wrist and he looks up, puzzled, seeing Jeo's eyes full of strange light.

"My father . . ." Jeo says.

"What?"

Jeo raises the hand with the paper and Mikal sees that it is one of Naheed's letters.

"My father . . ." Jeo says again, pulling out the others from his pocket.

"The letters are old, Jeo. From before you two were married. You can check the dates."

But Jeo's mind is on something else. "My father . . ." He is trembling, breathing fast as he looks at Mikal with terror in his face.

"My father caused my mother's death?" Rapidly he goes through the letters. "It says here . . ." He can't find the one he is looking for and then releases his hold on all of them, letting them fall as he looks at him and asks pleadingly, "My father killed my mother?"

Mikal shakes his head. "That's not what happened."

On his knees among the scattered papers, Jeo pushes some aside to uncover others, reading disjointed phrases from them, searching both sides of the sheets. "She was dying and he didn't want her to be damned eternally. He withheld her medicines till she let go of her doubts, forcing her to embrace Allah once again before it was too late. Some people say she had a heart attack during those moments . . . The sudden lack of drugs . . ." He raises his hands to his forehead. "Oh God. Why did you read them?"

He moves towards him but Jeo lets out a strangled bark. "Get away from me."

Mikal stops.

"Naheed." Jeo drops the letters, one of which has seven coloured flowers glued to it like stains on the page. She had gone to collect them from Rohan's garden, without knowing she would marry Jeo within months.

"She loves you," Mikal says.

Jeo gets up and pushes him hard into the wall. "How do you know?" The shock emptying the breath out of Mikal, his head slamming against the deep blue paint and Jeo has now picked up the gun and is trying to work it, keeping it pointed at Mikal. The gun is capable of firing four hundred bullets every minute and it goes off eventually, Jeo's finger pressing the trigger for two or three seconds, a duration long enough to release thirty bullets, gouging a curved line of chips from the wall behind Mikal.

For a while Mikal's wildly beating heart is the only point of reference in the formless darkness that has filled his eyes. The empty cartridges fall to the ground like a chain rattling. You told the mendicant to add a link to one of the chains hanging on his body for your sake, a link representing a need of yours, a wish. And as he wandered through the land he prayed for the need to be alleviated. When and if it was, the link disappeared miraculously from about the fakir's person, the chain shortening. To him it was proof that Allah had taken pity on him and somewhat lightened his burden, that he was forgiven a little for his transgression.

And now they hear, both Mikal and Jeo, what they hadn't before—

the rocket-propelled grenades being fired into the fort's main gate. They hear the splinters exploding from the wood as the gate begins to cave inwards.

There are a few seconds of utter silence and then more than a thousand attackers penetrate the smoke and dust, firing and being fired on, kissing their guns before pulling the triggers, both sides shouting Allah's name. A panic spreading like a flicker in a shoal of fish whenever there is a sound from an unexpected direction. Noises from the mouths of humans and the mouths of guns. In the form of screams, in the form of bullets, as if the men are shouting at the weapons and the weapons are shouting back. Mikal knows they will be in this room in less than five minutes.

"Remember," he tells himself. "Short controlled bursts." He turns around to where he last saw Jeo, a second or a lifetime ago.

Jeo is motionless and then begins to collect Naheed's letters. Calmly walking across the room to place them in an alcove.

Six Taliban men enter and bolt the door from the inside. Eight humans and their fate. "Not one of you is allowed to die until he has killed twenty of the enemy," one of them says; he was the driver who brought them here, the owner of the leather lash reinforced with Saudi coins.

Mikal crouches by the window and raises his head to look out. Rooms, trucks and trees are on fire, as is the golden dome of the mosque, and he cannot believe the intensity of the fight, hundreds of guns firing at the same time. The attackers are advancing and are being brutal with each person they find. They had expected more Taliban in the fort, and—disappointed at the small number—they are pouring the rage and violence and metal meant for several men into just one. Each man is dying ten, twenty or thirty deaths.

Someone is trying to break down the door, the wood receiving forceful blows. And all the while someone injured out there is screaming with pain, "Help me, somebody help me, somebody please help me!"

A rocket-propelled grenade—fired from the other side of the courtyard—lodges itself in the room's wall, emerging halfway into the interior without going off. It remains there and begins to vibrate. Grit and plaster falling to the floor and onto the man standing directly below it. He—and Mikal and Jeo, and everyone else—watch the grenade with rapt fascination for a few seconds, everything reduced to fear and marvel. It should've exploded but it can't because the wall is constraining it. It begins to burn instead, sending a stream of brilliant liquid flame and metal directly onto the chest of the man below with a piercing whistle. The man's torso melts, is consumed, and the rest of him falls backwards and the blinding red and white lava continues to shower onto him, the high-pitched sound echoing off the walls.

The second RPG comes and gets stuck in the wall directly above Jeo and Mikal, vibrating again but without any loudness. Nothing except a hum, the sound of a finality beyond all illusion. Mikal breaks out of his paralysis and moves Jeo and himself from under it. Because there hasn't been a blow on the door for a while Jeo opens it and looks out while Mikal reaches for Naheed's letters. The base of Mikal's neck erupts in blood, Jeo looking back and seeing him fall. The corridor outside is filled with dense smoke and the young woman who comes rushing out of it towards Jeo wears a look of wildness on her face, her eyes crazed with a radiant power. When was the last time he saw a woman? The tip of the foot-long dagger enters Jeo's face through the left cheek—going through the gap between the lower and upper jaw. The sharp metal cuts through the roof of the mouth and reaches under the brain. The blade grates against the bone of the skull that it splinters, and it grates again immediately afterwards when she pulls it out. He hears both sounds—from the inside, between the ears. The pain is something he could not have imagined. "This is for what your people did to my man," she says, armed with love's vengeance. Part of his mind remarks on the woman's beauty, notices the blossoms on her dress. He has fallen with his face to one side and he sees Mikal lying prone on the other side of the room, the red coming out of his mouth as though it is something he is saying, his last words.

How easy it is to create ghosts, he thinks as he begins to die a minute later, feeling his mind closing chamber by chamber, the memory of Naheed contained in each one. And despite it all it means much to have loved. Just before the world vanishes, a hope surfaces in him that this wasn't necessarily everything, that he will return somehow.

His arm rises, remembering when it used to be a wing.

8

"Night" was the word employed for the long period during which Muhammad did not receive a revelation from Allah.

Naheed lies awake in her mother's place, looking into the darkness. Five days ago there was a telephone call from Rohan in Peshawar, saying Jeo and Mikal had disappeared towards Afghanistan. Basie and his wife—Jeo's sister Yasmin—had immediately set off for Peshawar to join Rohan. They are still there, searching, and they ring Heer every evening but don't have any news.

The clock sounds its alarm to awaken her mother, Tara, for her predawn prayers. The amplified call from the loudspeakers attached to the mosque's minarets cannot be relied upon, because electricity is sometimes absent. So Tara sets the alarm as a precaution.

But Tara remains asleep now. This happens on occasion, when she has stayed awake late into the night with her seamstress work, her back bent over the sewing machine.

Naheed will not rouse her. So what if she misses a prayer? Allah understands. Sometimes Naheed even gets up during the night and switches off the alarm so it won't go off. Let her rest.

Naheed sits up, with a need to be in the room where she sleeps with Jeo. There is a series of minute scars where her glass bangles had broken accidentally against his chest on the wedding night. Where the skin on a man's body is soft, it is softer than any place on a woman's body. She had discovered this fact by touching Jeo.

Invoking protection from the angel who looks after the fifth hour of the night, she steps out into the darkness. From the balcony she looks down, hearing the splash of water as the owner of the building, Sharif Sharif, performs his ablutions downstairs. Freezing in winter, burning during the summer months, Naheed grew up in this first-floor room that Tara rents from him.

Descending noiselessly she raises her hand to undo the latch of the front door.

"Where are you going at this hour?"

She doesn't turn around. "I need to go to the other house for something."

"At this hour?" he says behind her. "Wait, I'll come with you."

"There is no need, it's only a few minutes away."

Arms and shoulders as powerful as a gravedigger's, Sharif Sharif's large body is taut with animal life, erect and distinct in its bearing. As Naheed had entered her teenage years his conduct towards her had taken an inappropriate turn. One day last year he came upstairs with a book and asked her if she knew the meaning of the English word he had underlined. When Tara returned from her errand, Naheed told her about the incident. Tara had reacted calmly but it was obvious that she was frightened. After several hours of careful thought Tara had gone to see Rohan, who—and Naheed was unaware of this—had promised some years ago to make Naheed his daughter-in-law. "I am too old and weak to look after her now," Tara said. "She's eighteen, a grown woman, and she belongs to you. I beg you to do something." Her acute trepidation meant that Jeo and Naheed were married within a fortnight, and Naheed moved away to live at Rohan's house.

She is not sure if she is being followed. It could be the sound of her own feet echoing differently in the silence, more audible than they are during the day. She quickens her pace and takes the next turn, and looking back she is sure she can see a figure in the shadows a few yards behind her. Resisting the thought of breaking into a run, with her veil floating off her head, she goes past the shop that djinns are said to visit in the dead of night, to buy incense sticks and perfume. A hope surfaces in her that the neighbourhood watchman might be making his last rounds in the vicinity. The English word Sharif Sharif had underlined was *Nude.*

The air is cold and blue and the street appears white as salt in the moonwash. As she is unlocking the padlock on Rohan's gate, a grey saluki appears and stands looking at her from the other side of the street. The animal tilts its head and then perhaps a man appears and stands behind it, and the next time she looks they have both vanished. Blackness nestling within deeper blackness around her, she walks through the garden, the paths forking, returning, disappearing in every direction, the shadows washing over them, and there are movements and sounds overhead but they could be the birds trapped in the snares. The bird pardoner has not returned to the house as he said he would. The earliest birds must have been caught the day Jeo left and they must be long dead by now.

She bolts the bedroom door. She leans closer to the windowpane to look at the garden, the paths that at night lead to the constellations in the pond or the shattered reflection of the moon when there is a moon. Crossing the tiled floor of the veranda the saluki stops and looks in her direction and she stills herself, unable to recall if dogs have night vision. The hound moves on but she is not sure if she isn't hearing its sporadic growl, isn't sure she is not hearing intermittent human footsteps just outside the room.

The sun has risen and she is carrying a chair through the garden. She places it under the large Persian lilac tree, against the trunk twisted as though struggling with some unseen force. Standing on the chair she looks up into the high leaves made luminous by the early morning light. The brilliant rays fall onto her face as patches of heat. A pair of scissors in her mouth, she reaches up and begins to climb, her soles against the roughness of the bark as her hands grab on to the branches and knotholes, branches thick as human limbs, making her feel she's being helped up. There is a massed chatter of birds, but there is no way for her to know which of the songs are those of free birds, responding in elation to the coming day, and which those of the trapped, calling out in distress. How many songs are missing from the chorus she is hearing? She doesn't know.

She climbs higher into the mighty sighing organism. Arriving inside the canopy she looks around and realises the sheer size of it, sees all around her the several dozens of captive birds. Some are upside down, hanging by the claws, by the wings, hanging with nooses around their necks. The brightness of the eyes has become opaque in several, the insects roaming over the bodies, the ants entering the open beaks or disappearing under feathers. But others are struggling. A golden oriole beats its wings like a wind-maddened fire. A few others are motionless but begin to strive when they feel her. She can identify the sound of flies in her ears.

In momentary madness she tries to whistle, thinking it would calm those who are panicking at her presence, making them think she is one of them, but her mother had thought whistling rakish and had discouraged it, and so now she cannot manage it.

Becoming sure of her balance inside the seldom motionless sea of leaves, she leans forward with the scissors and cuts a wire so that the green bee-eater, spinning slowly in the air by its claw, falls onto her other hand. She blows her breath onto it gently and sees how delicate it is, how small. She places it on a branch and slowly moves her hand away. It remains sitting low on its claws for a moment and she gives a small cry when it falls off and lands on the ground thirty feet below, and the jerk she gives makes her head touch a wire and a knot appears and closes around a trailing lock of her hair. A large heron crashes into the canopy as she is freeing herself, the sandy-gold beak coming at her like a lance. She sees the knot closing around its neck to trap it, feels the wind from its ghostly white wings on her face.

The nearer she gets the more it struggles, the noose tightening so that blood issues and lands with a sound on the leaves below. As fast as she can she cuts away the wirework, ignoring the black vulture, the fierce beak as thick as her wrist—they can swallow bones, she knows. It has come to consume the dead birds and inside its eyes moves the knowledge of another world.

Holding the blood-drenched heron against herself with one arm she begins to climb down, suddenly aware that she has been hearing a knock on the gate for some time, realising also that the sound of the flies had disappeared a minute or two ago, as though they had gone elsewhere.

"Is this the house of a Rohan-sahib?" the man asks when she opens the door.

Buraq—the winged, woman-headed horse that took Muhammad to Paradise from the minaret in Jerusalem—is painted on the side of the truck parked behind him. Flying through a rain of roses.

"Yes. But he's away," she tells him. "Have you brought us more books?"

"Books? No, I have the body of his son in there." He looks at the piece of paper in his hand. "Jeo, his name is, it says here."

The heron falls onto the ground and makes no effort to stand, its bleeding neck slowly relaxing along the ground. The man is saying something and pointing to the back of the truck whose tailgate has been dropped for two other men to take out a body lying on a cot. Draped in a white sheet.

Naheed looks to either side of her. It is an ordinary morning. The sound of a radio is coming from an open door on the opposite side of the street—a woman listening to music as she does housework. Sure enough, the woman comes to the door holding a dripping broom and stands watching the body being borne towards Naheed, raises her hand to her mouth, and then goes back in and the music is switched off. Confirming the disaster for Naheed. Two vultures are sitting on the roof of the house next door and Naheed watches as another raises its head from the top of the truck.

The body is coming closer, with the shirt she had made for Jeo lying on top of the white sheet, the shirt's grey fabric soaked in blood with flies circling around it. Her hands reach about in the air and finally take hold of the frangipani tree, the weak branch snapping and beginning to bleed thick white milk drop by drop, extremely fast.

She steps back as the gate is opened wide by the men, and she notices the puzzled expressions on their faces as they look upwards into the canopies—seeing the trapped birds whipping the air up there as though drowning, the feathers of all colours slowly sinking towards the ground.

They set the cot in front of her, beside the dazed heron, and they lift the white sheet and open the folds of the shrouds underneath to expose Jeo's swollen, pulped, blood-smeared face for her to identify.

Tara is looking through her basket of fabric cuttings. A little girl who lives in the same street as Rohan has come to ask for them, to make dresses for dolls.

When Tara awoke Naheed's bed was empty so she knew she must have gone to the house to wait for the bird pardoner. Tara had overslept and missed her predawn prayers. It is a sin to miss a prayer, but she is allowed to offer the compensatory *qaza* prayer this afternoon. Allah has full knowledge of human weakness and has made provisions. "Why are you crying?" the little girl asks.

"I am not."

"Yes you are. I can see it."

"There is a war."

She woke up thinking of Jeo and his decision to go to Afghanistan. She has been wondering if Mikal is responsible for this crisis, Mikal who came here to ask Tara for Naheed's hand last year—just days before Naheed's wedding to Jeo. Has he now taken Jeo to Afghanistan so he will be killed? But, no, she mustn't give in to these thoughts. Allah will bring Jeo home any day, perfectly safe. And since Allah disapproves of slander she mustn't think or say anything about Mikal until she has full knowledge of all the facts.

The knees of her trousers are minutely wrinkled from the extra prayers she has said over the last five days to ask Allah to look after Jeo in the war zone. But she cannot jettison her fears completely because 2001 had begun on a Monday, a sign according to the almanacs that the weak would suffer greatly at the hands of the strong and the unthinking during these twelve months.

She hands the scraps of fabric to the girl who is thrilled by their brightness and colour, the garden of printed flowers and geometric designs.

"You shouldn't be out here this early," Tara tells her as she leaves.

"There is a big crowd near my house," the girl says. "I think it's a wedding. I came out to look at it and then came to your house."

Tara fills a bowl of water and sprinkles it on the henna tree that grows in a fractured pot on the roof terrace.

She thought she was facing a madman when Mikal had appeared here and said he loved Naheed. The unfairness of it had almost reduced her to tears—just when she thought she had put her daughter out of Sharif Sharif's reach. She knew Mikal of course, knew of his troubled past and his disappearances, having seen Jeo and him together at Rohan's house.

"Surely you see that as her mother I cannot allow Naheed to marry you," she had said. "You cannot provide a better future for her than a doctor."

He said that he would tell everything to Jeo and Rohan and have the wedding cancelled, his eyes intense, the eyebrows meeting in the middle so his glance seemed weighed down by some dark mystery.

"We love each other."

"Is that how you will repay Jeo, by stealing his bride? The boy whose family took you in." His face had crumpled at that but she had continued, her own dreads and distress too great. "You cannot betray Jeo."

"I cannot betray Naheed either."

"I would like to know where you will live. In that room they say you rent in a dogfight and rubbish-heap district?"

"There is nothing wrong with where I live," he said quietly. "My parents lived there."

As if the story of his parents didn't frighten her. The father vanishing as he tried to bring about a revolution after which there would be no God, and the mother wearing herself out searching for him, slapped by policemen and officials from whom she thought she could demand answers.

Tara had said this to him and he was perfectly motionless, almost as though he had died standing up. Without knowing it, the unfortunate boy had become the outlet for the loneliness and suffering of her own life.

"Even if she loves you, you should do her the kindness of never seeing her again. Her life will be better with Jeo."

She promised Allah she would say five hundred prayers of gratitude if the wedding went ahead as planned. And she followed the trail of the chained mendicant as he passed through the streets of Heer and asked him to add a link to his chains: her wish was Naheed's happiness, for Mikal to disappear.

And it was granted—the link must have vanished from about the mendicant's person.

Now, as she waters the henna plant, she tells herself to trust in Allah again.

There is a note of feedback from the mosque's loudspeaker and the cleric clears his throat. Tara becomes alert. No prayer is called at this hour, so it must be a special announcement, and they are mostly about a death in the neighbourhood, or a lost child. She thinks of the little girl who just left with the fabrics.

"Gentlemen, please listen to the following announcement . . ." Sometimes on hearing this, Naheed mutters to herself, "And what about us ladies?"—earning herself a look of admonition from Tara, who is unable to accept criticism in any matter concerning the mosque. The man announces that Jeo, the son of Rohan-sahib, the former headmaster of Ardent Spirit, has died, that the body is laid out at home and the funeral will be held after the noon prayers. The words are like a blow to her head and chest but for several seconds their meaning eludes her. There is pain but it cannot find its focus as she descends the stairs slowly and goes out of the door.

The ground threatens to dissolve under her feet when she approaches Rohan's house, where there is indeed a crowd as the child had said. She negotiates a way through the mass and walks into the garden, knowing where to find Naheed, at the head of the corpse, but there is no corpse and no Naheed.

She touches the face. It is broken but it is him. There is a cut in the cheek, the flesh swollen around it and the blood congealed in dark colours under the skin, the features that would be unrecognisable if she didn't know them as well as she does. The mole on the back of the ear that even he didn't know he had. Women have been knocking on the door ever since they discovered that she had locked herself in here with him but she ignores them, looking instead now into his eyes that are open, the ruined porcelain of them looking back at her. Carefully she uncovers him entirely. There are incisions and bullet wounds throughout and she imagines him crying out as each of these wounds was made. The stomach has been cut open in two diagonal strokes, deep enough to slice through the intestines. The bruises so vivid she thinks they would stain her fingers, but they remain fast, as though painted on the reverse side of the skin. She touches the mouth which is a purple blotch, full of syrupy plasma and clots of blood, the lips and tongue that came together to form a word or a kiss, and she bends to sniff the dead air inside the nostrils and she sniffs the riven shirt, the cold moth smell of it. Normally the body would be taken away to be washed at the mosque and brought back smelling of vetiver and the essence of camphor, but she heard someone say earlier that he must not be bathed, that a martyr is buried with the blood of the battle still on him.

Dipping the nib into an inkpot filled with his own blood, the cleric at the nearby mosque has been transcribing the Koran into a blank book for more than a decade, intending to complete the entire Holy Book out of his own body. But occasionally, when he is delighted by an act of piety performed by a child, the cleric allows the child to donate a speck of red from a fingertip. As a child Jeo was proud to have been asked to make a contribution—a pair of dots in the name of the prophet Ayub.

She rebinds the shroud carefully and covers him with the sheet and then walks to the door to let them in.

Nothing anyone does can alter the fact that he is dead. Not even God can change the past.

By nightfall most people have gone—just a few men lingering outside the house, someone looking for their child's lost shoe on the veranda, a few women in the kitchen washing and putting away dishes, and then they too leave. Messages have been left in Peshawar for Rohan, Yasmin and Basie but they cannot be located—gone away to look for Jeo and Mikal, following rumours to nearby towns.

The neighbourhood women had taken control of the house and of the situation—apportioning tasks, taking flowers off the vines to cover the body and later the grave, sending young men up into the trees to remove the snares. Surrounding and comforting Tara and Naheed, each woman recalled the last time she saw Jeo, offering memories of his intelligence and kindness and remembering details of their wedding.

Naheed wanders through the large house. It is ten o'clock and candlelight is all there is, the electricity having disappeared. She walks down the darkened corridor towards Cordoba House with a flame, then stops and leans against the wall, the wax dripping at her feet. On the wall hangs a picture of Jeo and she stares at it questioningly. The three men who brought the body did not have much information. All they said was that they were employees of an ordinary truck-hire company in Peshawar and that a man had come to their depot and paid them to deliver Jeo's body to this address in Heer.

But at one level it is too soon for such details to matter. When a woman had asked Tara, "How did he die?" Tara had said, "I don't care yet."

The house drifts in darkness. The girl thinks of the time the garden had pulled her into its brilliance, the sunlight and the invasion of delicate insects, the smells from the Tree of Sorrows and the Sorrowless Tree. She knows it will never again be the same because, tarnished, exposed, corroded, stained, blinded, her eyes have been made different, imperfect.

Where is Mikal? She sits down on the floor with her back against the wall and becomes still. When she and Mikal began to meet, there was something like embarrassment in her initially. It had all seemed a pretence, and she had perhaps tried to make light of what they were doing. But his intensity had compelled her to take her own life seriously, made her see that beauty and happiness were her right too.

Eleven p.m. and Tara is in a nearby room with a lamp and a Koran. Midnight and there is a perfect quietness as if the house has become detached from the earth and floated clear. The two of them alone with a war, the gutted burned insides of it. The times have something to tell them through this occurrence but neither knows what it is.

Soon after the body arrived a rumour spread in the neighbourhood that American soldiers had killed Jeo. One man had loaded his rifle on hearing this and rushed out of his house, thinking the American army had actually invaded Heer.

The ash on Naheed's clothes has marked her wrists and neck. Upon learning that Tara had sent for ash, for the mourning clothes to be dyed with it, almost all the women had become perplexed, saying that these must be poor people's customs, those of villagers. They wondered once again how a seamstress had managed to get her daughter married into this big house. Rose-ringed parakeets have to be buried under neem trees, so when Tara's had died two decades ago she had come here and asked if they would allow her to bury the bird under their neem. That was how she had met the family, though Rohan was also a very distant relative of her dead husband.

Naheed sits in Rohan's room with the telephone receiver in her hand. One a.m. She has tried contacting Rohan again in Peshawar but there is no answer.

There is a ruby on the table. It was discovered in Jeo's stomach and its surface is carved finely with Koranic verses, the colour brilliant and clean. It is polished to a perfect smoothness in the areas where there are no words and it had made people gasp, such loveliness had entered them at the sight, in spite of the occasion. A woman remembered that it had belonged to Sofia and that it had disappeared from the house long ago, presumed stolen. The cleric said that the drops of blood Jeo had donated as a child to the calligraphy of his Koran had appeared as a jewel within him.

Naheed is still sitting beside the telephone at two o'clock, the candle long spent. She gets up and searches for another. There are some hours when a human being needs company even if it is only a small flame. In its light she lowers herself onto Rohan's bed.

9

Rohan dreams of an American soldier and a jihadi warrior digging the same grave.

He opens his eyes and looks out of the car, moving towards Heer along the Grand Trunk Road, vast stretches of it without light. They have been travelling all night and the dashboard clock says 4:30 a.m. They'll be home around eight in the morning. Basie is driving and Yasmin is asleep in the back seat. They have been unable to discover any clues to Jeo and Mikal's whereabouts, and are returning to Heer exhausted after the various searches they have conducted in and around Peshawar—all three of them stunned by the past few days.

Earlier in the evening they telephoned home but there was no answer. Naheed must be at Tara's place, and there is no telephone there. In all honesty they were relieved that no one had picked up. They have no news to give and would have had to tell them that they would be returning empty-handed. It can wait until they get home.

The thought comes to him that Jeo and Mikal might die, a terror in the black leaf-encumbered forest that is his mind, but he turns away from it immediately, almost cowering.

Out on the plains a river is shining like poured metal now that starlight has caught it at the right angle and hundreds of bats can be seen passing over the sheetwater on their leather wings as they hunt for moths. Just ahead of them a church has come into view and then Basie has to bring the car to a sudden screeching halt. A bearded man, of Rohan's own age, has appeared before the vehicle, crossing the road less than five yards ahead. He carries a weak lamp whose flame is lost in the white glare of the headlights, and he presents an extraordinary sight because he is bound heavily in thick chains. They are wrapped around his torso like thread on a spool, covering the entire area from his hipbones to his armpits. At least two dozen chains also hang from a metal ring around his neck—they fall to just below his knees and then rise, half of them joining a ring that he wears on his left wrist, the other half attaching themselves to the right wrist.

He looks directly at Rohan as everyone in the car recovers from the shock.

"Should we get out and help him?" Yasmin asks.

"He just needs time to get across, I imagine." Basie looks back to see if there are any vehicles behind them but there is nothing and the man is in no danger.

Basie makes a small courteous detour around him and he doesn't acknowledge them as he continues his slow walk to the other edge of the road. His beard is matted and dust-filled like the hair on his head and he is thin, his face deeply lined and sunburnt, but there is a peaceful expression.

A thick metal garment.

"As a child Mikal thought he was our father," Basie says quietly as they leave him behind.

The chains must weigh as much as two healthy men at least and must be a very heavy burden—they account for the slow progress.

"I have heard about him but never seen him," Rohan says, looking back. He is soon lost to view as they pick up speed but then they hear the hard metallic sound like a colossal hammer coming down on an anvil of equal proportions. A noise so loud the air itself bends.

"Someone just blew up the church," Yasmin says.

"Turn around."

"He could be hurt. He was crossing towards it."

This is the second attack on a church in two days. Yesterday it was during the daylight hours and it had injured several people. Those claiming responsibility had said that since Western Christians were bombing and destroying mosques in Afghanistan, they were beginning a campaign to annihilate churches in Pakistan.

The blaze can be seen from two hundred yards away, the building engulfed in a powerful inferno and the smoke billowing up into the black sky. The explosion was on the ground floor and long flames are emerging from the windows to climb the facade. At the fire's height the tips of the flames break off again and again, vanishing into the darkness.

They park by the roadside and get out and Rohan feels the light like a hard rain on his face, on his eyes, and he has to look away every few seconds. The fire inside the church is brighter and hotter—the outside flames dull by comparison. One blaze seems to be escaping another more ferocious blaze.

Even though it is night there is soon the beginning of a traffic jam and in the chaos people are getting out to help, bear witness or complain. Yasmin and Basie tell Rohan to stay beside their car as they themselves go forwards, to see if they can be of assistance.

Though he doesn't say anything, standing with his back to the bright light, he doesn't want them to go. There could be a secondary explosion, meant to injure the people who are trying to save the building. Or men on motorbikes could drive by and spray the rescuers and onlookers with machine guns. Fearfully he looks over his shoulder and watches them leave.

The burning gives off a roar that reaches the last little place inside him, where each man keeps his courage, and when the wind pivots there is nothing but that roar, a reminder that the noise of fire had resounded on earth before the speech of man.

Basie and Yasmin both teach at the Christian school in Heer, and the thought comes to him that they could be in danger when they return, with their school and the church attached to it a possible target.

A few in the crowd around him are delighted. To them this isn't madness but, on the contrary, is *beauty*.

Rohan is some way from the Grand Trunk Road when he sees the lamp lying on its side in the grass, still intact, still burning. He sees the knee-high mound of chains under a wayside cypress tree, each link someone's wish, and his first thought is that they have been torn from the fakir's body by the explosion, that he would find the body somewhere nearby, but now the heaped-up metal gives a stir and an uncertain hand comes into view.

Rohan moves forward with the lamp as the fakir sits upright in a dazed condition, and begins to pick the debris off his chains. He must have been close to the church when the device exploded, and has come away and collapsed here. In all probability he has been saved by the chains, the armour of other people's needs.

Sometimes when Allah does not take pity on him—does not hear his prayers on others' behalf, making the links vanish—the chains continue to grow, so that he has to drag several yards of them behind him.

Rohan watches him as he stands up in a series of gradual accomplishments—that incredible weight.

He begins to walk away, removing bits of brick and stone that the explosion had thrown onto him to be embedded in the links, as another man might brush off dust from his clothes.

"Brother, are you all right?"

He stops, the chains continuing to swing.

"I didn't mean to disturb you," Rohan says.

They are a dozen or so steps from a pond and with his lamp and the clinking of his chains he walks in up to his knees, making the water golden with the lamplight as he leans forwards and lowers his face to the water. As if to take its odour. Then he begins to sip. Rohan watches him alertly lest the weight make him lose balance, fearing he would drown within the coils, but he straightens and returns successfully.

He places the lamp on the ground and then lowers himself onto the ground beside Rohan and they look towards the east from where the sun will rise.

"I am waiting for my daughter and son-in-law." Rohan points to the line of trees behind them, where the sky is a dark orange from the church fire.

The fakir looks for a long moment in that direction, his breath steaming weakly in the air of the October night. The chains must be cold, Rohan thinks. The wrists are calloused where each thick ring or bracelet has been rubbing against the skin for decades.

"We have been away from home for some days," Rohan says, surprised by the tears he is trying to control. "Looking for my son and foster son."

A need to talk. After trying to appear courageous before Yasmin and Basie over the past few days.

The man gazes ahead. He appears to be a soul without a self.

"How can anyone explain the world?" Rohan says to himself, looking down at his hands. "Sometimes I despair that it can't be done."

The man clears his throat gently and the voice is almost all rasp when it comes. "It can be."

With great care, as though writing the words instead of uttering them, he begins to speak. "It can be done. *Ahl-e-Dil* and *Ahl-e-Havas*. We all are divided into these two groups. The first are the People of the Heart. The second are the People of Greed, the deal makers and the men of lust and the hucksters." He pauses to gather sufficient energy to continue. Some say that he is a djinn, and also that God has graced him with the lifelong innocence of dervishes, and also that he had used the chains to capture a djinn in the wilderness who had then converted to Islam. After his silence he says, "The first people will not trample anyone to obtain what they desire. The second will. Here lies this world."

Rohan says, "That could be one way of reading the world, yes."

"If I take dust in my hand and ask you if that is all the dust there is, you will answer that dust is everywhere on earth. More specks than can ever be numbered. So I can give you a handful of truth only. Besides this there are other truths. More than can ever be numbered."

The earliest glimmers of light are appearing in the sky, and they sit without words and a scent comes to Rohan and he looks around for its source because he has the same tree growing in his garden. The blossoms produce this roaming perfume but are green and very small, almost invisible to the eye—choosing to be represented, rather than revealing themselves.

The last time he spoke to Naheed the bird pardoner had yet to return to the house.

He touches one of the chains. "Why do you carry these?"

With the tip of his index finger the man writes a word in the dust, the dust in which his chains had made swirls when he sat down.

"You were once one of the *Ahl-e-Havas*?" The man remains silent.

"You hurt someone?"

"It cannot unhappen."

"Someone was harmed?"

The word he has written is *Desire*.

"I made mistakes when my son was a child," Rohan says. "His mother had died in the state of apostasy and as a result I enforced an extreme form of piety on myself and on my children, making them pray and keep fasts, revealing to them things inappropriate for their ages. The transience of this life, the tortures of Hell and, before that, of the grave. I stopped eventually, seeing the error, but it must have marked them. I wonder if that is why he went to Afghanistan."

The fakir looks at the thousands of chain links surrounding him, perhaps wondering if any of them have vanished in the night. The light is caught in hazy smears on the metal.

"We believe my two boys are in Afghanistan. What you said about *Ahl-e-Dil* and *Ahl-e-Havas,* does that explain what is happening in Afghanistan? The armies from the West. The extremes of the Taliban."

He is not sure if the fakir is listening, his eyes on the first sunlight, the rays spanning the gap between the unseen and the seen, but then the man looks at him. "Whoever has power desires to hold on to power. That is the case both with the Taliban and the West." He sits breathing in the morning air and then with careful movements of his hands—as diligent as he was when he was writing—he erases the word he has written, letter by letter.

"What did you do before this?"

"I worked with law. Twenty years ago, thirty." He shakes his head. "Nothing is ever over. Time is unimportant."

"You were a policeman."

"Worse." The man extinguishes his lamp. "A judge."

The sun is an orb of boiling glass before them, the light remaking the world once again, and now the fakir rises slowly and begins to walk along the rim of the dawn-lit pond. "My day is only a day, my name only a name," he says with one hand on his breast in the gesture of swearing fidelity. Rohan watches him disappear as the sunlight erupts from the water in shards.

It is late morning when they arrive in Heer. The gate to the house is locked and Rohan lets them in with the key.

He is immediately relieved to see that the bird pardoner's steel wires are lying in a tangle at the foot of the young mango tree. So the snares have been taken down. He spends a few moments examining the health and progress of the tree. Jeo loves its fruit, with a tinge of turpentine to its flavour, the pulp almost liquid and having to be sucked through a hole one makes at the top.

Turning around to move deeper into the garden he notices with unhappiness the branch that has been broken off the frangipani tree. He touches the wound and from the consistency of the congealed latex can tell that the damage occurred sometime yesterday.

Basie walks along one of the red paths towards the house. He enters a room but emerges a minute later with a sense of an unidentifiable wrong. The corridors are unswept—which is understandable since Naheed has probably been staying with her mother—but there is evidence of many footsteps in the dust on the floors. It is as though the characters and personalities from the boxes of books had come alive and wandered the house.

Yasmin stands looking at the garden from the veranda, wondering why the vines and the branches are flowerless, wondering why there is a ghostly impression of a figure in coal dust or ash against a wall.

At the pond Rohan sees the heap of dead birds, insects rising from it in a glittering black vortex as he lifts a paradise flycatcher with its pair of long white ribbons for a tail, three times the length of its body. He walks towards the clothesline strung between the eucalyptus tree and the tall glad jacaranda. He had passed the line earlier without really seeing what was hanging on it: a single item and it seems to be the shirt Jeo wore to Peshawar six days ago. It is pinned upside down, the sleeves almost reaching the grass. The fabric has many gashes in it and its original grey colour is stained by what appears to be blood or dark red ink. A rag with which someone tried to clean something rusty. Did Naheed make two of these? This must be one of the earlier practice ones. And he stands examining it for seams.

From a shelf Basie picks up the large sphere of ruby-coloured glass with verses of the Koran indented into it. It must be glass—too heavy and too clear to be plastic. It is a pendant for a necklace or a talisman to be worn around the neck on a black cord. He has never seen it before and he brings it to the window and holds it up to see the sun enter and inhabit it, illuminating the verses from within.

He walks to Tara's place but there is no one there. A man is sitting in the sun in front of the neighbouring house. He has wet henna paste on his hair and a sheet of newspaper is protecting the collar of his shirt from stains and he tells Basie that the two women are at Naheed's in-laws'.

"I have just come from there," Basie says.

The man shrugs. "Then maybe they have gone to the doctor. Or the bazaar. Who can understand women and their whims?"

Basie returns and hears Yasmin and Tara, hears Naheed and Rohan. He doesn't know what they are saying, only their voices reaching him from somewhere, and then he sees Naheed walking towards him, dressed in ash as though she has been caught in a lightning storm.

10

A follower of Allah knows nothing of chance. In this life everything is significant and meaningful. So why has this happened? A drop of his bloody soul struggle, the ruby shines in Rohan's palm.

He looks at the clock with its black hands. Before Jeo was born, he had placed his ear to Sofia's skin, just above and to the left of the navel, and listened to the small second heartbeat, there in the darkness before life began. Now the boy is in the other darkness and Rohan doesn't know where to find a sign of him, what wall or barrier or skin or veil to place his ear on.

In the night garden the hibiscus blossoms sway on the vine like birds, their crimson darkened by several shades. The berries of the Persian lilac trees are poisonous so they remain on the branches throughout the year. The bulbul is the only bird that seems to have immunity and all day they were feeding noisily on the clusters.

"Uncle."

He turns to see Basie on the red path, a storm lantern in his hand. Behind him is Tara.

"Aunt Tara says she would like to speak to the two of us."

"Just a few moments of your time, brother-ji," Tara says.

He points towards the bench under the Mysore fig tree.

"I want to talk to you about Naheed's future," she says, sitting rigidly.

"Naheed's future? As long as I am alive, sister-ji, the girl will be provided for. This remains her home."

Basie, sitting beside her, assents too.

"No." She shakes her head. "I want her to marry again."

Basie and Rohan look at each other.

"Of course," Rohan says. "She should. She's only nineteen years old."

The light of the lantern is caught under the dark canopy of the tree, shadows washing over the ground as they converse quietly.

"I know it's too soon to talk about these matters," Tara says, "and I feel ashamed for having brought it up when Jeo is buried not even ten days, but I just didn't want you to forget that you have a responsibility to Naheed."

"That will never happen," Rohan says. "She is like Yasmin to me."

"I don't want my daughter to spend the rest of her life as a widow."

"We'll find a good man for her," Basie says. "Let's allow a period of time to pass, and then we'll begin to look."

"That is all I wanted to hear," the woman nods.

"You mustn't ever think you are alone, Aunt Tara," Basie tells her. "You have us."

"What does Naheed think?" Rohan asks.

"I haven't yet spoken to her about this matter."

"Of course."

They remain where they are, surrounded by a penetrating silence until Naheed appears at the kitchen door with a candle, the banana fronds made luminous by the light, and she looks at the three of them across the distance. "The food is ready."

She comes forward and takes Rohan by the hand and leads him away, Tara following. Very quickly after she came into the house as a bride with her forehead decorated with starlike dots, the girl had taken responsibility for the everyday affairs of the family. Yasmin's work had flourished because of her; Naheed cooked, and insisted that Yasmin and Basie come here after school instead of going to their own place. She took over the running of several aspects of their household too, allowing Yasmin to concentrate on her teaching, and at the weekends—when Jeo returned from medical school in Lahore—the entire family gathered here, and it was all arranged and organised by her, with unobtrusive advice and guidance from Tara.

"I'll join you in a minute," Basie tells them.

He sits on the veranda where Jeo's motorcycle is parked beside the pillar. Basie has visited several organisations that have been sending boys to Afghanistan but has been unable to discover who sent Jeo and Mikal. He doesn't even know who managed to bring Jeo's body back from the war. Nor do they know where Mikal is, alive or dead.

On Fridays the dead person is said to recognise the visitor to his grave. Rohan, accompanied by Tara, Yasmin and Naheed, arrives at the cemetery to say prayers for the comfort of Jeo's soul.

At the entrance there stand four women veiled head to toe in black and holding yard-long sticks. Around their heads they wear green bands with the flaming-swords motif of Ardent Spirit's flag. The black-clad figures bar their way and one of them says, pointing to Naheed, Tara and Yasmin, "You three cannot enter."

"What do you mean?" Tara asks.

"Women are not allowed into graveyards according to our religion."

They express their disbelief but are told the same thing again:

"It is not allowed in our religion for women to visit graveyards."

"Since when?" Rohan asks. "Muslim women have been visiting graves for hundreds of years."

"That is an innovation and has to be put an end to. We are here for that purpose."

Confronted with the necessity of exposing their eyes through the slits of their cloaks, the women are hiding the true colour of their irises by wearing coloured contact lenses, the green, red and blue circles darting.

Yasmin gives a sound of annoyance and tries to move past them but the women stiffen and raise their canes.

Yasmin stops. "I have to see my brother. He died in Afghanistan." They seem to consider the fact for a moment. "It doesn't mean anything as far as this matter is concerned. You will not go in, it is Allah's wish."

"My mother is buried here," Yasmin says, adding with a gesture towards Naheed: "And her father."

"You can say prayers for the soul of your dead at home. And rest assured that we too will do that for the man martyred in Afghanistan. He was our brother and died defending Islam."

"You are stopping a martyr's widow from visiting him," Tara says. "This is my daughter and she was married to the dead man."

"If you are a martyr's widow," a woman turns to Naheed, "what are you doing stepping outside the house with your face uncovered?" All of them look towards Naheed now. "You should be ashamed of yourself. He gave his life for Allah and you are disgracing him."

Another woman visitor who has been barred from entry is standing under a nearby tree. "My one-year-old son is buried in there," she says to Tara.

Yasmin moves and one of the figures swings at her face with the metal-tipped cane twice in quick succession, coming a step closer with every swing, Yasmin taking a corresponding step back each time. The tip passes just an inch from her face.

"It's because of people like you," the woman points to them all with her cane, "that Islam has been brought so low. Filthy, disgusting, repulsive infidels are attacking Muslim countries with impunity." And to Rohan she says, "Don't you know better than to walk around with your women uncovered, you vile pimp?"

Yasmin, the gentlest and most congenial of women, raises her voice. "Don't talk in that manner to someone three or four times your age."

"Age doesn't mean anything," says the woman furiously. "If he is wrong I am his superior in Allah's eyes and He gives me authority to reprimand the abhorrent wretch."

It is obvious that nothing can be done. Rohan goes in alone to say a prayer while Tara, Naheed and Yasmin wait outside. They will have to visit the grave in the darkness, deep at night.

11

Naheed's face appears among the reeds and she gasps for air, her eyes filling up with light after the minutes under the water. She climbs out of the river, her hair falling with a shifting weight along her back. She stands coughing up water while around her brilliant groups of butterflies sun themselves on the muddy green slime. They often leave the garden to roam the arches above the worshippers in the mosque on the other side of the crossroads. She walks through the garden, where spots of sunlight are going in and out of focus as the foliage shifts overhead, and enters the house and changes into a dry set of clothes. She lowers herself onto the bed, lightly brushing the counterpane, white with a geometric pattern of raised white threads.

Out there Rohan is sitting in a square of mild sunlight and he opens his eyes at her approach.

She crouches beside him.

"Do you say the prayers I told you to?" he asks. "To atone for the sin of having seen Jeo's body after his death."

"Yes."

The marriage contract is dissolved at the moment of death. A wife becomes a stranger to her husband and must not lay eyes on him.

"Strictly speaking you shouldn't even have looked at the face. But Allah understands. We humans are weak so it's hard to avoid committing sins." He closes his eyes. "It is always better to begin atoning for them as soon as possible. That way we won't have to fear the consequences in the grave and later on Judgement Day."

She looks around.

"I wanted to see Sofia's face before she was buried," he is saying, "more than anything, but I knew I shouldn't."

Suddenly she gets up and, leaving him there, goes back to the house with hurried steps and enters the room she shared with Jeo.

She stands looking at the far corner, the heart beginning to beat painfully in her chest. She raises her hands to her forehead, eyes fixed on the dark brocade of the armchair.

She moves towards it and drops onto her knees and reaches underneath, the open palm skimming the floor as it moves blindly forwards. When her fingertips make contact with the cold metal object down there she almost cries out. She withdraws her hand and looks at the fingers as though expecting to see an injury there.

She reaches out with both hands—as when trying to capture a bird—and grips the toy truck that has been standing stationary against the back wall since the evening of Jeo's departure.

Her fingers grip the painted wheels so they won't spin and empty out the energy that had flowed into the toy from Jeo's body when he wound it up with the key. She stands holding it tightly, locking the gears and cogs of its mechanism.

She is shaking. As a test she releases the pressure on the wheels for a fraction of a second and the wheels turn in the air and she gives out a sound of pain.

At last she places it on the floor and watches it move away from her. She walks alongside it to the other end of the room and then continues out of the door, overtaking and leaving it behind, unable to bear witness to the moment it stops.

12

Mikal sits with his back against the wall in the cold interior, the chain at his ankles rattling with every movement of his body. Never away from his mind, not even for a single second, is the thought of flight. Not since he regained consciousness at the Taliban fort in October.

He doesn't know where Jeo is.

The last thing he remembers of the fighting on that October day is the battle-torn smoke and a bright burst of poppy before his face. They tied him up with lengths of barbed wire while he was insensible and carried him outside, and when he opened his eyes he couldn't move and near him a pack of dogs was eating the blood-soaked earth of the fort's courtyard.

He caught a brief glimpse of the group of American soldiers who had co-ordinated the battle against the Taliban fort. The Americans were now confronted with the corpses of more than a hundred enemy men, and they told their Afghan allies to dispose of them as quickly as possible before they were filmed by a passing satellite.

Mikal became the prisoner of a warlord, who cut off the trigger finger on each of his hands and nailed the two pieces to a door frame along with those taken from dozens of other captives.

Fearing gangrene, he begged them to extract the bullets from his body, but to no avail. But then two nights later, while he slept, a large group of them came at him with scalpels and blades. A rumour had circulated that the Americans had used solid gold bullets.

He spoke to ask them where Jeo was, asked if they knew someone named Jeo, but received no information.

Carefully he pulls his bandaged hands into his sleeves for warmth. His body is combat-seamed and a little raw elsewhere too, where the bullets went in, where the bullets were taken out. The left arm, that was torn open by a dagger-tip in search of gold, is restricted in its functions—he can touch the right shoulder with it but not the left one.

He must escape and find Jeo and then both of them must go back to Heer.

13

Naheed enters the room where Tara is sitting in a chair.

"Mother, I am pregnant."

Tara is attaching a red glass button to a tunic. She completes the stitch she has begun and only then stands up, carefully, placing both her hands on her knees.

"Mother, did you hear what I said? I am pregnant."

"Are you sure?"

The reaction is more muted than Naheed had expected.

"Yes. I have counted and . . ." She shakes her head. "It doesn't matter. I am pregnant."

"When was the last time you and Jeo—?"

"Just before he left." Naheed comes and stands in front of her. She links her arms around Tara's neck and rests her head on her shoulder. Tara embraces her with reluctance.

"We'll have to tell Father," Naheed says. She is about to part but Tara won't allow the embrace to be broken, their faces inches away from each other. The woman looks directly into her eyes and says, very firmly,

"No."

It is a few moments before Naheed realises what Tara means. She steps away.

"We are not telling anyone about this." Tara moves towards the door and shuts it while Naheed looks on aghast. "No one will marry you if you have a child."

"I don't care about that."

"I do."

"I can't contemplate even for a second what you are suggesting."

Tara is standing with her back resolutely against the closed door. But after a while, in a softer voice, she says, "I am not suggesting anything. I just think we should wait a little before telling Rohan." She doesn't meet Naheed's eye as she speaks. "Don't you think he is in enough anguish already? We should wait until completely sure. If it turns out that you are mistaken, you would have raised the poor man's hopes needlessly."

Tara moves away from the door.

Naheed sits down on the chair but then shakes her head and stands up.

"Stay away from the door, Naheed. I can marry you off if you are just a widow. But a widow with a baby—you'll be alone for the rest of your life."

Naheed can hardly believe she is living through these moments. Tara strikes her face with such strength that she has to back away and lean against a wall. In the few seconds it takes her to recover, Tara has gone out and bolted the door from the other side.

The emergency deepening around her with every minute, Tara tells herself to think fast. She knows a woman who can be of help in this matter.

Hundreds of thousands of poor defenceless Afghanistanis have been murdered by the Americans in cold blood. No one tells you about it . . . From outside comes the sound of a loudspeaker fixed on top of a van, telling everyone that it is a critical moment for the holy war in Afghanistan, encouraging them to join the jihad. Several such vehicles have been roaming Heer of late, all with the Ardent Spirit flag painted on the sides.

Tara reaches for her burka.

And hundreds of thousands of American soldiers have been killed by the brave Muslim fighters. No one tells you about those either. The Americans are on the verge of defeat so we need just a few more volunteers . . .

Fastening the ties and buttons of the burka, she goes down the stairs and out into the street. Once again she is taken aback by the silent implacable passing of time, the months and the years. The truth is that she hadn't noticed Naheed growing up until the day she found a blood-soaked handkerchief in a corner of the room, and her first thought was that a cat must have brought in a dead sparrow and eaten it there. Naheed meanwhile was under the impression that something like a large pimple must have burst somewhere inside her, and was stanching the blood with whatever piece of cloth came to hand.

She visits the woman who lives in Soldier's Bazaar and then stops to buy a padlock in a narrow alley that is full of jobless young men sitting outside the shops, angry and humiliated, some of them former students at Ardent Spirit, and they look longingly at every girl who passes by, frustration and unemployment causing them to erupt into passion and violence at any time, while the students at the good schools like the one where Basie and Yasmin teach want only to emigrate to Western lands, saying young men like these have made this country uninhabitable.

She recognises one of them and calls out to him and tells him she will sew the item that he had asked her to the previous week, something to which she had said no at the time. But now she will need the money. The substance she will administer to Naheed is very strong, even life-threatening, and she will fall severely ill after taking it. There will be medical expenses.

She gives a rupee to a beggar and asks him to pray for her daughter's health and happiness, and getting home she puts the padlock on the staircase door, blocking the only way out.

She stands at the closed door to the room, listening intently to the heavy silence on the other side. In the kitchen she begins to prepare the medication. Then she cooks the evening meal and when it is ready she unlocks the room, on alert in case the girl tries to rush out. But Naheed is sitting still in the chair and remains that way. Tara places the plate of spinach and two chapattis wrapped in a white napkin before her.

"You've put something in it."

"I haven't."

Naheed touches the rim of the plate with a fingertip and slowly begins to slide it away from her. It goes over the edge of the table and shatters on the floor.

Tara brings another.

"In your condition a woman must eat to maintain her strength." There is no response from Naheed.

"I didn't put anything in it," she encourages. "Surely you know you'll damage the child's development if you don't eat."

Naheed breaks off a piece of chapatti and scoops an amount of spinach from the new plate and raises it to her mouth but then drops it.

"I didn't invent this world, Naheed. Your life will be ruined."

"This is Jeo's last reminder in the world."

"He didn't think of you when he went to Afghanistan, why are you thinking of him?"

"This is my child. I'll bring him up myself."

"How exactly will that happen?"

"I'll get a diploma and become a teacher and when he grows up he'll look after me."

"He? What if it's a girl? Where will we get the money to marry her off in twenty years? Or will she too get a diploma and prepare her own dowry?"

"I am not listening to any of this."

"And are you sure you are intelligent enough to get a diploma? You didn't even pass high school."

Naheed looks fiercely at her, stung. "I failed my classes because of you. Your imprudence, that landed you in prison for two years. And you were mad even before that."

Tara takes a step closer. "Why are you speaking to me in this manner?"

"When you came back from prison, I had to contend with the months of madness yet again. You and your djinns."

"What do you mean by these remarks?" Tara says.

"Nothing. Forget it."

"I was ill a few times, that's all. I did my best to bring you up."

"As will I."

She is silent but then she speaks. "What do you mean by those remarks?"

Naheed looks at her. In her childhood she was afraid of Tara. Terrified of the djinns that visited her. Tara would not speak for days and just lay in bed facing the wall. Naheed learned to cook and care for her from very early on. One day a child even threw a stone at Tara as children do at lunatics. Naheed has always wondered how much of those weeks and months her mother recalls. They have never been mentioned by either of them with any directness. When she became a teenager, Naheed acquired the idea of becoming a teacher, of one day carrying a purse and walking confidently, clipping the front strands of her hair to rest on her cheeks. But her schoolwork was suffering. She remembers the humiliation of having to repeat her classes, and then Tara was arrested.

"Father will help in bringing up the child."

"He hasn't much of anything," Tara says from the armchair. "I thought he was wealthy but I was mistaken. Even the house belongs to the people who own the school, and they might want it back one day. Jeo becoming a doctor was the only secure future he, and you, had."

Naheed looks at the plate and then pushes it away.

"Your Jeo's last gift to you will be you becoming the plaything of that man downstairs, or of someone else like him, for the next decade and a half. And then you will be cast aside. Do you wish to make a life around that? Once a month, in the dead of night, you and your child can walk through the dark streets to pay a visit to Jeo's grave."

Naheed carries the tray back into the kitchen and returns with a rag and begins to clean the mess of the first plate from the floor.

"I will wait for a few days, until I am absolutely sure, and then I will tell Father and Yasmin. I'll find someone to marry me, with my child. You can win great merit from Allah for marrying a martyr's widow. Everyone says that."

"It's all talk."

Naheed rises to her feet and looks at her. "Then I'll live on my own."

As Tara stands on the prayer mat and bows down towards Mecca, she has a sense that the girl is standing behind her. From the small metallic sound she knows that she is holding the pair of scissors. After twenty years of handling them Tara knows every possible sound they make. When she finishes her prayers, however, and turns around the girl is still on the bed. The scissors have moved from the shelf to the windowsill. Or perhaps they were there to begin with.

Sometimes Tara thinks she has asked too little from life. Sometimes she thinks she has asked too much.

When Naheed was fourteen years old, Tara had been assaulted by a man she had recently met. She went to the police and they demanded—in accordance with Sharia law—proof from four male witnesses that it was indeed an assault and not consensual intercourse. There were no such witnesses, of course, and Tara was jailed for adultery. Naheed went to live with her village grandmother while Rohan tried to have Tara released.

It was while she was incarcerated, terrified of the future, that Rohan had reassured her by promising to make Naheed his daughter-in-law.

And that madness of hers that Naheed mentioned, her djinns—her mind would feel broken into during those hours and days. A young widow, her youth slipping away, she had wanted her husband to be alive again. She cannot believe she is thinking this while sitting on a prayer mat—recalling the days of combatting desire, the feeling of guilt in her whenever she thought of a man, feeling like a criminal for wanting something as basic as love and an end to loneliness, feeling maimed in her very soul. What will Naheed do about these things? Sharif Sharif used Tara for a few years after she was widowed and then threw her aside. He already had two wives and her hope of becoming the third came to nothing. She wants to stand up but her knees won't let her so she raises herself a little on her haunches and pulls the velvet prayer mat from under her and folds it with a kiss and puts it on her lap. Sitting on the cold floor, she knows she mustn't allow the girl to repeat her own mistake. The matchmakers said again and again that the presence of the daughter reduced her chances of remarrying, and they advised her to have Naheed adopted. "They change their mind when they hear you'll be bringing another mouth to feed. A girl whose upbringing will have to be provided for, whose honour and virginity protected, for whom a dowry will have to be given one day."

She sent the child away to live in the village, but even then the marriage talks failed to progress beyond a certain point. People were invariably delighted to learn that she was descended from the Prophet, the idea that through her they could connect with Muhammad's bloodline, but she would invite the prospective inlaws to this roof and of course it would be a mistake to let them see the poverty. One room with a small balcony at the front, the steep stairs, and a cubby she called kitchen. The last man who came here ended up marrying someone whose family owned a business in Riyadh, the bride no doubt bringing a car and a washing machine in the dowry, a colour television and a VCR. "So much for Muhammad's blood unaided by Saudi gold," said the matchmaker.

She brought Naheed back and the years kept passing. She began to fantasise about a man she saw walk by in the street regularly, and one day she talked to him briefly at someone's house, convincing herself that he loved her too. She wrote a long letter to him and he came up here and according to him it was not an assault, her letter being the proof of his innocence.

The lock on the stairs remains in place, its key in Tara's pocket, and for two days and two nights Naheed does not eat anything Tara brings.

"One reason I can't do what you want me to do," Naheed says, her face turned away, "is that I know he is alive."

"A woman can't feel the child inside her at such an early stage."

"I am talking about Mikal."

"Mikal?" Tara looks at her. "Have you heard something? Has he been in touch?" Then she stiffens. "Why are you waiting for him anyway?"

"I know he is alive and that he will come back to me. We loved each other."

"I didn't know."

"Yes you did. He didn't say anything but I think he came here to ask for my hand. You must have made him feel like a worthless beggar. I know. We planned to disappear from here before the wedding, we agreed on a time, but he didn't come. I waited, and I never really stopped." She pauses and takes a deep breath. "Maybe this new waiting is just part of the old one."

"Did you two plan all this?" Tara says quietly. "He took Jeo away to have him killed and now you'll wait for his return? Is this Mikal's child?"

"It's nothing like that, Mother. I just know he's alive, I feel him."

"You can't build a life on a feeling, Naheed. I may be mad but I know that much."

"There is no body, there is no grave."

"That doesn't mean he is not dead. Some boys who went to Kashmir or Bosnia or Tajikistan didn't come back, just the news of their death."

Naheed breaks into tears. "Oh Mother, I don't know what to think. But please understand I can't do what you are telling me. And I did not say you were mad."

Tara gets up. She stops at the door. "He did come here and I sent him away. You've known all along?"

"Yes."

"And you were going to run away?" She looks devastated as she asks this. "Leaving me behind, with those wedding preparations I'd made, having to explain to Jeo's family and the entire neighbourhood what happened? Everyone would have said that I, being a wanton woman, had raised a brazen disgraceful daughter."

There is a pained silence from both and then Tara comes back and takes the key from her pocket and places it next to Naheed on the bed.

She brings in a tray of food, telling her it is unadulterated, but Naheed still cannot bring herself to trust her.

"You'll fall ill with weakness. Believe me and eat something," Tara says, pointing to the tray and then to the fridge in the corner—the kitchen is too small to accommodate it so it stands here in the bedroom, their only room, filling the air faintly with the odour of chemicals that have been leaking from its mechanisms ever since it was bought second- or third-hand a decade ago.

Finally Tara unlocks the door to the stairs herself.

"Then go to Rohan's house and eat something from there."

It's almost midnight.

"I'll go in the morning," the girl tells her.

Hunger awakens her a few hours later, deep in the night, and she comes out of the room and stands under the star-coated sky. There is a pomegranate in the kitchen, from the trees in Rohan's garden, that she had brought for Tara some days ago. It has been skinned and the seeds lie glitteringly in a steel bowl, surrounded by their own reflections, the red making her think of the ruby. She lifts a seed and places it on her tongue, then expels it. Tara could have sprinkled something on them.

She looks down from the roof into Sharif Sharif's courtyard. Towards his family's kitchen, almost dizzy with hunger. She walks down the stairs and the screen door squeaks as she enters the kitchen, a small bird noise, a cicada. She stops and looks around more or less frantic with the thought that she must nourish the life inside her. Her fingers reach out and blindly lift the lid of a jar and she can tell from the syrupy smell that it is sugar. She places a large pinch onto her tongue, feeling the crystals melt in the saliva. She hears a sound, a breath suddenly drawn in. Or is it the rasp of a matchstick being struck? Will a small yellow flame soon illuminate Sharif Sharif's face somewhere in the blackness? She drops the jar and hears it break with a sound louder than she would have expected, hears the smaller sound of sugar scattering within the breaking of the glass, a muted hiss. There is graininess under her feet as she rushes out.

Upstairs she eats the pomegranate, lifting the seeds to her mouth with both hands.

When Tara gets up an hour later for her predawn prayers, she is still awake. She asks Tara for breakfast and ten minutes later Tara brings her a paratha and an omelette with coriander, onions and green chillies. When the sun comes up she walks out towards Rohan's house.

She takes a sip of water and a crimson thread swirls into the glass.

She puts it back on the table and lies down on the bed again, shaking with fever. Her skin burns and she feels as though she is looking out through fire.

"What time is it?"

"Night," Tara says.

"What day?"

"Thursday."

Tara places her hand on her forehead—the hands of kindness and a weak human mercy. Naheed looks into her eyes, the eyes through which she had seen tears enter the world for the first time. She hears Tara say, "This isn't anything to do with me. I didn't put anything in your food."

On Friday morning the amber eyes open and she sits up in bed and asks if she can help with the housework. Tara gives her a basket of peas to shell. Ten minutes later when Tara comes into the room she finds her asleep in the chair, with the basket fallen on the floor, the peas scattered.

On Saturday she works on the hem of a tunic that Tara has sewn. Afterwards she goes to the bathroom—Tara reminding her yet again not to lock the door—and spends a long time in there, Tara standing anxiously outside, sounding a knock on the door now and then, gently like a heartbeat, but there is no response.

When at last she emerges Tara asks, "Did something happen?"

She gives a nod. "It's over."

She sleeps for a long time but the body temperature remains high, Tara sitting beside the bed with her Koran or her seamstress work.

"I heard someone say that you sew things, good aunt," the young man had said, appearing on the stairs the week before.

Tara makes women's clothes, but sometimes boys come to her to have their trousers and shirts altered—usually tightened, which their own mothers refuse to do for them.

"Would you stitch an American flag for me?"

"An American flag?"

"Yes, we have to burn it at a protest rally in the bazaar."

Tara was reluctant. "I don't make such things," she told him as she said no. "And I would rather not get involved." She had imagined herself being arrested for a crime involved with public disorder.

But now she is glad she saw the boy at the shops again. If Naheed's fever does not abate, the visit to the doctor will cost twenty-five rupees.

In all probability, Naheed will not manage the walk to the clinic, and the doctor will have to come here, and that will cost more.

"What does it look like?" she had asked the boy.

She brought him into the room and he drew a picture of the flag on a piece of paper. "This bit is blue. These stripes are red, and these white."

"Oh." She held the picture at arm's length. "It's not as plain and simple as our flag, is it? Would I have to stitch on the stars too?"

"Yes. I think there are supposed to be a hundred. Or is it eighty? I can't remember. Just fill the whole blue area in the corner with rows of them."

"When do you need it by?"

"It's for after the Friday prayers next week. It has to be large, about the size of four bedsheets. And can you please make sure that it is of a material that doesn't burn too fast or too slowly? The flames have to look inspiring and fearsome in the photographs."

Just before leaving he had asked her respectfully if there was anything he could do, and she had told him to replace the dead lightbulb at the top of the stairs, the socket being too high for her to reach even when standing on a chair and she did not want to ask Sharif Sharif.

She spends the rest of the day setting fire to small strips of cloth to measure the texture, intensity and evenness of the various flames— linen, cotton, the textiles named after women's films and novels, *Teray Meray Sapnay* and *Dil ki Pyas* and *Aankhon Aankhon Mein*. She settles eventually on a mixture, interspersing the fast burners with the more languidly flammable. She cuts up strips from a bolt of white KT—as pure as the pilgrimage to Mecca—and she makes red strips from a length of red linen. For the dark blue rectangle in the flag's corner there is a large leftover piece from the indigo tunics she sewed for the uniforms of a nearby girls' school. Blue as the colour a candle flame is said to become when a ghost is near. As she measures it she says a small prayer for the school's caretaker who cannot afford the expensive operation he needs for his heart.

For the stars she makes a template with a piece of cardboard and begins to cut them out of white satin, pleased with the fact that the material is shiny, dropping them on the floor one by one where they lie around her full of gloss. She must do this well, in case the boy is dissatisfied and pays less than the agreed amount, and so again and again she consults the picture he drew for her, rubbing her knees occasionally because there is a touch of November in her joints. But pain at her age is no longer a surprise and she continues with the work, wondering what the various elements of the flag signify.

Are the white and red stripes rivers of milk and wine, flowing under a sky bursting with the splendour of stars?

Or are they paths soaked with blood, alternating with paths strewn with bleached white bones, leading out of a sea full of explosions?

Perhaps the blue in the flag means that the Americans own all the blue in the world—water, sky, blood seen through veins, the Blue Mosque in Tabriz, dusk, the feather with which she marks her place in her Koran, her seamstress's chalk, the spot on the lower back of newborn babies, postmarks, the glass eyes of foreign dolls. Muhammad swore by the redness of the evening sky, and Adam means both "alive" and "red." Do the Americans own these and all other reds? Roses, meats, certain old leaves, certain new leaves, love, the feathers under the bulbul's tail, dresses and veils of brides, dates marking festivals on calendars, garnets and rubies, happiness, blushes, daring, war, the Red Fort in Delhi, the spate of violent robberies after which people from the neighbourhood had gone to the police and were told to stop being a nuisance and hire private security guards instead, soda pop, the binding of her Koran—these and all the other shades of red, crimson, vermilion, scarlet, maroon, raspberry, obsidian, russet, plum, magenta, geranium, the tearful eyes of the woman from three doors down, who had told Tara she did not want her to sew her daughter's dowry clothes after discovering that Tara was possessed by the djinn, fearing Tara would stitch her bad luck into the garments, the red flags of the revolution dreamt by Mikal and Basie's parents, the Alhambra in Spain, the paths in Rohan's garden, carpets woven in Shiraz, shiny cars that the rich import into Pakistan only to find that there are no good roads to drive them on. The setting sun. The rising sun.

She works without pause, the large flag materialising slowly in the interior as the hours go by, half the size of the room. She looks at Naheed but the girl remains asleep, hair sweat-pasted to the edges of the face. Winter will arrive soon like a blade opening and the room is cold. She lights a brazier of coals and places it next to Naheed whose body is now chilled. She turns up the volume of the radio a little when it is time for the news and the bulletin informs her that Kabul has fallen earlier today, that the Taliban have fled, after looting everything in sight including six million dollars from the national bank. Afghanistan is liberated and American troops are being handed sweets and plastic flowers by the free citizens of Kabul, music shops are being reopened, but while men are shaving off their beards, the women are choosing to remain hidden in their burkas for the time being. And Tara knows they are wise. During her adult life there has not been a single day when she has not heard of a woman killed with bullet or razor or rope, drowned or strangled with her own veil, buried alive or burned alive, poisoned or suffocated, having her nose cut off or entire face disfigured with acid or the whole body cut to pieces, run over by a car or battered with firewood. Every day there is news that a woman has had these things done to her in the name of honour-and-shame or Allah-and-Muhammad, by her father, her brother, her uncle, her nephew, her cousin, her husband, her husband's father, her husband's brother, her husband's uncle, her husband's nephew, her husband's cousin, her son, her son-in-law, her lover, her father's enemy, her husband's enemy, her son's enemy, her son-in-law's enemy, her lover's enemy. So now Tara commends the women of Kabul for being wise enough to stay in their burkas, because more often than not there are no second chances or forgiveness if you are a woman and have made a mistake or have been misunderstood.

She works until midnight and then 1 a.m. and it seems no one is awake but her. She alone is Islam.

Naheed opens her eyes and sits up.

"You do believe me when I say I didn't do anything, don't you?" Tara asks. "I threw the substance away. I didn't put it in your food after the first few times, I swear on the Koran."

"I know," Naheed says weakly.

"Sometimes Allah Himself does what He knows is the best thing for us."

"I went to a nurse and asked her to give me some injections," the girl says. She looks at Tara. "It wasn't Allah. I did it myself."

14

The leaves of the Sorrowless Tree are abrasive and therefore ideal for polishing. Workers from the furniture shop at the crossroads often come to ask for them. As he answers the doorbell this morning, that is who Rohan thinks is outside the house.

"You don't recognise me?" the man says.

"Forgive me, but I don't." Perhaps he is a seller of bees.

"I came to your house back in October to put up bird snares. I am Abdul, the bird pardoner."

In his mind's eye Rohan sees the bicycle with the giant cage attached to the back.

"I have come to get back my wires." The man looks up into the canopies above the boundary wall of the house. "I can't see them. They must have been taken down."

Rohan finds himself staring speechlessly at the small soft-featured man, the light brown skin stubbled white at the jaws, a side tooth missing in the mouth.

"You don't seem to remember me at all," Abdul says.

"I do. Come in, we have your wires." Rohan had spent an entire morning untangling them and then neatly winding them around foot-long sections of a rosewood branch.

The bird pardoner is a few paces behind him as they walk towards the garden shed. The north corner is full of smoke because he has been pruning, burning the twigs and branches that would otherwise carry disease. A golden-backed woodpecker crosses their path with its undulating flight, dropping out of the whistling pine to escape the smoke and then rising to disappear into the tamarind tree, several of whose branches, bare in winter, are like a net of nerves overhead.

Rohan stops and turns to face the man. "I fail to see why you cannot make a living by another means."

The bird pardoner lets the words hang in the air between them for a moment. Then he says, "I am sorry I didn't come the day I was supposed to."

"You should be." Rohan is surprised to discover anger in his voice, and equally surprising is the speed with which the man's eyes fill up with tears. But Rohan's anger persists. "What excuse can there be for your conduct?"

Abdul wipes his eyes by lifting the loose front of his shirt to his face. "I can't apologise enough for having inconvenienced you."

"I was speaking on behalf of the birds, who remained trapped up there for five days. Hungry, thirsty, terrified."

The bird pardoner takes a sheet of folded paper from his pocket and holds it towards Rohan. "This will explain what has happened to me."

Rohan takes the paper—with hesitation, nor does he unfold it.

"After I put up the snares that afternoon, I got home and learned that my fourteen-year-old boy had run away to fight in Afghanistan. I couldn't come to your house the next day to collect the birds because I had to go and find him. I took the train to Peshawar that very night."

Rohan gazes at him and then at the piece of folded paper in his hand.

"I couldn't find him in Peshawar, and I have spent these months looking for him. Every time I enter the house his mother asks, 'Do you have any news of him?' She has gone half mad and cries as if he's already dead." The man points to the paper. "And then suddenly yesterday we got this letter. It was pushed under the door. He is being held in a warlord's prison in Afghanistan. They captured him fighting for the Taliban, and the warlord's people want to meet me in Peshawar to discuss how I can free him."

Rohan slowly unfolds the sheet and reads the few lines.

Be present at electricity pole number 29 in the Coppersmiths' Bazaar in Peshawar. Eight in the morning on Saturday 22 December. We will bring your son so you'll know we have him.

"The date is two days from now," Rohan says.

"Yes. I thought I would come and see if you would let me put up the snares again, to catch some birds. I have no more money for the train fare to Peshawar. My wife has already sold her earrings and I my bicycle. They were the only bits of wealth we had."

"You must forgive me but I cannot allow you to put up the snares."

"Then I'll have to find another place full of trees. The bicycle is gone so I'll carry the cage filled with them on my back."

Rohan looks at the letter. *Don't go to the police. We will kill him or hand him over to Americans to be tortured.*

"You probably don't know," Abdul says, "but thousands of our boys have gone to Afghanistan."

"I do know."

"All I can say is if September's terrorist attacks had to happen, I am sorry that they happened in my lifetime. They have destroyed me. And I live so far from where they took place. What does Heer know about New York, or New York about Heer? They are two different worlds."

"Is that your son's name?" Rohan asks, looking at the place in the letter where it is mentioned. "Jeo."

The man nods and Rohan hands the paper back and turns and they continue towards the shed. Rohan takes the rosewood spools of wire—knotted branches like bones of trees—and puts them in a cloth bag and then watches the bird pardoner leave down the path and out of the gate, the ground littered with the last flowers of the rusty shield bearer. The exhaustion in the man's eyes resembles the exhaustion in Basie's eyes, who has been following rumours of Mikal ever since they came back from Peshawar, his spirit almost defeated, for now. His energy will revive with time no doubt. Whenever a boy from the neighbourhood ran away to help liberate Kashmiri Muslims from Indian rule, people continued to speculate, bringing true or false leads to his house for months and years. The missing boy was seen in a forest in Anantnag and was suffering from amnesia. He had started his life over again in China. He was abducted by dacoits and was being held for ransom right here in Pakistan, in a lime kiln near Quetta. The ghosts of the missing boys were said to haunt mansions in Delhi, they were said to have been strangled by gamblers in Mansehra, and burnt in houses in Srinagar. Once a young man appeared at a house claiming to be the missing son but he was an escaped mental patient.

Rohan walks to the gate. The bird pardoner has almost reached the end of the street, but Rohan has never raised his voice in public. He looks around for a child who can be asked to shout out and draw the man's attention. Just then the bird pardoner happens to look over his shoulder and Rohan lifts his hand and beckons him.

"I will go to Peshawar with you," he tells the man. "We will meet the warlord's people together and see what can be done to bring back Jeo."

He fears being unable to convince Naheed, Yasmin and Basie about the journey. He is prepared to remind them that in his youth he had visited Saudi Arabia, Iraq, Spain, Egypt, India and Turkey with little money or guidance. He is sure they would argue that that was a long time ago, so he does not tell them about the bird pardoner's son. He tells them he is going to Peshawar to see his former pupil's family, to thank them for the boxes of books, something that had had to be postponed during the last trip.

At the Coppersmiths' Bazaar in Peshawar, they locate electricity pole number 29 and wait to be contacted. They are just outside a rickshaw repair shop, across from a stall collecting money and blood for the Taliban. Sounds of grief were heard from a number of houses in Rohan's neighbourhood in Heer when Kabul fell. The cleric at the mosque near Rohan's house had wept for most of his two-hour Friday sermon, the tears broadcast over the loudspeaker. The person in the Ardent Spirit van said that he had been reading the Koran when the news came of the West having conquered Afghanistan—and the Holy Book, overcome with shame, had disappeared from his hands.

It's 8 a.m., the time specified in the letter, but a six-year-old boy is the only person who approaches them, asking if they want their shoes polished.

They continue with their wait and at ten o'clock a man wearing a Kalashnikov over his shoulder appears and asks them curtly to identify themselves.

He says it'll take twenty thousand rupees to free the bird pardoner's son.

"I don't have that kind of money," Abdul says, and the man sighs with irritation. The mountain peaks cut white fangs into the sky around the city, the December cold intense. The rivers and streams must be flowing with shards of ice.

"The note said you would bring the boy," Rohan says.

The man points to a red van at the other end of the bazaar. They walk towards it and he opens the back door and tells Rohan and Abdul to climb in, the door closing behind them immediately. The interior is windowless, a pitch-black metal box, and Abdul snaps his cigarette lighter. The light it produces is sparse and he adjusts the lever on the side to lengthen the flame. They look around, holding their heads at an angle because of the low ceiling, and realise that the huddled shape at the other end of the space is a boy and not a pile of rags. He flinches and lets out a squeal when the bird pardoner moves towards him.

Abdul stops and looks at him and then moves to the door. "That's not my son," he says, sounding a knock.

Rohan sees that the boy is weeping. "Please take me away," the little voice says finally, looking down. "They keep us in a prison. They do things to you that make you want to kill yourself. Please take me away," he whispers.

"Suicide is a sin," Rohan says. "You mustn't talk like that." Abdul is knocking on the door but there is no response from the other side.

"They have this game, they call it 'Nail.' They start with the youngest prisoners and ask their ages. If the boy says twelve, they send twelve men to him. If he says fourteen, he gets fourteen. They take him to a room and take off his trousers and hold him down and then the whole place fills with screams. The men yell louder than the boy—like they have gone mad or have turned into wild animals. They are shouting, 'Nail! Nail! Nail!' as they do it to him."

It would terrify even the stars. And Abdul's fists are hitting the door louder now, the lighter flame jerking and then going out. "Please help me," says the boy's voice. "Allah will reward you and your wife." And then suddenly the door is opened and the light floods their eyes.

Rohan and Abdul are let out and the door is closed on the boy who screams desperately for the last time, "I will kill myself," just as the van jerks forward and drives off.

"That's not my son," Abdul says, and the ransom seeker takes out a set of photographs twice the thickness of a deck of cards, and asks Abdul to look through it. Towards the end of the sheaf, Abdul recognises his Jeo.

"We will bring him next week. Same time."

"I have no money for the ransom, or the journey," Abdul says. "Either I or my wife will have to sell a kidney. It'll take some time. Can we meet again in a month?"

"A month?" The man considers.

"Have you no shame?" Rohan finds himself saying into the man's face, having pushed Abdul aside, unable to control his distress and fury. People stare at him as they walk past and he feels at the centre of a swarm of eyes. "How can you hold children to ransom and force the parents to do such a terrible thing to themselves?" He cannot even bring himself to raise the other subject, so traumatised is he by it.

The man is outraged and looks as though he will lunge at Rohan.

"I will cut the boy's throat and I will kill you!" he says while Rohan glares at him. "Your boy was caught fighting against us. He probably killed some of our men. We need money to make sure the widows and the children of those dead men don't become beggars."

Abdul tries to placate him. "I will come back in a month and I will bring the money. Please treat my boy well in the meantime."

"No," Rohan says, suddenly determined. "No. We want Jeo and we will go and get him today."

"He's in Afghanistan."

"Then we go to Afghanistan."

"It's four, five hours away," the man points to the east of the city.

"Afghanistan is not four or five hours away," Rohan says.

"Six, seven, then."

"It's more even than that but I don't care. I want Jeo back."

"Yes, come with me if you want. The official ways into Afghanistan are still difficult, but I can get you there and back without any problems via old smuggling routes."

He is aware of the dangers. Defeated and banished, Taliban and al-Qaeda gangs are roaming Afghanistan, and of course the place is full of Western soldiers.

"The journey will cost you," the man says. "And I'll have to make a phone call to arrange everything, to make sure it's acceptable to my superiors."

"What about the twenty thousand rupees?" Abdul asks Rohan. Rohan reaches into his pocket and takes out the ruby on its black cord. Both Abdul and the ransom seeker are taken aback by the size and beauty of the jewel, the unimprovable red light collected inside it. They cannot take their eyes off the stone, and they stare at the pocket where it is when Rohan puts it back into his coat.

Rohan looks around. "The Street of Storytellers is that way. Which way is the Jewellers' Bazaar?"

The ransom seeker has a car and, after the ruby has been appraised at the Jewellers' Bazaar, they drive towards the eastern outskirts of Peshawar. The legitimate path into Afghanistan is the Khyber Pass, but they are taking narrower roads, slipping through hillocks overgrown densely with mesquite bushes. In the limestone Maneri hills there are veins of marble mottled black, green and yellow, or pure green and pure yellow, and the rosary in Rohan's hands is made from these, the two-coloured beads alternating. On the boulders on the riverbanks the words *Jihad is your duty* are daubed, white against the grey and black. They were not there in October when Rohan was roaming these areas with Yasmin and Basie. *Victory or martyrdom. Telephone now for jihad training.* There is a phone number.

The gem merchant valued the ruby at fifty thousand rupees. The sign above the shop said the proprietor was a genealogist of precious stones and could tell the origin and race of every precious stone on earth. Rohan asked him to write down the amount while the ransom seeker watched.

"I will give your warlord this gem instead of the money, and he will give us Jeo."

As they drive towards the Afghan border, the ransom seeker talks. "Seventy people from my village were killed when the Americans dropped a bomb," the man says. "I blame America but I also blame the foreign fighters—the likes of your boy—who the Americans were trying to kill."

And repeatedly he wants to be handed the ruby.

At a secluded place near the border he stops the car and asks them to disembark, saying he has to go away for an hour. And yet again he wants the ruby. "It'll save you the journey. Give me the jewel and I will bring the boy to you."

But Rohan refuses and he drives away. The valley of Peshawar has the appearance of having been, centuries ago, the bed of a vast lake, whose banks were bound by the cliffs and peaks of the surrounding Himalayas, and Rohan has the feeling of being submerged within that vast inland sea.

I was given the following words of the Prophet by Adam bin Ayaas, who was given them by Ibn Abi Zyeb, who was given them by Syed Makbari, who in turn was given them by Abu Horaira. The Prophet said, "If anyone has been unjust towards someone, he should secure himself a pardon from the victim before it is too late. Otherwise, on Judgement Day, when the only valid currency will be a person's good conduct on earth, the good deeds of an unjust man will be transferred to his victim. And if he has no good deeds, then the victim's sins will be transferred to him."

Rohan is reading the *Book of Prophet's Sayings*, turning the pages at random—pausing on this, the saying number 2,286, for a few moments. He shivers in the cold. It has been two hours since the man left with the car. The bird trapper is asleep, wrapped in a blanket under a tree.

"Why do you look so troubled?" a woman's voice asks.

Rohan looks up—her hair is white, the features of the face caught in a net of wrinkles. He smiles and shakes his head.

She points to the boulders and the screen of bushes on the other side of the road. Rohan sees that behind the leaves and branches there is a low mud wall.

"Go there."

Rohan returns to the book. *Number 2,279: I was given the following words of the Prophet by Osman Ibn Ani Sheeba, who was given them by Hasheem, who was given them by Obaidullah bin Abu Bakr bin Uns, who was given them by Hameed Tavail, who in turn was given them by Uns bin Malik. The Prophet said, "Always help your (Muslim) brother, whether he is a tyrant or victim."*

The woman is hovering and now touches his shoulder. "It is a grave-yard. The body of a boy who died fighting the Americans in Afghanistan was brought out and is buried here. He is a martyr and will intercede on your behalf with Allah. Go and ask Mikal for your suffering to be alleviated."

Rohan closes the book and places it in his shoulder bag and stands up. He crosses the road and enters the graveyard that contains about a hundred souls, a few decaying tombs and thorn trees. The mountains loom overhead vertiginously, the land and slopes marked with evidence of the lost sea, the effort of currents, waves, springs, streams and rivers. Verses of the Koran are on every headstone—as though the graves are quoting them, carrying on a conversation with one another using nothing but holy words. One mound just on the other side of the boundary wall is at least ten yards long, heaped with bright flowers, river soil with pieces of freshwater shells, and chips of soft blue slate quarried from the nearby hills. A group of women is reciting verses of the Koran over the mound. A man is lighting an incense stick at its head, the smoke rising in sluggish blue strands through the cold air.

"He was a giant." A woman looks up at Rohan as he approaches.

"He wasn't," the man with the incense stick corrects her, walking the ten yards to light the ones at the other end. "He was of normal height, but he became this size on the battlefield."

The tombstone is carved with stars along the edges. There is Mikal's name, the date of birth, and of death—the day after he and Jeo went to Afghanistan.

"They say he brought down six fighter jets single-handedly and saved thirty women from being ravished by American soldiers."

He stands looking at the blossoms piled onto the boy. The dazzle of the sun is in his eyes and his body feels suddenly tired. Claw prints of an eagle were found heading away from the martyr, the warrior saint, someone tells him. His soul must have been an eagle.

How did Mikal's body end up here? The mayhem and chaos of war. He looks up at the cliffs. The vegetation everywhere is profuse; after the level of the sea decreased this was a tropical marsh, the resort of rhinoceros, flamingo and tiger, thick with reeds, rushes and conifers. Under his breath he reads the verse of the Koran that is etched onto the ruby. *Wealth and offspring are transitory adornments of the nearer life.* How long he stands there in that disordered state of mind he doesn't know, coming to himself only when he hears Abdul calling out his name from the other side of the wall.

Through hillside, across bridges, through a dust storm a mile long, and through streams in which float—by the dozen—the shaved-off beards of fleeing al-Qaeda militants, the journey to the destination in Afghanistan takes seventeen hours. In deep twilight they cross a broad flat valley with a river and river flats in it, every bit of it scorched black where a Daisy Cutter bomb had been dropped, reducing everything to ash, pumice, lava, the sides of the hills torn up into segments, and scattered over it all is the yellow haze of the unrisen moon, the cold night falling on them out of the east, the stars beginning their slide through the black slopes. It looks like the site of a cosmic incursion such as a meteorite, not the work of men. The US casualties number twelve in the two-month war, whereas countless thousands of Afghanistanis have perished, fighters as well as bystanders, and Rohan doesn't know who will speak the complicated truth, and he watches with attention as though at some point in the future he himself will be asked to tell what he has seen. Towards the end of the journey a convoy of American soldiers goes past their vehicle.

He wonders if he can ask them to help secure the release of the boys imprisoned by the warlord. He watches the convoy disappear just as the car radio brings news that a British Muslim has been arrested trying to blow up a passenger airliner over the Atlantic Ocean with explosives hidden in his shoes.

Arriving at a compound at 3 a.m., they are shown into a room full of the odour of dust and are told to spend the remains of the night there. The walls are of grey cement and hundreds of broken statues lie in heaps on the floor. The Buddha and the various people from his life—torsos, arms, feet and faces of all sizes. He looks at the exact arc of the eyebrow made above a man's eye by the carver's chisel. The flowers as though growing out of the hair on a woman's head. There is barely room for Rohan and the bird pardoner to stand, and they clear a space by stacking a number of the pieces onto each other, the bird pardoner lying down against a yard-long fragment of drapery—hewn from the skirts of a nymph or temple dancer. As she lay dying, Rohan remembers burning a sketch of a Bodhisattva statue that Sofia had made. And he knows some people in the neighbourhood, on hearing the news that his vision is slowly deteriorating, comment that it is Allah's retribution for tormenting her during her last hours. "He didn't want to see what she had painted, now he won't be able to see the real things."

He falls asleep looking at the photograph on the far wall. The warlord is shaking hands with an American colonel. The date on the frame says it was taken soon after the Taliban regime was toppled last month. The opposite of war is not peace but civilisation, and civilisation is purchased with violence and cold-blooded murder. With war. The man must earn millions of dollars for guarding the NATO supply convoys as they pass through his area, and for the militia he must have raised to fight the Taliban and al-Qaeda soldiers alongside American Special Forces.

He wakes up before the stars are down and says his predawn prayers. He had slept on the palm of a seven-foot hand, using the swollen base of the thumb as his pillow. He thinks he hears shouts of "Nail! Nail!" from some nearby room and he interrupts his prayers and moves from point to point within the compound's darkness, but the howling has stopped, nothing but the waning moon overhead casting his faint shadow on the ground, and the clear chart of the constellations that makes him think of Mikal, the bone geometry of stars.

A man with grave coal-black eyes enters the room, late in the morning, and asks Rohan and the bird pardoner to follow him. Guided by him they descend into the warlord's underground prison, going along the buried hallways lined on both sides with barred cells. There is a large pool through one wide arch, but it is full of stored gasoline, the grimy walls painted with the still-beautiful flowers and parakeets and bulbuls from when it must have been used for indoor swimming. There are pumps to put the gasoline into tins for vehicles or electricity genera-tors. As they continue along the hallways, shadow-people thrust their arms through the bars of the cells and shake dirty beakers and call out, "Water." The place smells of sweat, urine and excrement, of rotting wounds and flesh. These prisoners must all be insignificant, because the important ones are handed over to the Americans for $5,000 each.

A barred door is unlocked and the guide motions for the occupant to step out. The boy who emerges is in a daze, standing at an angle in the half dark, and the man pushes him towards the bird pardoner. He wears a dirty shalwar kameez and is ghostly thin and his hands shake as he lifts them to wipe away tears. When the father embraces him the boy's arms come out of the torn sleeves and Rohan sees that the skin is crisscrossed with deep cuts. Abdul keeps up the glad words of reunion but the child is silent, looking as though he would rather understand than speak.

Rohan hands the ruby to the guide when they are back in the original room. Immediately he says that it is not acceptable.

"This is mere glass," the man says.

"It is not glass," Rohan says. "It's an authentic and indisputable jewel."

The man stands with it in the palm of his hand. Then he sighs and tells them that the warlord is not present and that they must wait for his return. He goes away with it and Rohan walks to the door to see which of the many rooms lining the courtyard he will disappear into. Posters of the warlord are pasted to the walls in the compound. He clearly hopes to have a role in the government.

"How did you end up here?" Rohan asks Jeo, but the boy won't speak—unwilling to recall the time and the place where his ties with the human had broken. He looks at his father and whispers, "Have you come to get me back?"

"Yes."

"One boy's father came last week. He is an ice seller and said he is trying to save ten rupees a day to free his son. It'll take him twenty years. You have to take me with you today."

"We are here to take you away, this morning, don't worry," Rohan says, looking in the direction the man went with the ruby, gently placing a hand on the boy's head.

The boy recoils under the touch.

"You don't need to be afraid of him," Abdul says. "He is a good man."

"How many prisoners are down there in the cells?" Rohan asks, looking at the floor. They are perhaps directly under his feet.

"About a hundred. The others who came with me died."

Rohan recognises the warlord from the photograph on the wall the moment he enters the room, holding the ruby in his hand, clearly delighted by its beauty. He is one-eyed with a big head and chest, the breast thrust forward as though by the force of the heart beating unafraid of any man or thing.

"I have come to see the man who has brought me this gift." He smiles as he walks towards Rohan. "You can take the boy," he says, holding out his hand to be shaken.

Rohan looks down at the hand but does not take it, unable to hide his feelings, and the man stops smiling. His servants gathered behind him stiffen: the proffered hand remains hanging in the air and Rohan might as well have slapped him. Everyone waits while the ruby shines in the man's other hand. Valour is associated with this gemstone. The courage to seek the truth at all times. To be able to look tyrants in the eyes. This world of havoc, malice and destruction, where the blood of the innocent is of no consequence, is perfect for him and his kind.

Rohan walks out of the door, followed by Jeo and the bird pardoner, leaving the men of war behind. But he is beginning to regret his act as it could jeopardise the safety of Abdul and the boy.

They go out through the gate, not meeting the eyes of the armed men standing guard. People are gathered outside the front gate, all there to pay homage to the warlord or seek money and help. The moment the guards open the gate to let the three of them out, the crowd begins to shout out its needs, frenziedly waving pieces of paper in the air, asking to see the lord. The voices of women coming from under the folds of blue or cream-coloured burkas. Near the road people are eating breakfasts of tea and packets of biscuits. Jeo stares at a cat walking along a wall. He says to his father, "They forget to feed you for days sometimes down there, and one day I was hungry this cat brought me a dead hoopoe to eat."

Rohan sees the convoy of American vehicles coming down the road.

"The other prisoners are just there," Jeo says pointing back to the warlord's compound, his eyes almost vibrating with intensity. "See that row of barred windows at the base of the wall? They are the high windows we looked up at, in our underground cells."

The Americans' six-vehicle convoy has drawn near and Rohan steps into the middle of the road before it.

The lead vehicle stops ten yards away from him and the white boy-soldier behind the steering wheel looks at him through the windshield. His companion in the passenger seat leans out with his gun after a few seconds and shouts, "Get out of the way!"

Above him the sky has suddenly opened into the cold of the cosmos.

Tormented by dreams of justice on earth, Jeo wants to do something like a star shooting off light to make itself. Before his father knows what he is doing, he picks up a section of broken brick lying at his feet and throws it solidly at the men guarding the building, missing one of them by a mere two feet. He stands defiant, as though gaining strength from being under the open sky, having found this way of announcing his place in the world, the family of man. One of the guards comes running towards him with a raised rifle but Abdul moves forward to placate him. Taking a cigarette from his pocket, Abdul puts it in the guard's mouth and even lights it, keeping up words of apology.

"Get out of the way!"

Rohan does not heed the order. Instead he begins to walk towards the jeep. The other vehicles have halted behind the first one and soldiers are leaning out with weapons at the ready, some in confusion, some in alarmed fear.

"I need to talk to you," Rohan says in English.

"Get out of the way!"

Rohan puts up both his arms. The soldiers will not see him as a harmless aged man. "I need your help in getting some children out of this building," he says, pointing with his head.

"Not our problem."

"They are being abused in there."

"Not our problem. This is your last warning!" They are aiming at him and in every other direction, behind them, to the left, right, at the crowd of petitioners, the gun barrels unceasing as the panic mounts. "Move! Now! This is your last warning!"

Rohan catches a glimpse of Jeo, who has walked towards the windows of the dungeon and is peering down through them.

Slowly Rohan walks to the very edge of the tarmac—unable to bring himself to vacate the road completely, still searching for words he might say to these soldiers, and the vehicles begin to come towards him suspiciously, in extreme slowness, the zigzag pattern on the tyres moving down inch by inch, and he watches as the gate to the building opens and the warlord emerges. He stands looking at Rohan.

One of the warlord's men has rushed forward to drag Rohan away from the road, throwing him forcibly onto the ground. As he falls he sees the American convoy speed up, he also sees that Jeo has taken off his shirt for some reason, revealing the gaunt, sickeningly bruised body. Snatching the lighter from Abdul's hand the boy sets the shirt alight and with this burning rag he runs—towards the row of windows to the underground cells.

Rohan lies in the dust, thinking that the warlord's man had wished nothing more than to remove the obstruction from the path of the Americans. But the man is still holding Rohan down—and now others have appeared, pinning him so hard against the ground he thinks it is an attempt to bury him alive, that using nothing but their arms they want to push him into the earth. The warlord is standing above him with his hand extended, the hand he had rejected. Time slows down as the warlord lowers the hand and Rohan sees that the pulverised remains of the ruby are in the palm, the stone crushed into tiny fragments. Calmly the man presses a fingertip into the shattered jewel, coating it with the razor grit, and brings the fingertip towards Rohan's eyes.

One second, two, three—and the pool of gasoline erupts, Jeo having dropped the burning shirt onto it from above.

Rohan stands up. The light is so strong everything disintegrates in it—it is like being in a field of pure energy. Rohan sweeps at his head to remove the white cloth that has come to rest over his eyes but realises there is no cloth. The world moves away and everything becomes smaller but then the vision returns for a few moments and he sees the fire eddying along the ground. He is tired, tired of living without Sofia, and as he stumbles against something and falls, feeling a patch of meagre grass under his hands, he knows he is blind.

15

To one side of the house in Heer, between the window to Rohan's study and the cluster of the towering silk-cotton trees, a bathroom sink is affixed to the wall. As children Jeo and Mikal loved to wash their faces there in the mornings, amid birdsong and the breezes of the garden. At certain hours the sun's rays shine in the mirror that hangs above it, and above the mirror is a bougainvillea with its heart-like leaves and tissue-paper blossoms, its long branches sometimes covering the mirror so that they have to be parted for the face to be seen. Sometimes they are tied back or are cut away in a square shape to expose the mirror. The colour of rust on apple slices, the deep orange blossoms of the bougainvillea fall into the sink by the dozen and have to be lifted out before the taps are turned.

Naheed splashes water onto her face, avoiding eye contact with her reflection. She tilts her face to the December sun and stands there for a minute, feeling the water dry on her skin. I know he is alive, she had said to her mother, I feel him.

Walking back to the chair she picks up the book she had been reading, having selected it out of one of the boxes. Rohan went to Peshawar two days ago to thank the family of the kind donor. They are no longer a recent presence in the house but still she forgets them at times, emerging out of a doorway and walking into a column of boxes as though she wishes to enter and disappear into it.

There is no body, there is no grave. She will keep telling herself this. If the sun and the moon should doubt, they would be extinguished.

She looks up from the book now and then, her tunic patterned with grey flowers and black leaves, a garden at dusk, due to the ash.

Love does not make lovers invulnerable, she reads. *But even if the world's beauty and love are on the edge of destruction, theirs is still the only side to be on. Hate's victory does not make it other than what it is. Defeated love is still love.*

II

The Blind Man's Garden

If there is no God,
Not everything is permitted to man.
He is still his brother's keeper
And he is not permitted to sadden his brother,
By saying that there is no God.

—*Czeław Miłosz*

16

Adam was pardoned in winter.

The thought comes to Mikal as he stands in the cold air, his breath appearing and disappearing before him. In his bandaged right hand he holds the small dried flowers he has kept hidden in his pocket. The index finger is missing from each hand. The flowers are faded and torn, but with all the grey around him they are still the brightest things in his gaze. He shields them as he would a candle flame, as though preventing their colours from being extinguished. He runs a finger along the centre of one, the parts small yet feelable, fine as thread with minute swellings of pollen.

He turns and walks back into the building.

It is the mountain house owned by the warlord who is holding him prisoner. The chain at his ankles is long enough for him to walk at a slow pace but not to run. He goes through the kitchen without pausing and climbs the staircase and then continues along a long corridor, towards a room filled with voices at the end.

He saw the Quadrantids meteor shower three nights ago so he knows what month it is. Meteor showers occur at approximately the same time every year and the Quadrantids are seen at the beginning of January.

He was trying to escape from here the night he saw it. The house is surrounded by towering pines and snow-covered peaks, most of its rooms locked, the only human presence being a retinue of six of the warlord's men.

He still doesn't know where Jeo is. During the months since his capture in October, he has been bartered and sold among various warlords, and as the weeks have gone by there have been fewer and fewer words from him, none at all on most days. The current warlord doesn't even know his name.

He comes into the room to find the men huddled around a coal brazier. The warlord is a bandit and the son of bandits, and Mikal has heard stories of how much his bloodthirstiness is feared. Once, having received word that he was about to mount a raid, the inhabitants of a village had left their jewellery and valuables out in the streets at night, the thousands of banknotes blowing about in the air as he rode in.

Mikal lifts a pomegranate from a dish and squats in the far corner of the room, listening to them as he opens the fruit with his teeth and fingernails, careful as he manipulates the fruit because the wounds from the missing fingers are still tender these months later. Every warlord has told him that he would have to be ransomed. He had refused to give any of them a contact address, no matter what they did to him. The only way anyone could gain financially from him was to send him to work on construction sites every day—a school being built, a prison for women being expanded—and he laboured while wearing his chains, becoming thinner with each week, his clothes hanging on him in rags. His hair became long and lay on his head like a thick ungovernable cap, and he still wore the boots he had been wearing back in October, having washed the blood out of them. He worked as hard as he could because he feared they would otherwise shoot him for being just a mouth to feed. But then being worked to death was another fear.

He chews the pomegranate seeds and drips the red liquid from his mouth onto the bandaged areas of his hands, knowing it is a potent healer.

One of the men is lamenting about a pistol that keeps jamming. It is an M9 Beretta and Mikal knows how simply the trouble can be fixed. He could tell the man to put a piece of electrical tape over the hole in the bottom of the pistol's handle to keep the dust out. But he remains silent, keenly alive to the possibility that the weapon could be turned on him at some point as he attempts to flee.

He has been brought here to the mountain house to assist in a mission, a theft. Around the fire the men are finalising the details of the plan. The Prophet Muhammad's 1,400-year-old cloak has been kept at the mosque in Kandahar since 1768. But when the American bombing started back in October, the cloak was brought into the mountains for safekeeping, and it hasn't been sent back to Kandahar yet. It is still there in a high-altitude mosque a distance of fifty miles from this house, and the warlord wishes to acquire it to increase his prestige, to benefit from its miraculous powers.

The warlord's most expert thieves will go with Mikal to acquire the Prophet's cloak, a father-and-son team, the son the same age as Mikal. The sacred garment is no doubt guarded and if they are discovered during the crime a fight will ensue. Mikal would rather not take part in the theft but he has to obey. In addition, the warlord has said that he will consider granting Mikal his freedom if the cloak is successfully brought to him. Mikal doesn't believe the man would keep his word, so he resolves to remain alert to every possibility of escape during the journey.

They stand up when they are ready to go, everyone beginning to walk out to the front courtyard to see them off. Mikal lingers in the room and is the last one through its door: with as much swiftness as his chained legs allow, he picks up the bullet he had seen lying under a chair the moment he came in. He works it into the waistband of his trousers as he walks behind the others in the dark corridor, the metal cold against his skin even through the fabric.

Outside, as they walk towards the van, minute specks of frozen moisture float in the otherwise dry air. It glitters in the late morning sun like shining sand or a dust of glass. The mansion has high walls of stone with lookout posts, and five large Alsatians roam the compound at night. In spite of this he has made three attempts at escape, getting further on each successive occasion, and it was only the sub-zero cold that forced him back. He had wrapped his ankle chain in rags to muffle it but in the end he couldn't walk fast enough to generate the necessary heat, the mountainside locked in the white iron of winter.

The father gets behind the steering wheel, and he and his son utter in unison the Arabic phrase all good Muslims are meant to use before setting out on travel: "I hope Allah has written a safe journey for us."

Mikal climbs into the second row of seats. He must be ready to act at the first chance. He has known for two days that something is wrong with the vehicle, that it could break down during the journey. The day before yesterday they had gone hunting for deer in the woods, and when they came back the Alsatians had not recognised their approach, had barked as they would at the noise of an unfamiliar vehicle. Some mechanism inside the engine is about to fail, a fracture spreading in the chassis.

He touches the painful arm as they drive off. For a while his wounds had made him manically alert to bees, following the progress of each one in the air with the hope of being led to the hive, coveting the yellow colour sealed inside the cellular wax, knowing that honey can mend flesh as nothing else can, healing wounds that have remained open for a decade.

The air inside the van becomes colder as they climb towards the snow line, moving through the rocks and the immense boulders, the landscape ripped to pieces by its own elemental energies. They interrupt the journey when it is time for the afternoon prayers, getting out and spreading a blanket on the rock-strewn ground while the wind howls in a gorge to the left of them. Standing next to each other on the blanket with their faces turned towards the mountains in the west, they begin to bend and bow towards Mecca hundreds of miles away.

Mikal finishes earlier than the father and son and hurries back into the vehicle, his hand working the bullet out of his waistband as he goes. It's a .22 calibre, and working as fast as he can he replaces the fuse of the van's headlights with it. The procedure requires about thirty seconds and all through it he fears the father and son will conclude their prayers and look towards him, but his luck holds. The bullet is a perfect fit in the fuse box which is located next to the steering-wheel column. After about fifteen miles the bullet should overheat, discharge and enter the driver's leg. It'd be as though he had been shot with a gun.

Afterwards Mikal sits looking out, waiting for them to finish praying, the sky composed of horizontal pink, yellow and grey bands repeated in Allah's strict order above them. When they come back the father scolds him for hurrying his communion with Allah, and then they move on. The headlights—that have been in use since before they stopped to pray in the afternoon gloom—illuminate giant slabs of stone thrust out at all angles as though the place had been attacked from the inside with pickaxes and sledgehammers, resulting in entire zones of star-shaped fractures.

The days are short in the mountains and the greyness intensifies as one hour passes and another begins. While they are making a narrow turn, Mikal notices that the soles of several boots have left deep imprints on the muddy ground of the bend. America is everywhere. The boots are large as if saying, "This is how you make an impression in the world." After the victory in November, the war had quickly devolved into an endless series of raids and manhunts for terrorist leaders and lieutenants. And these must be Special Forces soldiers looking for a possible Osama bin Laden hideout or grave site.

He sits leaning forward from the back, his head between the two front seats. When the bullet enters the driver's body it will cause an accident: the vehicle will be damaged and it is possible that his son will not be able to drive them to safety, that they will bleed to death here in the wilds. A part of him wants to cancel the plot he has set in motion and after a while that is exactly what he tries to do.

"Stop the van," he says.

"What?" the son asks, turning around to look at him.

"We must say the evening prayers."

"It's a little early for that," the driver says, and the van remains in motion, the headlights burning into the mountainside. Mikal reaches out and grabs the steering wheel and it swings violently to the left for a moment. The son takes hold of Mikal at the collar and pushes him backwards and shouts for him to be still. Mikal sits back in and the father strikes his face hard without turning around, the back of the fingers paved with coloured gems. The vehicle continues to move beyond any hope of influence, and again Mikal says, "We have to stop."

After that it's only another few seconds before the van has entered the air above the gorge with a loud tearing of steel against stone—it's preceded by the noise of the exploding bullet but Mikal hears it only in retrospect. Twenty feet below is a river overhung with weeping trees, and as they begin their plunge towards it everything out there becomes darker, because the bullet leaving the fuse box has broken the electric connection to the headlights.

"It's a bullet wound," says the father with a mixture of shock and confusion, turning his back to the two of them and opening his trousers and looking down at his thigh. "I have been shot."

They've splashed ashore, the man limping badly, barely able to stand upright. Every pain in Mikal's body has been awakened, a jolt to the spine when the vehicle landed in the shallow river.

"Shot? How is that possible?" the son says, going around to look at the wound. "Maybe a part of the van pierced you."

"I know what a bullet wound looks like," the father says. He is a large man but at this moment just the effort to raise his voice seems too much for him.

Beyond them in the glacial water a thick rope of blood emerges from the driver's side of the wrecked van and goes swaying down the slow current. It is as though the metal itself is bleeding.

"We need to bring it out," says the father, gesturing towards the van. Mikal can see that apart from everything else both father and son are terrified at having ruined their master's property.

"It's not going to move now," Mikal says. He looks under his shirt for any injuries. There is a pause while everyone reflects on what has happened, the drenched bodies shivering in the terrible cold, the son wincing as he touches the two-inch cut on his forehead. "It's a warning from Allah," the boy says quietly. "This is a wicked and sinful thing we are attempting, stealing the blessed cloak. I think we should turn back . . ."

His father looks at him sharply. "You have no knowledge of this matter. Stop talking nonsense."

The boy shakes his head. "We have to turn back. You've been shot with an invisible pistol. It's a warning from Allah . . ."

"Be quiet," the man says, attempting to remain in control, and the son looks away, torn between who he fears more, Allah or his father. The man is losing blood very fast, the red-black liquid spreading on the pebbles at his feet. It seems to be something seeping up from the earth due to the weight of his body. "We can't stay here," he says. "We have to walk the five miles to the mosque."

"Go and see if you can rip out the seat belts," Mikal says to the boy. "We need to bind your father's leg." And he asks the father, "Are the keys to my chain in the van?"

"I didn't bring them."

Mikal is aghast. "How did you think I would help you steal?" He doesn't believe the man is telling the truth. "What if I'd had to run?"

The thief lifts his gun and aims it at Mikal unsteadily with shivering hands. The pain is making his eyes murderous. "I don't have them. And don't think you can run away from me. Now go and get the seat belts."

After applying the tourniquet they begin to walk, finding a path that leads them back up to the level from which they fell, the thief leaving a glistening trail. Moving through freezing air in wet clothes, the footsteps of all three soon become less sure but they continue, wordlessly, Mikal's chain the only sound. Two years ago in Pakistan he had gone hunting at the same latitude as this, and had prevented frostbite by duct-taping his entire face, leaving just a half-inch slot for the eyes and another for the nose. Now he watches the father and his son as they weaken. He knows they'll fail sooner than him, the father leaning on the son as they stagger along. He must summon the last bit of warmth inside him. Naheed. The word in which all meanings converge.

The father is the first to collapse among the grey rocks just as they are approaching a ridge. The son succumbs a moment later as though he had needed permission. From where he lies the man swipes at Mikal's shirt in sudden desperation, to hold on to him, but the mountains have sucked out all his strength, the slopes and summits that stand around them like solidified silence—time made visible in a different way, ancient and on an elongated scale.

In a trance of liberty Mikal keeps walking towards the ridge. In another half hour the darkness will be complete. He looks over his shoulder and sees that the injured man, lying on the ground, is attempting to aim his gun at him, the barrel jerking as though he is trying to shoot a butterfly that won't settle.

He goes over the ridge and stops in his tracks, seeing what lies on the other side. "What the hell?" And only after a long moment does he take another step forward.

He is facing a graveyard of planes and helicopters, Russian MiGs and Hinds, all resting at odd angles with cockpits slung open and the glass smashed, the tyres ripped and rotted. There are several dozen of them, a swathe of hulks stretching all the way to another ridge half a mile away.

He moves towards a helicopter and looks inside. There is Russian graffiti scratched onto the tarnished walls. Names, sentences, and hearts with initials in them. The interior has been stripped of everything, from the seats to the instrument dials. Each aircraft is little more than a pod or shell, a coffin meant for a giant, and the metal of each must weigh thousands of kilograms. At some point each has had a growth of lichen on it, layer upon thick layer dried now to a crust. He continues to walk in an almost straight line through and between them, climbing in and out of the doors, speaking quietly to himself as he goes, to stop the mind from losing focus. "Mikal is free at last. Mikal keeps walking. Mikal hears the sound of his chains. Mikal cannot feel any of his fingers. Mikal is not going to die in this metal cemetery. Mikal has probably caused the death of a man. Mikal wants to see Naheed's face. Mikal wants to live with her in the room in Heer. Mikal must find Jeo." After a while he stops and turns around.

He arrives back at the first helicopter gunship and sees that the father and son have attempted to follow him—they'd made it over the ridge but have collapsed once again on this side, one prone, the other supine. He approaches and astonishingly the father raises his wildly trembling arm with the gun towards him once again. The son's eyes remain closed but even in the state of unconsciousness his body is shaking. Mikal, shivering almost as much as them, frees the weapon from the father's grip and standing with his feet as wide apart as possible points the barrel at the taut chain. The action is stiff from the cold, an equivalent of his own bone-deep chill, and since he is having to use a hand that has no trigger finger, there is little precision in his aim. He fires into the hard ground twice, powdered granite and the blue smoke of the gun rising very slowly towards his face.

He puts the gun in his pocket and prises loose the one from the son's rigid fingers too. From the father's pocket he takes out the brass cigarette lighter. The man stares up at him helplessly, too far gone. Under the darkening blue sky and the already countless stars, and with his feet still bound in chains, Mikal walks up to a MiG.

The MiG is fifteen feet high. He stands under the wing coated densely with the dried lichen and raises his hand and snaps the lighter. The lichen catches on the sixth try and an area of it glows indigo for a moment, then the glimmer spreads sideways and becomes a sheet of scarlet combustion. He steps back: at first it's only the wing, but then the entire plane becomes sheathed in the bright flame, the tinder-dry lichen flaring abruptly with an explosion of heat. There is a brilliant upwards suck, a one-moment-long vacuum. The machine is on fire from top to bottom, back to front, in about twenty seconds, a burning transparency rushing over the fifty-foot metal shape. A bird made of flames.

He is still cold, his clothing wet, but his hand has become a little steadier and he takes the gun from his pocket and shoots into his chain, shattering the seventh of the thirteen links.

Though they are still lying where they fell, the blood of the other two is beginning to revive also, life returning to their limbs. A great roaring fills the air. Brought out of sleep to find itself in flames, the metal is screaming, and it is as though the plane might take off with the blaze.

"Come closer," he calls over his shoulder.

They rise and slowly walk towards the source of heat, a blast of August temperature in January. Hand's-breadth pieces of lichen are separating to float up as flakes of blinding light. And then, as suddenly as it had begun, the blaze completes itself and the plane starts to creak emptily and smoulders here and there. Fragments of charcoal lie on the ground with bright crimson points worming along their edges.

The scorched metal continues to give off heat and the father and son stand as close to it as they can tolerate. With a wave of the gun Mikal tells them to follow him as he walks over to another plane, flicking open the lighter once again.

They move from hulk to hulk, from one bright roaring platform to the next, the rotor blades of the Hind helicopters burning like fifty-foot-wide gold stars above them, bathing them in light. They leave a crooked wandering path behind them through that necropolis of steel, their clothes steaming.

When it begins to snow, the snowflakes hiss upon encountering the heated metal.

Eventually both Mikal and the son stop shivering, the released river-grit falling away from their dry clothes, but the father himself has lost too much blood and his condition deteriorates, his face pallid, the lips dark.

"He'll be fine when we get to the mosque," says the son.

Mikal looks at him. "I hope so. But I am not coming with you. I have to go my own way."

"Please don't disappear," the boy says softly. "We'll be punished by the master."

Mikal shakes his head. "I have to go. Release that tourniquet every fifteen minutes."

"We will be beaten if you run away. Already there is the matter of the ruined van."

"I can't help you. I have to go."

"He will kill us."

"Then don't go back," Mikal says, suddenly full of fury at the world. "You disappear too."

"We *have* to go back," the son shouts. There is an edge of desolation to the voice. "Our family is where the master is. If we run away he'll torture them to find out where we are, to force us out of hiding."

Mikal looks to the ground, then shakes his head. "I can't."

Sitting in a half-faint, the father opens his eyes for an instant and points to Mikal's fingers. "Maybe when you touch the Prophet's cloak, the pain in your wounds will stop."

Mikal begins to walk away, still shaking his head.

"How can you abandon fellow Muslims like this? Just help me carry him to the mosque. After that you can leave."

Mikal stops and looks back.

"I can't carry him on my own, you can see that," the son says, on the verge of tears. "He'll bleed to death."

"All right. You and I will take him to the mosque and then I will leave. And we are not stealing anything."

It's past midnight when they see the mosque in the far distance, a glass moon shining above it. The sacred building stands on the expanse of blue and white snow, appearing separate and singular like something presented on the palm of the hand. The son was here on a reconnoitring trip last month but the area has been transformed by snow and ice. He whispers, "Glory be to Allah who changes His world and then changes it again but Himself changes not."

The father has been babbling, hallucinating as he begins to die.

"Run to the mosque and get help," the son tells Mikal when the man falls silent; then he lowers his father onto his back and, brushing the snow away from his chest, listens for a heartbeat. In his other hand he holds the torch they'd made with a branch and a torn turban. Although it has stopped snowing the snowflakes lie so thickly on them that almost half of their bodies are invisible.

Mikal shakes the whiteness off his face and clothing, patting himself into visibility, and sets off towards the mosque, at a slow pace—if he runs he grows faint. His mind retains very few impressions during the distance to its giant door. Now and then his two pieces of broken chain catch on something behind him, and thin plates of ice break under his feet when he encounters frozen puddles. He arrives at the mosque door but instead of knocking he convinces himself that there is no harm in lying down for a few minutes of rest. How long he lies there at the foot of the door he doesn't know, but at one point when he tries to turn his head he discovers that his hair has become locked in ice, and later that the two sections of the ankle chain are also fused with the ground.

He lies looking up at the mosque that has the entire Koran inscribed on its exterior walls, domes and balconies. The calligraphy is said to be there on the interior walls and ceilings too. He watches the facade in the moonlight through half-open eyes and it is as though there has been a rain of ink—every drop that had landed on a surface had formed a word instead of a splash.

He looks at the sky as he sinks into sleep. Arabic is written up there in the cosmos too, he knows. Of the six thousand stars visible to the naked eye, 210 have Arabic names. Aldebaran, the follower. Algol, the ghoul. Arrakis, the dancer. Fomalhaut, the mouth of the fish. Altair, the bird . . . He falls asleep and there is a city under the stars in an undiscovered country, no lamp in any window. The only light is the constellations and the city's minarets, each one of which is burning, a tall plume of fire, the flames streaming in the wind now and then. He enters the deserted city knowing that a group of black-clad figures is following him. Though he cannot see them he somehow knows that they have the natural fighting power of mountain lions, and he passes under several burning minarets before pushing open a door and entering a house and some time later he hears his pursuers come in. They spread out through the rooms and they make no attempt to lower their voices, to conceal their search for him. He climbs over the wall into the mosque next door. He picks up a book from a niche and removes a page and crumples it in his hand and then straightens it and places it on the floor. He does this with another page—introducing wrinkles into it and then putting it on the floor beside the first one—and then with another and then another, and eventually with all of them, lit by the light of the burning minaret, moving backwards as he leaves the paper on the floor. If anyone steps on them, he'll hear it. When the floor around him is lined with the pages, he lies down at the centre of them and closes his eyes—a rectangular clearing, the exact dimensions of a grave.

There are moments of faint awareness through the dark. People moving near him. Hands that touch. Candlelight. Eventually he is able to awaken fully and things are called into being. He is on a sheet spread out on the bare floor, no pillow, and he is wearing a dry set of clothes. An aged man is tending to him with a gentle pensiveness, his beard falling to his stomach in two silver divisions.

"Did you get them out of the snow?"

"Who?"

"I left two people outside." Mikal sits up slowly and looks around.

"There's no one out there."

"Maybe you can't see them because it's dark."

"It's no longer night. It's morning."

The mosque is a ruin, and the man is burning a reed prayer mat and a heap of straw prayer caps to keep him warm. Propped up against the pillars are words that have fallen away from the walls, lines of calligraphy that curve and knot purposefully, collecting force and delight and aura as they go.

He stands up, wrapping the sheet around him as he rises. "In which room is the Prophet's cloak kept?"

The man offers him a piece of bread. "The Prophet's cloak is in Kandahar. What would it be doing here?"

"I was told it was brought here."

"No. It's always been in Kandahar." The man touches his forehead. "You are tired. Lie down and rest."

"I dreamt I tore pages out of a book of hymns to protect myself." The man thinks for a moment. "There is a kind of tree whose leaves do not fall," he says, "and in that it is like an ideal Muslim. But Allah understands if we don't succeed in being perfect in this imperfect world." He smiles at Mikal.

Mikal begins to eat the bread, its core humid and porous. The man tells him that he is from Yemen, a foreigner trapped in Afghanistan. Scattered in various areas of the mosque, Mikal finds others like him, smelling more like wild animals than humans, entire families from Arab countries, destroyed-looking women and children. They have been on the run since October, making various journeys towards places of safety, to find some path back to their homelands. One little girl stands apart from other children, not participating in their activities, and he realises only after a while that she has no arms.

Though still very tired and weak, he opens the door to the south minaret and begins to climb up, looking out through the small recessed windows as he goes, the landscape altering with every turn of the spiral. Emerging into open air at the top, he examines his surroundings, the sky a water stain on paper. He is unable to understand why he was told the mosque contained the cloak, why he was sent on this trip.

Beside him on the facade, an ant is wandering in the shallow trough that forms the word "Allah," carrying a wheat grain in its mouth, trying to climb out of the word but falling back into it again and again.

He turns around to leave and everything slides into place when he notices the large boot print in the snow next to his feet, a quick ray of recognition: the warlord sent him here to be picked up by the Americans. They were *delivering* him.

The Americans pay $5,000 for each suspected terrorist.

He rushes down the spiral—as fast as he is able, the two pieces of chain falling ahead of him and getting under his feet—and asks if they know the warlord who'd been holding him prisoner.

"Yes," the bearded man answers. "He was the one who sent all of us to the mosque. He told us to gather here and wait to be taken out of Afghanistan."

Mikal counts the men and they are twenty-two including him.

$5,000 x 22 = $110,000.

And now his hearing picks up the outermost ring of a wave of sounds, something just on the limit of being audible, his heart giving a great leap and then seeming to go still in recoil. There is a questioning stir from everyone and then they too catch the reverberation of American helicopters arriving overhead. Cautiously, Mikal moves towards the mosque door and reaches out his hand to part the panels, but the door is opened suddenly from the other side just then and blinding snowlight fills his eyes and there is a confusion of shouts. Several figures overpower him and he watches the aged gentleman begin to run to the other side of the prayer hall, watches as an American soldier picks up a chair and launches it towards the man across the long space: a clean, effortless arc is described and then the chair connects with the fleeing man's shoulders and he falls with a sharp cry. Mikal's hands and feet are fastened with zip-locks and he is carried outside to the big bird with the twin propellers. He hears gunfire from the building and the screams of women and children. They leave him on his stomach beside the machine and go back inside and he watches as one by one the other men are brought out and made to lie on their stomachs beside him.

17

Naheed is in the glasshouse with Rohan.

"I have been thinking," Rohan says. "The best method of recalling the colour red is to touch a warm surface. That sensation to the hand is what the colour red is to the eye."

"Your eyes will heal, Father." She makes sure to say it with a certain lightness, hoping the words will contain audible hints of her smile.

There are bandages over his eyes.

"And the stars," he says, "the twinkling of them. I will remember them by holding the palm of my hand in the rain."

She imagines him trying to find equivalent sensations for everything that is lost to him. The sky. His own hand. The transparent case of a dragonfly's head.

There is still a certain amount of vision in the eyes but the doctors they have consulted have said that it is the very last, that it too will disappear within a few months.

"You'll be fine," she repeats. "The specialist we will see this morning is said to be the very best in the province."

They are tending to his Himalayan orchids. He feels along the stem and tells her where to make the cut. She holds the scalpel inside a brazier of glowing coals to sterilise the blade every few minutes, dusting the cuts with powdered cinnamon as a guard against infection. His hands rest on the table as if to steady the world, or to make it stay there. Whenever she removes the bandages it is like taking the hood off a falcon's head. He is alert as he hunts colours and shapes. He doesn't know when he will be given a sighted day, and on most days he sees nothing at all.

He moves closer to the brazier.

"Are you cold? I will take you in."

"They are saying the snow is very thick in the north this year. May God help the poor up there."

She guides him into the house and then along the corridor into his room. Mecca House. He settles in the armchair of faded blue brocade. On the table are some of the books she had been reading to him, having taken them out of the boxes. There is a volume of letters that an American poet wrote to the families of American soldiers, during a war within America a long time ago.

Washington, August 10, 1863. To Mr. and Mrs. Haskell.

Dear Friends: I thought it would be soothing to you to have a few lines about the last days of your son Erastus Haskell, of Company K 141st New York Volunteers . . .

She looks down at the finger she has accidentally cut in the glass-house. Incising her flesh it's Jeo's blood she sees. And that of Mikal. Rohan came back from Peshawar without his vision and with the news of Mikal's grave. Basie has visited it since. They considered reburial in Heer but it has been turned into a shrine and they will leave it there, a profusion of myths and legends around it.

"How is the bird pardoner's boy?" Rohan asks. "I must visit the family."

"Basie and Yasmin went to see them yesterday," she tells him. "The boy won't let any man come near him."

He nods. "For now, Tara, Yasmin and you can visit him. We have to help the family any way we can."

"Yes, Father."

She closes the book of letters and under it the *Dictionary of Colour* lies open.

Dragon—A bright greenish yellow.

Dragon's Blood—The bright red resin of the Indian Palm tree, Cala-mus draco (or perhaps of the shrub Pterocarpus draco).

Drop Black—An intense black pigment made from calcinated animal bones.

He had wished to have colours described to him one by one, all shades and subtleties.

Jeweller's Rouge—A powdered red oxide used to polish gold and silver plate.

Womb Red—Illustrated as scarlet but with no clues as to the origin of the term.

She walks out and crosses the garden towards the kitchen, entering through the banana grove.

"Have you given any thought to what I said?" Tara asks, as she bandages the cut finger.

She leans against the wall beside her mother.

"Naheed, have you given any thought to what I said?"

"I am not getting married again."

"You said you were waiting for Mikal. We now have confirmation that he too is dead."

She doesn't say anything. A minute later she takes the bowlful of flour from the shelf and trails her hands through it, holding the injured finger aloft as she parts and combs small ridges and peaks, working away the lumps. She pours vanilla essence and ground almonds into her half-folded hand and adds them to the cake mixture. Then she reaches into a pan and scoops out the white butter. Deftly she squeezes it through the flour. Water-thinned milk streaming down the three undamaged fingers, she forms the dough with the other hand.

"The dead don't return, Naheed."

She looks at her mother and says after a while, "I don't want to think about it."

"I don't want to think about it either, but I have to." Tara reaches forward with the salt jar and adds a pinch to the bowl, something Naheed always forgets. "How will I face your father on Judgement Day? What will I say when he accuses me in Allah's presence of not having given you the best life possible?"

The girl shakes her head slowly.

"I am going to start looking for a suitable match," Tara says.

Naheed turns away from her. Wetting a muslin cloth to cover the bowl of dough. "I have to take Father to the doctor. Would you go out to the crossroads and get us a rickshaw? Tell the driver we are going to the corner where Lumber Bazaar meets Savings Bazaar."

Tara had wanted Yasmin and Basie to accompany Rohan to the doctor. To keep both of them away from the Christian school where they teach, for however short a period. There was another explosion at a church the day before yesterday. Their safety is a constant anxiety throughout the day. She gets up and begins to put on her burka, doing up the long row of buttons at the front. "I hope this new doctor will say something different from the others."

Through the window Naheed watches her go past the pink mulberry that has a honey-like taste but only if eaten under its tree, so tender is it that it cannot even withstand being transported. But Tara is back only a few moments later, followed by Sharif Sharif. Dressed in white he has a flat brown crocodile-skin bag under one arm, its zip golden. Upon noticing Naheed he takes a comb from his pocket and passes it once along each side of his head.

She moves to the kitchen table and holds the empty cup her mother left behind. There is warmth in it still and it is transferred onto her skin. The colour red.

Tara leads the man along the corridor. She'd met him just outside the gate and he said he'd come to see Rohan.

She announces him and withdraws without a glance in his direction. Hate is a male domain. When she has to think of this man she feels anger instead.

"I am here on a delicate matter," Sharif Sharif says. Sitting on the chair beside him he is still holding Rohan's hand from when he shook it. "It concerns your daughter-in-law."

"Naheed?" Rohan hears the rustle of his starched clothes, the metal clank of his wristwatch.

"Yes. I care deeply for her."

"You have been good to her and her mother. The entire neighbourhood is aware that you have been taking only the minimum rent from that poor lady for some time."

"I do what Allah allows me to do. I seek no reward in this world. But I see that bad times have fallen on the two women again. And on you, as the only male decision maker in Naheed's life." Sharif Sharif sighs. "But these days, with this war, it appears that Allah has decided to test *all* us Muslims. Anyway, I am here to tell you that I would be willing to ease your burden."

"I don't understand."

"I am willing to marry Naheed to put an end to your worries and her widowhood."

Rohan sits up in the chair.

"I have two wives already, but our religion allows us to marry again if we can prove that we can look after the new wife financially and emotionally . . ."

"Sharif Sharif-sahib, I must say I am a little surprised. She is nineteen years old."

"That makes her a grown woman."

"Indeed. But I was attempting to point out the age difference."

He is silent. On the table are various magnifying glasses brought out of Sofia's study and Rohan hears him touching them. With them she would study twigs, petals, beaks, feathers and pollen grains before beginning to paint, and in his sighted days Rohan has been examining the world with them, storing up information. Sharif Sharif says at last, "Be kind enough to think about it. You are a wise man and must know that it's not good for young girls to be without a man once they have *been* with a man. It can cause them to seek out what they once had any which way."

Rohan stands up. "Thank you for your interest and your kindness."

"A woman's heart is soft and trusting, she can be corrupted all too easily."

"Thank you for your interest and your kindness."

"Do think about it and let me know. But that is not the only reason why I am here. Please be seated. Please. I wished to ask about your eyes. You must need funds for treatments and operations, and I was wondering if I could help in any way."

What exactly could this person be implying? Does he think Rohan would contemplate giving him Naheed in exchange for money? "I thank you for coming," he says curtly.

There is a silence and then he hears Sharif Sharif begin to walk out of the room. Tersely he says in the man's direction:

"The girl will be looked after very well as long as I am alive. And after I am gone she has Basie, who thinks of her as his sister."

"It appears I have offended you," Sharif Sharif says from the door.

"I have raised one daughter who makes an honest and honourable living, and I will make sure Naheed too takes that path if she wishes."

He sits down and realises he is shaking with fear and rage.

He listens to the streets as he travels with the girl, the rickshaw crossing the major roads and entering the density of the bazaars. She holds his right hand, her own two hands placed gently above and below it. Beneath the bandages and the closed lids there are specks of light like coloured sand in his eyes, a vast visual song of the cells expressing their internal life, and out there is another song called Heer, called Pakistan, the people buying, selling, asking, shouting, the minarets insisting on Paradise at every street corner, and in his mind he sees the shop signs painted with heartbreaking precision and beauty by barely literate men and he listens to the slap of wrestlers against each other, gleaming with oil, the arcades under which pieces of meat sizzle, cubbyhole shops selling Japanese sewing machines, English tweed and Chinese crockery, the fruit sellers standing behind walls of stacked oranges, and women's clothes hanging in shop windows in sheaths of pure lines and colours, teaching one the meaning of grace in one's life, and he wishes Sofia were here so he could ask her to describe these things for him, she who had made an entire life out of seeing, possessing an enraptured view of the everyday, who knew which section of the house received the most moonlight on any given night of the lunar calendar, and he wonders if this is how the dead mourn the world they have left behind, if this is how she mourns it below ground.

The doctor is studying Rohan's files when they enter the office. He is a young man and has recently returned from studying in the West. He looks up, and in utter silence stares at Rohan's face.

Removing Rohan's bandages he lifts the cotton pads from the eyelids, parting them gently with his fingers.

"Can you see me?" he asks.

"No."

The doctor guides Rohan into the examination room adjoining the office, Naheed catching a glimpse of the heavy-seeming machinery in dull grey steel and shining chrome as the green curtain is released behind them.

She sits alone in the office, looking into the book she has brought. This specialist is the final hope. One of the others said they should stitch shut the eyelids permanently. Last week Tara had visited the cleric at the mosque, to see if any specific verses of the Koran could be read for the restoration of vision. "Why could you not have come to me sooner?" the cleric had said, unable to conceal his wounded feelings. But he was not saddened or aggrieved on his own behalf. "You thought you were modern people, wanted to visit as many doctors as you could before turning to Allah. It seems to me to be a case of 'We might as well give Him a try too.'"

Twenty minutes go by and the green curtain is lifted and the doctor leads Rohan out.

Rohan gropes for Naheed's hand as he settles in his chair.

"So. As I have just explained to your father-in-law," the doctor says to her, "we need to carry out a number of procedures over the next six to eight months to restore the vision."

"He will be able to see again?"

Before the doctor can respond, Rohan says, "We can't afford the operations, Naheed."

Naheed tries to swallow but can't.

The doctor looks at the files. "I am sure we can correct his original condition too. With the new medical advances in the West there is no reason why he should *ever* be blind." Naheed cannot help but express an elated astonishment at this but again Rohan says,

"We can't afford the operations, Naheed."

"Could you not sell something?" the doctor asks. "Do you still live in that building with the garden that used to be the school?"

Rohan looks towards him. "I wasn't aware that we knew each other."

"I was a pupil of yours. You expelled me because my mother was a sinner."

Rohan is still.

Naheed knows the story of the prostitute's son. The boy who tried to steal a spade from the school garden. He wanted to go to the cemetery and dig up what his mother had always said was his father's grave.

The doctor, his face utterly serious, has his eyes locked on Rohan.

"I recognised the name the moment I saw the report, and I recognised you as you walked in."

"I have had occasion to think of you not a few times over the years."

"And I about you."

"You are a doctor now."

"The clinic is named after my late mother."

Naheed sees how this has shaken Rohan. "So these operations you have suggested . . ."

The man swings his black chair towards her. "We will have to act fast. You will need to get the funds together soon. Unfortunately in a case like this almost every day counts."

"And the original cause is reversible too?"

"Yes. You seem to have been given outdated advice. There has been much scientific progress."

Is he trying to destroy Rohan? Are these operations beneficial or necessary? Will he just waste the money on unneeded procedures and then claim he did his best? But, no. It is said that something in people's souls will not let them take advantage of the blind or deceive them. The Koran admonishes a personage—some believe it to be Muhammad himself—for ignoring a blind man in a gathering of influential tribal chiefs.

"My reasons to expel you from Ardent Spirit seemed persuasive at the time," Rohan says suddenly.

The doctor ignores the comment. "When should I schedule the next appointment?" He holds out the reports. Rohan extends his arm towards the sound and takes them, the hand groping in the air before grabbing, like a bird trying to alight on a branch in a strong wind. "When did your mother die, may I ask?"

"The year I graduated from medical school."

"The name didn't bring her to mind," Rohan says. "I am sorry to hear of her death. May Allah have compassion on her soul."

"What do you mean by that?"

"I just meant . . . Allah is all-forgiving . . ."

"She was the most decent human being I knew."

Naheed watches him concentrating on the man's words. She knows from Mikal the power the voice has to reveal someone. Sometimes when he sang she would close her eyes and realise that every emotion that had been present in his facial expressions was also present in his voice.

"I am sorry to hear of her death," Rohan says again. "There are many ways to live a good life, and Allah is all-forgiving."

The doctor looks at him and then in a calm controlled gesture rings the bell for the next patient to be shown in.

"Thank you," Naheed says, getting up. "We'll contact you about the next appointment."

"I look forward to hearing from you," the doctor says without looking up.

Night, and he walks in his garden, hands outstretched, touching the skin of the world in the darkness. He moves beside the night scent of flowers, feels on the bark the names Jeo and Mikal had scratched when they were children.

That afternoon thirty years ago, when the boy was brought into his office, Rohan had no intimation that one of the darkest years of his marriage was about to begin. The child was amiable and conscientious but was brought in because he had attempted to steal from the school's garden—this garden, here. Some of the more daring boys often did that, picking fruit from the trees or taking bird eggs. But he was attempting to steal an implement from the shed. At first he would not explain his motives. Eventually he said, "I want to dig up my father's grave to see if it matches the picture that my mother keeps on the shelf." His fellow students had been taunting him. Some of them were summoned to the office and the complete details of the entire affair came to light. There was no father, the mother was a fallen woman.

Rohan went to see her that very afternoon, knocking on the door of the house and waiting while a youth, no older than the senior boys at Ardent Spirit, came out. Suddenly he had a vision of the woman corrupting his student body. There was no prejudice at Ardent Spirit. There were all sects of Islam at the school. Shias, Deobandis, Wahabis. When Rohan heard that a teacher had given a Shia student fewer marks than he deserved, he had investigated the matter immediately. But this was different.

To his utter shock the woman was unrepentant. He offered to waive her son's fees if she would put an end to her commerce. He visited her every day for a week to try and persuade her. Almost every student knew about it by then and a number of alarmed parents had visited Rohan, threatening to withdraw their children. He went to the classroom mid-lesson and asked him to collect his things.

"Sir, I am sorry for stealing the spade."

"That is not the reason for your expulsion," he remembers saying, looking directly ahead. "Your mother is a sinful woman."

They got into the rickshaw and putting his hand into his satchel the boy brought out an eraser. "Sir, I borrowed this from Fareed Chaudhuri. Can you give this back to him please?"

Rohan put the item in his pocket. "I will do that later."

The woman came to the door of her house and took the child in wordlessly.

Sofia raged at him. She wanted to go to the woman's house and bring back the boy—a thought that stunned him. There would be no eye contact with her for over a year after that day. He felt persecuted, believing he had done the only correct thing possible under the circumstances, and he had begged Allah for strength and begged Him to forgive Sofia for some of the words she had uttered in fury.

In the garden one dawn, the house lit red by the sunrise, she said she was leaving him.

They had both attended Punjab University in Lahore, though at different times, he being five years older. Born and raised in Heer, and possessing an intense shyness of character, he had not fitted in at the university, or into the large city. His efforts to understand himself and his times were lonely ones, and he lived in fear of—and perhaps even a mild revulsion at—the behaviour of the other students. He stood out to the extent that he could not even bring himself to wear Western clothes—those trousers that had pockets in appallingly inappropriate places, front and back, from where items of food could then be pulled out and eaten, hands removed to be shaken, documents produced and handed over. She—who was also from Heer—had thrived at the university however. A laughing confident beauty. He was already teaching at a government school when he met her. She was the new English teacher, and a month after they were introduced she caught him opening a notebook in which she had been writing earlier: full of longing for her, he had wished to see her handwriting. Some glimpse of a thing that was intrinsically her. Intimate. And he knew she might be his only chance at happiness. At the year's end she entered the room and, lowering herself into a sitting position before him, told him he must ask her to marry him. Covering his lying mouth with her hands when he tried to protest.

Her emotions were always closer to the surface than his.

Now she placed the large suitcase on the dresser in their bedroom and emptied her wardrobe into it, and it remained there for a year. She herself moved into her study. Some nights he would hear her come into their bedroom and he would pretend to be asleep. Two a.m. or 3 or 4. And she would sit in the chair for a while and watch him. Then she would rise and take a few items out of the open suitcase and leave. Then one day her clothes were back in the wardrobe. Her parents were dead and her brother had his own family. She had nowhere to go, the brother reminding her that she had chosen to marry Rohan without seeking his counsel. "Now go and be a modern woman," he said. "Live somewhere divorced and alone." He had waited all these years to avenge the slight to his honour.

He turns his face upwards, where the visible planets must be burning in the eastern sky. He reaches the overgrown *thor* bush and slowly raises his hands towards the spike-filled branches, wondering how he will know which of these limbs must be amputated next year to restore symmetry.

18

The air of the February evening is dabbed with fog and the saluki appears and disappears within it. Major Kyra walks into Ardent Spirit's Baghdad House. The boy who had opened the school's gate for him is a few paces ahead, calling to the hound. He is in his late teens and is known for his passionate nature, his limbs full of disciplined movements, and eyes capable of a sudden flaring as when straw is thrown onto a fire. He owns a deadly dagger as beautiful as a toy, and his name is Ahmed. Five months ago his father was at work in the ice factory when a rectangular block of ice slid down a ramp and shattered. A foot-long splinter flew up and pierced his diaphragm from below. It continued through the left lung and entered his heart. He fell backwards onto the floor and that was where he was discovered half an hour later. By then the ice fragment inside him had melted away. The neighbourhood women insisted he had been killed with a ghost dagger by Ahmed's mother, who had died the previous year and who had known nothing but contempt and ruthlessness from her husband while she was alive.

He joined the jihad in October and went away towards Kabul, returning only a fortnight ago.

Major Kyra follows him along a corridor, having tied the saluki to a chair leg in the hallway.

The day-to-day affairs of Ardent Spirit's six houses—Mecca, Baghdad, Cairo, Cordoba, Delhi and Ottoman—are the responsibility of six senior boys, Ahmed being one of them. And they are all gathered in the room when Major Kyra and Ahmed enter.

The candlelight casts oversized shadows on the walls. Kyra lowers himself onto the woollen carpet bought from the smugglers' market in the North-West Frontier Province. The six boys position themselves before him in a semicircle.

With his flame-scarred hands—they look as though they've been put together from scraps of leather—Ahmed holds a piece of paper towards Kyra. On it are the layouts of Heer's Christian school and church. All sides of the two buildings have their lengths written down next to them, and all the surrounding roads are named.

"Bombing the church or the Christian school will not achieve anything," Kyra says. "Such explosions in other places have not deterred the West from continuing with its war, nor forced the Pakistani government to withdraw its support for the Western occupiers."

"We are the world's seventh nuclear power," the boy from Ottoman House says quietly, "and yet our government does the bidding of the Americans, as though we were nothing but beggars." The knowledge of his helplessness is making him angry, he the brother of someone who had gone to Afghanistan in October and is now believed to be in US custody.

"Twenty or thirty Pakistanis, be they Christian or Muslim, dying in an explosion in Pakistan isn't going to matter at all," Kyra says. "Neither our own government nor anyone in the West will care about it."

The head of Ottoman House says, "If we don't send a message now they will attack other Muslim countries."

The boy from Delhi House extends a hand towards Ahmed.

"Tell him."

"Tell me what?" Kyra asks. There is a companionship among the boys that will probably never be bettered in their lives.

"Why don't we raid the school and hold everyone hostage? The teachers and the students. Release a list of demands. We should ask for the Americans to leave Afghanistan and free all our brothers who are being held prisoner by them."

Kyra studies the paper. "Do we have enough men for such an operation?"

"The six of us will form a sufficiently strong core. Beyond that we need a dozen or so others. We can find them."

"The siege could last several days," Kyra says.

"Yes," Ahmed says. "We need to calculate exactly how many weapons we'll need and of what kind. We'll have to buy some."

With Ardent Spirit no longer linked to the Pakistani military and the ISI, the influx of funds has disappeared. Arranged by the ISI, there used to be donation boxes in many cities across Pakistan. Two years ago, during the festival to mark the Sacrifice of Abraham, Ardent Spirit had received contributions of almost $2 million, mostly from the hides of the sacrificed sheep. During the same month millions more were raised from the 675,000 Pakistanis who live in Britain. Money also came from Muslims in India—Kashmir, Andhra Pradesh, Tamil Nadu, Karnataka, Maharashtra and Gujarat. But access to all of this is now denied Kyra. He will have to use his own money.

"It will be hazardous but it is a cause worth dying for," Ahmed is saying. "And as for the other side, the founder and headmaster of the school, Father Mede, is an infidel. The teachers at the school are Muslim but traitors to Islam, filling the heads of the children with un-Islamic things like music and biology and English literature. And the students too are traitors."

"They laugh at us," says the boy from Ottoman House. "They refer to us who attend schools like Ardent Spirit as 'donkeys.' They say we and our like have made Pakistan unlivable."

"Father Mede is white," Kyra says. "An Englishman. It'll become an international affair."

"Exactly," says the head of Mecca House, leaning forward. "They will pay attention if something happens to a white person. We could kill a few teachers to indicate our seriousness and hold him as the chief bargaining and negotiating asset."

"There will be no bargaining or negotiating, brother," the head of Cairo House says.

"Leverage, then."

"He is over seventy years old," Ahmed says.

"Do you think they are asking to see birth certificates before dropping bombs in Afghanistan?"

"Brother," Ahmed says, "you misunderstand me. I was just thinking that it would make the authorities act with speed. It's in our favour. How do you feel about capturing him and bringing him here?"

"It's not good to have infidels in the house," three of the boys say in unison.

The doorbell sounds and Ahmed leaves the room to answer it, making sure his back is never turned towards the Koran and other religious texts on the shelf.

Kyra opens the *Book of Prophet's Sayings. Number 813: I was given the following words of the Prophet by Hukm bin Nafa, who was given them by Shoaib, who was given them by Zehri, who was given them by Abu Salma, who was given them by Abu Horaira. The Prophet said, "The End of the World won't be until two armies have gone to war proclaiming an identical goal."*

When Ahmed returns he is accompanied by a middle-aged woman wrapped in a shawl, her face marked with the deep lines of resignation and self-control. Maintaining a pointedly respectful distance from the sphere of candlelight in which the men are, she greets everyone and sits down in the far corner.

"How can I be of help, sister-ji?" Kyra asks.

She smiles. "I am the mother of one of the former students at Ardent Spirit. He is about to go abroad to study."

"I am delighted to hear that one of our students is prospering."

"He was given a good start here by your elder brother, may he rest in peace," the woman says to Kyra. "My boy was at Ardent Spirit for just the first two years of his education, then we moved to another neighbourhood so I had to take him out."

"May Allah grant him continued success so he can make Pakistan and Islam proud. Which country will he be going to? Indonesia, Malaysia, Egypt?"

"He has a scholarship to America. His entire education will be paid for by a university there."

Kyra considers this. "It would have been preferable if he had chosen a Muslim country instead of the West with its bloodstained wealth. Which city in America will he go to?"

The woman gave a nervous laugh. "I can't remember the name. I will send him to you, you can ask him yourself."

"Do send him."

The woman is now leaning towards the candlelight. She appears to be someone who knows she is having one of the most important conversations of her life. "I have a favour to ask of you, brother Kyra. On his application form, he has chosen not to mention that he attended Ardent Spirit. You must be aware that schools such as these have developed certain connotations of late. If the Americans discover the truth they could refuse him his university place altogether. Or they could arrest him at the airport."

Kyra watches the shock of the boys, the glazed smile appearing on Ahmed's face as he begins to contort the rosary tightly in his hands, his jaw muscles working.

The woman seems not to know where to rest her glance. "Also, with the news of his good fortune spreading in the neighbourhood, some envious person could alert the Americans to my boy's two years at Ardent Spirit. This frightens me."

With glacial politeness, Kyra says, "The aim of Ardent Spirit is to teach decency and love of Islam to the young, sister-ji. That was the case in the past, it is the case in the present, and it shall be the case in the future."

"*Insha-Allah*," say the boys in unison.

"I agree, but still, brother-ji, if someone comes and asks you about it, my request is that you deny my son ever attended your school."

"What is more important to you, good aunt," Ahmed asks with a sharp indrawn breath, "the truth or your children?"

"Both. I want the truth to live in my children. I don't think I have to sacrifice either."

"And yet you are asking us to lie for you."

"I feel terrible to have come to you with this," the woman says, confused and distressed. "I am an illiterate woman, so you know better than me what is occurring in the world ever since the Jews carried out the terrorist attacks in America. You know perfectly well that there is a possibility my son could lose this golden opportunity." Suddenly she begins to weep, covering her face with her shawl, and is unable to speak for almost half a minute. She says eventually, "I have nothing but him. He must become an educated and wealthy man. He has four sisters whose dowry he has to provide for."

Ahmed stands up and gestures towards the door. "Let me show you out, good aunt."

"My brother never wanted anything but the best for his students," Kyra says. "Why can't your son stay and study right here in Pakistan?"

The head of Ottoman House looks at the woman with an unkillable light in his eyes. "Good aunt, a dollar is worth seventy-two Pakistani rupees. Do you know why? Allow me to tell you. It is because each American person loves America seventy-two times more than each Pakistani person loves Pakistan. That is why."

"Almost all of us are traitors," says the boy from Cordoba House, his head low with anguish. "Now, good aunt, please allow brother Ahmed to show you out. It is dark and you should be home."

The woman wipes her tears on her shawl and gets to her feet and whispers a farewell. As the two of them leave, the other boys sit in a silence that seems more and more like a seeking. Nothing remains in the room but the truth and they see the enormity of their struggle, the light from the candle weak but undeceiving. They are all aware that across the planet words are being said about them in ten languages, sinister ungodly plans being hatched to eliminate them.

"It's a test," one of them says quietly. "We, our very souls, are being attacked by the West from many directions."

"We mustn't lose heart," Kyra says. "Remember the anvil lasts longer than the hammer."

Ahmed returns and takes his position in the semicircle. "We should begin planning the siege." He unfolds the paper with the two drawings and studies it carefully. He turns to the boy from Cairo House. "What is the latest news about Father Mede?"

"He's not in Heer. He has gone on his annual tour around Punjab, visiting the school's other branches. And he is inaugurating a new branch in Faisalabad."

"It's provocation," the head of Mecca House says. "I stopped one of their teachers in the street last month and told her that they need to curtail their activities, not expand the Christian school, or carry out repairs and refurbishments of the building, but she looked at me as if I wasn't there."

Ahmed takes a pen from his pocket and draws arrows indicating all the entrances to the school. "They'll notice us," he says. "We'll drag his and his teachers' corpses along the Grand Trunk Road if we have to. They'll notice us soon enough."

19

The helicopter, as it brings Mikal to the American prison, is filled with the curses and prayers of the other captives. Some of them were shot as they tried to escape or resisted capture and Mikal can smell the blood, and he can tell that some of them have lost control of their bladders with fear.

His arms and legs zip-locked, a hood covering his head, he is carried out of the Chinook and the place they bring him to has the scent of the inside of a balloon. When they remove the hood he sees that he is in a tent that has white sheets of rubber insulation buttoned onto its green canvas. There are a dozen hospital beds but he is the only one here. One of the two Americans in attendance writes the number 121 on his shirt in black felt-tip pen. *I am the one hundred and twenty-first prisoner here?* But it is altered to 120 when a third white man comes and says something in English to the others. They had miscounted or perhaps one of the other prisoners has just died.

Getting him to open his mouth they shine beams of light into his throat and then his ears and eyes, a pair of surgical scissors cutting away the old bloodstained strips of cloth that serve as bandages for his hands. He hears the barking of dogs. Perhaps the prisoner who has just died was trying to escape. Quickly but expertly, they clean the wounds and dress them, the new bandages overlapping each other like a basket being woven, a brilliant clean white that is painful on his eye, reminding him of the snow out of which he was plucked, and then they look at the bullet wound on his neck and expose his chest to examine the blade and bullet lesions on his torso, and the medicines they apply bring an astounding reduction of the pain. He wishes to cry out at the relief.

In another room where the dogs are louder they overpower him when he refuses to accept the removal of trousers and they cut off all his clothes and as he stands there naked they bring a circular electric saw and slice the manacles off his feet, throwing jets of soft sparks along the floor and into his leg hair. He struggles in terror when they must perform a cavity search and he snarls, roaring, and they have to pin him down and afterwards they put him in a jumpsuit and lock his ankles in their own manacles, shiny and complicated as puzzles, his wrists also in chains. *Where is this place? Is he still in Afghanistan?* They photograph him against a height chart and then they shave his beard and hair off and photograph him again.

His head disappearing into a hood again they leave him somewhere for a short while, just a few minutes during which he falls into dead-weighted sleep, the exhaustion making each bone feel as though wrung tight as the horn of a ram, and then they come and lead him to another place. When the black hood is removed he sees that he is in a small room, no bigger than ten feet by twelve. A cabin or a booth. A large white man sits in the left corner under a poster of the Twin Towers, the moment the second plane hit, the fireball attached to the side of the building.

There is a table with two chairs on opposite sides, facing each other, one of which Mikal is made to sit in. Another white man—equally bulky and over six foot tall—comes in with a man whose skin is the same colour as Mikal's own. The brown-skinned man says in Pashto that he is the interpreter, and then—when Mikal does not react—says the same thing in Urdu, Punjabi and Hindko. Mikal does not alter his blank expression and he tells Mikal in all four languages that at no point must he attempt to get out of his chair. That the man in the corner under the poster is Military Police and this other white man is here to ask some questions.

"My name is David Town," says the new white man through the interpreter. "From the US government. The doctor said you were well enough to speak to me. What is your name? I want to notify your family that you are here."

Mikal does not answer.

"Tell me your name and how to reach your family."

The white man has very pale skin. Mikal has never seen a real white person at close proximity before today. The paleness is actually astonishing.

What will they do to make him talk? Hold a pistol to his head, pull out his fingernails, like the Pakistani jailers did to his father.

"We know you can speak. You spoke in your sleep. Sometimes in the language of an Afghan, sometimes in the language of a Pakistani. Are you a Pakistani, an Afghan, or an Afghan born and raised in Pakistan?"

Mikal does not answer, his shackled hands resting on the table. *Was he asleep long enough to have spoken?*

The man puts a book of photographs on the table. "Tell me if you recognise anyone in here." Slowly he begins to turn the pages, Mikal staring down at the men in Arab headdress, Palestinian scarves, clean shaven with neckties, young and old, beards long and short.

Just then another white man comes in and motions for David to step out.

When David returns a few minutes later he is an altered man. He begins to shout at Mikal even before sitting down.

"You were found in a mosque from whose basement we recovered drums of white powder. What is that powder?"

Mikal does not answer.

"Is it anthrax or ricin?"

Recipes for ricin were found in an al-Qaeda safe house back in November, Mikal has heard, and there are videotapes of al-Qaeda's experiments on dogs with sarin and cyanide gas.

The man goes on shouting questions at him, his face inches from Mikal's at times.

"Or is it something else?" As the man speaks Mikal keeps his eyes on his mouth, listening to the sounds coming out of it, and not looking at the interpreter beside him who turns those sounds into words. It is as though a disembodied voice in the air is making him comprehend what the white man is saying. "What is that substance, and where did you people get it? What were you doing at the mosque?"

Every man at the mosque was picked up. The women and children had been left behind. The man takes out a silver digital camera and shows Mikal shots of women on its flat-screen monitor. "These were the women at the mosque. Which one is your wife? Your sister or mother?"

All the women carry an identical expression. Afraid of the gun but contemptuous of the hand that wields it.

"Maybe we should bring them here. Maybe they can tell me what your name is and who brought the powder to the mosque."

He closes his eyes and the Military Police soldier shouts at him to open them.

"If the powder does not belong to you, and was left there by someone else, you should tell us. We have done some tests and we think it could be anthrax. You must tell us what you know and tell us fast because the whole area might have been contaminated. The women and children in there must be evacuated. The only way we can get US chemical teams out to neutralise the stuff is if you tell us what you know. Don't waste time, those women and children need your help. What is your name and what do you know about that powder?"

"I don't know anything," Mikal says. "I am not from the mosque. I am just a prisoner. At first someone else's, now yours." He speaks Pashto, to keep them as far away as possible from his real identity.

"What's your name?"

"I don't know anything about the powder."

"What happened to your hands? How did you get the bullet wounds on your body? Did you fight with the Taliban against the Americans?"

"The powder could be insecticide. I saw a large kitchen garden behind the mosque."

"We are sure it's not, we have done initial tests. What's your name? Did people in expensive Toyota SUVs ever visit the mosque?"

"I am not from the mosque."

He is very tired and his head nods and the Military Police soldier shouts at him to stay awake and David wants to know whether he had spent time in Sudan, whether he had fought in Kashmir, if he had any links with the man who planned to blow up Los Angeles airport in 1999, if he had been to Bosnia.

"Say something. At least tell me we infidels will never win against the likes of you because we love life while you love death."

As punishment for his silence David asks him to get out of the chair. He is made to lower himself onto his knees and hold out his arms at the sides. David and the interpreter leave the room, and he stays in this position for thirty-five minutes, the Military Police soldier shouting at him every time his arms droop or he slumps forward out of fatigue and the need for sleep.

When David returns he wishes to know whether he has met Osama bin Laden, Mullah Omar or Ayman al-Zawahiri. Mikal refuses to speak and they take him to a bare windowless room, attach a chain to his wrists and, asking him to raise his arms above his head, fasten the chain to a ring on the ceiling. The room is filled with brilliant light. A sleep deprivation cell.

Every time he falls asleep the arms shackled to the ceiling wrench him awake.

The prison is an abandoned brick factory. In a vast warehouse inside the main building there are two rows of metal cages, filled with boys and young men, some with hoods over their heads, industrial white lights shining down on them at all hours.

After he loses consciousness in the sleep deprivation chamber, he awakens to discover that he has been stripped naked and is being washed with a hosepipe. A Military Policeman dries him and walks him naked to the tent that had smelled of balloons where his wounds are dressed again. They put him in a jumpsuit, put the metal back onto his limbs, and he is brought to one of the cages in the warehouse and he curls up on the floor.

"Where are you from?" the boy in the next cage asks.

Mikal doesn't know whether he has reacted to the question, to the language.

"My name is Akbar," he says to Mikal in Urdu and then Pashto.

As he lies on the floor the boy tells Mikal the nationality of the other people around them, pointing to each cage. Algerian. Sudanese. Russian. Saudi Arabian. His face is serious and beautiful, as is his voice, and he says he was a taxi driver in Jalalabad when he was kidnapped and sold to the Americans for $5,000.

"What's your name?"

Mikal closes his eyes, telling himself not to react. He has been placed in the next cage to make Mikal reveal information.

"Where are you from? The man on my other side is from Morocco. See him, the one with his head bandaged? He is a bit unmanageable. He speaks English but his accent is terrible so he needs an interpreter, and always wants his answers to be translated precisely." Mikal hears the chains of the boy as he moves. "He hates America and feels it's necessary to keep telling the interrogators that fact, becoming angry when the interpreter refuses to translate his full answers and says instead 'and so on and so forth.' Or 'Now he is prattling on about the Koran and the Crusades and the glory of Islam and the Day of Judgement,' or 'And now he's off again on his obsession with death.'"

The boy continues to talk as Mikal hears the noise of someone weeping in a nearby cage, the sound of someone praying, the barking of dogs. Though full of fatigue he focuses on everything in an effort to remain awake—fearful that he might talk in his sleep and reveal something. But the struggle to keep his eyes open is only intermittently successful. During sleep he sees someone rinsing a red garment in flowing water. Moving it around in the current. He approaches and sees that it is not a garment, but his blood, the liquid taken out of Mikal's body as one article and entity, and being sluiced in the river, all his knowledge being extracted from it.

Three white men enter the interrogation booth—that smells of vomit—and begin to shout at him without the interpreter translating any of the words, just screaming into Mikal's face for more than ten minutes. Then suddenly they stop and leave.

"Did you get the women safely out of the mosque?" Mikal hears himself asking David.

"Tell me about Jeo."

Mikal looks up from the table.

"Jeo has told me everything about you two."

"You have Jeo?"

"Stay in your chair."

"I want to see him."

"Impossible. Stay in the chair."

"Where is he?"

"He has told us everything."

"There is nothing to tell. Where is Jeo? Is he all right?"

"Tell us which escape routes the Arab fighters are using to get out of Afghanistan into Pakistan and Iran."

"I want to see Jeo."

"He says you took a *bayt* of loyalty to Osama bin Laden two years ago." He uses the Arabic word—*bayt*, a blood oath.

"You are lying."

"Either I am or he is. I am telling you what he told me."

"I want to see him."

"So it's a lie?"

"Yes."

"Why would he lie to us?"

"I don't know." Suddenly a terrible possibility enters his head. "What did you do to him to make him confess to that?"

"Stay in your chair," the Military Policeman says loudly from his corner. He stands up to his full height which is well over six feet, obscuring the poster behind him. Talking about the Moroccan and his bandaged head, Akbar said that a female interrogator had asked him how he'd felt when he heard about the attacks on the Twin Towers. The Moroccan said that he had been ecstatic, and when she told him that the first boy she had ever kissed had died in the Towers, he had said, "You kissed someone you were not married to? If you were in my family I would cut your throat and wipe the floor with the blood, you disgusting bitch." He had spat on her and the Military Policeman had become uncontrollable and beaten him savagely.

"According to Jeo you have committed to memory the satellite phone numbers of several al-Qaeda lieutenants," David says. "Give them to me."

"Did you beat him? He's so gentle. He'd say anything to stop the pain."

"If a person would say anything to stop the pain, then he would probably start with the truth. No?"

Mikal closes his eyes and incurs the wrath of the Military Policeman who bellows at him to stay awake and pay attention.

"Let me tell you something," David says. "The reason the United States isn't torturing you, hooking you up to electricity or drilling holes in your bones, as some countries in the world do, is not that torture doesn't work. Torture most definitely does work. But we don't do it because we believe it is wrong and uncivilised."

"I want to see Jeo."

Did Akbar say to him, while he was going in and out of sleep, that he must never give in to the temptation of grabbing the interrogator's gun? "I think they wear it in the room because they want you to grab it and try to shoot them, so they can charge you with something." The soldiers wear them even when they are washing and dressing the prisoners, the prisoners' hands and feet free of iron.

"You are lying about Jeo. If you have him then go and ask him what my name is. Come back and tell me."

"So what he told us is a lie? Duly noted. We'll have to make sure he knows what the consequences are for lying to us. Now tell me what your name is and where you are from."

"Ask Jeo."

"When we captured him he had thousands of Omani rials, American dollars and Pakistani rupees on him. Why do you think he had those?"

"Ask him."

"Did you ever transfer money into Afghanistan from Pakistan— given to you by your al-Qaeda handlers in Pakistan?"

"Ask Jeo."

.   .   .

He dreams that his father and mother are travelling across land and sea, their path lit by a soul flame. They arrive and deliver him from his chains and lead him out of the cage. He dreams that he has turned into a boar and in mysterious happiness is rushing through the bright colours of various maps, an atlas, pursuing his female and when he finds her he becomes a man in a world so intense that the sound of a flower bud opening can kill and the bulbul is in the letters that spell the word *bulbul.* No longer bound to their flesh, the pair of them are among the ancient stars, enclosed in perfect crystals shaped like heroes and heroines and demons, true books and instruments of music. Outside his sleep, night has sealed all mirrors but in the clear glass of the dream both of them move fearlessly across the firmament towards knowledge not only of how the world began but of how it will end.

"Did you try to count the teeth of a wolf?" Akbar asks, pointing to the missing fingers.

"Why are there pictures in the corridor?" Mikal says. Their bright colours had pained his eyes. He passes them whenever he is taken to the medical tent where the dressings on his torso and hands are changed, to receive what he is told are antibiotic injections.

"They are from children in America."

Drawings of butterflies, flowers, guns shooting at men with beards and helicopters dropping bombs on small figures in turbans.

"They are letters to the soldiers from schoolchildren. The words say, *Go Get the Bad Men* and *I Hope You Kill Them All* and *Come Home Safely.* I saw one that said, *We are praying for you, and said the Rosary for you today in class.*"

"I am going to escape," Mikal says to Akbar.

"Don't. They shot and killed someone who tried."

He will have to locate and free Jeo within the factory and then they will break out. Or will he escape and come back for Jeo later?

"How many guards are there?" Mikal counts the MPs gathered near the cages. All captured Arabs are eventually sent to Guantánamo Bay. The others must be assessed to see if they should be. A shipment will leave today and since noon yesterday the MPs have been making preparations, laying out new jumpsuits, manacles, leg chains and spray-painted goggles on the floor in plain view of the cages. They pull on the leg chains, and lock and unlock the shiny chrome manacles, to make sure everything is in working order. No one can remain unaware of the rattling, and no one knows who will leave.

Now suddenly it is time, and the MPs are having great difficulty in getting some of the prisoners out of the cages. One prisoner clings to the wire of the cage and sobs as they pry him loose. Another falls to his knees, howling and shouting something in English. "He's imploring for mercy," Akbar says. "'You promised you wouldn't send me, Andrew. You promised, Steve, you promised.'" Kissing the hands of the white men. Others though are just walking out, resigned to their fate, reciting the verses of the Koran.

An MP moves towards Mikal but continues past and enters the adjoining cage, which contains a Nigerian called Mansur. From him there had been complaints that everything in Afghanistan was inferior to Africa, even the rain and wind here were of an inferior quality. A Christian who had converted to Islam, and in the interrogating booth was constantly trying to convert the Americans, he is now being readied to be put on a plane.

"What is your name?" David asks.

Mikal sits still.

Just then there comes the sound of screaming from the other side of the wall. Someone in terrible agony.

"Who is that?"

"Who do you think?" David says. "Jeo lied to us, so now we are making him tell us the truth."

The boy next door sounds like an animal in sacrificial torment.

It's not Jeo. He must remain composed.

"What is your name?"

It's not Jeo. Does anyone in the world know where the two of them are? Is anyone searching for them?

"What is your name?"

But he is unable to bear it and says at last, "Stop beating him."

"We are just making sure we know the truth. Stay in your chair."

"Please stop it. Don't hurt him, please. You said you wouldn't torture." He stands up and reaches for David with his hands, then in the same movement turns and rushes towards the door in disordered confusion, to go and help Jeo. As he falls to the floor—given a blow to the kidneys by the MP's club—he is struck again on the shoulder and he hits the man with his handcuffed wrists just above the ear and once again below the ear with greater force, and the man leans over him and punches his face, once, twice, three times, Mikal's neck pressed against the concrete under the man's boot. He tastes blood and is not sure which of the screams are his and which from the next room. Then he is snatched back into the chair.

"He's telling the truth," he says, "he's telling the truth. I *did* take the oath with Osama bin Laden. Stop hurting him, please, stop hurting him. I was the one who lied, not him." Drops of blood fall from his face onto the table, joining up and becoming a large blot with an amazing quickness.

"What's your name?"

Next door Jeo continues to scream, and there are other sounds, of him being slammed against the walls. The cubicle shakes with each impact.

"What's your name? Where are you from? What happened to your hands and body, and when were you shot?"

They could bring his brother here—they could bring all of them here from Heer—and, armed with suspicions and false accusations, do to them what they are doing to Jeo. Basie and Yasmin and Rohan and Naheed. They'll put them in the cages next to him.

"I am a prisoner. They sold me to you for money. I have nothing to do with this war." His ribs and face in agony from the strikes, the pain in the bullet wounds fully awakened.

Next door Jeo is whimpering.

"What is your name? If you are innocent we will free you the instant you eliminate our suspicions. You must show us that you support justice by co-operating with us. All the people who were captured with you have already been released. You with your behaviour are going to end up in Cuba."

"I will tell you everything if you let me see Jeo."

"Impossible."

He looks at the wall separating him from Jeo whose sobs have become fainter now.

Finally he says to David, "I will tell you everything, if you ask Jeo to tell you something only I would know."

He is brought to a chamber whose walls, floor and ceiling are painted entirely black, and his raised arms are shackled to a ring overhead. After the Military Policemen leave the light is switched off, the room becoming a perfect vacuumed blank. It is like the shadow darkness of the grave after death. He is not sure when last he saw a star or the red dawn light pulsing like the bloodbeat of a living creature, but now time ceases to exist altogether as he stands or slumps in the measureless void—for half a day, two, a week? He is sure that men have died in the chamber, and he sees their ghosts. At some point the light comes on and a white man Mikal has never seen before makes his entry. Nineteen keepers are appointed over Hell, according to the Koran. The man stands before him and suddenly bursts into laughter, and he doesn't stop—the soulless glance fixed at Mikal and laughing loudly at him for having made the mess on the floor, for being worthless, for the disaster that is his love for Naheed, for not being able to help Jeo, for Pakistan and its poverty, a laughter tinged with contempt for him and his nation where the taps don't have water, and the shops don't have sugar or rice or flour, the sick don't have medicines and the cars don't have petrol, his disgusting repulsive country where everyone it seems is engaged in killing everyone else, a land of revenge attacks, where the butcher sells rotten meat to the milkman and is in turn sold milk whose volume has been increased with lethal white chemicals, and they both sell their meat and their milk to the doctor who prescribes unnecessary medicines in order to win bonuses from the drug companies, and the factory where the drugs are made pours its toxic waste directly into the water supply, into rivers and streams, killing, deforming, blinding, lacerating the sons and daughters of the policeman who himself dies in a traffic accident while he is taking a bribe, an accident caused by a truck the transport inspector has taken a bribe to declare roadworthy, a country full of people whose absolute devotion to their religion is little more than an unshakable loyalty to unhappiness and mean-spiritedness, and the white man continues to laugh with eyes full of hatred and accusation and hilarity and mirth at this citizen of a shameless beggar country full of liars, hypocrites, beaters of women and children and animals and the weak, brazen rapists and unpunished murderers, torturers who probably dissolved his father's body in a drum of acid in Lahore Fort, delusional morons and fools who wanted independence from the British and a country of their own, but who now can't wait to leave it, emigrate, emigrate, emigrate to Britain, USA, Canada, Australia, Dubai, Kuwait, Singapore, Indonesia, Malaysia, Thailand, Japan, China, New Zealand, Sweden, South Africa, South Korea, Norway, Germany, Belgium, Chile, Hong Kong, Holland, Spain, Italy, France, anywhere, anywhere, anywhere, anywhere but Pakistan, they can't wait to get out of there, having reduced the country to a wasteland, their very own caliphate of rubble. Like a malevolent god the man pours his laughter into Mikal, his skin becoming red as he laughs, sweat welling from his brow, and even though he makes Mikal relive every shame, indignity, humiliation, dishonour, defeat and disgrace he has ever experienced in his twenty years, Mikal begins to whisper back at him now: "What about you? What about you? what about you what about you . . ." He struggles against the chain and begins to shout. "What about the part you played in it?" He wishes he knew how to say it in English. *If I agree with you that what you say is true, would you agree that your country played a part in ruining mine, however small?* He wonders if the man is real, despite the fact that his laugh is continuing to swell in the air of the room, roaring like a giant wave getting louder as it encircles his head. He remembers how after they had interrogated a prisoner for twenty-nine consecutive hours he was brought back to the cage hallucinating, was seeing people and things that were not there. And then suddenly the light goes off and the laughter stops, nothing in the room but his own breathing. The pain in his arms is so intense it is screaming at him in a real voice, using human words.

"I want to see Jeo," he says in the interrogation room.

"Shut up. When did you take the oath with Osama bin Laden?" He must say something or they'll begin to hurt Jeo again on the other side of the wall.

"I can't remember. What date did Jeo give?" He is having trouble focusing his eyes after the dark chamber.

"You don't get to ask me questions. Get on your knees and stick your arms out."

Mikal does as he is told, the MP unlocking his handcuffs, and David and the interpreter leave the room, the MP remaining in his corner.

Half an hour later David returns and tells Mikal to sit back on the chair, his wrists locked again.

David indicates the Twin Towers poster. "If you think we will let you repeat what you did five months ago you are severely mistaken." And then, holding Mikal's eye, he says, "How did you feel when it happened?"

"It was a disgusting crime."

"Most of your people didn't think so. They were pleased."

"Now you know we don't all think alike." The man's eyes have not left his for even a fraction of a second. "How many of my people have you met anyway?"

"I have met enough of them here."

"Do you want me to base my opinion of your people on the ones I have met here?" *Let him ask me to get on my knees and stick my arms out.*

David leans back in his chair. "You wanted us to ask Jeo about something only the two of you would know. He has given us one word."

The man utters the word and it travels through Mikal, journeying along his blood vessels and then something ruptures in his mind. He is feeling weightless suddenly, what the arrow must feel when it leaves the bow. The muscles of his arms are in indescribable pain from having been in the stress position, and before that there were the ceiling shackles in the chamber, and yet he lunges at David across the table with his teeth bared, his only weapon—the animal part of him.

Naheed.

20

I curse this city. Its king erred in killing the man I love . . . She looks up from the page she has been reading and then closes the book. She has imagined an arrival, the presence of someone on the other side of the front gate. Perhaps there was even a knock. She emerges onto the terrace and gazes at the gate through the trees, surrounded by the natural noises of the garden. The ashes on her clothes deposit an indistinct impression on the white pillar beside her. These half-ghosts appear elsewhere in the house too, as she brushes against a wall in passing or forgetfully leans against a cupboard for support. They are faint—only she can see them—and as with the others she will brush this one away soon after becoming aware of it.

It is the first morning of steady heat this year, and she sits down on the stone steps. She opens the book on her lap and begins to read. *Shilappadikaram.* A text from the third century AD. *The story of Kannagi who, having lost her husband to a miscarriage of justice at the court of the Pandya king, wreaked her revenge on his kingdom.* When she looks up the gate has opened to admit Mikal.

His eyes locate her.

The jacaranda is in bloom and after a shower the smell enters the house at twilight so thickly she can lie there wondering if it will ever stop. It marks half the distance between Mikal and her, and she halts when she reaches it. Is it his ghost, here to convince her to build a life without him? Or is he real and her thinking has summoned him into her presence?

She backs away and he takes a corresponding step towards her.

"When someone thinks of us, or dreams of us with enough longing and love," Tara had said to her once, "we disappear from where we are." Naheed had become afraid lest she think about Mikal strongly enough to make him appear in the room, unable to explain to Tara who he was.

She turns and begins to walk away, looking over her shoulder to see him following her. But when she reaches the terrace he is no longer behind her. She had taken a sideways step on approaching the walnut tree, and it is as though he had continued in his momentum and disappeared into the bark.

She touches the tree trunk.

She waits for him to emerge for ten, fifteen, twenty seconds, and then she looks around, searching inside the light that breathes down everywhere through the canopies, her glance passing over the mulberries that have both foliage and flowers on their branches now, the thick softness of the leaves gleaming amongst all the other greens of the garden, the banyan's wide clear green, the cypresses almost black in comparison, the apple-green poplars. Eventually she sees him standing next to the peepal tree near the far boundary wall. She imagines him ascending through this trunk and then travelling along the joined crowns overhead to enter the peepal. Or perhaps he had gone down into the earth and walked through all the darkness and soil, the roots like wooden bolts of lightning around him, and then risen into the peepal.

21

As Basie and Yasmin come into the school, Father Mede stands at the window of his office and watches them. They are walking as close together as propriety allows in this land that is both less and more innocent than any other. They are lit by the March sunlight that is thick as felt. As a child he used to wonder why Eve was taken from Adam's rib. Now, at the other end of his life, these decades later, he knows it was because the rib is close to the heart. Both Basie and Yasmin have lost a brother and he can see that they have yet to recover, if they ever will. He doubts whether he has been able to express his feelings to them adequately. He held each of them in turn and just repeated the two or three phrases humans have for grief. Two thousand years have passed since man became brother to every other man on the planet, and yet words remain uninvented for the alleviation of certain burdens.

"Who is that young man on the cypress path?" Yasmin asks, as she passes by Father Mede's office. "Good morning, Father."

"Good morning, Yasmin," he looks up from the letters stacked on his desk. "Could it be one of the gardener's helpers?" Father Mede walks to the door and looks out towards the cypress trees. "He sometimes brings in his grandsons."

The sky is a blue so clean it verges on joy.

"He's gone," Yasmin says. "He was there a minute ago."

"Must be the gardener's grandson."

Children are coming in through the gate to begin the school day, the girls in white with red sweaters, the boys all in navy. *And He placed at the east of the garden of Eden cherubim, and a flaming sword which turned every way, to keep the way to the tree of life* . . . He looks at Yasmin. "You are wearing your mother's watch."

She glances at it.

"It cost her two hundred and fifty rupees," he continues. "She purchased it with her first pay cheque, the late 1960s. She came here to show it to me, I still remember. She said she had done a hundred and fifteen rupees' worth of shopping at the Army Canteen Stores. Biscuits. Coffee. Condensed milk. Chocolates. All the luxuries. And the Favre-Leuba watch." Father Mede taps the dial. He smiles. "And from the look on your face it is obvious that I have told you this many times before."

Yasmin puts her arm into his and walks into the office with him. "How was your trip?"

"Tiring."

"You are getting old."

"I don't feel old. I just feel like someone young who has something wrong with him." He settles in his chair. "How is your father?"

She looks away for half a moment.

Father Mede nods. "I wish him well." Rohan had requested that Father Mede stay away from his house while he dealt with Sofia's crisis of faith, had asked Sofia not to see him. The fracture was never really mended. "Is that ash on your sleeve?"

Yasmin tries to brush the small mark away. "My sister-in-law."

"The Greeks maintained we sprang from ash."

"This tunic belonged to my mother."

"I know."

As she is about to leave, he indicates the paperwork that has accumulated on his desk in his absence. "You and Basie must spare an hour to help me deal with some of this."

"Father, you take advantage of us."

"I know. First the Raj and now this."

The girl leaves with a smile—her mother's daughter. When Sofia went to Punjab University in Lahore for her MA, she had become distressed by the big city within days, and had returned to Heer, insisting she wouldn't go back. Her father—who had dreamed of having educated children—had summoned Father Mede urgently. Father Mede had been her teacher here at St. Joseph's, and the two of them had persuaded her to return to university. She agreed but was back a few weeks later, telling them that she felt a sense of exclusion from the other students, the modern Lahore girls and boys, a few of whom laughed at the way she dressed and spoke, laughed at her burka. Her father thought all week and then uttered the four words that shook the entire family to its very foundations, even the most distant branches in remote towns and villages:

"Take off your burka."

Sofia was speechless.

"Can you do that?"

"Of course not."

"Would it make you feel less noticeable?"

"It might."

"Then try it. Modesty and decency dwell in the mind, not in a burka. I want you to get an education and it seems that this issue is distracting you from that."

And she had gone back without her burka, much to the horror of her mother and brother, who knew that the chances of her making a decent marriage were in complete ruins now. It was bad enough already that she, an unmarried girl, was living away from her parents in a big-city hostel where there was no parental supervision.

Whether she had panicked too early at finding herself in an alien environment and would have settled in time with only minor adjustments, there was no way of knowing. What did happen was that after she went back she prospered at the university. She did try the burka again in the third year but by then she had lost the habit. She bought five Kashmiri shawls to cover her head and body when she was teaching at Ardent Spirit, and there was a dazzling wine-coloured coat with a fur collar for the coldest days of winter, pinned to whose left shoulder was a brooch shaped like the turban pin of an emperor.

Father Mede stands up and crosses the room that has a pattern of black and white griffins on the floor. He comes to stand before the small painting on the wall that Sofia had made for him. The crucified Christ, and the weeping figures at the foot of the cross. They are his mother and his friends and they are weeping because this—the crucifixion—is taking place, and it is powerful because the suffering of the tortured man and the suffering of those watching him are in the same picture. Are in the same glance. Injustice is not occurring in a distant hidden pocket, and the grief of the victim's relatives is not in a far removed place, disconnected from the crime. He will die, and those who love him are watching him—and all of it being watched by the viewer.

"Father, who are those two young men I just saw by the piano room?" Basie asks, entering the office.

"Were there two of them? I think they might be the gardener's grandsons or his helpers."

"I know his grandsons. And that wasn't them."

"I'll find out."

"How was your tour?" Basie asks, and he walks back to the door and casts his eyes about. "I think they were too neatly dressed to be the gardener's helpers."

Father Mede smites his forehead. "They must have come with the angels."

"The angels are back?"

Father Mede opens a drawer and takes out the key to the assembly hall.

Together they walk out onto the colonnaded corridor, the row of classroom doors stretching along on one side of them, the blazing March garden on the other. It's early so only a handful of students have arrived and there is a conspicuous silence in the classrooms. They pass the fourteen-year-old girl who had broken down one day three years ago as she held Father Mede's hand and wept with love and perplexity. "You are so good, how can you be a Christian? Why won't you convert to Islam?" She said she didn't want him to burn in Hell, and he had asked her to pray for his salvation. He has always maintained a cautious attitude over religion in this country. Although St. Joseph's is a Christian school, it is no longer a mission school as in a previous age, and both the Bible and the Koran are read at public functions, the festivals of both faiths marked through the year.

Father Mede unlocks the assembly hall and reveals the floor crowded with large shapes wrapped in newspaper. There are one hundred of them in total and he removes the paper from one to reveal Raphael's face. The angel responsible for healing the ailments and wounds of human children.

These human-sized wooden figures will be winched up on steel wires to hover overhead in the assembly hall. They were sent away to be repainted by an establishment that decorates Heer's trucks and rickshaws, and they have returned bathed in vivid colour, Raphael's cheeks rouged with cyclamen pink. Each eye is a turquoise disc of glass held in place with a slender nail, almost a pin. They lie on their stomachs on the floor and the wings of each rise up from their backs taller than Basie and Father Mede.

Basie removes the newspaper from the flank of the figure nearest to him. A hand holding a black chain is revealed. He uncovers the face and breast.

"After the Fall, Gabriel was sent to comfort Adam," Father Mede says, "and Michael to comfort Eve."

Michael, who is Mikal in Islam. Described as having emerald-green wings and being covered in minute saffron-coloured hairs, each of which has a million faces that ask Allah in a million languages to pardon the sins of the faithful.

Father Mede places a hand on Basie's shoulder. Basie touches it and then covers up Michael's face.

"They are all here," Father Mede says. "The Angels of the Seven Days of the Week. The Angel of Earthquakes. The Angel of Fascination. Of Dust. Of Doves." He looks up at the rings attached to the ceiling from which they will be suspended.

"So they were brought here by the boys I saw?"

"It is possible. They arrived in three trucks and there was a small gang to unload them."

"I must ask the guard at the gate," Basie says. "We have to be careful."

"Don't frighten the children."

Yesterday the Ardent Spirit van had mentioned reports that a religious school had been bombed by the Americans in Afghanistan, killing a number of small children. The van slowed to a crawl outside St. Joseph's. "We'll reduce America to the size of India, India to the size of Israel, Israel to nothing," the loudspeaker said as it lingered near the public monument at the end of the road, a giant fibreglass replica of the mountain under which Pakistan's nuclear bomb was tested. Its colour marks the precise moment the device exploded. Unstilled after millions of years, the mountain had turned a pure white. Its insides are hollow and it is lit up from within at night: in the pale evenings from the balcony of his room above the school, Father Mede watches it come on— one moment it is dead and grey but then suddenly, like a fever rising from its very core, a glow spreads on the slopes and it swells and brightens until its radiance rivals the moon, and the beggar children who shelter in there can be seen moving in silhouette on the brilliant sides.

The crinkled newspaper is straightening and coming away, and after Basie leaves Father Mede watches the figure of Michael reveal itself here and there out of the newsprint—allowing glimpses of the golden robes, the chains with which he holds Satan, the sword in the other hand. It is said that cherubim were created out of the tears Michael shed over the sins in the world. The Chief of the Order of Virtues and the Chief of Archangels, he is also the Prince of the Divine Presence, the Prince of Light and the Prince of God. He is the Angel of Repentance, Mercy and Righteousness, the Guardian of Peace and the Angel of Earth, and the patron of policemen and soldiers.

Father Mede turns the key in the assembly-hall door and walks back towards to his office.

> *Restore us again, O God of our salvation,*
> *And put away your indignation towards us.*
> *Will you be angry with us forever?*
> *Will you prolong your anger to all generations?*

Michael is said to have written these lines. Psalm 85. The lines that are employed to invoke him.

22

"Don't step on that piece of ground," Naheed cautions Rohan as they walk in the garden. "I buried the dead birds there back in October."

Rohan looks at the soil. He can see a little today, the places where the sunlight is clear and unrestricted. She had found him with the Koran open in his hands earlier, one of his great torments being that he cannot read it for the comfort of Sofia's soul.

"Is the pomegranate in flower?"

She guides his hand and he touches the blossoms, the tough outer cups, and the scraps of wrinkled silk at the centre that are the petals, and as he takes in their scent he tells her that the name Granada derives from the pomegranates that grew in that region of Spain. Basie and Yasmin have had a number of conversations with the eye specialist since Naheed and Rohan visited him, and the procedures he suggested are the only answer.

"Spain was once a Muslim land," Rohan says, cupping the flowers in his hands. "In October 1501, the Catholic monarchs ordered the destruction of all Islamic books and manuscripts. Thousands of Korans and other texts were burned in a public bonfire."

She lets him talk as she looks around for Mikal. Nothing but a kingfisher stitching together the two banks of the river with the bright threads of its flight.

"A shopkeeper was arrested because he muttered 'O Muhammad!' after someone refused to buy his wares. Another man, brought before an Inquisitor for washing his hands in a suspect Muslim-looking manner, confessed under torture to being a Muslim and denounced a number of his neighbours, only to revoke his confession immediately afterwards. He was tortured a second time and died of his injuries in prison."

She holds his hand in hers. These days she is having to make sure he eats everything on his plate, disregarding his objections that he no longer feels hungry. She and Tara make his chapattis bigger and thicker, with the result that when he thinks he is eating just one, he is in fact eating one and a quarter, or one and a half.

She is relieved Basie and Yasmin are dealing with the eye specialist himself. Seeing the nurses at the clinic had provoked anxiety in her. The mind fighting phantoms, a strange fear had appeared that one of them could be the nurse who had given her the injections to destroy the child back in November, that the doctor—enraged at Rohan—could reveal this fact to him. *Why am I afraid?* she had asked herself initially. *What could anyone do to me if they learned about what I had done?* But, no. She is not concerned for herself, she is afraid of distressing Rohan, Yasmin and Basie. The truth would hurt *them.* That is why the matter has to be kept secret.

Rohan has noticed her silence. "What is it?"

"Just a headache."

"Has your mother said something?"

She shakes her head. Then, wondering if he has seen the gesture, says, "No."

"I had a conversation with her yesterday."

She doesn't reply. A movement in the grape arbour where the very first green beads have appeared on the branches; by June they will have grown and the skin will slip liquidly from the pulp.

"She is concerned for you."

"There's no need."

"You should think of getting married again."

She looks up where the tamarind tree shifts its branches, in its stately thirst for movement. The dying leaves that had covered it in a copper haze last month are gone, replaced by a luminous green.

"It's too soon," she says.

"It probably is. Your mother has selected a boy, but by the time the necessary enquiries and arrangements have been made, an appropriate amount of time would have passed. These things move slowly. I know the marriage with Jeo was rapid but that was an exception."

Last week Naheed had said to Tara, "This year I will help Father through the trouble with his eyes. After that I will begin studying for a diploma to become a teacher." She has discovered a sudden appetite for books as though the boxes had arrived at the house just for her. She dips her hands into them at random. Lyrics and fictions from all periods, volumes of photographs and paintings, works of Eastern and Western history. Some telling her to exchange reason for wonder, others to replace wonder with reason. She lifts the slender gossamer paper from a painted page and a bandit in a glowing orchard is revealed, the Persian sky coated entirely with gold leaf above him. Mikal surfaced when she looked at and opened al-Shirazi's fourteenth-century work entitled *A Book I Have Composed on Astronomy But I Wish to Be Absolved of All Blame.* Late into the night she reads stories from South America, Iceland, India. *She turned herself into a doe and sped away from him, but he transformed himself into a stag and—overtaking her—coupled with her. Afterwards she was a peahen running away from him but he became a peacock and mated with her again. Next she was a cow pursued by him in the shape of a bull, coupling with her a third time . . .*

"You mustn't be concerned," says Rohan as they walk back to the house. "We will check everything thoroughly. Once Tara has asked the initial questions, she will tell me and Basie, and Basie will conduct a full investigation. He is your brother."

Suddenly she is overwhelmed. The tears coming so fast she needs two hands to catch them.

"Why has this happened?" she whispers.

Rohan turns and after groping in the air for a few moments—coming in from the sunlight has dimmed his vision further—encloses her in his arms.

He strokes her head gently. Distant acquaintances continue to arrive to give condolences for Jeo's death, having heard about it only just now. They come and find his own eyes in bandages. With Jeo and Mikal's deaths he was just as wounded, and it is an astonishment that no one could *see* that wound. It is one of life's great mysteries, human beings living with secret grief, unseen, and unsympathised. And so it is that Naheed carries Jeo's death secretly inside her, the mountainous weight of it. Yasmin and Basie carry it too. And Tara. But if all of them were to walk into a place, it would be Rohan who would be seen to be afflicted. The wounds in the souls and the hearts remain unsensed. Requiring another kind of vision.

When the girl is somewhat comforted he lets her go. He had intended to ask her in detail about the bird pardoner's son, she and Tara having visited the family last evening. The boy is making a slow recovery but still the subject is a melancholy one and he decides not to broach it.

She takes him forward and lowers him into his armchair.

"It's eleven o'clock," she tells him.

He no longer has any need to wear a wristwatch. His blindness almost coincided with the death of the two boys. They seem the same event. In the coming years when he is asked how long he has been sightless, he would ask himself how long Jeo and Mikal have been gone.

"He said he'd come about this time."

A message had arrived at the house from Major Kyra last week, requesting a meeting with Rohan. Rohan had attempted to visit him on hearing the news of Ahmed the Moth's death, but again and again the boys at the Ardent Spirit gate had informed him that he was not on the premises, something like hostility appearing in them as soon as Rohan gave his name.

"I have no doubt they are planning to invade Iraq and Iran," Kyra is saying to Rohan, as Naheed enters with the tea tray. "And then of course it will be Pakistan's turn, if our government disobeys them."

Naheed pours a cup and hands it to the former soldier.

"The US President used the word 'crusade' in the first speech he gave after the terrorist attacks," he says. "And they said if Pakistan did not help them in fighting al-Qaeda and the Taliban, they would bomb us back to the Stone Age. These were their exact words."

She leans against the door frame. She has a feeling she knows why he is here, even if Rohan doesn't.

He looks at her and then turns to Rohan. "Well, now we must talk about why I have requested the meeting."

"I am glad you have come," Rohan says. "I was thinking about contacting you soon . . ."

The man ignores him. "It is a delicate matter. There are not many donations for Ardent Spirit anymore. The cowardly government has cut off funding to honourable patriots like us. Things are very hard since the conspiracy of last September, and people like us are being accused of sowing something called terror. I wanted to meet you to see what can be done."

"I don't know how I can be of help in this matter."

"I was hoping you could find alternative accommodations."

"Alternative accommodations?"

"Yes."

"He wants us to move out of here," Naheed says.

Kyra doesn't acknowledge the comment. "It wouldn't be straight away," he says to Rohan. "I can give you six weeks, two months, to find another place. But we do need this house."

"It's my home." Rohan raises his hand and Naheed comes forward to take it.

"Yes, but I own it." Kyra produces a set of papers from his pocket. "The school belongs to me. And so does this house. My brother let you live here out of the kindness of his heart, and due to the respect he felt for you. In spite of everything."

"I don't need to see any papers. I remember what I signed."

"Then I don't know how you can claim that this house is yours."

"I was thinking of contacting you to say that you must give the house back to me. It is a shameful thing to divulge but I have contemplated selling it to raise funds for my eyes."

He can be protective with his emotions, but Naheed knows how terrified Rohan is of being blind. He hasn't revealed the full extent of this to anyone. Perhaps because he doesn't wish to be judged for his despair, by humans or by Allah.

"I think you should leave," Naheed says to Kyra.

Kyra turns to her, his manner a mixture of cordiality and woodland bandit.

"You heard her," Basie says, coming in.

Kyra straightens. "You must be Basie."

"I want you to leave," Basie says, a glare in his eyes. Kyra stands up slowly, squaring up with Basie.

"One way or another I am going to destroy you," Basie says, a startling and violent contempt in the voice. "I have asked around and I think it was you who were responsible for the deaths of my brother and Jeo." He takes the papers from his hands and tears them up. "I spoke to one family," he says, "who told me you sent their son to Afghanistan. You gave the father full assurance that the boy would be given training before being sent to the battlefield. You gave your word that the boy would be looked after. But he was butchered."

"I had to tell the father that. He is a eunuch and a traitor and an infidel in all but name and was not granting the boy permission to go to jihad. What are we supposed to do? Bow down before America?"

"Get out."

"So this is what you have learnt by being around Christians," Kyra says from the door, "by being a teacher at that Englishman's school. Contempt for true patriots."

After he leaves the three of them remain in the shared silence. Eventually, looking at the photograph in the newspaper on the table, Basie says, "And you can go to Hell too, Mr. President."

"What happened?" Tara asks Naheed, coming into the house to help her prepare lunch.

"Major Kyra wants us to vacate the house."

Tara utters the verse of the Koran one is supposed to upon receiving bad news.

"Basie asked him to leave."

"We have to be careful, they are dangerous people." Tara looks towards Rohan's room. "He signed every piece of paper they put in front of him. Now he sits in there stroking his deceived beard."

"No one deceived him, Mother."

"Yes, they did. He was half mad after Sofia's death. You could have made him do anything." Tara brings the basket of green gourds to

Naheed. "But I don't want you to worry about the house. I'll go to the mosque and ask the cleric to give me a talisman and we'll pray . . ."

"Pray," Naheed mutters. "Who listens to our prayers?"

"How dare you talk in this manner? One or two prayers going unheard doesn't mean none will ever be heard."

"One or two?"

"Be quiet. It was praying to Allah that got me through my time in prison."

"It was Allah and His laws that put you there in the first place."

Tara takes a step towards her. "Be quiet! Don't you ever utter anything like that again."

Naheed gives her a look of fury, her eyes swimming at her entrapment and yearning, and turns away.

"Did you hear what I said?"

"Yes."

As they work in the kitchen both remain locked in their anger, both silent, though Tara's lips move in soundless recital of Koranic verses.

After a quarter of an hour, and without looking up from the gourds she is cutting into wedges, Naheed asks, "What did Sharif Sharif want when he came to visit Father that day?"

"Nothing," Tara says, though not immediately. "I told you it was just a neighbourly visit. Asking about Rohan's eyes."

"Mother, please."

"He asked for your hand in marriage."

Naheed puts down the knife.

"He offered to pay for his eye operation in return."

After minutes of further silence Naheed takes the bowl full of green and white pieces of gourd to the other side of the kitchen. Turning on the tap she submerges the pieces in water, to remain fresh until cooked. "One more thing," she says quietly from there.

"Yes?"

"Father says you've found someone for me."

"I have a boy in mind." And not having received a reaction from Naheed, she adds, "It's the only way."

Naheed smiles tensely, her eyes on the point of igniting. "It's not the only way, Mother. There are a thousand other ways. I am tired of being afraid all the time—"

"The world is a dangerous place."

"Let me finish, Mother. It was wrong of you to frighten me into destroying my child. It was wrong of you to frighten Mikal away. I don't care what you have been through, but you should never ever frighten those younger than you with your own fears. Caution is one thing, but you filled me with terror. Just leave me alone please. Just take this world of yours and go away with it somewhere and leave us alone. All of you."

"What if—"

"What if, what if. What if the world ends tomorrow?"

"It could. The signs are there."

Naheed comes and places her hand gently on Tara's shoulder.

"Mother, you can't be *this* afraid. The world is not going to end tomorrow."

23

Kyra and the six boys from the six houses of Ardent Spirit are discussing the St. Joseph's operation.

"The siege will go on for several days," Ahmed says. "So we'll need sacks of almonds to take with us for energy."

The boy from Cordoba House has produced a precisely detailed diagram of the school—the height as well as the length of each wall is marked, the number of windows in each classroom—and it lies on the carpet before them.

It has been decided that each of the six young men will bring along just four trusted companions—as the Prophet had four companions. So in all twenty-four men have to be found. They have begun the search and made a partial selection. Some of them will be students at Ardent Spirit, while others are from outside, chosen for their commitment, strength and boldness.

"Given the possible length of the siege," says the head of Mecca House, "each of us will have to take five or six rucksacks, containing spare ammunition, medicines, bottles of water in case the authorities try to kill us by poisoning the taps."

"May Allah reward him somehow," Ahmed says, "the guard who stands at St. Joseph's entrance has been very helpful in providing details of the building, of the routine and flow of the staff and student body." The guard is a devout man in his fifties, and said he knew what kind of suspect humans the St. Joseph's students would grow up to be. Over the years he had guarded the mansions of any number of Heer's rich people, and he was repulsed by what he had observed—the indecency of the women, the abominable traitors' talk, the superior attitude towards the unprivileged, the consuming of alcohol, the constant blasphemies—and he had lost his job several times for daring to speak up, or had abandoned it in shame for not having the courage to say what he wished.

They said to the guard that they needed the information in order to rob and vandalise the place.

"Once we are inside the building," the head of Cairo House says, pointing to the drawing, "this line of trees along the south wall will restrict our view of the outside. The police and army could storm the school from that direction."

Ahmed studies the drawing. "We need to do something about them."

He gets up and walks to the window, looking out. He has been feeding tactics, strategy and vigour into the boys. While in the military he had developed a silencer for the AK-47 rifle, hitherto available to only a select few internationally, and he developed what he referred to as a "guerrilla" mortar gun, of a type available to only some of the world's most advanced military forces, so small it can be hidden in a medium-sized holdall. He had specialised in urban assault training, his ideas proving to be the most important element in the series of fearful guerrilla attacks on Indian barracks in Kashmir. In February 2000 the commandos of the Indian army had raided a village in Pakistani Kashmir and killed fourteen civilians, returning to the Indian side with abducted Pakistani girls, the severed heads of three of whom they threw back at Pakistani soldiers. The Pakistani guerrilla leader who crossed into Indian-occupied Kashmir the very next day with twenty-five fighters, to conduct a revenge operation against the Indian army in Nakyal sector, had been trained by Kyra. They kidnapped an Indian officer and beheaded him, bringing the head back to be paraded in the bazaars of Kotli in Pakistani Kashmir.

He has given every aspect of the St. Joseph's operation deep thought, and has just returned from a three-day visit to China, where he had gone to procure weapons and night-vision glasses. The biggest task was to clear them through customs in Pakistan. He had called an old friend, a captain, who is the President's security officer. The captain came to the airport in the President's official car and received Kyra at the immigration counter. In the captain's presence no one dared touch Kyra's luggage. So there are some in the army with their honour intact. He visits his old military comrades regularly and tries to shame them for their weak Islamic beliefs, for continuing to serve in the Pakistani army, and he is delighted on being told that some of them are thinking of leaving, like him. After St. Joseph's, he and several others will leave to fight and kill British troops in Afghanistan's Helmand Province.

"So we need to do something about the trees along the south wall," he says, returning to the boys. "And we must purchase a camcorder—to film the beheadings."

24

Yasmin comes into the assembly hall to find Basie standing amid the paper-wrapped angels. No movement within his body. His head low-ered. She bolts the door behind her and walks up to him, making her way through the newspaper shapes. *At any given moment we are entangled in all the past of mankind. Our heads encircled by the echo of every word that has ever been spoken.* These words were written down in one of his father's journals. Standing behind him she flattens her body against his, her arms around his waist. A moan comes from him, the most ancient of human conditions, and a shudder of grief that she absorbs into her-self, the most ancient of exchanges.

He turns within the ring of her arms. "I want a child."

"Me too."

It is as though he has not heard her. "I want a child," he repeats, the voice muffled.

"Let's go home."

From the corridor come the sounds of the school having ended for the day, the din and hum of voices, snatches of intense high-pitched conversations. She leads him out into the corridor, into the current of children that parts and converges about them.

25

Mikal knows the Americans are about to execute him. What they have said is that he is being set free, but he knows it is a lie. They are about to execute him.

David Town, the interrogator, has informed him of his freedom through the interpreter. His chains have been removed, they have given him some money, and there is a new set of clothes—a pale blue shalwar kameez with a light jacket whose softness indicates it is quilted with feathers. He is being freed because the warlord who had betrayed him to the Americans has now himself been arrested. David said the warlord was firing on Western soldiers, attacking military convoys and installations, and then picking up random people to hand over to the Americans for reward. "He is in custody," David said. "Being held right here in the brick factory, awaiting transport to Cuba."

But Mikal knows that these are lies. It is all preparation for his murder.

"The freed prisoners are always dropped off at the place where they were picked up," David tells him as he walks out of the brick factory with him. "You are being taken to the mosque where we found you back in January." He points to the helicopter on the other side of the compound, the blades churning the dust into djinns. Ready to fly him to the wilderness and a shallow grave.

Mikal looks up at the sky, feeling lightheaded and exposed to be under it after the prolonged period indoors. "Where's Jeo?" he asks.

Although the interpreter translates the question, it is as though David does not hear it. He continues to walk, looking straight ahead. "Where's Jeo?" He turns to the interpreter. "Ask him where Jeo is."

But again there is no reaction.

"What month is it?"

"April."

When they arrive at the edge of the dust being raised by the rotors, David stops. Two white Military Policemen are standing beside the helicopter, inside the churning dust, and David motions Mikal towards them.

"I am not leaving without Jeo."

David looks at the two MPs and they advance towards Mikal, one of them taking him by the arm.

"I am not leaving without Jeo."

"Good luck with the rest of your life," David says, extending a hand towards him.

He looks out of the helicopter window as they begin their descent towards the mosque. No longer winter, the snow and ice are gone. The mosque is on the edge of a lake and the released water is full of movements.

Mikal knows both the MPs. One of them had put his gloved fingers into his mouth an hour ago to see if he was hiding anything under the tongue. The man wears a battle-dress jacket onto whose sleeves have been stitched cargo pockets taken from a pair of trousers. Over several days of interrogation David had convinced a severely wounded Arab prisoner—his wrists zip-tied to the frame of the gurney as he hallucinated—that this man was his father and they had extracted useful information from him.

From the beginning of January to April. More than three months during which Mikal was administered intravenous fluids and drugs against his will and was forcibly given enemas in order to keep his body functioning well enough for the interrogations to go on. Questionings from the CIA, FBI, MI5, MI6. Restraint on a swivel chair for long periods, loud music and white noise played to prevent him from sleeping, lowering the temperature in the room until it was unbearable and then throwing water in his face, forcing him to pray to Osama bin Laden, asking him whether Mullah Omar had ever sodomised him.

Threats of deportation to countries known for torturing prisoners. "After they are through with you, you will never get married you will never have children you will never buy a fucking Toyota." Threats made against his family including female members, strip searches and body searches sometimes ten times a day, forced nudity, including in the presence of female personnel, threatening to desecrate the Koran in front of him, placing him in prolonged stress positions, placing him in tight restraint jackets for many days and nights, and in addition to all this there were the times when he was actually beaten for his "threatening behaviour."

As they touch ground Mikal wonders if his murder will take place inside the ruined mosque, enclosed by the words of the Koran inscribed on the walls. The wind coming off the water has a smell like metal. Are the women and children who were left behind in January, after the men were picked up, still in there?

The two MPs climb out of the machine with him.

The three of them walk to where the rotor diameter ends, and there the two men stop, gesturing to Mikal to continue.

Keeping his eye on the mosque door ahead of him, he takes one step and then another, and then he smells it, the whiff of sulphur that is the unmistakable clue that a bullet has been fired. The noise of the rotors is too great so he doesn't *hear* the gunshot. He holds his breath for a pearl diver's minute. The sulphur intensifies and then he turns around and lifts the pistol from the hip holster of one of the Military Policemen, amazed at the freedom of movement in his unchained arms, amazed that his incomplete hands are now allowing him to place the pistol directly against the man's throat and effortlessly pull the trigger. The air behind the neck balloons in a red mist. There is a small funnel of shock wave and in a frozen moment he sees himself reflected in the man's American eyes. Next to Mikal in each eye is the reflection of the sun, the two placed side by side in each intense blue circle. He sees now to his astonishment that he has pulled the trigger a second time and now there is a bloody wound on the man's breast. He swings the barrel towards the other man and shoots him too, the bullet entering the arm at the elbow and coming out through the wrist. He realises too late—his trigger pulled for the fourth time, the bullet travelling towards the white man's face at point blank range—that someone is aiming at the helicopter from the mosque, that a hail of metal is coming towards them from the minarets, the sound lagging.

He is running upwards into the mountain. The slope is abrupt on the east and south but gentle to the north and west. Above him the day is withdrawing from the sky in long lengths of gold and soon he is high enough on the gradient to be able to see the mosque below him, the lake whose water he had crossed in a boat. The helicopter took off without the two fallen bodies. He can see them. The pilot made several attempts to come out to collect them, to capture Mikal, but the firing from the mosque was too intense. Mikal had dropped the pistol and run towards the boat that stood in a patch of reeds and poisonous dog's mercury at the edge of the lake. No doubt they'll return soon in greater number to begin their hunt for him.

If this were summer he would take handfuls of wild rose petals and eat them for the sugar, for the sweet water in them, but in spring there are only the cream white blooms of the wood anemone, his fingers plucking them as he goes, the traces of pink, the faint bitter scent reminiscent of leaf mould and foxes. He fills his pockets with them as he runs. There are mountain villages in Pakistan he has been to where the first wood anemone of each year is sewn into clothing, with the idea that beauty wards off pestilence and plague. Coming to a plateau he sits by a spring and makes a small boat with one of the banknotes the Americans had given him and sets it on the current. He enters a cave but leaves it a few minutes later, having found a collection of passports in a crevice and a list of thirty-three Jewish organisations in New York City. Darkness falls but he continues to move, the overcast sky a slab of unreadable black stone above him and as always the silence of the mountain is physical—a thing, with weight—and there is a wish in him to keep walking, to continue up into the mountain and into the high ice deserts, becoming God's neighbour.

Arriving at a small village, twenty single-storey houses around a crooked street, he knocks on the first door. After salutations, he asks the man in Pashto whether he would like to own his clothes.

The man touches the material of his shalwar kameez but says he has no money.

Mikal explains that he only wishes to exchange them for another set.

"Is someone pursuing you?"

"No."

"Are you a bandit? A lover who has killed a rival?"

"No."

The man is suddenly anxious about the possibilities he has raised and closes the door.

The knock on the next door produces a younger man who agrees readily to Mikal's proposal, fingering the jacket lovingly, the small logos embroidered on the shoulders and pockets in orange and raspberry thread.

"Why do you want to exchange them?"

"I don't like the colour."

The boy looks at him. "Are you an American?"

"What?"

"Are you an American?"

"No."

"Do you know where I can get a visa to live in America?"

"No, I don't."

Mikal steps into the house and changes into the clothes the boy brings for him. He sees a knife on the floor in the corner. "Can I have that?" he asks.

The boy picks it up and pulls the six-inch rusty blade out of the brass liners. It is a lockback knife with a cracked deer-antler grip and nickel bolsters. He makes a face, but on sensing that Mikal has some need for it, he erases the expression. "I can't give it to you, it's very dear to me."

"I'll buy it."

At the other end of the street he shouts into a window and asks if he can sleep in the stable. An old man's face appears and then a woman's beside him, their clothes marbled with grease and grime, and from the

stable the goat looks at him with its agate eyes. They are poor like everyone else in the place and they smell of smoke, wax and sweat.

"Where are you going?" the man asks. "Where is your home?"

"I don't know. I am alone."

The woman lifts both her hands to her ears, overcome with despair
at being told such a thing, on meeting someone who can believe such a
thing. "No one is alone on earth," she says. "No one."

They invite him in and he sits with them on the earthen floor of
their one-room house. The man tells him that Pakistan is over the
mountains, through the cliff passes, and the woman brings him a bowl
of milk with a triangle of stiff bread.

"Someone must be waiting for you," the man says.

"Listen to me." The woman touches the side of his head. "You must
find your way back. In the past merchants and soldiers would go away
for years to other lands. But they returned, to find people waiting for
them."

"I returned after decades and she was here," the old man says.

It is cold in the night and he hears helicopters hovering overhead,
real or imagined, and when he wakes in the dawn light the woman is
already up and has a fire burning in the corner of the room used as
a kitchen, huddling over it in her thin clothes. Mikal crawls out from
under the blanket and puts on his boots and walks out to study the
morning as it shapes itself out of the darkness rich with gleams.

When he is ready to leave, after drinking a bowl of tea with them,
the man decides to walk with him partway into the mountains, through
the corridors of various limestones, often much contorted, and there,
over ancient hieroglyphs carved onto calcareous flagstone, he draws
Mikal the route to Peshawar, his marks moving over and through the
Buddhist writings, between them and incorporating them. Mikal makes
him take some of the money before they part.

Around noon he spends an hour on the edge of a cliff, sharpening
the knife. A white lamb's skull lies in an eagle's nest just below him on
the cliff face. He licks the back of his wrist and tries the blade on the
hair. It is sharp but there is nothing to kill. In the evening he scoops out
termites from a hollow tree and eats them, spitting out the bitter heads

like pips, and has to enter the tree a few moments later on hearing helicopters, the insects climbing onto his face and clothes. Did the boy who wanted to go to America tell them about him?

He walks all through the night, Venus appearing as the hours go by and moving with him. Lyra, Pegasus, Piscis Austrinus, and all the other constellations that he hasn't seen since he was captured at the beginning of the year are now pulsing above him, but he cannot read them fully, the shapes tangled, or threadbare like beads missing from a piece of needlework. He has forgotten some of the names, while in other cases it is the shapes and locations associated with the remembered names that he cannot recall.

From the faintly rotting corpse of a jackal he extracts the bones with the knife, cracking them open to suck out the marrow sealed inside, still without taint. He had gained some weight from the food the Americans had fed him at the prison but now he is exhausted. At dawn he falls onto his side with his eyes closed, lying on feldspar grit and stiff clay at a river's edge. At noon he sees a rabbit in the meadow twenty feet ahead of him. He stops walking and puts two fingers to his teeth and whistles and the rabbit freezes. He takes the knife from his pocket and opens it and he watches as the blade slices the tips of the long grass on its way towards the animal. Catching the sparks from a struck rock onto a piece of dry moss, he builds a fire and roasts the skinned rabbit, eating every last morsel, not knowing if his mutilated hands will allow him the same luck again.

They don't. He fails several times and the next day in despair he picks up a snake by its tail and, like a whip, slams the head against the rock under which it had been sheltering. And then once again to be sure. Severing the head he peels back the skin, a mute sheath of nibs, and pulls it downwards to separate it from the body. The guts are pulled out along with the skin, leaving the meat. He traps one end between a splice in a stick and wraps the length in a spiral around the stick and ties the other end with stalks and roasts the snake over an open flame.

The journey to Pakistan takes him eight days, staying away from villages, stealing from an orchard, a planted field, nests, staying away from humans because he knows the Americans are looking for him. This time they'll lock him away for the rest of his life. In Cuba or in America itself. Or he could get the death penalty. When he climbs down out of the mountains at the outskirts of Peshawar, a storm overtaking him in a hail of ice, he hasn't eaten in two days and he is running a constant body temperature that must be 106.

He is still trapped, the cage is just bigger. On several occasions he stands with the receiver of a pay phone in his hand but cannot dial in case the Americans are following him. When he leaves after the call, they will trace the number. They will go to Heer and take away Basie, Yasmin, Rohan, Tara and Naheed, to put them in the cages in the brick factory. He makes several haphazard journeys into surrounding towns, within the coronet of mountains and hills that surrounds Peshawar. Getting into a bus without asking the destination, he disembarks halfway and changes direction, or continues in the same direction but on the next bus. When he is convinced at last that there is nobody behind him, in a small town thirty miles outside Peshawar, he breaks into a place called Look Seventeen Beauty Parlour and from there dials the number of Basie and Yasmin's house. No one picks up. He rings Rohan's house and Yasmin answers, her voice like electricity through him. Hearing her and not being able to respond makes her feel further away than she is. He is an exile in his own homeland, his eyes filled with uncrossable distances. What ghosts must feel. He hangs up and stands there, shaking from the fever. The interrogators at the brick factory had said one day that the woman screaming in the next room was Naheed. Was he told that or is he just imagining it? He knows he must go to Heer to see if they have captured Naheed. *And I still have to find Jeo.*

He opens his eyes and sees Akbar's.

For a moment he thinks he is back in one of the cages. But then he sits up and recognises the place where he had taken shelter—the cramped windowless space under the mosque in Coppersmiths' Bazaar in Peshawar, where the torn copies of the Koran are kept.

"Are you talking much nowadays?" Akbar smiles.

He tries to speak but his throat hurts. His flesh is burning, the earthen floor under him damp with sweat.

"The Americans let you go too?" Akbar says. Mikal nods. *For now.*

"I saw you from the other side of the bazaar. You were on the roof."

"I was trying to find the constellations," he says. He raises his trembling hand and places it on Akbar's. "I don't remember you telling me you were from Peshawar."

"I am not. Just visiting."

Mikal lies down again. "What time is it?"

"Three."

"Day or night?"

They talk for a few minutes, Mikal telling him about shooting the two Military Policemen, and though Akbar wishes to know the details he is too weak to continue, is exhausted from the few words he has spoken, lowering his head onto the wet pillow of Koranic pages and closing his eyes, lost between several worlds.

He senses daylight and there are movements and words near him. From time to time there is a bitter taste in the mouth, or a needle punctures his arm, after which the darkness returns. Eventually he manages to keep his eyes open long enough to see a girl standing beside him and he does not wish to breathe or blink for fear of breaking the spell, just remaining there on the very edge of inhabited time. She wears a white shalwar kameez, the sleeves coming down to her wrists, her fingers pale as porcelain.

Over several drowsy moments the details assemble into a complete picture—the room is large and clean and the walls are whitewashed. There is a tree outside the window whose foliage grows in seven-leafed fans.

She is supervising an older woman, who appears to be a servant but is respectfully addressed, and is pressing a piece of ice wrapped in flowered cloth onto Mikal's forehead. The moment the girl notices that he has regained consciousness she pulls her veil down onto her fine-boned face and withdraws from the room in utter silence. The grey-haired older woman continues to tend to him until Akbar enters, and then she too leaves.

"I've brought you a visitor," Akbar says, holding a snow leopard cub pressed against his chin, the fur so soft there are furrows in it from the boy's breathing.

"How long have I been asleep?"

"Five days. And I think the word is unconscious."

"Five days," he whispers. "This is your home?"

Akbar nods and places the animal on his chest and Mikal sits up and cradles it. The pads are like pink-grey raspberries attached to the undersides of its paws, and the fur has dark markings that look as though another cub with sooty paws has walked all over it.

"It's about three weeks old. My sister sent it in for you. In October, her husband and my twin brother and I went to fight the Western armies in Afghanistan. They were both martyred."

Mikal remembers Akbar telling him at the brick factory that he had had nothing to do with fighting, that he was a taxi driver and the Americans had captured him in Jalalabad on false information.

He gets up and walks to the door and looks out, suddenly untired, desiring movement. The cub is pure innocent trust as it clings to him.

The house is painted yellow, and is located in a dense grove of trees, all the same kind. One of them grows in Rohan's garden in Heer, its small green-white flowers filling the winter evenings with a rich smell. Rohan had planted it because its wood is used for making writing tablets.

"It used to be a clinic," Akbar says, as they walk in the grove, the sun falling through the sieve of leaves here and there. "A small hospital, owned by a doctor in the 1930s. He planted these trees. He was famous in the region for providing wooden noses to the women whose real ones had been cut off by their families. The wood of these trees was used for carving the new noses."

"Where am I?"

"South Waziristan. The clinic was abandoned when it was discovered that it had links with English missionaries."

The new pale leaves stand out against the darker foliage brightly.

"I won't ask you your name," Akbar says. "I know you'll tell me when you are ready."

Mikal nods.

"The men you shot," Akbar says. "Do you think they are dead?"

"They couldn't have survived."

"I know what charges the Americans will bring against you. I telephoned a friend in Peshawar and he looked it up."

"Tell me."

"Are you sure?"

"Yes."

Akbar takes a piece of paper from his pocket and unfolds it. "Let's assume they didn't die. For each wounded man you will be put on trial for one count of attempting to kill US nationals outside the United States. One count of attempting to kill US officers and employees. One count of assault of US officers and employees. One count of armed assault of US officers and employees. One count of using and carrying a firearm during and in relation to a crime of violence . . ."

"How long?" Mikal interrupts.

"You will go to prison for almost two hundred years."

"And if they have died?"

Akbar looks at him, his eyes containing the answer.

Mikal places the cub on his knee and it lifts a paw as if to test the air, the soft leather nostrils expanding.

"I thought they were about to kill me."

"I know."

Silently they walk back to the room where two male servants are setting out dishes for their lunch, both of them with rifles over their shoulders, the straps decorated with small coloured beads and sequins.

Corn bread drenched in clarified butter, yogurt, a dish of chicken and spinach, another of lentils and potatoes, sliced onion in a saucer, oranges. A large bowl of custard with a layer of coin-like banana slices on top. Akbar sends the custard back to remain cool in the fridge until they call for it.

A few minutes into the meal Mikal says quietly, without looking up from his plate, "There is no way out of it, is there?"

"I don't know."

"There isn't. They won't *ever* stop looking. They'll be trying to find me in twenty, thirty, forty, fifty years."

"It's strange how much their government cares if something happens to its people." With a morsel of bread in his hand, Akbar extends his arm and touches Mikal's shoulder with the back of his wrist. "You'll just have to make sure they can't find you."

"I don't understand how I could have smelled the sulphur of the bullets fired from the mosque. The rotor blades should have dispersed the smell. But I smelt it. I don't know how it's possible." The leopard is perched on Mikal's knee as he eats. They descend trees head first and he imagines the cub moving down his shin towards his foot.

"I don't want you to feel any guilt about it," Akbar says. "You are even with the Americans for what they did to you."

"They didn't kill me."

"They've killed plenty of others."

"That's not how it works. Not with me."

The yellow house is just over a mile from the town of Megiddo. The town was ransacked by the British on three occasions during the Raj, the last when they were fighting the Fakir of Ippi, Akbar's maternal grandfather, the guerrilla leader who fought a war against the British from 1935 onwards and killed thousands of soldiers in numerous pitched battles, demanding nothing but the infidels' withdrawal—*we want neither your honey nor your sting*. It was said that he had supernatural powers and could predict when the British were about to attack so he could vanish long beforehand. The British convinced a few members of the clergy to speak out against him in the mosques but it was to no avail. His support and appeal continued to grow steadily, Muslim soldiers having to be court-martialled for not shooting straight at him and his fighters, or for leaking plans of attack to him. Muslim brigadiers in the British army would leave ammunition for their hero in prearranged places.

In 1940 Adolf Hitler sent two German advisers to improve the Fakir's gun-making and help him in guerrilla training. He was the most logical person for the Axis powers to have approached in this region, in order to spread mayhem for the British in the tribal belt of their own colony. It had taken a whole year to establish contact with the Fakir and he had informed his prospective German allies that he would require a sum of £25,000 every month to keep undermining the British, as well as supplies of weapons and ammunition. The support of the Germans ended eventually, when Germany attacked Russia and it became impossible to send in the necessary arms.

The war in Europe came to a conclusion but the fighting against the enemies of Islam in the wilds of Waziristan continued. By 1947, forty thousand British troops were arrayed against Akbar's grandfather as he hid in caves and forests and ravines, turning sticks into guns and pebbles into bullets with Allah's direct help, some of the stone bullets still owned by Akbar's family.

For a long time the town of Megiddo was one of the region's major weapon-producing centres, the local clans manufacturing their guns from the iron they smelted there. Within days Mikal learns that the talk of weaponry is more or less constant in the house, the young men proposing a shooting competition a minute after meeting him.

Behind the yellow house, one dawn during the second week of his recovery, Mikal finds a courtyard that is an expanse of scrap metal, old car doors and transmissions, rotting hubcaps and cast-off motor parts lying at the base of those *saptaparni* trees. There are empty rocket shells from the war years in Afghanistan.

The grass is clogged with dew and out of it three enormous Airedale dogs stand up at his approach long before he notices them, revealing legs that have been dyed with henna to keep them cool. Aggression has clearly been bred into them but they are chained to the tree trunks and he lets the leopard cub walk beside him in the dawn light, its fur tinted by the orange light where it is dry, darker where the dew has wet it. Its calls resemble the thin notes of birds.

Mikal looks through the window of the gun factory, owned and supervised by Akbar's father and elder brother. When Akbar told him about it he understood why he had kept hearing gunfire through his fever, the workers testing the weapons they were making. The floor is covered with ash and strewn with pieces of metal the thickness and size of books and magazines, out of which the shapes of pistols have been cut like stencils. There are piles of wood meant to be burned in the smelting and there are carved pieces of wood that will become stocks of rifles and shotguns.

Long low skeins of mist rise from the river that flows in a half-circle around the house, its densely wooded bank enclosing three sides of the large building. The cub wanders away towards the side of the building and when he follows it he sees the girl under an arch, the mist drifting on the young silky air while above her the last stars cling to the white sky, and the zone of containment and poise about her person remains intact as she begins to withdraw into the darkness of the house on seeing him. *Human contact is as vast as any wilderness,* he remembers thinking the day he approached Naheed for the first time, *and demands all daring,* but he lowers his eyes as he advances towards the animal, like someone looking for a lost coin or key, gathering the cub to his chest like a collection of loose things, the creature's ears flattening with fear at the sudden upheaval, and he turns around under the flashing gaze of the chained Airedales, the disc of the sun both blinding and illuminating. "Where do you think you are going?" he says into the fur, walking away fast. "Do you know what they'll do to her if they catch her near a stranger?"

"You need to see this." Akbar hands him the leaflet.

A column of text in English and two black-and-white photographs of Mikal. Taken at the brick factory back in January, one with the long hair and beard, the other after they had removed the hair on the head and jaw.

"Where did you find this?" Mikal asks.

"Someone brought it from Peshawar. I'm told there is one in Urdu as well."

He tries to read the text but soon gives up. "What does it say?"

"They are searching for you. There is a description. Your height, your complexion—"

"Akbar. You know what I am asking."

Akbar doesn't answer immediately. Eventually he nods and says, "They both died."

Twenty days. Strong moons hang above the house at that season. After spending months indoors, he sleeps on the twenty-five-foot boundary wall that encircles the house, the leopard curled with him under the folds of the blanket, and he wakes in the night to see stars imprinting their numberless fires on the blue-black sky, and in the centre is a golden moon, serene and distended, and then there are the bronze moons, ugly and threateningly dagger-like to him in his convalescent state, resembling the ones that had come at his fingers. He works in the gun factory with Akbar's brother and the men he employs, one of whom says his joined eyebrows are evil luck. He operates the six-inch Herbert lathe for the heavy work and the three-and-a-half-inch Myford. The Boley watchmaker's lathe. The Senior milling machine. The Boxford shaper. The large and small drill presses. On the walls are several rifles and he levers open the breeches and looks down the barrels and he runs his hands on the stock of a hundred-year-old gun, etched with a scene of warriors on horseback going off to meet the Crusaders, with proud pennants and spears and large empty cages in which they hope to bring back captive infidel kings.

One night he walks up to Akbar's bed and very gently shakes him until the boy awakens. He lowers himself onto the edge of the bed. No light except the sweep of the moon through the window.

"My name is Mikal."

He hears Akbar swallowing drowsily, taking deep breaths in the dark air.

"I come from a town in Punjab called Heer, it's next to Gujranwala. I went to Afghanistan with my foster brother Jeo last October. I don't know where he is."

"I think the pedestal fan in the corner is made in Gujranwala," Akbar says, sitting up and feeling for his pack of cigarettes and lighting one.

"It is. The city's famous for them."

"So your name is Mikal."

"Yes." Mikal feels his gaze on him even without the light.

"Let me have that for a second." Mikal takes the cigarette from him and inhales the smoke and then hands it back and lights one for himself. He rises and goes to sit on the windowsill and looks out at the wildflowers that had closed at sunset but have opened once again in response to the moonlight.

"I have to leave soon."

"You can stay as long as you like. You are my brother."

"I have to find Jeo. Or maybe I should go to Heer first. What if Jeo has already gone back? I need to go and see."

"The Americans could be waiting for you there."

"I know. They don't know my name, but there are the photographs and my fingerprints."

Akbar gets up and turns on the light. "Stay until you are stronger. You are perfectly safe here." He takes a piece of paper and a pen from a drawer. "Let me show you something, now that we trust each other." He makes a thick dot and surrounds it with several concentric circles. He points to the dot with the tip of the pen and says, "This is you right now."

"I am the target?"

Akbar smiles. "These concentric circles are walls. Invisible ones. Defences that insulate al-Qaeda leaders who are on the run from the Americans."

"What al-Qaeda leaders?"

Akbar holds his gaze.

Mikal smokes the cigarette in silence for almost a minute, holding it between the tips of the thumb and the second finger. Then he says, "In this house?"

"Yes."

"Where?"

"The entire wing on the southern side."

Now Mikal knows why the doors there are of welded metal.

"When I brought you here there were objections, concerns that you could be a spy. They said they wouldn't pay the agreed sum for the use of the wing, that they would leave immediately."

"I didn't realise I was so . . . *discussed.* I live mostly inside my head."

"I told them how the Americans had tortured you at the brick factory, how you had killed two of them, how you lost your fingers to infidel-in-all-but-name Muslims who were fighting for the Americans. So they reconsidered."

"I don't know them but I know you, and I would never betray your trust."

"When I told them you were a fugitive, having killed two Americans, they became unhappy for another reason. They said you will betray them to the Americans in exchange for having your own crimes pardoned."

Mikal smokes, the red light opening and closing before his face.

"It is an understandable reaction," Akbar shrugs. "They are being hunted and have to think of every possibility. Two of them worked with you in the gun factory one afternoon and they were very taken by your seriousness. They had had trouble believing you shot anyone with those hands, but when they saw you at work they finally believed it." Akbar gets up and turns out the light and walks back to his bed in the darkness. "I don't want you to worry. The Pakistani military is helping the Americans hunt down al-Qaeda heroes in these parts, but those circles of protection mean enough of an early warning in the event of a raid."

Out there the light of the moon dissolves all hardness from the world and the grasses are becoming milk and murmuring, and the bats are plunging through the leaves in their soft songless flight.

"Is that why your father doesn't like me? All these suspicions."

"My father likes you," Akbar says after a while.

"I am jeopardising his income."

"He likes you. Go to sleep."

He looks at the map, planning his four-hundred-kilometre route back to Heer.

From Megiddo he will go to Tank by the local bus. Then a bus from Tank will take him to Dera Ismail Khan in about two hours. From Dera Ismail Khan—through the salt marshes and barren parched distances that had led to the British administrators and missionaries calling it Dreary Dismal Khan—he would go to Rawalpindi by bus again, this journey lasting four or five hours.

And from Rawalpindi to Heer on the train will be another five hours.

He will have to ask Akbar for money. He could do labouring work in the bazaar but he suspects it would sully the family name to have someone associated with it do menial work for others.

The bus ticket from Tank to Dera Ismail Khan will be about eighty rupees. From Dera Ismail Khan to Rawalpindi about four hundred, and the train fare from Rawalpindi to Heer about three hundred . . .

But there is a chance of police checks at the Rawalpindi bus terminal—Rawalpindi being the home city of Pakistan's military—so maybe he should go through Sargodha . . .

The cruelty of distance. When living in his parents' painted room in Heer, with Naheed married to Jeo, he would think how close the neighbourhood with Rohan's house was in some respects. It was just three miles away. It was just an hour away. It was just a nine-rupee rickshaw ride away. But it was an eternity away because his dream was there. Now Heer is probably two hundred years in prison away. Or a thousand volts of electricity fed into his body away. A lethal injection away.

He cannot jettison the feeling that the dot at the centre of the concentric circles had looked like a target. There is a dizzy sense of convergence and he feels himself being watched, now that he knows there are others here whose presence he had been unaware of. It's dawn and he sits on the riverbank with the snow leopard on his knee, the white spot at the end of its tail curving in the air restlessly, the pulse of impatient blood. He looks into its eyes. "The expression on your face says, *Why do you keep looking in that direction?* My answer is, 'No particular reason.'"

You were looking for the girl.

"I wasn't."

You were.

"So what if I was?"

I am actually glad. The cub nudges the air with its nose, sniffs his hand. *Do you think Naheed is going to leave Jeo for you?*

From his pocket Mikal takes the small white ball he has carved out of a block of *saptaparni* heartwood in the gun factory. The wood is white when first sawn, soft and fine-textured, and coffins are also made from it, and tea chests and masks, and he rolls the ball on the ground, watching the cub set off towards it in dives. In the wild a grown snow leopard can leap seven times its body length. "Let's change the subject," he says.

No. What do you think is going to happen between you and Naheed?

"Are you sure you are a leopard and not a serpent?"

You have to move on.

The ice the cook had pressed into his forehead was wrapped in flowered cloth and when he unfolded it he realised it was a sleeve torn from an old kameez and he had briefly wondered who it had belonged to.

But even the most distant prospect of forming an attachment, daring to approach another, when his only experience of it so far has ended in suffering, fills him with intense dread.

From behind him a shadow advances on the slope towards them and the small desert doves drinking from the water's edge rise in coils and he turns and sees her standing behind him.

"I thought I heard talking," she says. He stands up just as the birds pass overhead in their circular flight and return to settle on the river at another spot further down, the wingbeats sounding in the cool air and scattering the haze. She turns around to leave. "I am sorry. I didn't mean to disturb you."

"I was just talking to myself," he says. He is too stunned to say anything more. Akbar said he could speak English because the younger children—meaning himself and his twin, and this sister—had been sent to be educated at the best schools in Lahore. She was brought back here to be married at sixteen, to the young man who would die in Afghanistan. Perhaps the time in Lahore counts for her courage in approaching him now. There were four other brothers, who had been murdered over the course of the past three decades, all involving blood feuds whose origins were several decades old.

"I woke up when Father left for the mosque and couldn't go back to sleep."

"Me too," Mikal says. The man drives the Datsun pickup to Megiddo to say his dawn prayers. The other four prayers of the day he might say at home, depending on the circumstances, but he likes to be at the mosque for the first one.

"I should go."

He inhales and realises that he had smelt the perfume on her clothes during the days he lay unconscious. "Thank you for the cub."

"He has grown." There is a fraction of a smile. To reveal more to this stranger would be indecency. "He shouldn't be here, of course. He should be up somewhere in Chitral. One of our guests brought it with him. The mother died soon after giving birth. It hadn't even opened its eyes when they arrived."

"They stay shut for the first ten days or so."

She seems to think for a few moments. "It was exactly after ten days that he opened them. So he was probably only hours old when he was given to me."

He lifts the cub and hands it to her and she holds it, the tips of her fingers disappearing into the fur. She must be eighteen years old, nineteen at most.

"My name is Mikal."

"Yes, Akbar told me." She holds out the cub. "I should go."

"I am sorry to hear about your husband and brother." He lifts the *saptaparni*-wood ball and moves towards her and holds it before the leopard's face, both of them almost joined through the sphere and the creature.

"I approved of him going," she says. "I wanted them to defend Afghanistan, he and my brothers. I would have gone myself if it was permitted. Father blames the clerics who arranged for them to go, he says rageful things against al-Qaeda and the Taliban."

That explains the man's censoriousness towards Mikal. He thinks Mikal is a jihadi, the killer of American soldiers, the hardened militant who hadn't even revealed his name while in American captivity. He must be in torment at the fact that Akbar and his elder brother have given shelter to al-Qaeda fugitives. One evening he had heard an argument between him and the brothers.

"He was crazed with grief when the two bodies arrived, and Akbar was still missing. We thought Akbar's return would bring him some peace, but—" Suddenly she stops speaking and lets the cub slip to the ground, Mikal hearing the Datsun coming in through the gate in the boundary wall a few seconds after she has heard it.

"My name is Salomi," she says as she walks away, disappearing into the grove, and he climbs up from the riverbank to see the father emerge from the pickup and go into the house, the vehicle's paintwork smeared here and there with petals where the roadside wildflowers, dew-covered, must have thrashed against it during the journey.

After breakfast he drives to Megiddo to have the kitchen's gas canisters refilled, parking the Datsun near a herd of black and brown camels just outside the mosque. A caravan of *powindah* gypsies is passing, descendants of tribes who crossed from Central Asia and Afghanistan all the way to Calcutta in the far east of the subcontinent, trading goods, song and news, the British taking them and their camels to open up the Western Australian Desert in the nineteenth century. The men of the bazaar recognise him as belonging to Akbar's family and he is obliged to sit and drink tea. There has been a raid in a town a hundred miles away: Pakistani soldiers—assisted behind the scenes by Americans, no doubt—have raided a compound and, after a fourteen-hour battle, killed or taken away al-Qaeda figures sheltering there. Women, children, the old and the innocent—anyone who happened to be in the way— have been killed.

The person who betrayed them was a member of the family that was sheltering them—and he has been found butchered by al-Qaeda in retaliation.

He drinks the apple-green tea from a bowl. One man asks him why Akbar's father had not attended the dawn prayer at the mosque today. "It just isn't the same without him," the man smiles. "It feels like a wedding procession without a bridegroom."

"He has been unwell," Mikal says, draining the bowl and standing up, chewing the softened leaves.

"Yes, the martyrdom of his son and son-in-law has been very hard on him," the man says, nodding. "The bodies arrived with their hands and feet tied with barbed wire."

"Those boys fought the thugs of the West very bravely," another man says. "They knew that a coward dies but his screams last forever." And all the while the adze in the shop next door, that sells coffins and ladders, is repeating, "*. . . black as night . . . black as night . . . black as night . . .*"

He returns to the house and enters the gun factory to work. He has no desire to handle another gun as long as he lives but he doesn't know how else to repay the family for their hospitality, telling himself that it is only for a few more days. After an hour he interrupts his work, his hands black with metal dust. He takes off his shirt and wipes under his arms with it. He throws it aside and takes a clean one from a cupboard and puts it on while standing before the window, looking out at the Datsun.

He walks out to the Datsun and bends towards the door and picks off one of the flowers pasted onto the paintwork. Dried now by the sun to a scrap of crisp onion skin. He looks at it for a long time and the Airedales watch him from the shade of the trees, their dyed legs making them look as though they have waded through blood.

He has not seen these yellow flowers anywhere along the route from the house to the mosque.

Around noon when he drives into Megiddo to collect a consignment of scrap metal that a new set of gypsies has brought, he goes slower than usual so he can inspect the vegetation on either side of the narrow road. There is nothing much, just thornbushes and certainly no yellow flowers.

On the way back he turns onto a small path, the dust blowing from under his tyres and twisting away sideways, and after fifteen minutes he comes to a field at the base of a row of hills, a meadow the size of four cricket grounds, full of tall yellow flowers, the colour so intense it makes the eyes ache.

He conducts a brief search among them but not knowing what he is expecting to find he just stands looking at the hills in the end. *Who did he meet here at dawn? The Pakistani soldiers? The Americans?* The hills are infested with bandits and from this distance look like pyramidal heaps of coloured earth, piled there by man instead of having an origin in nature, some taller than others, some red, others with more yellow than ochre. *Was he hiring an assassin to murder the cleric who sent his boys to their deaths?*

The next day the paintwork is dotted with yellow again when the father returns from the dawn prayers and Mikal watches him from the riverbank, the sky above him soaked with a gentle merciful light, and a few hours later the men in the bazaar ask him again about the father's health. He watches the tide of movements around the house throughout the day, feeling the girl's presence behind the slabs of walls, and suddenly they are all bodies assigned for wounds, sites of destruction.

26

He climbs down from the night wall.

Carrying the leopard in his arms he walks into the empty kitchen. Onions and coriander in a basket. Eggs. Clean pots. There is a tassel of corn silk in the basket and he strokes its softness. It is in filament form but essentially it is the same material out of which flower petals are made. On the far side is a whitewashed arch and he is looking at it—the section of the house he has never entered, where the women are. He walks towards it eventually and lifts the curtain draped across the arch to reveal a wide room with sofas against the left and right walls, a table with a mirror framed in ivory, a clock in the shape of a proud-looking mosque. In the wall directly opposite are two doors. One is set in a recessed arch, identical to the one in which he is standing, but the other is narrower and not as tall. He puts the cub on the floor to see where it will go but it remains at his feet and he squats beside it and gently encourages it to explore. Failing, he picks it up and walks towards the smaller door and opens it.

An enclosed passage hung with framed verses of the Koran.

He looks over his shoulder before entering. There is a window directly before him at the other end of the passage, the *saptaparni* trees visible through the diamonds of stained glass, and there is a door on either side of the window. Both have clear glass panels and when he looks in through the one on the left he sees a desk and a shelf of gold-spined religious books. The stuffed head of a black bear with a pink mouth. A framed family tree that displays only the names of the males. The right door gives onto a stone staircase but instead of climbing it he turns and rushes back, the audacity leaving him.

Five minutes later he is back, and he goes up the stairs and emerges onto a balcony lined with pots that have intensely scented orange trees blooming in them. Two whitewashed steps lead to a door.

He stands on the first step and looks in through the glass square. But only after another turning back, and returning ten minutes later, does he open the door and place the cub on the floor, and it touches the stone tiles with its nose and sets off to the other side of the room, a stride both purposeful and beautiful, and he watches it disappear through a curtained arch.

"I have to leave here soon," he says quietly. "I have to go back home."

Nothing from the other side of the cloth.

He turns to leave but stops on hearing the rustle of the curtain.

He returns to the top of the wall just before dawn, the leopard in his arms. "Don't say a thing!" he tells the animal in a low voice as he lies there. "Don't you dare say a thing!"

27

Father Mede leans down towards a rose to take in its scent. It is the striped variety named Rosa Mundi. He is seventy-five years old, and as he walks towards the south boundary wall of the school, he stops now and then at various plants. Now he is at the hedge of wild jasmine. For how many generations have the children taken off the small green cap from the back of a wild jasmine flower and sucked the sweetness out of the thin tube? Making sure that he is unobserved, he does it now, and he is astonished that the drop of nectar tastes the same now as it did all those decades ago.

He knows what the word means. From the Greek. *Nek tar.* That which overcomes death.

He is descended from Joseph Mede, the Cambridge don and teacher of Milton, and although the family is from Wiltshire, Father Mede's childhood was here in the Punjab during the Raj.

He resumes his walk. At the south wall is a grove composed mainly of dense rosewoods and cypresses, and one of the children had reported a hornets' nest in an alcove somewhere along there. Father Mede wishes to determine whether it poses a threat to children, in which case the gardener will have to be told to remove it. The lines from Moses' valedictory song go through his mind as he recalls eating the saccharine substance from hornets' nests.

> *He suckled him with honey from a rock,*
> *And oil from a flinty stone.*

Soon after entering the grove he hears a sound that resembles the long dry crack that a tough cloth would give on being torn. The ground shudders and he looks around, earthquake being his first thought. He attempts to steady himself against a rosewood but the mighty trunk lightly swivels away from him, and overhead the entire crown swings sideways and the tree begins to fall. He tries to support it out of reflex and the trunk pulls him off his feet and it is like holding a fishing rod with a thousand-pound fish on the hook. He realises that the trunks of all the trees here have been severed, someone's blade going through them at sternum height. They were just standing in place waiting for the merest touch, the meshed canopies providing the minimum steadiness until now, and they are crashing around him, the falling boughs generating a wind. In Joseph Mede's *Key of the Revelation* a historical meaning was given to the various symbols of Revelation and "winds" had always meant "wars." Dust fills his eyes, nothing but the torn leaves and branches around him as he attempts to gain a place of safety, the dark red flowers of the Madagascar *gulmohar* erupting into the air as the green limbs come down and he stands mercifully unscathed and watches how the place has suddenly filled up with light, the sky painfully exposed.

28

Naheed slows down as she climbs the stairs, taking the last five steps one at a time. She can hear someone in the room ahead of her.

"Mother, is that you?" Even though she knows Tara has gone to the haberdasher's in Anarkali Bazaar.

She enters to discover Sharif Sharif. He stands up from his crouching position beside the bed. In his left hand is the box in which she keeps Mikal's letters. One of them is in his right hand. It falls onto the bed as he stands up, surprised.

"I just thought I'd come up and see how things are."

She looks at him, unable to speak.

"I wanted to see if you needed something. Do you need anything?"

Naheed shakes her head.

"How are you managing? I haven't asked after you for a while."

Naheed looks at the letter on the counterpane.

He takes a step towards her. "Who wrote you those letters? They are all signed 'Mikal'?"

She back away and he asks,

"Is that Mikal as in Basie's brother?"

She looks at the table where the scissors lie. He notices.

"I am here to fulfil your every need. You don't need anyone else."

She sees how carefully he has placed himself between her and the scissors.

"I have my family. My mother, my father-in-law."

"I will pour all my money at your feet. You could have anything you wanted."

She shakes her head.

"I'll buy you a house, here or in Lahore. You won't have to live with the other wives downstairs. Come away with me." He glances at the box on the floor. "Are they love letters?"

"You have to leave," she says.

He goes back to the bed and picks up the letter. "Come away with me. I will even pay for Rohan's eyes."

There is the sound of someone on the stairs and Naheed moves forward and snatches the letter from him.

"What are you doing here?" Tara says to him fiercely as she comes in.

"I came to see if you needed anything."

"We don't need anything." She points to the door. "You must leave or I will scream. Now go."

Buttons, snaps, collar stays and a seam ripper have spilled out of the plastic bag that Tara had let drop onto the floor as she came in. "I don't know why you must pretend to be so innocent," he says as he steps over them to leave. "Both of you."

After he has left Tara comes and holds Naheed. "What happened?"

Tara is thin. The months have taken so much out of her.

"Nothing. I am fine," Naheed says, folding the letter and placing it in the box, securing it with a rubber band.

"You have to throw them away," Tara says.

She places the box in the suitcase under the bed. She turns the key and takes it out of the lock.

Tara comes forward, holding out an envelope towards her.

"What is it?"

"It's a photograph of the boy you will be engaged to soon."

About to unseal it, Naheed lifts her finger away from the flap immediately.

29

Not a day goes by when a living person's eventual burial site does not call out in a clear and unambiguous voice, "O child of Adam, you have forgotten me."

In Baghdad House, Rohan is reading the Koran for Sofia, recalling the verses from memory.

Allah created four homes for Adam. Eden, the Earth, Purgatory and Paradise. And He has given four homes to the Children of Adam too. The womb, the Earth, the grave, and then Paradise or Hell.

After the burial a person is asked by the angels, who have materialised inside the grave, "What do you think of Islam?" The second question he is asked is, "What do you have to say about Muhammad?" If the answers are satisfactory, he is shown a glimpse of the tortures of Hell. "You have been spared this," he is told, and a vision of Paradise is granted him. "This will be your eventual home." The grave widens and seven doors open in its sides to allow the fragrant breezes of Paradise to circulate until Judgement Day. The opposite is true if it is a sinful person: seven entrances to Hell open up and the grave shrinks until the ribs crack past each other, the demons descending on the body to begin the tortures.

Rohan makes his way around her room and stands at the window, listening to the garden. The Prophet said there will be no tree in Paradise whose trunk is not of gold. Paradise, which Sofia will enter after Judgement Day, he is sure. Though about himself he cannot say anything.

He moves his head in the air of the room, aligning his dead eyes for a chink of light. Her voice seems present in the walls. Everything in this room has outlived her: he senses the lamp looking at him with that knowledge, the paintings of flowers on the walls, the ink-stained table. It's all here except her. It is as though she still exists but is choosing to stay away from his eyes.

"Naheed."

Tara calls out to the girl.

"Naheed."

"She's not here, sister-ji," Rohan answers.

He comes to the veranda, feeling along the walls. The tips of his fingers are the precise length that his gaze can travel now—his eyes bandaged.

"I thought she was here," Tara says, looking around, and she calls out again.

"I have been alone all morning. I thought she was with you."

Tara takes his hand and guides him back into his room. "You've been alone all morning?"

"Yes. What time is it?"

"It's past noon. I just came in to help her prepare lunch." With the beginning of panic in her voice she shouts the girl's name once more.

"She'll be here any minute, I'm sure," Rohan says as she lowers him into his chair. He sighs and slowly reaches out for the notebook on the table. "I have been trying to write."

The pages are empty because, unknown to him, the pen doesn't have any ink in it.

"Where could she be?" Tara says, moving towards the window.

"Perhaps she's gone to the bazaar."

"She would have told me, brother-ji. Her behaviour has been some-what erratic these past few days but she wouldn't go anywhere without telling me. Or leave you here all by yourself."

She enters the garden hoping to see her step out of a pocket of greenery, dressed in ash, and she walks towards the pond where the water lilies burn in the sunlight and then recoils at the thought that enters her mind on seeing the moss floating at the water's edge, looking like long hair.

As she cooks in the kitchen—and attends to the disorder Rohan has unknowingly created in making himself breakfast or pouring a glass of water—she remains alert to every movement out there, every sound.

By the time Yasmin and Basie return from St. Joseph's, at three, she is close to tears.

"I am sure there's a perfectly simple explanation," Basie says. "Don't be alarmed."

"Yes. She'll be here soon," Yasmin says.

"Have you asked the neighbours?"

She shakes her head.

"I'll go," says Yasmin.

Tara reacts with pain. "Don't."

"Someone might have seen her, Aunt Tara."

"No," she says firmly. "We have to be careful who we ask. If we tell them she is missing, the thought will enter their minds that she has a secret life, and later they'll easily accuse her of immorality and unchastity."

Yasmin half-heartedly comes back to her chair.

"Let's just wait for a little while longer," Basie says. "I am sure she'll be back any minute."

As the afternoon advances, Tara ties on her burka and goes back to her room five streets away. Before climbing up she stops to exchange a few words with Sharif Sharif's wives but they don't mention Naheed. On a shelf in her room there are stacks of clothes, folded as neatly as newspapers. They are the sewing work she has finished over the past week, and she carries these around the neighbourhood now, taking them to the customers' houses. In each house she mentions Naheed's name several times, with a pretend casualness, in case someone says something about having seen the girl, in case someone remembers something Naheed had said recently and provides a clue to her disappearance.

When she returns to Rohan's house it is almost dusk and the stars are beginning to come out in the east, where it is darkest.

She is sitting with Yasmin and Basie in the kitchen when Rohan makes his way towards them through the banana grove. "Where is Naheed?" he asks from out there.

Basie goes out and offers him his arm to lead him in but Rohan refuses to take even a single step. "Where is Naheed?" The voice is louder now.

Basie makes to say something but then stops.

"Answer me, someone. I know you are all here. Basie? Yasmin? Tara? Where's my Naheed?"

"She's not here, Father," Yasmin says.

"Where is she?"

"She'll be here soon, brother-ji," Tara says.

"What time is it?"

Nothing but silence from them. Basie wondering whether it is possible to lie to him as he had tried to earlier. But the night prayers have been called from the minaret so he must have a very good idea of the hour.

"I said what time is it? Eight? Eight thirty?"

"It's just gone past nine, Father."

He reacts as though a sword has fallen onto the back of his neck. "Why are you just sitting here? Why aren't you out there looking for her?" He turns around and rushes through the banana trees into the garden, seeing with the light of his grief. Terror is not knowing where the pain is coming from—and so in his desperation he begins to shout, the word echoing through every dark canopy and trunk, turning in every direction, batting at various things. As Yasmin and Basie try to help him, Tara sits holding the envelope containing the photograph of Naheed's prospective husband, still unopened.

At midnight Yasmin and Basie are sitting on the steps of the veranda. An insect-swirled candle burning beside them. There was rain earlier and hundreds of snails are roaming the garden, their shells conical in shape, and tiny, no bigger than the exposed lead of a well-sharpened pencil. The bodies are bright yellow.

"She'll return," he tells her.

"I wish Father would stop insisting we look in the pond and the river."

"He can still frighten me when he is angry."

"Me too. We should keep reminding ourselves we are twenty-eight years old." She leans her head against his shoulder in tiredness. "After Mother died he'd make me pray five times a day for her. Even Jeo when he was five or six was being made to do it. He was so strict, a disciplinarian. I joke about it with him now sometimes, and he claims not to remember being severe."

He looks towards Rohan's room. From a confused anger Rohan had slipped into melancholy and despair. Saying this place was ill-fated. This building defines the line of the trench in which the horses were buried during the Mutiny. The surrounding lands were gifted to Rohan's great-grandfather by the British as a reward for his loyalty during the rebellion. But in the decades since 1857, several members of the bloodline refused the tainted inheritance. Businesses begun on it would fail. Locusts descended on the wheat fields. Orchards rotted. Rohan too had wanted nothing of it, and only at Sofia's pragmatic insistence had decided to build Ardent Spirit here, only at her insistence had he used the parcel on the other side of the river to build the bigger building. It is possible that he gave it all away to Ahmed the Moth with relief.

Basie inhales the damp scents in the air, the cold moonlight. The Rangoon creeper above them has been adding new leaves to itself every day this month, a dense opaque green, branch crowding branch, while the new leaves on the banyan and the peepal are a soft red.

"What are you thinking?"

"I am thinking when will I see my husband smile again."

She feels him hold his breath at this, the mechanism of the body becoming still.

"I am sorry," he says after a while.

"And when will I hear my husband use a swear word? Mikal said you taught him such filthy things as a child."

He tightens his arm around her. "Motherfucker."

She gives a small sleepy laugh.

When Rohan brought them home all those years ago, the ten-year-old Mikal had a book of constellations and the eighteen-year-old Basie was dragging the trunkful of his father's jazz records. This veranda was where she had seen him for the first time.

"I am married to a Pakistani nicknamed after Count Basie," she says now, wanting him to talk, to be comforted by his voice and to make his own mind disappear towards another topic for however brief a period. Even if she has heard what he will say many times already.

"Hey, hey," he responds, heavy-eyed but play-acting to make her happy; if he had the energy he would smile. "Jazz and Pakistan have a long history. Chet Baker was married to a Pakistani woman. Halema Alli. There is a song named 'Halema,' for her, and their son is named Chesney Aftab."

"Fiction."

"She is the beautiful woman with him in the famous William Claxton photographs. I have a print of one hanging on the wall at home. The woman who is now my wife bought it for me on my twenty-first birthday . . ."

Six days later he walks into the police station on the Grand Trunk Road and asks to see the house officer. As he waits to be shown into the office he wonders what is occurring in the room on the other side of the wall directly in front of him. It is difficult to suppress a shudder every time the police solve a crime in Pakistan. There is no knowing if the confession is genuine, and there is no knowing how many innocents have been tortured to get even that.

When the government began hunting Communists in 1980—for criticising it and the USA—Basie and Mikal's father had gone underground and then one day the police had taken the child Basie away to make the father give himself up. Basie still remembers being held up towards the rotating ceiling fan at this very police station, as they tried to force him to tell them where his father was hiding. A plot had been uncovered—some of the younger comrades were planning to kidnap American citizens in Pakistan. "Your father is doing this to you, not us," the policemen told Basie as they struck him. When he came home his legs and face were blue and his mother's initial thought was that they had spilled ink onto him for some reason.

Now Basie is shown into an office and he finds the police inspector seated in a black leather chair behind a large desk. Beside him on the floor squats an old emaciated woman, toothless, her meagre hair in a short plait. Her eyes are closed and she's holding on to the man's khaki-clad knee. She's perfectly still, her face wholly expressionless, and his ignoring of her is total—it is as though she is not there.

"How long has your sister-in-law been missing?" the inspector asks.

"Since Thursday." He cannot help but glance towards the woman.

"Why have you come to report it only now?" the inspector asks.

"We thought she'd gone to visit relatives."

"Does she do that often?"

"What?"

"Does she do that often? Go to visit relatives without telling you?"

"No."

The sparrow-like woman must be about eighty. Is she begging the release of a grandson picked up on a false charge? Begging the police to do something about a missing son? A daughter threatened with gang rape by enemies?

Basie wonders if he recognises the inspector. Was he the one who beat him?

"Your sister-in-law is a widow, you say."

"Yes."

"Have you considered the possibility that she has run away with a *yaar*?" He uses the lewd Punjabi word for a woman's lover.

"She wouldn't do that."

The chart hanging behind the inspector lists the six qualities a Pakistani citizen can expect to find in every member of the police force.

Politeness. Obedience. Loyalty. Intelligence. Courteousness. Efficiency.

"You say you are a teacher," the man says, "and you look like a respectable man. You don't know what I witness every day. I have made you uncomfortable, I know, but you don't know how depraved humanity can be."

A constable opens the door and beckons the inspector. He gets up from behind his desk, detaching his knee from the woman's hand. "I shall return. Certain matters require privacy," he says to Basie with a smile as he leaves. "Among the sacred names of Allah, there is the Veil."

The woman slumps against the chair. Her scratched and grimy spectacles, lacking earpieces, are tied to her head with a fraying cord.

The children tell a joke about a man who had lost his horse. He went to the American police but it proved fruitless. He went to the British police and their investigation too failed. As did those of the Germans, the French, the Dutch. He came to the Pakistani policemen, who listened to him and went away. When they came back the next day they were leading an elephant by a chain. The animal had been severely beaten and was in bad shape and could barely walk. "I am a horse, I am a horse," it was screaming.

"Good aunt, what is the matter?"

But she doesn't acknowledge him.

"Would you like some water?"

She shakes her head.

The inspector returns but then goes to the door once again and shouts to someone out there: "Just make sure he has a bad night."

"So. What would you like me to do?" he asks Basie, settling in his chair, and extending his knee a little until the woman connects herself to it again. Metal reacting to nearby magnet.

"I was hoping you would look for her."

"Are you saying she has been kidnapped?"

"I want you to find that out."

The inspector opens his arms in exasperation. "How do you expect me to do that? It's a big country, there are millions of people."

"Inspector-sahib, I wish to report my sister-in-law as missing," Basie says firmly.

The man does not like the tone but ignores it for now. "Let me just say that an hour ago we captured a truck that contained two dozen machine guns, dozens of pistols, thirty Kalashnikovs and thirty sacks of bullets. And you want me to waste my time with a girl who has run away from home."

"How do you know she has run away? Anything could have happened."

The man waves the comment away as foolish. "She has run away with someone who has filled her head with his talk. When they realise how difficult life is, she'll return. Hunger is the best cure for illusions."

"I wish to report my sister-in-law as missing."

He wants a bribe from Basie before proceeding. Bribes exist in other countries too, he knows, but there they are an incentive towards performing illegal acts. Here they must be paid to induce an official to do what he is supposed to do.

"When was she widowed?" he asks brusquely.

"In October."

"Did you discover last week that she is pregnant and now she is buried in your garden?"

"You can come and dig up the garden."

"We might have to. Tell me again why you waited six days before coming here."

"We thought she'd return." When on the third day Basie had wondered aloud whether they should contact the police, both Rohan and Tara had been horrified, and Yasmin had almost cried out, "You might as well tattoo the word 'prostitute' on her forehead."

"She probably will return. Come back and see us in another month if she hasn't."

"A month?"

"Yes," he says, holding Basie's eye. "If she hasn't come back by then we'll come and take your statements. We'll have to talk to the neighbours about her character and personality, about her mother's character and personality." He notices Basie glance at the woman and shakes his head. "And stop looking at her. This doesn't concern you."

"What does she want?"

"What do criminals always want?" the inspector says with contempt. "To evade justice. Left unchecked they will destroy everything. Look at America and how it is behaving." He stands up, pushing the woman away. "Now I have other matters to attend to."

Basie vacates his chair reluctantly. "You are not going to do anything?"

The inspector ignores the question. "You teach at St. Joseph's? A school for the children of the wealthy."

"I wouldn't call them wealthy."

"Some of them are. The school must pay you very well."

"It doesn't."

The inspector smiles. "Don't worry. She'll probably return. And when she does I want you to bring her here."

"You won't look for her now but you want to see her when she returns?"

"Yes."

"Why?"

"We might have to investigate her for immorality and wantonhood. She must explain to us, as agents of decent society, where she has been all these days. A charge of decadence and wickedness might have to be brought against her."

Tara sits in her black burka on the steps of a shop in Soldier Bazaar, very early in the morning. There is no one around but her. She looks at the paper in her hand, the text she has composed to be printed as a "Missing" leaflet. Naheed's age, her height, the colour of her skin and her eyes. The distribution of leaflets—suggested by Basie—is something she has resisted till now, but last night was terrible, the various fears overcoming her in the sleepless dark, and after the predawn prayers she set out for the printer's shop.

She sits waiting for the owner to arrive and open up, her head leaning against the jamb.

Today will be the eighth day of the disappearance. From the pocket of her burka she takes out the photograph of Naheed that will be printed on the leaflet. It was taken by Jeo, a month or so before he died, and in it Naheed is standing in the garden, on the path on which she lost consciousness for several minutes when Jeo's corpse was brought home in the truck. When the neighbourhood women came in soon afterwards they found the truck driver and his assistants taking care of her, her head in the lap of the driver who poured water into her mouth. A memory comes to Tara from that day and she straightens suddenly. "She fainted in the presence of three men, three strangers?" she had overheard a woman say to another during the funeral. "How could she allow herself to do that?"

Tara stands up as quickly as she is able. She tears up the text and walks away down the street, horrified at what she had come here to do. At the corner she stops on seeing faint marks in the dust on the ground, and she follows them, thinking the chained fakir is making his way through Heer once again, but she turns the corner to see a woman road sweeper dragging her broom behind her, about to begin the day's labours.

Deep in the night thirteen days after her disappearance, Basie drives Tara and Yasmin to the graveyard, women being barred from visiting their dead during the day by the stick-wielding cloaked figures associated with Ardent Spirit. It's 2 a.m., and as they get out of the car and enter through the wooden gate they see a hundred scattered lanterns, the faint haze of light, where other women are making their way towards dead husbands, sons and daughters, leaning mournfully over mothers and fathers.

A quietness prevails, the only sound the lift and hushed fall of feet.

He is carrying a flashlight, known as *chor batti*—a thief's light. He looks at the women, their hearts seemingly in flood as they pray amid the mounds, having brought flowers, holy verses and letters—tributes in rock, ink and gesture. Tara and Yasmin, with light on their faces and on the pages of the Koran, begin to read the sacred words. And Basie stands and watches.

When he mistakes a girl in the distance for Naheed—a quick second glance confirms it not to be her—there is a surge of pain in him followed by sudden directionless anger. As he waits for it to pass even the murmur of the Korans becomes an annoyance. Whenever he is drunk, his feelings about religion can become vocal—revealing a sham, his own and his country's. "I'll announce tomorrow that I don't believe in Allah or Muhammad or the Koran," he'd said to Yasmin two evenings ago. "But I'll be beaten to death by a mob for being an infidel, or taken to jail and shot dead in the middle of the night by policemen or set upon by other prisoners. So I go on pretending. But I am not a hypocrite. I'd be a hypocrite if I was *free* to say and act what I believed in and didn't. But I am not free."

There is a commotion in the distance, beside the northernmost wall, and they see the group of black-clad women has appeared and is striking the visitors with canes, the mourners' lanterns hurrying in every direction. Each set of women is asking for help from Allah in ending the menace that is the other.

Tara stands up, kissing her Koran and closing it. "We should leave."

Some of the women are fighting back. The men who have brought them here too are receiving blows from the black-clad women, or from the zealous men who brought the zealous women here.

Two cloaked figures appear behind Yasmin, their draperies moving in urgent passionate waves, their heads tied with green bands with the flaming-swords motif of Ardent Spirit. "Women are not allowed into graveyards," one of them shouts and swings at Yasmin's head with the metal-tipped cane. "It's because of people like you," the other veiled woman says as she strikes Tara in the stomach, "that Allah is punishing the entire Muslim world these days."

Basie takes hold of both canes as they are raised again for further blows, but one of them is slippery—he realises it's Yasmin's blood—and it slides out of his grip and comes down on Yasmin's head again. She cries out. The other woman struggles to get her cane free and shouts, "We stop you from coming in the daytime and you start to come at night! There is no end to the ingenuity of the wicked."

Yasmin is trembling on the ground, thick lines of blood pouring from beyond her hairline and into her eyes. "My mother is buried here," she says, "and my brother."

Basie lets go of the other cane and bends down to her and the freed weapon is brought down onto his back, feeling as though he has been slashed with a razor.

Tara dodges the cane aimed at her and it strikes the Koran in her hand instead, brutally. "Look what you made me do," the assailant— only her contact lenses visible, her hands encased in black gloves— screams with distress and gives Tara a fierce fluent strike to the shoulder.

Around them some of the graves are in flames, from the oil that has been spilled by the broken lanterns.

"What strange times are these," says Tara as they wend their way through the dead to safety, "when Muslims must fear other Muslims." At home he examines the cut on Yasmin's head and bandages it. Agony gently vibrates out of her eyes as she tries to fall asleep.

He stays in the chair beside her and just before dawn listens to Tara and Rohan get up to say the first prayers of the day. He goes up to the roof and finds comfort in the brightening sky, receiving his share of the earth through the five senses, the dawn glow of ochre and cinnabar, the light calling things into existence, the thin voices of birds. As the sun rises higher he walks through the garden where a near-thousand flowers are opening and goes out into the streets to call the doctor, the neighbourhood waking up around him—the inevitable dailiness, the shops being opened at the crossroads, the butcher unloading the skinned carcasses he has brought from the slaughterhouse in a rickshaw, an early-rising child leaning against a door frame, a look of suspicion and hostility in his eyes about the world of the adults, a woman carrying a small Madagascar *gulmohar* tree on her head for fuel, the branches trailing behind.

He stops on realising that he had caught a glimpse of a figure in a side street that had had a gait resembling Naheed's. Two minutes ago. He turns back and breaks into a run, but she is just another one of the dozens of girls he has mistaken for her since she vanished.

The doctor says Yasmin's cuts are superficial and he places stitches on the scalp with a tiny crescent needle. He tells her to rest, perhaps take a day off work. Basie kisses her mouth when they are alone in the room and astonishingly she wants more, an intensity in her body as when adolescence's delight had first found completion years ago, in both of them, here in these very rooms, and he walks to the door and bolts it shut and comes to her, shedding his clothes on the stripes of light blazing on the floor. Mortality? When he is near her his impermanence has no power over him.

He bathes and eats the breakfast Tara has cooked, and Yasmin reminds him that Father Mede has asked for a few cuttings from the garden. Over half the plants at St. Joseph's are from here. At eight o'clock he gets into his car alone, to drive to St. Joseph's four miles away. A rose tree, bronze with thorns, sprinkles dewdrops onto his crisp white shirt just before he leaves the house, the cotton becoming grey in an everyday miracle.

The six head boys from the six houses of Ardent Spirit have been awake since before dawn. Ahmed, the head of Baghdad House, gives everyone the final instructions. But the assault and the siege have been planned meticulously over the past several weeks and there is little need for further words. They sit and collect their thoughts before setting off for St. Joseph's.

They are in a ruined seventeenth-century mausoleum that is approached along the blacktop road in an easterly direction from Heer, parallel to the old thoroughfare that disappears towards Amritsar. A large domed building with four stubby minarets at each corner, constructed on a high plinth from deep red sandstone but now in an advanced state of decrepitude. Avoided by the people of the vicinity because it is said to be haunted.

Deo Minara. Minaret of Demons.

In addition to the six Ardent Spirit boys and the twenty-four recruited men, there are two young women—to contain and supervise the school's female staff and children during the siege. Covered in black, they wear pistols under their cloaks and belts of ammunition are wound about their waists.

Among the twenty-six recruits there are seven who don't know what today's destination is, and what is planned once they reach that destination. Nineteen are in the know. There was pleasure in Ahmed's mind when he recalled that the number of men who were alleged to have carried out the attacks in the United States last September was nineteen.

"Who is buried here?" the head of Mecca House asks him as he approaches a crumbling arch to watch the 147 rucksacks of supplies being loaded onto a truck that was stolen by the head of Ottoman House late last night.

"The governor of the area during the time of the Emperors Shah Jahan and Aurangzeb."

Shah Jahan who built the Taj Mahal, which is now lost to Hindu India.

Aurangzeb who empowered officials to enter and break musical instruments anywhere they heard the sound of music, who barred women from visiting shrines to prevent lasciviousness in holy and sombre places, a virtuous and humble man who forbade the writing of the chronicle of his reign as an impious conceit, but whom they now belittle by saying he had no vision, only ambition, no reach, only grab.

Aurangzeb who in April 1669 had ordered the eradication of all religions except Islam in his realm.

Ahmed leans his head against a pillar and closes his eyes, his mind entering the nightmare of the battlefield yet again, in Afghanistan last autumn, the place where he'd learned what two hundred corpses look like. He had had to dig his way out from under them after the guns and rockets and missiles had fallen silent, emerging into the light that revealed the bodies full of insect scribble, the mouths that would ignite their red lament for him in the sunrise every morning from then on, the eyes ruined but still dreaming of returning to whatever Egypts, Algerias, Yemens, Pakistans and Saudi Arabias they had known, rotting men who were true believers and read the Koran as ravenously as they devoured meat and sugar and milk, and men who came to the jihad because, well, to be honest, Ahmed, there wasn't much else to do, and men who thought of death to the exclusion of all matters so that in the end life was easy to give up. They lay all around him then, slain, slaughtered, stinking, cleansed at last of the burden of being who they were on earth, the souls pulled clean out of them, the arms twisted, the heads severed, the feet separated from legs that had been separated from torsos, and the dark decaying mulch of the names, OmarFareedAbdulYusufKhalidSalmanFaisalShakeelMusharafAnwar-ImranRashidSaleemHusseinNomanIbrahimMansoorIkramMushtaq-NaimAsimTahaHanif, and he stood above their corpses, puffing out wide flowers of breath into the Afghanistani air, a dawn light so pure and undeceiving it might have been the dawn that Adam saw. For an instant he wanted Allah to appear and explain it all to him, not just watch from His high distance through unappalled eyes. He hadn't known he could summon such deep feelings, and in his madness he had wondered whether this earth was nothing more than a toy with six billion moving parts for Him. A thought for which he later asked forgiveness. And he was enraged at the peace that reigned at that very moment on other parts of the planet, and in grief he had cursed the lives that were continuing uninterrupted elsewhere . . .

"Brother Ahmed," one of the women says as she approaches him. "I have something to suggest."

He opens his eyes. "What is it, sister?"

"It regards the time when the police will surround the building and open fire on us."

"Yes?"

"We should make one of the children stand up on the windowsill wherever the firing is heaviest. It will silence the guns."

Ahmed says after a few moments, "I will give it some thought, sister. Thank you."

"It has nothing to do with me," she says, her voice serious and earnest. "The solution was revealed to me by an angel during sleep last night."

Her husband had gone to Kashmir some years ago. She had set off after him, spending two months of snowblindness and winter windburn in the mountains, evading Indian and Pakistani bullets. But she had come upon him eventually—he had stepped on a land mine and was lying unconscious beside a boulder. He didn't survive and her dearest wish is to follow him into martyrdom.

She returns to sit in a multi-cusped arch with the other young woman—who is among those from whom the truth has been withheld, who think they are on their way to attack a government building instead of a school. The pistol she has been given does not function. She had worked as a cook in the house of a Shia cleric and had poisoned him, so her brave-naturedness and commitment to the cause of true Islam is undoubted, but there are doubts about her willingness to do the truly unpleasant for the long-term benefit.

Beside the two women is a heap of smashed glass bottles. It is what remains of the shards that are packed around the eighteen bombs being taken into St. Joseph's.

The twenty-fourth man has now arrived. As lethal as a krait, in his youth he had murdered two men during a dispute over a woman's honour but had then discovered peace through Islam. Fighting the Russians in Afghanistan his arm was blown off and later his son was born without an arm, as though he had passed on the mark of holy sacrifice.

At just past seven o'clock they get into the truck and begin the journey towards Heer, avoiding the Grand Trunk Road as well as the other main routes, those sitting in the back of the truck feeling the jolts and bumps of the country lanes and dust tracks, the potholed minor roads.

Ahmed, behind the steering wheel, had hoped to avoid being stopped by the traffic police, but as soon as they approach Heer that is exactly what happens.

"Can I see your documents?" the policeman says to Ahmed. "Aren't you aware that this is not officially a road?"

The policeman does not extend the hand to receive the forged documents Ahmed proffers. All he wants is two or three hundred rupees and Ahmed gives it to him and they move on.

Soon after half past eight the main gate of the school is within sight, the words on the arch above it telling everyone that St. Joseph is the Patron Saint of the Dying, of the Fathers of Families, of Social Justice and Workingmen.

Ahmed stops the truck and leaps out to help an aged beggar woman cross the road, remembering what Abu Darda—one of the Prophet's forty-two nominated transcribers of the Koran—had said: "Do a good deed before battle. For one fights with one's deeds."

Basie parks in the narrow lane that runs behind the school, the shade from the dense bougainvillea overhead preventing the car's interior from baking during the course of the day. He enters by the small door in the boundary wall and takes the path lined with cypress trees towards his office. There will be dyed eggs hidden in the tall grasses at Easter here. He enters the room and stops.

"Naheed."

She stands looking at him. Her veil is arranged carelessly on her head, one end of it trailing on the floor.

"Naheed. What are you doing here? Where have you been?"

She continues to stare at him and he moves towards her. She struggles to speak, as though she hasn't spoken for days.

"Mikal is alive," she says at last.

"What?" He approaches and puts his arms around her. "Naheed, where have you been for two weeks?"

"Did you hear what I said? Mikal is alive."

"What are you talking about?" She looks thinner and exhausted.

"There's no one in his grave."

"His grave? His grave is in Peshawar." He is thinking fast, trying to understand. "You went to Peshawar?"

She nods. "I wanted to see it. Basie, there's no one buried there."

"How do you know?"

"It's just an empty pit. People say the Pakistani followers of the Taliban and al-Qaeda fired rockets into that grave, to stop women from coming there. But no remains were discovered there."

Basie raises his hand to his forehead.

"I saw nothing but a scorched pit. Some people say it wasn't the work of al-Qaeda or the Taliban, but of the American soldiers, who secretly took away the body to conduct tests on the bones to identify him. 'Even our dead are not safe,' the women were saying."

"You saw the empty pit?"

"Yes. The earth was black from the rocket fire."

"It doesn't mean he's not dead."

"He is alive, Basie."

He looks at her. "When did you get back?"

"Just now. I arrived at the bus station and was on my way home in a rickshaw but when we passed the school I got out. I knew you and Yasmin would be here by now. So I came in. Just a minute ago."

"How did you pay for the journey?" On the first Monday of every month Yasmin goes to the bank and withdraws money for Rohan's household expenses. The rubber-banded roll is kept at the back of a wardrobe, in the inside pocket of one of Sofia's paisley jackets. When Naheed went missing Tara had counted the money. But it was intact.

Naheed touches her empty earlobes to indicate that she has sold her earrings.

"You've been gone two whole weeks."

"I didn't want to come back, I just wanted to keep going. And I also got lost, several times."

"I wish you had told us."

She shakes her head.

"I'll get someone to take you home. And I'd better telephone Father right now." He moves towards the phone but stops, both of them hearing the unison shouts of *"Allahu Akbar!"* from outside, followed by automatic gunfire.

30

"The worse, the better," Ahmed murmurs, behind the steering wheel of the truck. "The more ruthless we are, the more visible our fury."

Every morning two-thirds of the 1,100 staff and pupils have arrived by eight thirty. The youngest children are the four-year-olds from the nursery, the oldest sixteen. A few of them notice in passing that the guard is absent from his post outside the gate this morning.

The head of Mecca House gets out of the truck's passenger side and walks up to the gate and opens it and the truck moves onto the premises.

Ahmed, holding a Kalashnikov and with a black hood over his head, leaps out among the children. He is wearing gloves to hide the flame scars from when he had emulated Ahmed the Moth as a child. A six-year-old is the first to see him, a fraction of a second before the others do, and he has watched enough movies to immediately raise his arms in the air.

The twenty-eight men and two women who were sitting locked in the back of the truck emerge and fan out onto the colonnaded verandas, while the head of Mecca House—a hood now pulled over his head too—begins to close the gate.

The sound of boots slamming onto the floors. Three hooded figures run towards the three other points of entry into the building, pushing the puzzled children aside, while behind them a dozen men have raised their weapons and—with those proclamations of *"Allahu Akbar!"*—opened fire into the air.

It is all done with such speed and efficiency that it takes a while to become apparent that the school is under attack, the panic beginning.

Running towards Father Mede's office, leaping over the wild jasmine hedges, the head of Cordoba House sees two fifteen-year-old boys escaping over the boundary wall—the gardener's grandsons—and he stops and takes aim and shoots at their legs, hearing their screams as they drop and land on the other side.

The only laws they are breaking are shallow laws, the head of Ottoman House tells himself as he tries to locate Basie, Kyra having given them specific instructions regarding him. It feels unreal but what is occurring here is believable at the deepest level, has a perfect legitimacy and even beauty. Any incongruity is a shallow incongruity.

In the assembly hall, angels hang from the ceiling. Only a few have been raised to their eventual height, the rest hovering from varying lengths of wire. They hover in many attitudes. The stiff white robes of the Man Cloaked in Linen, as Gabriel is described in the Book of Ezekiel, are low enough to be just a few inches above an adult's head. The unnamed Angel of Presence, who told Moses the story of Creation, is suspended at an acute angle and appears to be plunging headfirst towards the floor.

Half an hour after the gates are shut, all the children and teachers have been brought to the hall. The children, gathered on one side of the hall, are like bodies rolling in a sea-swell. The lower halves of the terrorists' hoods have a stuffed look due to their beards, and they are firing bullets towards the ceiling, perhaps in an effort to curtail the screams of the children, perhaps in an effort to make them scream louder so they can be heard outside. Or perhaps they just wish to destroy the angels as distasteful idols, splinters of coloured wood coming away.

The noise is deafening. A hooded figure walks up to Basie who is squatting beside an unconscious seven-year-old. "Where is the white man?" he asks but he is barely audible above the tumult.

"Tell everyone to shut up," he shouts at Basie, and adds, "Where is Father Mede?"

"This boy needs water," Basie says and reaches for a plastic flask lying on the floor a few feet away.

"Get up and tell them to be quiet."

"Tell your men to stop firing," the deputy headmaster approaches and says. The undeveloped quality in the terrorist's voice—he is almost a boy—has led to the teacher thinking of a student in need of discipline.

The terrorist grabs the teacher by the lapel, a tinge of death in the dark mask. "Watch your manner, you . . . you running dog of imperialism."

"You don't know what imperialism means," the incensed man says. "You're too stupid."

The eyes watch him through the holes in the black hood.

"Where did you learn to look down on people? One of those big villas in Model Town?"

"I grew up in a one-room house in old Heer, and I still live there. My father was a car mechanic and I am proud of him and grateful to him for teaching me to respect those who deserve my respect."

"You don't think we deserve your respect?"

"I know you don't."

"We are warriors of Allah."

"You are thugs with Korans."

The terrorist walks him by his necktie to the centre of the assembly hall. "Everyone must be quiet at once," he shouts, to no avail. He repeats his words but the children continue to scream, some of the four- and five-year-olds actually shrieking with terror at the guns bursting towards the ceiling.

"I will remember you," the deputy headmaster says with the starkness of a last prayer as the terrorist puts the barrel of his pistol to the back of his head and pulls the trigger. This bullet, entering a human body instead of empty air, sounds different from others and the effect on the assembly hall is immediate. The dead man falls to the floor in complete silence.

The shot leaves an echo under every skin. Over the next ten minutes, after the dead body has been removed—Basie wishing he could hold his hand over the eyes of each one of the children to stop them from seeing—the males and females are separated to either side of the hall and they sit in rows with the stillness and silence of hunted animals. The women and girls are made to face the wall so as not to provoke lustful thoughts in any of the males, and all boys have been told to take off their neckties, a symbol of the West.

"Where is the white man?"

When Basie says, "He's not here today, he had to go to Islamabad," several of the terrorists are beside themselves with wrath.

"He's not here today," Basie says again. He takes a step towards the hooded figure closest to him. "Look, these wounded people need medical attention."

"We want the teacher named Jibrael, known as Basie. Which one of you is he? He must be made an example of too."

Before Basie can identify himself the English teacher says from behind him, "He's not here either. He doesn't usually come in until just before nine."

Moving fast, the hooded figures are wiring the assembly hall with bombs, grenades and rockets, the skills taught to some of them by the Pakistani military for use in Kashmir. They ask children to hold the bombs while they climb onto chairs and weave a network of wires between the angels, each bomb slightly bigger than a briefcase and wrapped in either electrical or clear tape, this second allowing a glimpse of the ball bearings and glass shards packed inside. Once the cat's cradle is ready, the bombs are hung from it at various points. At the only unlocked door out of the hall there is a bomb attached to an improvised switch made of two pieces of plywood, one of the terrorists keeping his foot on it to prevent it from exploding. It is as though the very soul of each hostage has been packed with dynamite.

A terrorist walks to the centre of the floor and speaks into the massive immobility, asking all Christian, Shia and Ahmadiya teachers and children to come forward.

Beside the door, just behind the terrorist with his foot on the plywood switch, two ten-year-old girls are about to stand up when Naheed, sitting with her arms around them, tightens her grip by a fraction and slightly shakes her head once.

31

"You should not be here," Mikal whispers.

"I dreamt about you before meeting you," says the girl, ignoring his words. "It was the night before my brother brought you home."

"You should not be here."

She is with him at the top of his night wall, the snow leopard in her arms and the stars falling above the three of them in a tremendous living flood that reaches down to brush against them in slow currents of soft glass grit. The top of the wall is wide enough for four people to walk side by side, and there are raised edges to prevent a fall—edges meant to hide behind and shoot at the raiders or assailants outside during a siege. But now they are concealing the two of them. The constellations are sturdy or faint diffusions in the dark panorama and he whispers their names to her. So many intensities of light, all in flakes and bands and tilted shelves, of the light and within the light, sometimes blindingly brilliant especially to the west where the sky looks as if it is on fire from inside, blinking so forcefully it is a surprise they do not make a sound. Causing a dizziness. And down here there is her life-altering touch on his skin. He tells her of the number of occasions he was discovered lying horizontally on a bough thirty feet above ground in Rohan's garden, watching meteorites fall or peering up through the telescope, an instrument he called "a glass-bottomed boat for the sky." She tells him of an incident from her eldest brother's childhood. "Something has appeared on the other side of the hill," he had said to his parents and uncles one day. "It's black in colour and very strange." The men had armed themselves and left to investigate.

"What was it?"

"A road."

"You should not have come here."

"I turned back twice but had no alternative. You stopped coming to me."

He raises his fingers to his brow. The place where once there was a bruise, a faint swelling. Soon after Naheed was married to Jeo, he had struck his head against the floor one night. The torment of thinking of her with someone else. The pain has awakened of late though the discolouration has long since faded. Love is a distinguishing mark, something by which a dead body can be identified.

As the sun rises he is in the field of yellow flowers, listening to the breeze, to his own breath. He has been here since before dawn, soon after she left the wall. He had wanted to see if Akbar's father would arrive, and as he had waited three figures had appeared and then Mikal had heard the father's Datsun. The man drove into the flowers and met them. It was brief. Mikal had watched from where he hid as an object exchanged hands. After he pocketed it—Mikal suspected it was a satellite phone— the men had driven away. Before leaving himself Akbar's father had unfolded a prayer mat onto the flowers and had said his prayers, spending a longer period on them than was required.

Mikal thought they would be Americans, the three figures he met, but they were Pakistani. Military or the ISI, who will capture al-Qaeda terrorists for the Americans. And it might not be a satellite phone; it could be a vehicle-tracking beacon or a covert surveillance camera to be installed in the south wing.

When will the operation against the al-Qaeda guests be launched and how severe will it be? The raid that occurred at the village a hundred miles away had begun at 3 a.m. The forces had attacked five houses. Three helicopters had brought sixty soldiers but only two of the helicopters had landed and unloaded, the third remaining overhead, providing surveillance and aerial support. Someone said there was a fighter jet too, giving air cover during part of the fourteen-hour siege and battle. About twenty people, possibly including three women and four children, were killed. Whether the dead women were helping al-Qaeda is not known.

The sun is climbing gently, breaking free of the horizon to become rounder and solidifying the way liquid metal does. A sound behind him and he turns to see the Airedale dogs looking at him from ten yards away, standing beside each other on those blood-red legs, the eyes too appearing red in the long slow rising of the sun. He watches and listens, darting a quick glance to either side, but there is no one. At least no one who reveals himself. Suddenly certain that the three animals have killed humans he reaches into his pocket for the knife. Their heads— formidable, big of brain—are the same height as his neck. He looks down at the knife blade reflecting the rays and when he lifts his eyes only a second later the animals have vanished and he waits for something to happen, looking at the conical hills in the distance. Nothing. He walks back to the house, keeping the blade of the knife unfolded most of the way, and he goes in through the kitchen where the cook is singing a song to herself, giving voice to some quiet ache inside her. She pours him a bowl of tea. When he arrives at the gun factory the three dogs are chained up to the *saptaparni* trees.

The grass growing tall between the car husks and the empty rocket shells, he is digging in the area strewn with scrap metal outside the factory, yellow wasps flying in and out of a bullet hole in a rusting truck fender near him.

He digs to the depth of three feet until he has reached a pocket of sand and then puts away the spade and leans down into the pit, working the sand grains away with his fingers. The Mercedes-Benz of modern pistols, it is said about Glocks that they can be buried in sea sand for several weeks and removed and fired immediately. The replicas made at this factory must undergo a similar test. And so minutes after digging them up, Mikal and Akbar's brother are firing them onto targets painted on the scrap metal.

On more than one occasion during the course of the morning Mikal interrupts work with the intention of locating Akbar, to tell him what he saw at dawn. Again and again he comes to the door, where a boy of ten sits on a woven reed mat, refilling spent bullets so they can be used again.

After the buried Glocks have been cleaned and polished, Akbar's brother asks him to take one of them to the south wing of the house.

"Give it to the man on the veranda."

But there is no one there. Mikal clears his throat and stands looking around. On the wall is a plaque which has been painted over but is peeling and some of the text is visible. In any case he knows from Akbar what it says. "The Connolly Ward." A white man who was executed by the Amir of Bukhara in 1842, on suspicion of spying for the British. He moved through the Central Asian republics under the name of Khan Ali, adapting it for its resemblance to his real name, and he was the one who invented the term "the Great Game." Refusing to convert to Islam while the prisoner of the Amir of Bukhara, he was taunted for his faith and made to go through terrible suffering. After his death his sister would write to any new clinic or hospital when it opened, requesting to support a bed or ward in his memory.

Mikal clears his throat again and then pushes open the door and goes into the room which has light-absorbing cement walls and a cold terrazzo floor and he calls out a salutation and stands listening. Against the wall is a stack of cardboard boxes. Inside the one he opens there are hundreds of documents—booklets, instruction manuals on how to make and use explosives, training manuals for guerrilla warfare. There are notebooks, their corners rubbed off by handling and grimy like the ones in which butchers keep customer accounts. On the pages are techniques for kidnapping and assassination. He lifts out a folded letter dated 12 February 2001 to someone named Abu Khabab al-Masri. *Most respected Abu Khabab, I am sending five companions, who are eager to be trained in explosives and other methods of joyful bloodshed. Concerning the expenditure, they will pay you themselves. All are trustworthy . . .*

Killing the Pope. Killing the American President. Blowing up a dozen airliners simultaneously. Assassinations in Pakistan and the Philippines. Bombings in Iran and India among other countries. Attacks on consulates in Pakistan and Thailand. There is a drawing of a crude device for delivering anthrax, and in another box he finds gas masks and the final volume of an eleven-volume "encyclopaedia" on modern weapons, including notes on where to source high explosives, like RDX and Semtex, *that can be used in shaped charges to compress the nuclear core in an implosion-type nuclear device.* A map shows the location of a synagogue in Tunis. Nuclear power plants in Western lands. Sports stadiums.

A sense of defilement runs in his body. They want the birth of a new world, and will take death and repeat it and repeat it and repeat it until that birth results.

"I too was in a military prison like you and Akbar," he hears someone say behind him.

He turns around. "I was sent to give you this," he says quickly and holds out the gun towards the man. He is an Arab, young but with a large beard.

"When they released you, they took you back to the mosque beside the lake, and they took Akbar back to Jalalabad. Am I right? Guess what happened to my brother."

Mikal just wishes to leave.

"He was captured during the exodus of Arabs after Kabul fell on 13 November, so Kabul is where they should have returned him. Instead they flew him to an unknown city and put him on a bus that took seven hours to reach its destination. He couldn't speak the language, had no money or identification, and it was a while before he learned that he was in the country of Albania. No one believes his story, no one believes he was captured." He shakes his head pityingly.

Mikal gives him the gun and he turns it in his hand, holds it at various distances from his body. He gestures with it at the boxes. "If you find anything of interest in there you may take it." He smiles and adds, "The scholar's ink is holier than the martyr's blood, as they say."

"I was just curious."

"You killed two Americans. Single-handedly."

Mikal points to the door. "I have to go." He wishes he could pick up a telephone and dial Basie's number in Heer.

"I must shake the hand that did the blessed deed." The man gives what must be his happiest smile. "We have the right to kill four million

Americans, two million of them children. And to exile twice as many and wound and cripple hundreds of thousands. No?"

Mikal looks at the proffered hand. "I have a better idea," he says. He lets a few seconds pass for all sediment in the room to settle, to be able to speak into clear air. Looking directly into the man's eyes, he says what he wishes to say.

All day he searches for Akbar but cannot locate him.

The moon rises almost vertically, growing smaller as it ascends.

Entering her room he places the cub on the floor, watches it disappear through the curtained arch on the other side. There is a short leaf-like rustle from the other side.

She parts the curtain and looks at him, the animal in her hands. Astoundingly she is standing in a pile of loose banknotes. Every inch of the wide floor on the other side of the curtain is heaped with dollars and rials, pounds and rupees. It is a large room and the crumpled rectangles of paper are up to her shins in places. The surface of the bed is a large white square marooned in money, a chair submerged up to the seat. A spray of blue plastic lilies sprouts close to her, the vase itself unseen.

"I am to be married."

He doesn't have to ask who the bridegroom is. Al-Qaeda terrorists often cement relationships with the tribes by marrying the daughters and sisters of their hosts.

"Within the next few weeks."

"I leave for my visit to Heer in the morning."

"I'll come with you."

"I don't know what's waiting for me there. It could be dangerous."

"I don't care."

He shakes his head. "I will be quick. I'll come back and then we'll leave."

She picks up the leopard from among the banknotes, responding to its calls of unease. It opens its mouth and the whistle comes after a few seconds of silent effort, and is followed by a silence before the mouth is closed.

"Your father doesn't approve of this match. Am I right?"

"Yes. It was my brothers' idea."

The house is in darkness. Beyond the earth's curve, beyond its weather, the high distances are blank. The tops of the palatial trees silhouetted against it. In his pocket is the envelope of money Akbar has given him for the journey to Heer. He lies on the wall fully clothed and concentrates on sounds like a blind man. He gets up and climbs down into the courtyard. He walks through the trees to Akbar's room but the bed is empty. He knows he must disclose the father's betrayal to the son—but how severe will be the consequences?

He returns to the wall but comes down again after what must be an hour according to the stars and walks to the kitchen.

Akbar is at the window, his arms crossed on the sill. Mikal goes to stand beside him and Akbar drapes his arm familially around his shoulder.

"What are you looking at?" Mikal asks.

"There is nothing to look at. It's night."

He turns his face towards the boy. "Akbar, what's the matter?"

He still won't answer. After a while he takes his arm away from Mikal's shoulder. "I heard what happened in the south wing. Why did you say that to a man as great as him?"

"Akbar, are you weeping?" Mikal asks.

He shakes his head. "Why did you do it?"

"Why are you weeping, Akbar?"

He wipes his eyes on his sleeve. "It had to be done."

"What had to be done?"

"Dishonour has to be paid for." He takes Mikal's arm. "Come with me."

He stands firm. "Why?"

"Come with me."

They drive out of the house, moving through the darkness, the dust of their wake sidling into the thornbushes on either side of the car. Mikal's heart lurches as they turn onto the small path towards the yellow field, the hills in the distance. On the other side of the hills are wild and barren plains, stretching widely away mile upon mile towards Afghanistan. Akbar drives to the centre of the field and says, "Let's stop here for a while." Insects—different with each minute—come out of the night and fall around the headlights. Moths like golden-winged machineries. And Akbar is talking frantically about America and the West. Did you know what they did in Vietnam, did you know what happened in Bosnia, did you know, did you know, did you know. There are sallies of breeze in the flowers, the thousand sounds of the night, and the clouds lift and the countless white flames of the sky emerge.

"Akbar, why are we here?"

"Did the Americans ever ask you to collaborate with them?" Akbar asks. "Did they say they would let you go if you spied on al-Qaeda and the Taliban for them?"

"No. We have had this discussion already."

"The Malaysian boy three cages away from us was almost definitely turned into a double agent and sent back to Malaysia to spy on al-Qaeda. At the brick factory they gave him ice cream, pizza and apple pies and showed him movies."

"Akbar. What are we doing here?"

He looks at the dashboard clock and moves the car forwards through the flowers, towards the hills. Ahead of them their headlights illuminate the father's Datsun. Stationary on the hillside. Mikal raises his arms and places his hands on top of his head.

"Oh God." The vehicle's front—on the passenger side—is crushed against a boulder. Akbar stops the car ten yards from the collision site and they sit looking out. At the moment of impact the driver had been thrown out of the driving seat and through the windshield.

"Oh God." He is grateful eyes are incapable of seeing souls.

"Do you remember you told me the fuse of the headlights can be replaced with a twenty-two-calibre bullet? The bullet heats up and fires itself as if from a gun."

Akbar spends almost an hour looking for him, calling out in the darkness, Mikal having turned away from him and run into the bandit hills, and he stays hidden with his revulsion, the cold fury and confusion. He watches Akbar get into the car and drive away at last. His mind uncentring, he wanders in the darkness and sees a stream flowing upwards at dawn, but realises it is flowing downwards after all when he looks again, the sky full of quivering incidents of daybreak, the light slipping on the hillsides, inventing colours.

Early morning—and he walks out of the hills into Megiddo's bazaar and buys a cup of tea and then enters a shop and asks for four aspirin tablets, swallowing them with water from a tap on the outside wall, but they are chalk and he spits them out and stands looking at the shop. In another shop across the street he waits for his turn behind schoolchildren buying sweets and small booklets containing *mantar* spells to help them pass exams. After swallowing the aspirin he leans against the pillar that serves as a bus stop and waits to begin the journey to Heer, while a small child with a very solemn expression—as if visited by something terrible—comes up to him and tries to sell him two bent iron nails.

32

On the second afternoon of the siege, Rohan, Yasmin and Tara are standing in the crowd looking towards St. Joseph's, the chaos and fear out here no doubt matched by the chaos and fear inside the building, the interplay of glances, no one knowing how to drain the event of its power. They are under a tarpaulin that someone has spread from a silk-cotton tree and the tip of the fibreglass nuclear monument. The terrorists opened fire from the building soon after the siege began, to force everyone away, and this is the safest distance. And here they stand and listen and watch, face to face with this demon onto which sacred Arabic verses have been painted to make it blend in with the rest of their religion.

There is a dust-edged wind.

Yesterday all schools and colleges in and around Heer had closed at the news of St. Joseph's, in case it was a co-ordinated attack on several institutions.

"Has there been any change?" Rohan asks, his head bent as he stands. Because of the wind the trees around them sound as though things are crashing into them.

"No, brother-ji," Tara says.

He senses the two women on either side of him, full of that care beyond exhaustion that makes every woman in the world a heroine.

A large concentration of army, police and other emergency services have established a cordon around the school and the area has acquired the look of a zone of infection.

Tara's eyes are tired from the wait and search for Naheed, the endless night hours spent looking for her in her mind, to think where she might be. Now she hopes she might see Naheed among the people gathered around her, raising herself on tiptoe to look over shoulders every few minutes. Her knees no longer ache and to her it is evidence of the love Allah feels towards her, giving her a new pain but balancing it by easing another one.

At 11 a.m. yesterday, two and a half hours after it was shut, the school gate had opened.

"I think the siege is ending," Tara had said and she had immediately turned her face to the sky in gratitude.

"It's Basie," Yasmin said, moving through the crowd for a clearer and closer view.

Yasmin and Tara had watched as a soldier approached Basie and talked to him and received a piece of paper from his hand, with several people shouting, "Run towards us," at Basie.

He had turned and gone back inside and the gate had closed. Five minutes later they heard that the paper in Basie's hand was a list of the terrorists' demands. Folded within it was another sheet that was said to be a message to the entire planet.

"They want Father Mede to come to the school," Yasmin told Rohan and Tara. "The note says, 'If Mede presents himself to us we will release all children under thirteen years of age, except the Shias, Christians and Ahmadiyas.'"

But Father Mede has not been heard from since the siege began.

The phone lines into the school have been severed by the terrorists. The number of the satellite phone Ahmed carries was given out with the list of demands, and now he stands in the library, talking to the commissioner, reiterating his demands, telling him once again that there will be no need to send in food for the children, because the children have all announced a hunger strike in sympathy with the hostage takers' cause. He hangs up with the warning, "Do not try to storm the building."

He stands still for a few moments.

The library has been trashed, the books full of Western knowledge pulled out of the shelves and thrown onto the floor, the page upon page loud with lies about the story of the world, nothing but the blood-soaked abstractions of the so-called civilised world. As ephemeral to him as the Pyramids because they are un-Islamic and unjust.

He hasn't slept for two days. The floor-to-ceiling windows of the library are draped in trumpet vine, thick clusters of orange flowers hanging from the tendrils, full of bees and glistening black ants, and a plaque informs the children that the plant was *originally named after the Abbé Jean-Paul Bignon who was Louis XIV's librarian,* and that *its wood when cut transversely is marked with a cross.* All the pupils at this school are too young and impressionable to be taught anything but the Koran and the sayings of Muhammad. At his feet are dictionaries containing all the many meanings of the rose, and the seventeen words Urdu has for rain, and they are a blasphemy because they do not refer to Allah anywhere, just as the science books don't. Why not say that two hydrogen atoms and one oxygen atom come together if Allah wills to form a molecule of water? Through his speeding mind runs the text of the statement he has sent out with his list of demands. His outrage transmuted into language, the pain fixed into durable words. *This is a message from the warriors of Islam to all the world's Infidels, Crusaders, Jews, and their operatives in the Muslim Kinhood. We are the followers of Allah's mission and let it be known that that mission is the spreading of the truth, not killing people. Peace not war. We ourselves are victims of murder, massacre and incarceration. The West's invasion of Afghanistan—the only true Islamic country in the world—is an unprecedented global crime, and our brothers and sisters and children are being killed as we write this, abducted and taken away to be tortured. Jihad is obligatory under these circumstances, as it is for taking back Spain, Sicily, Hungary, Cyprus, Ethiopia and Russia, and for the restoration of Islamic rule over all parts of India . . .* These are not mere words. Out there is the truth of them played out with living figures, taking on dimensions through his energy and force, and he stands with his forehead pressed against a wall, his head rolling from side to side as he tries to breathe with a regular rhythm.

The second phone in his pocket rings and the delighted Kyra offers him his congratulations.

"The news has been spreading," he says. "It's on every national TV channel now. But they are belittling your achievement by giving the incorrect figure for the hostages."

They claim that there are only three hundred or so people inside.

Yesterday Ahmed was in the assembly hall at ten thirty in the morning when the man with his foot on the detonator had turned up his radio to listen to the news. The newsreader said that a school in Heer was under siege and then lied that "negotiations are under way." It was the fifth story in the bulletin and was given only two lines, and the holy warriors were enraged when it was said that only fifty or sixty pupils and teachers were inside the school. Two of his hooded companions had gone into the corridor and begun to slam chairs and tables into the walls, howling with tetherless fury, screaming, "Jihad! Jihad! Jihad!" until others from every corner of the school had joined in and they had continued until hoarse. The man with his foot on the pedal of the bomb had looked as though he would get up and join them.

Now Kyra says, "When you speak to the representatives of the government you must tell them you are unhappy about it."

"He said it is up to the journalists."

"The government is controlling them, making sure the news doesn't gain the attention of foreign news agencies. You must insist. Tell them you will be compelled to martyr a child if they lie again."

"We must have Father Mede. The Western press will not be interested unless he is here."

"They are saying they can't find him. Are you sure he is not hiding somewhere inside the school?"

"We have looked everywhere."

"And you don't have Basie either. I have been trying to get past the cordon to see if his car is parked at his usual spot outside the school. I'll try again."

You will say that the hostages here in this school are Muslims. But we know what kind of Muslims they are. We know that they and their kind approved of the destruction of the Taliban regime. Anyone over the age of thirteen who takes up arms against Islam can be erased. Any Muslim who approves of the West's actions in Afghanistan, and follows it into this Crusader war by providing material or verbal support, should be aware that he is an apostate who is outside the community of Islam. It is therefore permitted to take his money and his blood, as worthy of death as any American general with his braided glory . . .

The library door opens and the two women enter, or rather one of them is led in roughly by the other.

"I wish to leave, brother Ahmed," says the one whose total commitment he had doubted. "You're traumatising children. You said we were on our way to attack a government building."

"Sister, we have had this conversation twice already," Ahmed says quietly.

"What about the children being traumatised in Afghanistan?" the other woman says. "And this *is* a government building. These people are all instruments of the state."

The doubting woman listens to Ahmed as he explains once again. In movement, thought and gravity, he is older than his countable years, his point of view rooted firmly, and at times all his gestures seem to be ritual gestures.

"I don't want any part of your death-laden victory," the woman says after he has finished speaking. "I don't want to stay."

"You cannot leave."

"I will not watch Muslim blood on Muslim swords."

"You cannot leave," Ahmed says, raising his voice by a fraction. "We need to hold the children here until the white man is given to us."

"Most of these children are not innocent," the other woman says.

"And those who are?"

"You must believe me when I say that I too am upset about the innocent children. But I feel that Allah is asking us to sacrifice them to prove our love to Him, as He asked Ibrahim to cut the throat of his son to prove his obedience. With these few wounds we will heal Islam."

"You are comparing yourself to a prophet? Do you think you are sane enough to make these big decisions? You are half mad because of what you saw in Afghanistan, because your companions were captured or slaughtered."

"Take her away," Ahmed says, "and keep an eye on her." After they are gone the head of Cordoba House comes in.

"What did the commissioner say on the phone just now?" he asks Ahmed.

"He was insisting yet again that they don't know where Father Mede or Basie are, that they have no influence over the Americans to ask them to release captives, or withdraw from Afghanistan, that America is too big and too wounded at the moment for Pakistan not to obey it."

"We mustn't lose faith or hope. I came in here to ask you to come and look at what is happening outside."

They walk to a room that has a window looking out to the front of the building. A cleric has been brought in, in a van that has a loud-speaker attached to its roof. It has been driven as close to the school as possible. The man is quoting verses of the Koran against harming the innocent. He talks in minutes-long spasms and says that the passages of the Holy Book that *do* condone jihad have to be read in the context of the times in which they were revealed to Muhammad. "A verse in the Koran reads, *The nearest in love to the Believers are those who say, 'We are Christians.'*" He continues and once Ahmed has endured enough, he orders for the guns to open fire onto the van, onto the sickness of spirit emanating from it, and it drives away very fast towards the nuclear mountain, the tyres skidding and the terrified cleric calling for Allah's help through the loudspeaker while telling the driver to drive faster.

Basie watches Naheed from the other side of the hall, as she and a female teacher take a dozen children at a time to the bathrooms. The children are exhausted and hungry and are not even allowed to drink water. When Basie takes the boys to the bathroom he lets them drink and tells them not to get any drops on their clothes and not to speak about it.

Later she walks towards him in the corridor, becoming more famil-iar with each step. Her eyes are downcast, and he stares at her until she realises he is looking at her. To begin with there are no words between them during this encounter: it is late afternoon but for some reason it feels dark as though light has rejected the place. Homesick for lost assurances, the children are falling asleep in clusters, the limbs going limp. The hands are holding on to fistfuls of each other's clothing and the place feels somewhat calmer, almost hushed.

"How are you?" he asks eventually.

She nods, barely outlined, the face wearing the great stain of this experience, but unconsumed by the desperation he has seen in others.

"Did Jeo know about you and Mikal?"

Her gold eyes look at him in silence for a few moments. "I don't think so."

"I wonder. Do you think that's why he went off to Afghanistan?"

She is leaning against a wall. "So you know about Mikal and me?"

He nods.

"Who told you?"

"You did. Just now."

"It was before I was married to Jeo."

"OK."

"I think he's alive." A sense memory of him pulses in her blood.

"When this is over we'll go and search for him."

She gives a nod and looks around. "Basie, where are the Christian, Shia and Ahmadiya people they took away?" They were thirty or so, and they were removed from the hall with the words, "Go out and start digging your graves."

"I don't know." Seeing her jaw harden, he adds, "You won't cry, will you?"

She shakes her head.

"I'll keep telling myself I must get through this so we can go look for Mikal."

"I'll do that too," he says.

She wants to experience a simple feeling—laughing with a neighbour or washing her hands, complaining to the vegetable seller that one of the aubergines he sold yesterday had had a caterpillar in it.

"Basie, one of the terrorist women—"

"Don't say my name."

She nods, shocked at her mistake. He has thought several times of revealing himself, to induce the terrorists to release the children, but he fears the English teacher who lied about him being absent will be punished. Recovering, she says, "One of the women doesn't agree with all this. I have spoken to her to see if she might be willing to help us, if I and the other women teachers plan something."

"What are you doing?" A hooded figure shouts at them from the other end of the corridor and Naheed quickly walks away towards the bathroom. "Who told you you could wander around?"

As Basie turns the corridor to the assembly hall a terrorist appears and touches his shoulder and quickly passes him a handful of sweets, whispering, "For the children. I didn't know we were coming to a school," he says. "This has nothing to do with me."

"You must help me put an end to it."

"I have to go."

Basie grabs him by the arm. "Do some of the others feel like you?"

The man tries to free himself and raises his gun towards Basie, perhaps in reflex, perhaps in genuine affront at his audacity.

But Basie refuses to let go. "Find me during the night. Come and talk to me when you see I am alone." The man wrenches himself free and walks away with a firm-footed pace, the swagger of a street tough.

Michael took Adam to Heaven in a chariot of flames and buried him after his death with the help of the angels Gabriel, Raphael and Uriel. And Basie looks up at him as he enters the hall, thinking of Mikal, alive out there somewhere.

Father Mede heard about the siege an hour after it began. He was in his hotel room in Islamabad, waiting for a former pupil and now friend who was arriving on the flight from England with the various medicines his aged body needs to stay functional, some of which he has difficulty acquiring here in Pakistan. Chlorphenamine, pantoprazole, mebeverine, codeine phosphate, irbesartan, amoxicillin, ezetimibe, metoclopramide, Dicloflex, finasteride, doxazosin . . . A list as long as a catalogue of

Homeric ships. He tried to get back to Heer but was prevented by the authorities. His driver and car vanished and when he tried to arrange a taxi the telephone in his hotel room lost its dial tone. In the lobby, full of policemen, he was told that all phone lines in the hotel were down and would you very kindly return to your room, sir. It was only a few hundred miles away but he might as well have been in Borneo, Adelaide or Rio de Janeiro.

The government obviously did not want a white person being visibly linked with the affair. His frustration had turned to anger and some substance was administered to him through the cup of tea he asked for at noon. He was unconscious for almost thirty-six hours.

Now, 2 a.m, he is on the Grand Trunk Road, being driven towards Heer.

He is being followed by several vehicles that have made no attempt to disguise the pursuit. Their guns, their everywhere eyes. He had woken just after eleven this evening. There were puncture marks on his arms where he must have been injected with further drugs. Demanding to be let out of the hotel, he was told that he was free to go to Heer if he could. His driver and car had then appeared, the driver telling him that the vehicle had been mysteriously towed away and that he was sent from place to place by the authorities as he tried to locate it, that when he arrived at the hotel yesterday evening he was told Father Mede had left.

The public phones he approaches are always occupied, the person engaged in a long conversation, and thirteen times they have been flagged down by police for "random" security checks. There have been seven long detours, four of them ending in culs-de-sac.

Around four in the morning, as he turns off the Grand Trunk Road towards St. Joseph's a police car cuts him off and he is told that if he tries to go near the building he will be arrested immediately. He sits wordlessly looking out of the car window for several minutes, imagining the rain falling on the frangipani tree that Sofia had sent to be planted outside his office, the flowers large and beautiful like mysteries in a tale. Then he asks the driver to turn around. An hour later he is still trying to gain access to his home or a telephone, encountering repeated roadblocks and obstructions. As he stops at a roadside tea stall someone says that another school on the other side of Heer has been attacked with grenades, bombs and gunfire.

"But that is a Muslim school," Father Mede's driver says upon hearing the name. "Do they really want to destroy all schools, not just the Christian ones?"

"It must be the commandos rehearsing the storming of St. Joseph's," Father Mede tells him. "It is the only explanation."

"They will kill everyone inside," the driver responds, and begins to murmur the verses of the Koran under his breath to avert disaster. And he reassures Father Mede. "Allah is a friend to the broken-hearted."

On the outskirts of Heer, Kyra opens the back door of the Land Rover and gets in, the saluki jumping in after him.

"Whose idea was the siege?" the man behind the steering wheel asks. A sense of massed impending force in the voice.

"It was suggested by six students and I approved it."

"What are their names? I want—"

"Let me explain," Kyra says.

"I want you to write down the names of all thirty-two people in the building and if you interrupt me again I'll empty a syringe of mercury in your skull."

The man hands Kyra a small notebook over his shoulder, without looking back.

"I hope they are not stupid enough to reveal their faces to anyone. If any civilian has seen them without the hoods, I want that person or persons to be isolated, so they can be eliminated during the raid. Was the school's guard the only person approached during the planning?"

"Yes."

"He'll be found in a sack near Muridke in about an hour."

The man has short hair and precise short sideburns, the nape razored clean and neatly finished, much like Kyra's own. He wears a sky-blue shalwar kameez made of the fabric KT. Kyra can't see it but he knows that on the right side under the kameez is a handgun.

He is in the ISI, but not one of its ordinary tens of thousands of agents. He is a lieutenant general, wanted for questioning by the United Nations for supporting the Muslim fighters of Bosnia against the Serbian army in the 1990s. Despite the UN's ban on supply of arms to the besieged Bosnians, he had successfully airlifted sophisticated anti-tank guided missiles, which had turned the tide in favour of Bosnian Muslims and forced the Serbs to lift the siege.

The Pakistani government has informed the UN that the lieutenant general has "lost his memory" following a recent road accident, and is therefore unable to face any investigations into the matter.

He takes the notebook and quickly glances at what Kyra has written. A man used to getting things done and accustomed to being obeyed, a man who casts a shadow even in darkness.

"You tell this Ahmed that the building will be stormed late in the morning."

"I'll tell him," Kyra says, barely able to contain his rage. The saluki lifts its head from his knee and stands and clambers over to the front, the man reaching out his hand to lovingly stroke its fur.

"I can't prevent his capture or death. And you remain free because of your former connection with the army."

For several moments the man sits in a profound and expectant silence, like a prophet in the depth of receiving a revelation.

"Now was not the time for such an operation. Do you really think we don't have plans to undermine the American army in this part of the world, an army made up of homosexuals and women? Just who do you think you are—trying to do something of this magnitude without telling us?"

"The brothers and relatives of some of the men are being held by the Americans."

"What does that do, change every motherfucking thing in the world? Luckily the white man was away."

They sit in another silence and then the man turns his neck and looks at Kyra for the first time.

"What are you waiting for? Get out."

Kyra's own gun is in exactly the same place, under his clothes, as this man's.

He steps out and just as he reaches for the front door for the saluki the Land Rover drives off at great speed.

Naheed is in the corridor when through the arches she sees Mikal in the grove of crepe myrtles. Blue in the dawn light. He looks at her and then disappears into the fallen rosewood trees by the south wall. Crepe myrtle, Rohan has told her, is among the longest blooming trees known to man, capable of remaining in flower for up to 120 days.

She enters the hall, catching Basie's eye on the far side. The children and the teachers are asleep, and she leans against a pillar and closes her eyes.

"Dance," the man says, the man with the hood over his head. "Dance for me," he approaches and places his crazed hands on her shoulders. "Like the girls do in the films."

She takes a step away from him and glances towards where she last saw Basie. But Basie now sits with his foot on the pedal detonator of the bomb. The terrorist had asked him to take his position before coming towards her.

When the hooded man tries to touch her again she sees Basie and some of the teachers look up from their exhausted half-sleep. Basie knows he must keep his foot on the pedal, must accept another insult for the sake of going on living, for the sake of others. *There must be a place where it doesn't happen like this,* she thinks as the hooded man pulls her into the triangular space between two cupboards. She is thirsty. Basie is standing up, his foot still pressed on the pedal, his face full of confusion and distress, wanting to come forward but unable to. She calls out to him for help without realising. The hooded figure stops and looks in the direction she has shouted and she knows that by uttering his name she has ended his life as effectively as any bullet.

Ahmed sits in the library with his bright knife in his hands. A cold stone has replaced his mind. He has just spoken to Kyra on the phone. The building is to be raided.

Kyra also said that Basie's car is parked in the alleyway on the side of the school. That he must be among the teachers.

He turns and looks towards the door, all receptors working again. There is a sound of feet running in his direction, and the head of Mecca House comes in, out of breath. Less than a minute earlier Ahmed had sent him to question the teachers one by one, to bring him Basie. Now he comes in and says,

"We have Father Mede. He has just walked up to one of the small side doors and is knocking. He says he wants the children released in exchange for himself."

"Don't open the door. It's probably a deception. They are getting ready to storm the school." Ahmed walks to the head of the stairs and stops suddenly because two of his men are climbing the steps towards him with the white man between them.

And just then, from the corner of his eye, he sees the soldiers pouring in over the boundary wall.

33

Naheed is carrying a thick book towards the kitchen, the banana leaves crowding the windows. Two a.m. The house is dark and silent and it is raining and she is unable to sleep. Now and then a flash of lightning makes her think the light from the moon is briefly at her feet.

It is night, and the female relatives of the adults and children who died when the soldiers stormed St. Joseph's must be visiting their graves in secret, carrying umbrellas against the possibility of rain, lamps against the darkness. Her memories of the end are still fragmentary. The terrorists had forced women and children to stand on chairs in front of the windows, to stop the soldiers from shooting into the school from outside. She remembers the fires burning in various places, the escaping hostages shot because they were mistaken for terrorists, an explosion sending the head of an angel through the smoke and flames into the garden. Molten plastic dripping from the burning roof. The sound of a helicopter. Being brought out of her daze by a sharp pain in her scalp, realising that it was a teenager in his death throes unknowingly pulling her hair. At one point she had somehow found herself beside a soldier and, in a daze of his own, he had reached out for the edge of her veil to wipe the blood from his gun. And later she saw some other men wiping their weapons on the soft leaves of the fig tree. Outside there were not enough government vehicles and the wounded were being loaded into private vehicles, the blood-covered limbs hanging out of car boots. And a few hours later, when it was over, the bodies of some of the terrorists were shown to the television cameras, their faces mutilated beyond recognition.

She opens the large book on the table, the breath from the page tilting the candle flame. The book is a dictionary of dates and moves through the history of mankind, from the very beginning to the present.

According to the Islamic calendar, it is currently the early fifteenth century. The 1420s. She wonders what was occurring in Christian lands in the early fifteenth century of the Christian era.

1426. The Venetians go to war with Milan. The Duke of Bedford returns to England from France, to mediate in a clash between his brother Gloucester and the Bishop of Winchester.

1427. The Emperor Yeshaq of Ethiopia sends envoys to Aragon in an attempt to form an alliance against the Muslims. The Duke of Bedford resumes the war in France.

1428. The University of Florence begins teaching Greek and Latin literature. Venetian troops under Carmagnola conquer Bergamo and Brescia. The Treaty of Delft ends the conflict between Flanders and England . . .

When lightning flashes across the pages she looks up, then continues to read. She doesn't know who these personalities are, is unsure about most of the places too, but they do form a picture of their times in her mind.

. . . John Wycliffe's bones are dug up by order of the Council of Constance, burned and thrown into the River Swift.

Faith, the uncorrupted kind, and also souls hooked darkly to the corrupted kind. All the ways of error and glory.

1429. Joan of Arc, a seventeen-year-old shepherdess from Lorraine, has visions. She persuades an officer to provide her with armour and is taken to the Dauphin and liberates Orleans in May.

Naheed turns back to the previous page, to see if things had been better ten years previously. The book tells her that in 1419 an event known as the Defenestration of Prague had occurred, when the followers of the executed Jan Hus had marched on Prague Town Hall to insist on the release of imprisoned preachers. *They force their way into the Town Hall and throw Catholic councillors out of the upper windows. John the Fearless is murdered following a turbulent meeting with the Dauphin . . .*

. And what of the future? Were things better in Christendom ten years on from 1429? Would things be better for Pakistan and Islam in a decade?

1437. The Portuguese are defeated at Tangier by the Moors. The Moors extract a promise from the Portuguese to return to Ceuta; the King's brother Fernando offers himself as hostage but the Portuguese fail to return and Fernando is abandoned in the dungeons at Fez. James I of Scotland is stabbed to death by Sir Robert Graham, whom the king had banished. Graham is tortured and executed . . .

She leans forward and blows out the candle, and it is as though she has just breathed out darkness through her mouth, enough to fill up the room. Assaulted by answers, she walks away from the book, out into the lightning.

34

"So you have returned," the policeman says to Naheed.

He sips his tea, looking over the rim at her and then at Tara.

"Yes," Tara says. "She had gone to visit some relatives."

He had appeared at the house half an hour ago, a two-foot length of bamboo cane under his left arm.

The man puts the cup on the table. "We have to take you to the police station and ask a few questions," he tells Naheed. "Put on your shoes and veil." He lifts the cane from his lap and touches his earlobe with the tip of it.

"What kind of questions?" Tara says. "There is no more to tell."

The man's gaze is firmly on her face. "What did you say your name was? What does your husband do?"

"My husband is dead."

"Just like your daughter's." The man smiles and picks up the tea and sits drinking without further words.

The heat is intense despite last night's storm. A *tatiri* bird is crying out in the branches outside. "It's praying for rain," Tara had told her as a child and Naheed had wondered why it didn't take a drink from the taps like the sparrows. "It neglected to give water to a holy man and he put a curse on it," Tara said. "Now it can never drink through its beak, only through a small opening at the top of its head. It prays for rain so a raindrop might fall through that hole and into its throat."

"What are you waiting for?" the policeman asks.

"I don't want her to go to the police station," Tara says quietly.

"Well, Tara, Naheed," the policeman says, "both of you must agree that it is far from decent behaviour for a girl to disappear from her home without telling anyone."

"She did leave a letter but we didn't see it till later."

"Where is the letter?" The man touches his earlobe with the cane again.

"I can't remember where I put it," Tara says, wondering if she should wake Rohan. But he needs his rest—Kyra visited earlier, to offer his sincere condolences for the death of Basie, and to say that the St. Joseph's siege was the work of Indian agents posing as Muslims, but he also reiterated his demand that the house must be vacated, as soon as possible.

"You can't remember where you put the letter?" The man nods. "Tara, I am one of the moral guardians of this land. You cannot expect me not to have suspicions regarding your daughter's character, given that you yourself were arrested and put in prison for wanton behaviour. Your husband too was dead when it happened. Just like hers."

Tara, who has risen from her seat, having decided to call Rohan after all, sits down again.

"Yes," the man says. "We looked into your background." He turns to Naheed. "What are you waiting for? I won't tell you again. Go and get ready." He leans back in the chair and looks up at the ceiling, the tip of the cane touching the earlobe.

Tara removes her earrings and stands up and goes to him and turns his left hand palm upwards and places the earrings on it. Closing his fingers around them.

He stays in that position for another few moments, then he stands up briskly with a smile. "Well, I am glad you have returned safely to your family, Naheed. I think I'll go now. Everything seems to be in order here."

Naheed steps away from the door to let him pass.

"I'll be back regularly to ask after your well-being," he tells her.

35

As he approaches Heer it is as though he is looking at his own memories.

He gets off the bus two towns earlier and enters a fabric store to buy enough material for a new shalwar kameez. He intends it to be white linen, but the woman ahead of him is buying twelve yards of it for a shroud, and an uneasy thought enters his mind that he will wear clothing made out of the same bolt. When his turn comes no more of the white cloth remains in any case. He points randomly to another colour. Taking the deep green material to the tailor on the other side of the street, he asks how long it will take to sew a new set of clothes. He buys a disposable Bic razor from the general store next door and has a shave and bathes in the mosque bathroom. He goes up into a secluded corner and opens a copy of the Koran and keeps his eyes on the page so no one will approach him, and after a while he lies down and dozes, with his face turned to the wall. Two hours later when he goes back to the tailor his shalwar kameez suit is ready. He puts it on and resumes his journey.

It's ten o'clock at night when his rickshaw enters the central bazaar and then continues on towards the other end of Heer. Not wishing to be seen, he sits with his spine and head pressed against the back of the seat. At the Khan Mahal cinema he buys a ticket and goes into the main hall and falls asleep in the back row, while on the screen a woman sits at a piano singing a song, her eyes shyly returning to a man's framed photograph placed on the piano lid.

When he climbs the boundary wall of Rohan's house it is past one o'clock. Lifting himself from the top of the wall into the limbs of the peepal, going along various sturdy branches of other trees, he drops down into the garden and moves towards the veranda, his feet crushing a scent from the fallen guava leaves. He approaches the veranda where the entire far wall is covered top to bottom with nocturnal lizards, who flee at his approach.

Creak by creak, he opens the transom window above the main corridor. How many times had he done this in the past, coming home from a late film. He climbs down, as does his image in the glass of the far door, so that he is present at both ends of the passage for a few moments.

He enters Rohan's room and stands beside the bed, looking at him. A lamp burns on the bedside table. Rohan opens his eyes, but it is as though he doesn't see Mikal. The old man's eyes are fixed on him without any reaction or acknowledgement. He stands rooted to the spot with things shining softly in the lamplight around him. Were it not for the evidence of the lizards, he would feel he was invisible. Rohan's eyes watch him for a while and then Rohan blinks, on the verge of a word. But, no, he closes his eyes instead. Mikal looks at the Chinaman who supports the clock on the mantelpiece. Half past one.

He walks out into the hallway and glances towards the closed door to Jeo and Naheed's room.

In an alcove is the toy truck he had given Jeo back in October, a lifetime ago.

His feet scatter the melon seeds left out to dry on a cloth sheet on the veranda as he makes his way out. He scales the boundary wall and goes deeper into the darkened neighbourhood, looking up for several minutes at the window to Naheed and Tara's home. He is walking towards Basie's house when he stops and frowns and turns back.

Entering Rohan's room for the second time in less than an hour, he reaches out his hand towards the pillow and picks up the garment lying beside Rohan's head. It's the shirt Jeo was wearing when they left for Peshawar in October. It contains numerous gashes. One above the heart. Several in the stomach. Some in the arms.

He leaves the house with the bloodstained shirt in his hands, moving towards the cemetery, breaking into a run as he gets closer. There are thorns on fresh graves to stop dogs from unearthing the bodies. Some of them catch on his clothes but he keeps running between the mounds, towards where Rohan's family has its plots.

When he enters the garden around midmorning the next day he sees Naheed immediately. The grass is strewn with the red blooms of the *gulmohar* trees, a wide display of all their tints, holding on to light long after they are dead. She is at the opposite end of the garden and he walks towards her, stopping a few feet away. This is the other side of the wound. After the war and violence and the madness of being inside pain, and the ugliness of intention and deed, her beauty seems an improbability, causing a sense of gratefulness in him. What it means to be alive long enough to love someone. To be granted yet another day above ground.

She is tending to a vine and she comes towards him and looks him directly in the eye—and then continues towards the shed.

She emerges with a length of cord and goes back to the flower-laden vine—a brief look over her shoulder at him.

She ties the vine in three places, squinting when the petals fall onto her face, and they fall onto her hair and even enter the kameez through the neckline and her sleeves which she proceeds to shake out. The fourth tendril she wishes to secure is too high and she fails to reach it despite several attempts. This time she doesn't look at him as she goes back to the shed, no doubt for something to stand on, but her clothes almost brush his. He reaches up and ties the branch in place and walks away towards the pond, the hundred water lilies standing open on the water, the white of the herons too sharp to look at in the sun. He hears her walk back to the vine and then he hears her give a half-scream, the sound of someone just woken from a nightmare.

"It's not a ghost," he says. She has approached and is touching his incomplete hands tentatively, her own fingers so fine, the eyelids doeskin.

"I am not dead."

She looks at him. "If I thought you were dead I wouldn't be here."

"Don't say that," he places his hand on her arm. "I'd want you in the world whether I was in it or not."

"You look so thin."

"And you."

She sits down on the log that has always been here at the edge of the water, heavy as an anchor.

He kneels before her almost in a daze himself. "Are you all right?"

"Yes," she says, but then slowly shakes her head and keeps shaking it until she is able to speak again. "No, I'm not."

Gathering herself she adds, "I kept saying if you were here with me, everything would be fine."

"I wouldn't have been of much use."

"It's not that. None of the terrible things would have gone away, but I could have managed. With you next to me."

"I am here now."

"Jeo is dead."

He nods.

She looks at him for a long time, holding him in the relentless amber of her eyes.

"We haven't seen each other since that day Jeo brought you home and I asked you to go away. Sixty-six days into our marriage."

"I caught a glimpse of you a few times after that. Here and there, once in the bazaar."

"It's been four hundred and seventy-nine days since I saw you last. I feel like I have been in four hundred and seventy-nine wars." She looks up, past the nodding kite-high tips of the silk-cotton trees.

"Do you hold it against Jeo for not telling you he was going to Afghanistan?"

"I am angry at him for going, and going without telling us. I am angry at you for not telling us about his intentions. I am angry at myself for not having detected it myself. I am angry at the Americans for invading Afghanistan. I am angry at al-Qaeda and the Taliban for doing what they did. What does it matter?"

"It matters."

"Does it?"

"Yes."

He sits still, looking at her. So many dragonflies in a patch of sun behind her the air seems to be made of cellophane. The trees and all their various seasons of sorrow—the season of what has departed, the season of what has never arrived, of what refuses to be undone, of what will never happen.

"We can't tell anyone about me being here. I killed people."

She lowers her head and hides her face in her hands.

"Two Americans."

"They are looking for you?"

"Yes. They frightened and confused me. I was half crazed and thought they were about to kill me. They had lied to me before. That's not an excuse. I know I shouldn't have done it."

"If they catch you they'll take you away?"

"Yes. In all likelihood they'll imprison me forever. They might even execute me."

Pale leaves. A green shoot is growing out of the fallen log. Thorns as thin and as long as the hands of a pocket watch. "You said 'terrible things.' What else has happened?"

She remains with her head bowed.

"What terrible things have happened, Naheed?"

She takes a deep breath and stands up. "I'll tell you tomorrow." She points to the kitchen and says, "I need some water."

And with that she leaves and after a while he walks to the veranda and sits down on the steps. From there he hears Rohan in his room and he goes in to him, moving towards his armchair.

He comes and crouches beside him. "Uncle," he says, the image of the man dissolving before him because of his tears.

Rohan opens his eyes.

Mikal lowers his head into his lap and begins to weep—the deepest of sadnesses, wishing to empty everything out of himself. He feels Rohan place a hand on his head. "Who is this?"

"It's me. Mikal."

He looks up at the face and Rohan does not react, looking down at him blankly, the eyes tired.

"Mikal?"

"Yes. I've come back." He sobs uncontrollably, "I know Jeo has died . . ."

But something is badly wrong. Above all else, Rohan looks as if he carries news of some atrocious misfortune that no one else has heard of yet. They both hear Naheed come in and he looks towards her, Rohan continuing to stare at the wall. In a soft voice Rohan is saying Mikal's name again and again, questioningly, and he is touching Mikal's face, but Mikal still doesn't understand what Rohan is doing and then Naheed comes forward and begins to explain.

"We thought you were dead," Rohan says.

"Jeo's death wasn't my fault," he says. "Or maybe it was. I should have protected him."

"I wish you had told us he was thinking of going to Afghanistan," Rohan says.

Mikal does not respond.

"But I can understand why you didn't. Where have you been until now?"

"I was a prisoner, first of the Afghan warlords and then of the Americans."

He examines Rohan's face. As a child he had read that if a star falls into the eye of a blind man he can see again.

He stands up. "I have to go to Basie's house. How are they, he and Yasmin?"

Naheed looks at him and then at Rohan.

"What is it?"

But both of them are too distressed to speak. Eventually Rohan says, "Things became terrible while you were dead."

He opens the door and steps out into the dark afternoon of the garden. She is there, watching the rain, the gusts of wind injuring the bamboo grove, their delicate tresses littering the paths. How much more beautiful she is in life than in his memories. Its location now lost, somewhere here is the invisible and nameless _____ tree in which an aged djinn is said to reside, Tara having sensed it, advising them that they must take their clothes off upon encountering a djinn. It thinks you are capable of removing your skin and backs away.

He sits down beside her.

"Sometimes I think it isn't just you I've lost," she says, "but everything else in the world."

"You haven't lost me."

"I told you I have agreed to marry Sharif Sharif."

"And I told you it will not happen."

"He will buy the house for us."

He shakes his head. "It won't happen."

"He'll pay for Father's operations."

"Naheed. Look at me. I am not going to let it happen."

"It was after Basie died that I said yes. We were left all alone. Father, Yasmin and my mother were against it, they still are. But I didn't know what to do."

"I am here now."

"If he sees you as a threat, all he has to do is go to the police. You'll be picked up and handed over to the Americans."

"We'll see."

"He knows about you. He saw your letters to me. If he finds out you are alive, that you are here . . ."

There is a crack of thunder like a rending of the earth's surface down to the very core and they feel the glass rattle in the window-frames. He watches the trees as the rainwater pours itself from the higher tiers of foliage to the lower, moving from leaf to leaf in the canopies like unending stairs.

"What if I asked you to come away with me?"

"I can't."

"I know."

"I have to think of Father's eyes. My mother. Yasmin. I have to help them through all this. They need me."

"I know."

She turns her head to look at him. "They need *us*."

They look up at the lightning, her eyes shining with a dark brilliance, a warm wind in the leaves, the flashes illuminating the clouds.

"Your hands. They work?"

"Yes."

"So you keep them in the pockets just to make people think you are rich, holding on to your wallet?" A brief smile from her.

He looks into her face. "They work." The sound of a radio is issuing from a neighbour's house. A song lost and found again and again in the rain. *Kithay lai aaya sanu pyar, sajna. Kini dur reh gai vairi jag day nain . . .* How much is expected of the two of them, who in their union must conserve and maintain all those who are now apart, or have never been together.

"Yasmin, my sorrow," Rohan says quietly from the other side of the room.

Yasmin and Mikal sit side by side, their upper bodies turned in an embrace. She who has lost a brother and a husband. *They are gone but they are still here, in the hearts of those they left behind. War couldn't destroy* that. *War is weak after all.* He feels no consolation in such thoughts, in this sentiment.

"Who did it?" he asks. "Who held up the school?"

"No one knows," Yasmin says.

"When the soldiers raided the school," Naheed says, "the terrorists were either killed or they escaped."

"And Father Mede is still missing?"

Yasmin nods. "The surviving terrorists took him away with them. Some newspapers are saying the siege was the work of the CIA and Mossad."

He goes and stands at the window.

"Are you staying?" Yasmin asks.

"I don't know what I will do."

"It'll be more than a century in prison?"

"Almost two centuries. I keep thinking I could hide away forever but the reward on me is in millions. Someone is bound to report on me eventually."

"Some people will be reluctant to sell out a fellow Muslim."

"Some, yes."

Later in the evening he eats alone sitting on the steps in the garden and watches it rain. He sets the plate on the floor and gets up and goes out into the street, looking both ways before stepping out, looking out through the veil of water fringing the umbrella's rim, as he turns into the street where Tara lives. Where Sharif Sharif lives. Inside his pocket his fingers rest beside the knife. The weapon almost like the missing digit.

He crosses the courtyard and looks towards the door to the room where Sharif Sharif is usually found. He approaches and calls out but the man is not here this evening. After a while he climbs the stairs to Tara.

She is oiling her sewing machine, having dismantled it completely, the dozens of metal pieces lying on a newspaper beside her as she sits cross-legged on the floor. He leans against the doorjamb and watches and she doesn't look up after the initial glance. Naheed has no doubt told her about his return.

When she cannot shift a screw he comes forward and gently takes the screwdriver from her and loosens it for her.

"It has remained stuck for two years," she says quietly. "I wasn't able to unscrew it when I cleaned the machine last year either. I don't know where I got the strength to tighten it so firmly in the first place."

"You didn't," he says. "I tightened it, two years ago. I was visiting Naheed while you were out and the dismantled pieces were lying out on the table and I began putting them together."

She doesn't say anything, continuing with her work, handling the small curved and bent pieces and dripping oil onto them. They look like relics of metal saints.

She gets up and washes her hands. She smells them and then washes them once again, and then goes into the kitchen and begins to cook a handful of lentils. A woman who has spent most of her life in impoverished solitude.

"I will not allow Naheed to marry Sharif Sharif."

"He won't get a drink of that water while I am alive," she says. "I had found another boy for her. I haven't said no to that family yet."

Fate's renegade. A fugitive from international justice. He's still not good enough for her daughter. Or is she waiting to see what he plans to do?

He turns around to leave, thinking this is enough for now. He is halfway down the stairs when she calls out to him and he climbs back up.

She points to the chair. "Take a seat." She turns the flame low under the pot and carries a stool to him, sitting down to face him.

He doesn't understand immediately but then remembers that the dead have to be talked of with respect and formality. She says, "I am sorry about your brother."

Yasmin said he had been shot eighty-six times.

"He was a good man. I had grown to love him like a son."

"He was a good man. Does it get better?"

"I wouldn't say better." She lost her husband when she was very young: she knows her condition and her answer is instant. He might as well have asked her the colour of the sky.

"What then?"

"Life gets in the way of your grief." She begins to fan herself with a palm-leaf fan. "You make yourself forget about the pain because there are other things to take care of. But when you do remember it . . . well . . . it's a strange kind of hurting, like someone has lost a razor blade inside your soul."

"I don't know how long I should grieve or mourn, don't know when it would be right to stop."

She touches his shoulder.

"Would you stay and eat with me?"

"No, thank you. I'd better get back."

He returns through the rain-filled street and sitting on the veranda he counts to see what is left of the money Akbar gave him. The green shirt he is wearing has white buttons. The tailor said the plain white buttons were a dozen for a rupee, while the green would cost twice as much.

. . .

She looks out during the night to see him asleep on the chair on the veranda, his hands in his pockets. Gently she arranges a thin cotton sheet over him and lights a mosquito coil and places it next to him on the tiles, making sure her glass bangles don't rattle. She had started wearing the bangles and had put away the dark clothes because she had wished to signal to Sharif Sharif that she no longer mourns Jeo.

He wakes just after dawn when she is collecting fallen mulberries from the grass, the inked blue fruit that the rain has brought down, glossy blue clots, red, green, white, pink, the flesh sweet with sugar, turning the fingers sticky as it is eaten as though they contain blood, leaving stains on the tongue and hands.

He sits up in the chair, wincing from the stiffness and wrapping the sheet around himself against the mild chill. "I dreamt there was a city of burning minarets."

She leans against a tree, pushing back strands of loose hair with one hand. "Are you sure it's not something you saw in real life? The American bombing in Afghanistan? A photograph in a newspaper?"

He shakes his head. The dragon-ridden days of the planet.

"I keep seeing the burning angels when I fall asleep," she says. "But that really did happen. They hung in flames above everyone's head in St. Joseph's after the soldiers appeared. The school has been decimated from the explosions. Just a pile of rubble." In sleep she also sees again and again the thirsty children drinking urine at St. Joseph's on the second day of the siege. She sees again, on the first day of the siege, the deputy headmaster being shot and then males and females sitting on either side of the hall, a red dividing line having been created on the floor by two terrorists taking hold of the deputy's corpse and dragging it from one end to the other.

She is sitting beside him now, both of them looking silently at the garden. The mulberries' liquid is already beginning to slip out of the flesh.

"How does it feel to be back?"

He smiles.

"Could you not explain to the Americans what happened?"

"It won't work."

After a while he says, "I am sorry. About everything." And without turning towards her he adds,

"I am in Hell without you."

He had said this to her before, sixty-six days into her marriage, and she had not reacted. This time she answers him.

"I'll put it out with my breath."

She walks to the crossroads to buy a packet of Gold Flake for him, sensing his restlessness, a definite but quiet desperation in him at not being able to leave the house.

"There is someone outside," she tells him, trying to conceal her panic when she returns with the cigarettes.

He raises his head above the poet's jasmine on the boundary wall but there is no one in the street.

"I saw him when I left and he was still there when I came back."

"What did he look like?"

Will they raid the house? he wonders as he climbs down and stands looking at her, the trees bending in the wind around them as if borne forward by the earth's spinning.

It is 1219, the time of the Fifth Crusade, and Francis—the future saint of Assisi—and his companion, Brother Illuminato, have crossed enemy lines to gain an audience with the Sultan of Egypt, Malik al-Kamil. It is late September and the landscape they pass through is still littered with corpses from the battle that took place on 29 August.

Yasmin turns the page. For centuries artists have depicted the various episodes of the astonishing encounter, one of the most extraordinary in the history of belief. The bearded Sultan in his brocade robes and silk turban, and Francis in his rough and patched brown tunic.

According to some accounts, Muslim sentries fell upon Francis and Illuminato the moment they saw them, savagely beating them before putting them in chains. But according to others, when the sentinels saw them coming they thought they were messengers, or perhaps had come to convert to Islam. Soldiers on both sides of the Fifth Crusade had converted, and so the sentinels led them to the Sultan.

Yasmin touches the flames with her fingers. The fire burns in the book of paintings she is holding. St. Francis of Assisi is standing inside the blaze—entering a bonfire to prove that his faith was superior to Islam.

But that didn't happen either and was invented later. The Sultan and the future saint had talked of war and faith but the encounter was perfectly peaceful—no enraged and fulminating Muslim clerics had appeared, as is claimed, to demand that the Sultan behead the monk.

She closes her eyes, her hand on her belly where Basie's child is growing, small as a wren. He died before she discovered she was pregnant.

There are moments when Basie is not dead, when she turns around to share something with him, but then she remembers.

It is as though the house and the world are suffering from a kind of physical amnesia. They have forgotten him.

When they shot him they shot him dead in each one of her memories. Eighty-six bullets. One for the way he smiled, one for the way he frowned to himself when he read, one for the way his left hand sometimes rested on his thigh as he drove, one for the way he had become tearful when he said he had to find out who the old woman was who sat holding the police inspector's knee, one for the way he liked eating mangoes with skin still on them, one for the beautiful way he danced to Count Basie's "One o'Clock Jump," quietly concentrating to himself, one for the way he said about his father, slipping into a drunken impersonation of the man, "He had a beard but he would gently correct those who mistook him for a cleric. My beard is not religious. It's a revolutionary one, inspired by Castro, Che and Marx," one for the way he said with a smile, "Allow me to complicate you, your holiness," whenever Father Mede said, "I am just a simple man of God," one for the way he said Islam was a religion whose past could not be predicted, one for the way he didn't know how to say his prayers, looking for surreptitious guidance to the people praying beside him, one for the way he liked walking on dew-covered grass, one for the way he looked up from Tolstoy's big novel and said that the infernal summer heat was to Pakistan what snowbound winters were to Russia . . .

She listens for movements in Rohan's room. When after a quarrel with Sofia he would forgo a meal, saying quietly from his room that he was not hungry, she would take food to him in secret, and she would grin as he pretended not to care initially but would then ask, "What have you brought?"

She looks down at the book. The Sultan gave Francis the key to his private prayer room, and on parting he accepted one gift from the Sultan, an ivory horn, which is kept today in Assisi. The inscription on it says that Francis used it to summon people and birds to hear him preach.

The black shadow of the railing falls on her white tunic and makes it appear as though the fabric is patterned. The candle flame swaying on the floor beside her. He leans and places his mouth on her neck, his hunger shouting from underneath his skin. Every object around them is heightened, everything surprised. He feels ashamed for seeking happiness so soon after his brother's death. Something terrible will happen to him. He is inviting punishment. He thinks of Salomi, and he thinks of Jeo who has only been dead for four days—for him. Pushing past the confusion in the darkness he lifts her wrists and begins to break the glass bangles, eliminating the possibility of Sharif Sharif from her. "I want my breath," he says. His hand under the tunic on her breast on her stomach on the curve of her spine and now he panics. He has been in a world war and he can sense blood. She pushes him away gently because she knows about blood too—she is a woman. A breaking bangle has torn into her left wrist. They light the candle that had extinguished itself a moment ago and see the thin line of red emerging from the puncture. He lifts it to his mouth and with his teeth works out the small shard of glass lodged under the skin, not stopping as she stands up and leads him indoors, the glass disappearing into him the way the ruby had entered Jeo's body.

He crosses the Grand Trunk Road and enters the night-dark alley, moving towards the high painted rooms, visualising the doves and pigeons in one of them. When he notices a shadow behind him, there is a surge of anger in his body at not realising he was being followed. Squeezing through the narrow gaps between the fenders and bumpers of two parked trucks, he looks over his shoulder. *They won't just pick you up, they'll spirit away everyone you know.*

He climbs the stairs two at a time towards his room. It's Basie's birthday tomorrow and he has a bottle of Murree's whisky hidden behind a loose brick in the wall.

He looks down from the window. There doesn't seem to be anyone out there, at least not in the few areas where light is falling.

He turns and stands looking at the coloured walls, then leans against one of the painted angels and closes his eyes. "To them everything was about helping others," Basie said about their parents, getting drunk on the mattress in this room. "They'd always find that aspect. Once I wanted to see a cowboy film—it was on at the Capri cinema, I remember— and Father said he himself loved cowboy films because they were about someone coming to the aid of a town terrorised by the wicked and the powerful." They and their friends took poets into factories and mills, to inspire them to write songs about the terrible conditions the workers had to endure. They found itinerant storytellers and introduced them to the screenwriters in Lahore, so that the land's age-old tales of resisting the unjust could be incorporated into contemporary movies.

There is a sound outside the door.

"Akbar." The tension snapping into relief, of a kind. Akbar comes forward and embraces him.

"What are you doing here?"

The boy looks dishevelled and unslept, the eyes dark.

"They found out I killed my father," he says quietly.

"The military. The people he was trying to bring to your house?"

"Yes." He looks around him. He is carrying a shoulder bag and he places it at Mikal's feet. "You have to take this to Megiddo."

"What is it?"

"Salomi is married. She and her new husband need to get out of Pakistan. They will be safe in Yemen."

He tells himself not to let Akbar see his reaction.

"What's in the bag?"

"They need money to get out."

"I would have thought he had enough."

Akbar shakes his head. "He did. But before my father went off that night he burnt it all in the furnace in the gun factory. Not a single rupee was left. Everything turned to ash." He points to the bag. "You have to go and give this to Salomi, so the pair of them can leave."

Akbar unzips the bag. It is full of clothes but from under it he pulls out three bundles of American dollars, each the thickness of a telephone directory.

"When did she get married?"

"The morning you left." Akbar replaces the money and fastens the zip. "It's fifty-five thousand dollars."

"I don't think I can do this, Akbar."

"Please. The soldiers, backed by the Americans, will raid the house very soon, if they haven't already. The pair of them will have to bribe their way out of the towns and cities, find places to shelter. Otherwise people will hand them both to the Americans for the reward."

"I can't." At the brick factory the Americans had asked him if he had ever transferred monies for al-Qaeda. And yet he knows he must see Salomi and explain himself to her, if he can.

"Just go and give it to her and come back," Akbar says, and adds, "You are my brother."

He sits beside the bag, smoking, the room full of night's darkness. Three days have passed since Akbar gave him the money and it is still here. He moves towards the window and looks at the garden, the blossoms beautiful as Eden, where every memory of every man is said to have its origin, and after a while he turns and walks towards where she lies on the bed.

When he is naked beside her she sees the bullet wounds. She watches him, pale brown with calves and forearms darkly hairy, thin but sinewy and sheerly beautiful with the candlelight running over him.

From a book she has learned what a human body is worth. The chemical elements making up a living person are said to have the market value of about $4 or $5. His sweeping laughter, the merged eyebrows, the flavour of his breath and saliva when he leans every few minutes to kiss her for minutes at a time. Four dollars or $5. The features take shape under the red point of brilliance when he inhales from the cigarette in the darkness. It is as though he is sucking in light through the white tube, light that then runs under his skin to reveal him softly. She watches him as he gets up during the night and sits crouching beside the shoulder bag. Jeo came back wearing a tight-fitting suit of bruises, and now she doesn't want Mikal to go to Waziristan.

One night before she married, Mikal had broken into her and Tara's room. She was terrified to find him standing beside her bed in the dead of night, her mother only a few feet away. She had taken his hand and led him out to the roof. "I can't sleep," he had told her.

"Recite a poem. That helps. One that rhymes."

"I don't know any poems."

"You sing all the time."

"They are songs not poems."

"They are the same thing."

The next day she had bought him a book of poems by Wamaq Saleem from Urdu Bazaar, verses in which the dove called out in adoration to its lover the cypress tree. It was as though the poet knew nothing of the aeons of separateness that lay between these two things, and between the bulbul and the rose, and between the bee and the lotus blossom, and so the dove called and called, the rose continued to open for the bulbul, and the bee circled and circled and circled the lotuses.

"Will they allow you to receive letters in the prison?" she asks him now, when he comes away from the bag containing the dollars.

"What are you talking about? I promise you I will come back."

"What about visitors?" She is sitting up in bed. "Will the Americans allow you to have visitors?"

He encloses her in his arms. "Don't say that."

"I don't even know how much a plane ticket to the United States is. It must be thousands of rupees. I'll never be able to visit you."

What woke them was the sound of the rain stopping, the sudden calm in the middle of the night. A silence packed with distances.

"It'll be just a quick journey," he says. "Two days there, two days back. Four days—five maximum." On a map he has drawn a line from Heer to Megiddo. Taking small buses, avoiding all major stations. A long jagged stroke of ink resembling the constellation of Hydra. And now they speak quietly into each other's skin. *It is in the watches of the night that impressions are strongest and words most eloquent:* she thinks of these words from the Koran. His fingers are on the chain around her neck that has little leaves all along its length, a string of foliage. "Did you play with your mother's jewellery when you were a child?" she asks.

"Yes. I used to wear it as well."

She takes it off and puts it around his neck just as the call to the predawn prayers sounds and they remain in each other's arms, sinning in a time of holiness, and when he gets out of bed she feels for the clasp of the chain, to take it off. "Let me wear it," he says.

"But it's a woman's."

"I don't care." And then he adds, "Isn't the soul a woman?" Outside the sun would begin to rise in the bloody reefs of the clouds within the hour and the birds are already looking for light to fly into.

Tara is mending a broken umbrella. "You are leaving?"

"For a few days."

She continues to hold his eye.

"A friend needs help."

She nods.

"I just wanted to talk to you about Naheed," he says. "None of us wants her to marry Sharif Sharif, but you mentioned this other man you have found. There is no need for him. Naheed wants to get qualifications and become a teacher—"

"I know what my daughter needs and wants. She can get qualifications after she is married."

"Yes, she can." He looks at his hands. "I don't know what I want to say. I still can't offer her the kind of life you'd want for her. I could be caught anytime and taken away, leaving her on her own once again."

She puts the umbrella aside. "I stood in your way once, I won't this time. I suppose when it comes down to it it's a man's word that counts. That's all the security a woman needs. Who cares if the buttons on his shirt don't match the fabric."

"I will come back in five days."

"Then I will be happy to call you my son-in-law."

"I am sorry I didn't think of the consequences for you when I suggested to Naheed that we run away before her wedding to Jeo."

"It would have caused terrible difficulties for me, yes."

"I am sorry I didn't think of that."

"Would you do it again?"

"Wanting to do it is not what I am apologising for here."

She appraises him openly. "That's a good reply. Now I am going to be equally honest with you. You let down my daughter once, by not turning up when you said you would. I won't allow you to disappoint her again. Is that clear?"

"Yes. But didn't you say that her running away would have been bad for you?"

"That's a matter between me and her, nothing to do with you. As far as you or anyone else is concerned, I am on her side. Don't you ever disappoint her again."

"I am sorry I did it once."

"That's another good thing to say to me. And you might want to rethink some of the guilt you've been carrying around about shooting those Americans."

"I'll try. The men I killed had mothers, fathers, probably wives and children. I killed them and must pay for the crime."

"But there's no need to be so hard on yourself, at least until perfect order reigns in the world. Life is difficult at times and they goaded you and you were confused. Part of the blame lies with them. Don't hold yourself to too exacting a standard."

"That can be an excuse to not hold yourself to any standard at all."

"That too is true."

She tells him to go with Allah and he shoulders the bag and begins to climb down.

From the bus station he telephones Naheed just to hear her voice and they talk about what they have planned and envisaged for themselves after his return. He whispers a few obscene things to her and she laughs quietly, and then he stands listening to her breath until the money runs out, the sun rising above Heer and the sky changing colour like someone switching from one language to another, and as in a fairy tale he knows that he'll die if he takes off her chain from around his neck. When he hangs up it is with the bone-deep fear that beauty and loss might be inseparable, but then he thinks of a line from one of Wamaq Saleem's poems. *Love is not consolation, it is light.*

III

Equal Sons

                    . . . how he fell
From Heav'n, they fabl'd, thrown by angry Jove
Sheer o'er the chrystal Battlements: from Morn
To Noon he fell, from Noon to dewy Eve,
A Summer's day; and with the setting Sun
Dropt from the Zenith like a falling Star,
On Lemnos th' Ægean Ile.

                              —*John Milton*

36

As the bus nears Megiddo, the conductor and driver talk about a possible paramilitary cordon around the town. Mikal overhears the news that soldiers have been flagging down buses to check the passengers' papers. Four miles from the outskirts he asks the conductor to let him out. He leaps off into the dust, the afternoon's heat and intense light coming at him from the metal body of the bus and, as he begins to walk, from all points of the landscape, making him lose his sense of focus several times during the hour and a half it takes him to get to the outer limits of Megiddo. A wind shunting in from the open wild desert to the west. He stops when the yellow house comes into view and he stands looking at it, the material of the shoulder bag going soft in the heat. When he sets off again he has changed direction. Instead of approaching the house by the front door he will go along the riverbank, towards the kitchen at the back. Hidden in the grove of beautiful trees at the water's edge, he watches the entrance to the kitchen. There is no movement and no sound. There is the imprint of a boot in the expanse of dust between the trees and the kitchen door. Lying on his stomach he listens with his ear pressed to the earth for several minutes. The sound of loose water. He waits the three hours until the sun drops towards the west and the light becomes a rich amber, the birds beginning to return noisily to the trees around him, screaming and ascending as they quarrel about an over-loved branch. No one has gone in or come out of the house and at last he moves forward, going past the footprint. He is not sure if he recognises the pattern from his time in American custody.

The kitchen door creaks open at his touch and the first thing he notes is the spent cartridge on the tiled floor and he enters and walks through the room without a sound, the movements of the body honed down to the essential, the breath held. The door on the far side of the kitchen looks out onto the inner courtyard of the house and he peers through it, eyes surveying quickly. There is nobody and no light in any of the rooms lining the courtyard. Everywhere there is the red light of the setting sun as though the place is submerged in water-thinned blood.

He withdraws into the kitchen and lifts the cartridge from the floor and studies it for a long time.

He had glimpsed the car belonging to Akbar's brother, parked on the other side of the courtyard, and taking a rag from a shelf he goes out to it at a walking crouch. He tears off the side-view mirror from the car's body, wrapping the cloth around it to muffle the noise, a fast decisive twist like breaking the neck of a rabbit.

He uses the mirror to inspect the rooms before entering them, sending it in at the end of his arm from each doorway.

Several walls are scarred with bullets. The phones have no dial tone. He is about to switch on the light but then stops himself. Instead he plugs in the clothes iron and touches its base after ten seconds to see if it is getting warm. It stays cold so the electricity has been cut off.

The three dogs are missing from the front of the gun factory and as he walks through the long grass mosquitoes appear, abdomens swollen with sucked blood, and he doesn't know whose blood it might be. Inside the factory, the part of the floor before the furnace is covered with ashes of burnt money. An area the size of six or seven prayer mats. The patterns of ink that had been printed on the banknotes and the words, portraits and landmarks appear grey against the black of the crinkled paper—greys of various tints, depending on the original colour of the ink. Blue-grey. Orange-grey. Green- or red-grey.

His toes reduce one complete rectangle of blackness to a smear of black dust and as he moves around he is watched by the eye on each dollar bill.

The kitchen is filled with soft twilight shadows when he returns. He lights a lantern, almost wincing as the flame grows in the glass globe and the amount of light increases around him, as though someone is speaking louder than is prudent. He turns down the flame. The bag with the money has remained hanging from his shoulder. He lifts the terra-cotta lid of the milk pot to find that the milk has gone bad. He fills a glass with water and stands drinking in the semidarkness. There are chapattis stiff as cardboard in a basket but they can become like that within a day, so he can't really work out how old they are.

At last he picks up the lamp and goes to the south wing and he stays in there for the better part of an hour, trying to reconstruct what has occurred there. The metal door at the entrance has been blown off and he sniffs the hinges to determine what explosive was used. The battle seems to have been fiercest here. The room that had contained boxes of leaflets and other literature is completely empty, the glass in the windows smashed, the casements splintered. There have been explosions in several rooms. Rockets, bombs. The soldiers must have thrown in grenades before entering. Shot through doors. He moves through the wing like a sapper, room by room, and only when he unlatches the very last door does he find two of the three Airedales. The bodies have entered rigor mortis. They are lying a few yards apart in the middle of the floor—boot prints join one pool of blood with the other and then walk away towards a window. There is no sign of the third dog.

Returning to the kitchen he takes one of the dried chapattis and eats it with the curried potatoes and mutton he finds in a bowl in the dead refrigerator, chewing the stiff pieces until they soften. He finds a jar of carrots in sugar syrup and eats them in the dark light, lifting the long red pieces to his mouth two or three at a time, looking out through the window at the river flowing silently under the rising moon, the hatchery of stars in the most distant field of vision.

Wiping his hands on his trousers he walks into the women's section. Quietly he calls out to the leopard several times as he goes deep into the inner sanctums. Silence surrounds him in her room and he feels it is the silence of a trap. He is enclosed in an immense thing and he breathes slowly to remain calm, telling himself it shouldn't matter how deep the water is as long as you can swim.

He falls asleep on the kitchen floor, using the shoulder bag as a pillow, and wakes several hours later looking up at the dark blue sky. He has no memory of it but sometime in the night he had left the kitchen and come out onto the courtyard and resumed his sleep in the grass and now he lies looking up at the constellations in the warmly burning canopy and he feels the earth pressing up against his spine, sustaining him, lifting him inside the nocturnal space. He is held against the taut trembling solidity of the planet, the enormous living curve of the world under his body.

Even though it is still night, he walks out of the house through the kitchen door, the bag hanging from his shoulder, the moon casting blades of light on the river's surface. Going along the water he comes out to the road leading to Megiddo, and halfway along it he takes the narrow path which ends in the yellow flowers. He can smell them as he nears. It feels as though he hasn't seen them for several months instead of several days. Above him the craters and canyons are clearly visible on the moon's surface, and in the bluish light he walks through the flowers, still warm from the day's heat, and on towards the low light-capped hills in the distance, and three-quarters of an hour later he is crouched in the dry bed of a spring, watching the group of dark figures in the distance. He wonders if they are Americans. They are fifty yards away from him across a wide band of gravel. Between them there is a stand of small dark bushes. He moves forwards on elbows, the bag resting in the small of his back. They are moving slowly across the slope of the hill and seem to be searching the network of caves. Looking for terrorists. And suddenly a group of figures emerges from one cave and they run and struggle with the searchers. Each one as angry as a snake in an eagle's claws. Some of them fall to the ground and the dust blows in the air and the wind brings him their shouts along with Arabic words of praise for Allah, which the apprehended figures utter at each bit of pain and each restraining grip. The Americans, if they are Americans, are completely silent as though their words and sounds are incapable of travelling through the air of this land. Their existence here generates electricity that he can feel on his skin and for a fraction of a second he believes he sees the glittering eyes of a white man in the moonlight. But now he knows that the searchers are Pakistani soldiers because he hears them begin to talk in Urdu, Punjabi, Pashto and Hindko. The prisoners will be handed over to the Americans and the Pakistani army will collect the reward. The Arabs have probably just arrived from Afghanistan and were hoping to join up with their companions who have already escaped to this area. It is even possible that they were on their way to Akbar's house. Three of them have now run away down the hill towards the valley of flowers and five soldiers go after them, raising dust that shines palely under the moon, passing within twenty feet of where he lies, and they turn and move far out on the slope until they are the smallest of figures in the blue light and then they disappear.

"Get out of here, get out of here," he tells himself under his breath.

By the time he gets back to the house the darkness above him is splintering into light and it is almost dawn and a faint call to prayer is coming from the direction of Megiddo to the north of the house. He wonders if he should go to the mosque and try to glean information from the worshippers, and decides against it because someone could alert the Pakistani military or the Americans to his presence. He falls asleep in Akbar's room, listening to the muezzin, having locked the door and dragged a table against it—listening to the muezzin and to his own whispers, "Get out of here, get out of here."

Carrying the snow leopard cub inside his shirt, the American soldier steps across the international boundary line sometime around 3 a.m., leaving Afghanistan's Paktika Province and entering South Waziristan. The cub's small head sticks out from the top two undone buttons of the soldier's kameez. He walks through the night that is full of the schemes of terrorists and the plots of generals, the mathematics of war. There is a chalky wind and he carries a rucksack on his back and there is a large Thuraya satellite phone in a holster around his waist. Another, smaller satellite phone is concealed in the pocket in the shorts he wears under his trousers, in case he has to relinquish the Thuraya.

A Special Forces soldier, he found the snow leopard during a raid at a house in the town named Megiddo, and among the things in his rucksack are six of the several dozen tins of cat food he has had shipped from the United States.

There are night-opening flowers on the cactuses. He walks through the moths that are feeding on them, fluttering audibly around him. These mostly barren hills are being used by terrorists to flee Afghanistan and he is alert as he walks. His younger brother was murdered by a freed prisoner back in January.

There is no name, but the first finger on each of the prisoner's hands was missing.

Walking across an expanse of sand where the prevailing wind has produced corrugated wrinkles, like a broken staircase of white marble, he notes the angle at which he walks relative to the pattern, keeping it constant so as not to lose orientation. The maverick. He told the others in his team that he would be back in twenty-four hours, or would call them if he needs assistance. If he isn't back within twenty-four hours they will begin to look for him.

From time to time he makes sure that the leopard is facing his chest because he knows the eyes can be seen from a mile away in the desert.

Loaded into the memories of both satellite phones are the photographs of the prisoner who killed his brother, taken when he was originally captured. He should never have been freed—he never revealed his name and that should have been indication enough that he was a hardened terrorist, most probably belonging to the upper echelons of al-Qaeda. He should have been taken to Cuba for complete and advanced interrogation. The proof of it being that he shot dead two Americans the *instant* he was released. A detailed investigation is being carried out into how such a shrewd and astute prisoner, who was clearly a threat to the United States and to peace in this region, was given his freedom.

But it is difficult to be sure. The innocent and the guilty both weep in the interrogation rooms, leaving wet spots on the material of the jumpsuits as they wipe large tears on their shoulders. "I swear to Allah on my heart and limbs . . ." "I swear to Allah on my mother's grave . . ."

He stops and looks around as he comes to a river, to make sure he is travelling in the right direction. Most rivers in South Waziristan flow from west to south, he knows, and he remembers his brother's paranoia about crossing streams or rivers in Afghanistan, having heard stories about plastic Russian mines still flowing in the currents. But this is Pakistan.

There are American military bases in Germany, Japan, South Korea, Saudi Arabia, Kuwait, Bahrain, Albania, Bulgaria, Macedonia, Qatar, Oman, the United Arab Emirates, Hungary, Bosnia, Tajikistan, Croatia, Afghanistan, Kazakhstan, Uzbekistan, Georgia—a base in each vicinity, ready to mobilise and put down possible threats. And it is no longer a case of American happiness, American freedom, American interests, the American way of life. Now it is about the survival of America itself.

He is navigating by the stars as he walks, picking a new constellation every twenty minutes as the old one shifts direction with the earth's rotation. Hercules. Ophiuchus. He wonders if among them there is a spirit or god or goddess that walks the battlefield, collecting the last words of the dying, enumerating every drop of spilled blood.

What were his brother's last words?

Careful even when boisterous, as a Military Policeman his brother had never violated the rules, had in fact intervened one afternoon when an interrogator forgot himself during a session and made physical contact with the prisoner—grabbing the jumpsuit and shaking the kid. Most of the prisoners are so thin, small and undernourished that there is constant fear that one of them will die from the strictness of even the normal regime. He has yet to shed a tear over his brother's murder, willing the fact of the departure out of his mind as best he can, existing in the unexamined haze, stopping himself whenever he hears himself humming the song his brother had loved, taught to him by their mother.

Mikal is ravenous when he wakes after just two hours of sleep. The sun is up. Taking four eggs from the refrigerator he cooks them and carries the frying pan out to the riverbank, watching the water as he eats, a warm wind coming from the desert. He washes the pan and puts it back on the shelf and looks at his wristwatch. The woman who came to cook at the house every day lives a mile upriver, but it is too early to pay her a visit. He digs a hole and then goes into the south wing and wraps the two dogs in a bedsheet and carries them out. Rather than break the stiff limbs he widens the hole he has dug.

The bag with the dollars has stayed at his side at all times, but now he places it in the wardrobe in Akbar's room, arranging clothes around and on top until nothing can be seen. He is about to lock the wardrobe when he stops. Guns have been combined with keys, with knives, forks and spoons, and in Akbar's father's room there is a steel chest made to contain valuables which has a percussion pistol mounted inside it. If the lid is opened without setting a special catch, the pistol fires. This is where he deposits the bag. Afterwards he looks at his wristwatch once again and walks out of the house and goes along the riverbank.

A man is sitting on the cook's veranda reading a newspaper. He is in his fifties, with untidy pewter stubble and an Adam's apple as pronounced as his nose. He looks up and examines Mikal.

"Uncle, my name is Mikal. I am Akbar's friend," he says and nods over his shoulder. "From the house."

The man doesn't answer for a while. Then he calls into the house. "Fatima."

The woman appears at the door with one hand shading her eyes. Then she comes forward wiping her hands on her veil and stands beside the man. She has recognised Mikal.

"Have you just come from the house?" the man asks.

"Yes, I spent the night there."

The woman gasps.

They tell him about the ten-hour firefight. The army cordoning off a zone around the house. The assault included paramilitary forces from the Frontier Corps and Waziristan Scouts. This was Pakistan's first ever operation against al-Qaeda and the Taliban, under pressure from America. Members of the security forces as well as Chechen, Uzbek and Arab militants were killed. Many foreigners fled into the desert and the hills.

"All this was three nights ago," the woman says. "No one has gone there since."

"So you don't know where everyone is. Akbar's brother . . . and sister."

They both shake their heads and since there is nothing else to say he turns to go.

"Come back for lunch," the woman says.

"Thank you, I will," he says.

"Will you bring my rosary? It has green and white beads and is hanging on a nail near the—"

"I have seen it."

Arriving back he undoes the catch and opens the steel chest to see that the money is still there. He stands looking at it, his fingertips playing with Naheed's chain at his neck.

Half an hour later he is on the narrow path that leads to the yellow flowers. He walks through the field and on towards the hills. The western face of the range is composed of thick beds of Miocene rock, dipping west. On the eastern aspect several rocks of older formations appear under the Miocene and form a bold escarpment of white stone, which has given its name to the range. He climbs to the site where Akbar's father had died in the crashed pickup. Thin beds of lignite, of Jurassic limestone, and nothing but sections of broken glass and green flakes on the boulder where the paintwork had scraped against it.

"You son of a bitch," someone says behind him quietly.

He turns to see him squatting on the ground ten yards away. The man Salomi was betrothed to, the man he had met in the room with the boxes of books and other texts.

"What are you doing here?" the man asks.

"I could ask you the same question."

"Are you alone?" The man looks around. He brings his eyes back to Mikal and puts his AK-47 over his shoulder and stands up. He wears the same shalwar kameez he was wearing the day Mikal saw him last, now filthy with dust and grime.

"How much money do you have?"

"Just a few rupees," Mikal says.

"You son of a bitch."

He will give the dollars either to Akbar's brother or to Salomi, not him.

"What are you doing out here?" the man asks.

"I am looking for one of the Airedales. It ran away."

"Where have you been for the past several days?"

"I should leave," Mikal says and turns around.

"I asked you where have you been."

"I had to go away for a while."

"Just before the raid took place."

"What are you trying to say?"

The man spits in the dust. "I want the rupees in your pockets."

"I need them myself."

The man lifts the rifle. "I wasn't asking."

Mikal takes out the money and the man gestures for it to be dropped. "Where is the bag with the American money Akbar gave you?"

"It's at the house."

"Bring it here tonight."

"Are Akbar's brother and sister here too, hiding with you?"

"What concern is that of yours?" The man holds a pointed silence, then adds, "I saw the dog." He gestures towards a boulder ten yards away. Mikal walks up to it but there is nothing there. He rounds the curve and after a while he comes back. "That's a jackal."

"I know. The dog killed it."

"Couldn't you have warned me before sending me over there?"

The man doesn't say anything, his eyes half closed against the glare of the sun. "Be here with the money at midnight."

When he arrives for lunch he tells them he'll be leaving tomorrow. And also that he would like to leave a bag with them, to be given to Akbar or any member of his family should they return. The couple tell him that a friend stopped by an hour ago and brought some news.

"Someone saw Salomi in the hills," the man says.

"Whereabouts?"

"It wasn't Salomi," the woman says. "It was her ghost. Her ghost was seen."

"Fatima," the man says in consternation.

"Let me tell him," she says. "He fought in a war. No one believes in ghosts more than soldiers."

"It's nothing but talk," her husband says to Mikal. "Salomi has either been captured by the Americans, or she has gone away with the al-Qaeda people and joined the jihad. A woman's anonymity is an asset to those people. She could deliver messages in her burka."

· · ·

Since he is now without rupees he will take a few dollars out of the bag and exchange them in the bazaar in Megiddo. Going there is a risk but there is no alternative. He'll also find a telephone there and talk to Naheed, tell her that he will begin the return journey tomorrow.

He falls asleep in Akbar's room, using the pillow that is embroidered with verses of the Koran, meant to banish nightmares. Waking after sundown he opens the steel chest and sees that the bag is missing.

He is instantly desperate.

He examines the floor for blood and looks at the opposite wall for a possible bullet scar, sniffs the pistol within the chest to see if it has fired. He even goes back to Akbar's wardrobe where he had originally concealed the bag, and pulls out the clothes in severe dismay, separating them one by one, and then looks under the bed and behind the armchair. In the yellow light from the lantern in his hand he feels himself being watched.

From the gun factory he takes a hammer, a pair of wire-cutters, a flathead screwdriver and a crosshead screwdriver and walks towards the car whose side-view mirror he tore off last night. He smashes the window and gets in and pounds the flathead screwdriver into the ignition and turns it like a key but the car remains dead. He unscrews the panels of the steering column to expose the wires running inside it, letting the freed screws fall onto the floor. Cutting the red wires, he strips their ends and connects them by twisting them together. Then he cuts the starter wires: he touches the exposed ends and there are five blue sparks of varying sizes and a sputter and the vehicle comes to life. Lastly he unlocks the steering by jamming the flathead screwdriver in the slot between the top of the steering column and the wheel.

Past caring, he drives out of the front gate, which he hasn't approached since he arrived.

He travels haphazardly into the hills and then into the surrounding desert, the darkness so complete his eyes hurt as they try to see, a darkness resembling the black room in the American prison. Eventually the moon coins out and its light stretches in a white haze on the curves and plains of the desert. One by one the hills to the west offer their slopes to the moon in a pale glowing union, rising up out of the shadows.

At midnight he returns to where he was supposed to bring the dollars but no one meets him and now he begins to shout the man's name in all directions. He stands listening—nothing but wind and windborne echoes—and time no longer feels human to him, stretching and contracting, as unsettled as liquid. One a.m. and he is searching for her and her ghost and for the bag with the dollars and talking to himself, standing on the broken land at the edge of the desert, a flashlight in his right hand, remembering a story about a soldier who enters a night forest where the spirit of his dead lover is said to roam, transformed into a rapacious beast.

At the house he picks up the dead telephone and dials his parents' number in Heer, remembering it from the days of his childhood, and stands listening in the darkness, imagining the faraway painted room. Then he dials Rohan's house and talks to Naheed for almost an hour.

Two mock suns rise with the real sun, one on either side. His body a wreckage after only an hour's sleep, he opens his eyes and in a half-awakened state watches his hands on the bedsheet, the missing fingers making him think for a moment he's disappearing slowly. He sits up in alarm.

He walks to the steel chest but the money is still missing, and he wonders with stabs of shame and bafflement if the cook and her husband have stolen it.

The husband is on the veranda when Mikal arrives, reading the same newspaper as the first time he visited, newspapers being difficult to obtain in Waziristan. "Have you come to say goodbye?"

He shakes his head.

"I thought you said you were leaving today."

He stands there without words and says after a while, "I need to find some work to earn the fare back. I think I'll go into Megiddo."

"How much do you need? We can give it to you."

"Thank you, uncle, but I'd rather earn it." He can see that they are anything but wealthy.

"You could run an errand for me," the man says. "It'll save me a trip. You need to deliver some scrap metal to Sara. It's a small town about thirty-five miles—"

"I know it. Akbar mentioned it once."

"I'll give you directions. You take my pickup with the metal loaded onto the back. It should take about three hours to get there. Three hours back."

"I can do that. I need to get a little more sleep first."

"You can leave after lunch. You'll be able to get back before sunset. I wouldn't advise you to be out there after nightfall." The man folds the newspaper, his fingers full of ink. "This just sums it up," he says. "You have to wash your hands after reading this country's newspaper."

Mikal looks at the pages. To see if there's any news of Father Mede. But the country has moved on to other crises. *Carnage at the US Consulate in Karachi* is the headline in three-inch-tall letters. A truck with a fertiliser bomb, being driven by a suicide bomber, was detonated outside the building, killing twelve people and injuring fifty-one—all Pakistanis.

Enraged Mob Beats Suspected Thief to Death . . .

Illegal Pakistani Migrants Drown Off Italian Coast . . .

Senator Defends Burying Alive of Women Who Dishonour Their Menfolk . . .

"We levelled it," US Army Major General Franklin Hegenbeck said, *speaking of the destruction of three villages in the Shaikot Valley in Afghanistan. "There was nobody left, just dirt and dust." . . .*

He puts down the newspaper and watches the river sparkling under the three suns. This time tomorrow I'll be on my way towards Heer, he thinks.

"It's a bad omen," the man says, of the sun and the two sundogs. Going through a grove of pomegranate and henna trees, he is leading Mikal to the back of the house. Mikal enters a wooden shed and finds himself looking at a mass of chains piled up as high as his waist. This is the metal he has to transport.

He approaches silently and drops to his haunches before the heap, touching it gently.

"What's wrong?" the man asks from the shed door.

Mikal shakes his head, snatches of memory flowing through him.

"They belonged to a mendicant who wandered all over the place," the man says.

"I know," Mikal says after a while. He lifts the hoops that had attached the chains to the man's wrists. There is the hoop for the neck. "Where did you get them? Where is the fakir?"

"He was found dead by the roadside."

Mikal stands up, letting the strands fall from his fingers, and looks at the man with distress.

"The first time I ran away from home was to meet him. I followed his trail in the dust but couldn't catch up."

"Well. Now you have found him. Or some of him. He appeared in the bazaar here and the al-Qaeda Arabs became enraged and abused him. Saying how dare he pretend to intercede with Allah on Muslims' behalf. They beat him but people intervened, knowing how pious he was, but the next day the body was discovered."

"He wouldn't have been able to run," Mikal says under his breath. Bullet cartridges are caught in the links of the chains like little gold fish in a net.

"No. The chains were so heavy and so long he was having to drag them along with both hands. They trailed behind him for several yards. Some say he just vanished from inside the chains. They were the only thing that fell to the ground."

"I thought he was my father."

They drag the coils out through the trees to the pickup. He drops the vehicle's tailgate and climbs up onto the bed and pulls a fistful of the chains after him and the man begins to feed the rest to him very fast as Mikal walks backwards along the bed.

He was seen in Mecca once, never having left Pakistan physically, and several times he was seen in various parts of Pakistan simultaneously.

"Fatima is reading a chapter of the Koran to comfort his soul," the man says, a little out of breath, once the chains are up on the bed and Mikal has jumped down. "When she finishes she'll make us breakfast. There is only one town between here and Sara. It's called Allah-Vasi. And that is where Fatima's sister lives. She might want to go with you.

You can drop her off, move on to Sara, and then pick her up on the way back."

The sun and the sundogs follow the pickup across the sky, as he travels through open desert, an expanse of nothingness with low hills in the distance. There is not much traffic on the road but he examines each vehicle that passes him, in case someone is following him. Hasn't he seen that man on the motorcycle before? He is half an hour from Sara when a loud screeching noise causes him to pull over. He gets out and opens the bonnet to see the shredded auxiliary belt. What remains of it is hanging off the alternator pulley, fouling the timing-belt cover, and a diesel injector feed pipe has become disconnected, spilling liquid.

He looks at the thin road, the rocks and boulders giving off heat like mirrors. An hour passes and nobody comes along and he sits on the driver's seat with the door open, his legs hanging out, watching the dust djinns spinning across the desert floor, the interior smelling of the foodstuffs Fatima had brought as a gift for her family in several jars and baskets. He is sure the mendicant's chains are hot to the touch.

It is another hour before a truck appears in the distance, the driver agreeing to tow him to the nearest mechanic's shop, telling him during the journey that his cousin died fighting in Afghanistan last autumn and that his brother is in American custody in Cuba.

But by half past six in the evening the mechanics have still not finished with the repairs. Mikal realises he won't be able to leave for Heer tomorrow morning: he'll probably have to spend the night at Fatima's sister's house in Allah-Vasi after delivering the chains.

From the pickup he takes out the two empty bottles of Nestlé mineral water and fills them from the tap. "Can I make a call?" he asks the owner of the mechanic's shop, pointing to the grime-coated telephone sitting inside a cage meant for a bird. The little door has a padlock on it to prevent just anyone from using the instrument. "I'll pay for it." Fatima's husband has given him a few rupees for tea and a meal on the road.

Naheed answers on the fifth ring.

"Are you on your way back?" she asks.

"I was hoping to leave tomorrow morning and be in Heer late the day after tomorrow. But now it looks difficult."

Nothing from her. And he knows something is terribly wrong.

"What is it?" he says.

"Sharif Sharif wants to marry me."

"I know that."

"He wants to marry me as soon as possible. This week. In a few days. Just a quick ceremony with a cleric and two witnesses."

"How did this happen?"

"Father went to see him, to tell him that my agreement with him didn't mean anything, and he became enraged. He is demanding what is his."

"He can't marry you forcibly."

"He seems to think so. And Mother doesn't wish to get the police involved."

"I am coming."

"Father says he will not accept a single rupee from me if I marry him. He says, 'I don't want my eyes and I don't want to have a home if it'll come at the expense of your happiness. I'd rather be a homeless blind beggar.'"

"I am coming."

He hangs up and stands there in a daze for a few moments. The mechanic comes and tells him the pickup is ready. So happy is the man with his patching job that he asks Mikal's permission to sign the engine with a screwdriver.

Dusk will fall soon after seven. It's six fifty when Mikal sets off towards Sara to deliver the chains. The sinking of the sun dissolves all hardness from the landscape, the mineral brilliance of the hills increasing for a short period. In the setting sun he watches a cloud as white as snow, a bright scarlet cloud, a green cloud edged with yellow like a dying leaf, a pale blue and a bronze cloud. But soon the sky above him is deep blue and the stars have appeared. He leaves the road that winds between the hills and begins to guide himself by the constellations through the open desert, hoping to travel in a straight line. In a hurry to drop off the chains.

Within half an hour the desert has surrendered itself completely to darkness. When he sees the shape lying on the ground ahead, he applies the brakes with as much force as he can, the tyres screeching on the gypsum and sun-split shale. He waits for the dust raised in front of the windscreen to settle, the beams of the headlights boring into it, and then sits looking out, suspended at the very edge of his senses, his heart thumping. After a while he gets out. He stands motionless beside the vehicle's open door and then moves closer to one of the headlights, to be clearly visible. He undoes the buttons at his neck and wrists and takes off his shirt very slowly, performing each action emphatically. Remembering Tara's words about encountering djinns.

He throws the shirt sideways. Peeling off his skin.

He crouches and takes off his shoes and steps out of them and, again very clearly, kicks them aside.

Then he steps out of his trousers and throws them away from himself too.

Stars are falling across the expanse of the sky above him, innumerable and random, and, naked, wearing nothing but Naheed's necklace, he moves forwards with great deliberation. The headlights are reaching the figure lying on the ground and he is halfway there when he sees that it is a white man, sees the face. His pale skin and yellow-gold hair brilliant in the headlights. He is lying on his side, unconscious or dead, eyes closed and the right arm bloody.

Mikal stands still, breathing silently, and is about to take a step towards him when there is a movement in one of the hands.

He backs away and rushes towards the pickup, almost at a run. Collecting his clothes he begins to dress as fast as he can, looking around. If there is one there could be more. He glances up at the sky for Chinook helicopters and for fighter jets, a coursing of adrenalin in his veins. Someone will soon appear out of the darkness, he knows. He climbs into the pickup, wishing only to be out of there as quickly as possible, but just as the headlights swing away from the American soldier the snow leopard cub raises its head from behind the man's shoulder.

Carefully he brings the headlights back onto the white man, the daunting impenetrability of the face, onto the snow leopard's glowing eyes. The markings on the fur look as though the creature is in khaki camouflage.

He climbs out and calls to it but it doesn't come, the head turned sideways as it stares into the night with eyes full of a green and ancient calm. Watchfully Mikal draws near and with his arm at full stretch lifts it by the scruff of its neck, noticing the small increase in heaviness from the last time he picked it up. How many days ago? He runs his eyes onto the white man's body, the khaki shalwar kameez he is wearing. He walks around him in a wide circle unable to comprehend fully what he is seeing. He is much bigger than Mikal and looks to be five or six years older, though Mikal doesn't know how good he is at judging a white person's age. Moving closer, he places his hand on the chest to feel for the heartbeat but he's wearing a bullet-proof vest under the kameez. Mikal checks the pulse instead. The right arm is bleeding, the upper bone broken above the elbow, and the blood is warm on Mikal's fingers.

He looks for weapons. There is a folding-stock AK-47 slung over the shoulder and a 9 mm pistol strapped to the right thigh in a holster. There is another pistol in the small of his back. In the flank pocket of the kameez he finds two hundred dollars and a set of cards with English writing on them. There is a "blood chit" to be used in case of capture—it's in Pashto and English, and offers a cash reward to anyone who gives assistance to an American soldier in distress. Next he opens the man's rucksack and finds a spare magazine for the AK-47, enough Meals, Ready-to-Eat for five days, a water bottle and water purification tablets. Small heavy cans with pictures of cats on them. He checks for a lap-top computer. He extracts the large satellite phone from its holster and smashes it under his heels and then pulverises it completely with a rock.

The man is bull-necked and his body is hard, containing muscles full of health in every place. Hands like a stonemason's. He must be either a Special Forces soldier or a CIA paramilitary officer, thinks Mikal. He looks for a digital camera like the one on which they had shown him pictures of the women, after his capture at the mosque back in January, but there isn't one.

He looks at the dizzying height of the constellations and the stars, the thin millions of them stretching as far as the eye can see, southwards, northwards, eastwards, westwards, and he looks around the flat desert with its iron ore that is smelted by the Waziri tribes, the stone hills and the coralline beds and the waiting world. No sound except the pickup's idling engine. He takes the rucksack and the guns and puts them in the footwell on the passenger's side, placing the cub on the passenger seat itself. Getting behind the steering wheel, he swings the pickup around and puts it in reverse, backing it slowly towards the soldier, using his own footprints running from under the pickup to steer by. He stops when he is just a yard or so away from where the American lies. He alights to examine the distance and then gets back in and carefully reverses again until he is only half a yard from the soldier.

He gets out and stands looking at the face taking a dim red glow from the taillights. He looks at the bed of the pickup. The chains look like the heaped entrails of a slaughtered metal beast. Some of the links are covered in rust, prayers that have gone unanswered for decades. He drops the tailgate and begins the process of lifting the man up onto the bed. At first he braces himself and tries to lift the soldier the obvious way, with one arm under his knees, the other under his armpits, careful of balance and with fine elastic adjustments of his body—but he is too heavy. Out of breath, his sides caving in and out, he props the man in a sitting position against the tailgate, the legs sticking out like a doll's, and climbs up onto the bed and leans down and hooks his hands under the armpits. He doesn't know what he'll do if the man regains consciousness. Gathering all his strength into his arms he begins to pull the man up in swift and single-purposed hauls, unerring and untiring. Most of all he doesn't wish to jostle the injuries too much, in case the pain brings the body out of sleep. He is sweating by the time he has transferred the man onto the bed. He lies stretched out beside him like a sibling, noisily sucking in the night air, the dead weight of the white man's arm thrown over his stomach. Finally he rises, pulling free the looseness of his shirt caught under the American. The flashlight held in his teeth, a beam of radiance shooting from his mouth, he begins to separate the loops of the chains, identifying the neck, ankle and wrist rings. One bracelet is lying at the top of the heap of chains but he can't find the other and has to send his arm deep into the tangled loops. He fastens the neck hoop around the man's throat, removing the key once the lock clicks shut. He puts one of the wrist bands on the good wrist. The pickup's bed is ten feet long and six wide, and above the bed is a six-foot-tall rectangular framework of pipes, for a tarpaulin cover to be draped and fitted over it. He passes several chains through the base of the pipe frame on either side of the American, so that he is secured to the pickup's body. He will be able to manoeuvre himself into a sitting position but will not be able to stand up.

He climbs down.

He is sure he is being watched but he can see no one in the featureless night. He walks around to the front and takes out a bottle of water and returns and climbs back onto the bed. As he uncaps the bottle he rehearses out loud the question he will put to the man, preparing his voice for the venture. "Vere iz gurl? Vere iz gurl? Vere iz gurl?"

Moving closer to him he takes the man's head in one arm, the dust-covered face turned up, and gently opens the mouth and eases the two rows of teeth apart, feeling his breath on his fingers, and begins to pour in a thin strand of water. The swallowing function is asleep and the mouth fills up to the brim and the water slides out from the corners. Then it catches the back of the throat, a column of bubbles rising through the water that fills the mouth, and the alarmed mind wakes the body. The man splutters and then opens his eyes, struggling powerfully as he tries to sit up. He blinks in the light of the torch in Mikal's teeth. Mikal leaps away and the water drips from the bottle onto the bed of the pickup with a musical ringing. A loud half groan, half roar escapes the man as he feels the pain of his injury but even then he is so strong that his pulling at the chains can make the pickup rock slightly, twisting in confusion and then anger. It's as though above his shouting mouth his eyes are shouting too, contributing to the sound. Mikal fears the soldering of the pipe frame will give, tearing it off the sides of the bed. And he hasn't looked at Mikal beyond the initial eye contact. Mikal thought there was no need to secure the injured arm and the man tries more than once to lift it—failing and giving out an agonised bellow through gritted teeth each time.

Mikal stands at the tailgate, his torch shining into the man's golden hair and the face glistening wet where water has washed away the dust. The eyes are green with splinters of brown in them.

"Vere iz gurl?" he says after a while.

The man has stopped struggling and sits gasping, the half ton of chains shifting around his muscles, but Mikal's question remains unanswered.

Mikal looks at the sky. It's almost nine o'clock and he is drenched in sweat. He knows some of these soldiers understand Urdu and Pashto, so he puts the question to him in both those languages, but to no avail. He climbs down and goes to the passenger seat and returns with the leopard cub. Standing at the tailgate he holds the cub out towards the man and says, "Vere hiz gurl?"

The American doesn't look at him, examining the chains and the pipe frame intently. Mikal might as well not be here.

The stars move in the hot desert air and have a look of completeness to them, in comparison to the materials scattered about him here on earth, unassembled. When he sends the beam of the flashlight into the darkness the hills look like petrified clouds, ledges of hardened vapour.

The leopard calls out and he notices that its whistle has deepened from a songbird to an eagle. He sees the soldier lick water from his lips but when he moves forward with the bottle the man begins to struggle again, the eyes that needle and dare and challenge and threaten him.

Mikal gets back into the pickup, and with the heavy softness of the cub in his lap he begins to drive. "What have they been feeding you?" he says, stroking the fur on the leopard's head with one hand after they have been driving for five minutes, his breathing and heartbeat settling at last, the air from the window drying his clothes and skin. "Didn't take you very long to become friendly with him, I see . . ." He is still astonished at the power the animal's eyes have over him, the gaze captivating within an instant, a radiant dreamlike effect on his mind. And then he begins to talk to it in a constant stream. "Are you going to say something to me? It's probably beneath you to consort with someone like me these days. You've probably forgotten your own language by now, haven't you? . . ." As he drives he switches on the flashlight for a few moments to look through the glass window located behind his head. The soldier sits facing the other way and doesn't react to the light that falls onto his shoulder. The chains won't allow him to reach the glass of the window. "Don't worry," Mikal tells the cub. "I am not going to hurt your new friend. I noticed there was a school next to Fatima's sister's house. One of the teachers will probably know English. That's where I am taking him."

Raising dust, the pickup moves through the night. A flock of ghostly storks crosses his vision at one point with light pulsing on their wings as on a river, their throats rippling with language that he hears over the engine, the voices whipping the black air. He is moving through wild terrain and during one long stretch between two endless hills it seems as if he is standing still. Every now and then he drives onto the road, the tar melted from the day's heat, then drives back onto rough ground—travelling in a straight line as much as possible. Around ten thirty he sees a roadside mosque half a mile ahead, a single lightbulb shining over its door. In all probability it will be deserted at this hour and he will drive past but still he wishes he had a tarpaulin to put over the framework. Just as he approaches the mosque he looks back and sees that the American is slumped over. He brakes and gets out and runs to the back. The eyes are closed. He climbs onto the bed and moves forwards, ready to feel the pulse, to push aside the chains and thrust his hand under the Kevlar armour and check for the heartbeat, but the man stirs and sits upright.

Mikal backs away. The inscription on the mosque's lintel reads, *I have no refuge in the world other than Thy threshold, there is no protection for my head other than this door.* Just then a bearded man appears at the mosque entrance, holding an ablution pot in his right hand. The door is green as is the dome on the roof, the same colour as the pickup. The cleric approaches but stops when he sees the man in chains, dumbstruck.

"I thought he'd fainted," Mikal says.

"That's a white man."

"Yes."

"What are you up to?"

"I found him in the desert."

"Is he a soldier? An American?"

"I think so. His arm is broken. I am taking him to Allah-Vasi. I didn't think anyone would be up at this hour in the mosque."

"I am performing an overnight reading of the Koran. Just came out to get some water."

"You don't know anyone who speaks English, do you?"

"No." It's probably the truth, though people have been beaten for knowing English, suspected of being American informers. "Why are you taking him to Allah-Vasi?"

"I am hoping to find someone who speaks English there. He can ask the American if he knows anything about my friend and his family."

The cleric's face conceals nothing, a soul with no secrets, and he says, "I have never seen a real white person. During the First World War they were here. They used biplanes to drop bombs on us. The planes were considered a cowardice. Killing while being out of reach." Then he says, "If anyone sees him do you know what will happen?"

"I am hoping to drive through the darkness."

"He had something to do with the disappearance of your friend?"

"I don't know. I think so."

"If someone sees him they'll cut off his head . . . and yours too probably, for not doing it yourself. Did you say his arm is broken?"

"Do you know how to set bones?" Jeo would have, he thinks with a pang.

"Yes. But we shouldn't stand here on the road. I don't want to be seen tending to an American out in the open. They'll shoot me too. I know people who don't want to even look at a picture of them." The man turns to go back into the mosque. "Bring your vehicle to the back of the building. I'll see if I can find some splints."

"And I would appreciate it if you could let me have an old sheet to cover him during the journey to Allah-Vasi. A burlap sack or something."

Mikal brings the pickup to the back of the building to a dry river bed or a torrent that drains the hills in the rainy season, its limestone pebbles containing fossils. And the desert beyond is a dark wasteland of silence. With the water bottle he climbs up, holding it out as he moves forwards a step at a time. He unscrews the sky-blue cap with his teeth. The man is still. Mikal crouches and puts the bottle to the man's mouth and begins slowly to pour water into his mouth. The eyes have stopped moving, trained firmly on Mikal. Then he begins to swallow. When the bottle is empty Mikal steps away and the man watches him, breathing deeply.

Some minutes later, the bearded man emerges from the mosque with a sheet, a fistful of wooden splints and strips of torn cloth to be used as binding. He hands Mikal the sheet and he opens it to see that it's large enough to cover the soldier.

"He'll struggle while we set the arm but he won't be able to free himself," Mikal tells the cleric.

"Look at the size of his hands. If he gets loose he'll snap your neck like a twig."

"Why are you doing the all-night reading of the Koran? Has something happened?"

"My son is a cleric at a mosque not far away. He says the door to his mosque refused to open yesterday, not allowing anyone in. Allah is expressing His anger over some matter. Someone has committed an unconscionable deed in the vicinity and until he is forgiven the door won't open." The man has tears in his eyes and he slowly wipes them away with his hands, ancient fingers doing ancient work. "It's a catastrophe. No one knows what crime or sin lies behind the prohibition."

The moment Mikal and the bearded man climb onto the bed, the American begins to struggle against his chains, thrashing inside the coils. The cleric stops fearfully but Mikal moves forward to demonstrate that the American has been rendered harmless by the chains. He rolls up the sleeve of the broken arm and the bearded man feels for the fractures. The American has not stopped growling with anger, the features of the face contorted in Mikal's flashlight with spit seething between the lips. To inspect the shoulder bones for signs of harm, the old man loosens the collar of the American's kameez and unfastens the front of the Kevlar vest. He is looking down the back, feeling with his fingertips, when he suddenly cries out in horror. "Allah, I seek refuge in You!" When Mikal looks at the man's back he too cannot help but catch his breath. There is a large tattoo on the skin:

The word covers the entire space between the shoulder blades, and they stand looking at it, the American continuing to struggle. It says "Infidel."

But it is not in English, which would have meant that he had had it done for himself, or for others like him in his own country. It is in the Urdu and Pashto script so it is meant for people here. He is taunting. Boasting. I am proud to be an infidel, to be this thing you hate.

The cleric throws the splints away into the darkness. "Get him out of my sight."

"Please don't tell anyone."

"Get that beast away from here." The man climbs down off the bed, shaking with rage. "They want to wound not only our flesh but our very souls."

Mikal turns away rather than endure the man's eyes. "I'll leave. I'll leave. Right this instant. But please don't tell anyone."

When he is behind the steering wheel the old man comes to his window and stands looking at him, as if looking for an answer. There is a confused pity in the cleric's eyes too—why has the white man condemned himself in such a manner, daring to mark himself with the sign of His disapproval? Just before Mikal drives away the man says, "The West has dared to ask itself the question, *What begins after God?*"

Midnight, and he is moving through the hills with his eyes on a storm to the east, troubled flashes of brightness in the black sky, the dark shapes of the Pahari hills becoming visible for a moment and then disappearing and then the sound of thunder reaches him, strokes of lightning as fragile as filaments in a bulb. He enters a low pass in the westernmost spur of the Paharis and continues into the open desert. Once he sees the lights of an oncoming truck in the distance where the road cuts through the night. Half an hour later he passes through the last low cones of hills on that ground cracked like clay and after another half hour they are on the outskirts of Allah-Vasi. Before entering the town he gets out and covers the American with the cleric's sheet. He removes the 9 mm pistol from the rucksack and conceals it in the waistband of his trousers. But then, feeling loath, he puts it back in the rucksack.

Running east to west, a street turns off at right angles to the main road, descending and becoming a wide earthen path, and he drives along it towards where Fatima's sister lives. It's almost 1 a.m. As he drives on slowly the dead silence of the night is broken by the roused dogs in various houses. He continues eastward until he recognises the door at which he had dropped off Fatima and he cuts the engine and sits looking at the house, the dogs continuing their din. He studies the school building next door, the arch above the gate carrying a saying of the Prophet. *Seek knowledge. Even if you have to travel to China.* He pushes the American's rucksack deep under the passenger seat and gets out and makes sure the soldier is still covered with the bedsheet and then knocks on the large door to the house.

As he waits he puts the 9 mm back under his waistband.

It's several minutes before someone answers from the other side of the door, asking curt, suspicious questions, and he identifies himself and eventually they let him in. The man of the house, Fatima's brother-in-law, is holding a deer rifle and with him is his son, a young man a few years older than Mikal. Anxious to go back to sleep the son walks away immediately, leaving the father to deal with the inconsiderate, untimely guest. The father tells Mikal to bring the van in through the door and park it at the edge of the courtyard.

Mikal gets out holding the snow leopard and—looking around him, letting a breath go—says to the father who has just finished securing the door, "Uncle, I need to tell you something." The dogs in the neighbouring houses are still barking. Taking the man to the back of the pickup he pulls away the sheet in one swift movement to reveal the American sitting bowed in the mass of chains. Before the man can say anything there is a great howling from behind them, and when Mikal turns he sees that the son and five or six other young men are coming across the courtyard at great speed.

"No, no, no, no," Mikal says under his breath.

He places his left hand on the low wall that encloses the pickup's bed and vaults onto the bed, the cub held in the other hand. Reaching under his shirt he snatches the pistol from his waistband and kneels in front of the American, facing the oncoming men. The father has raised his hands to stay his son. Mikal looks over his shoulder to see that the American is sitting stock still behind him but with his eyes lit up intensely. The father moves towards his son who stops a yard away from him, and the other young men stop behind him. The father is physically a giant and has parental authority over the boy, but then suddenly the son lunges towards the pickup, scrabbling in the dirt of the courtyard, and in the skirmish Mikal hears the tearing of a shirt and he keeps the arm with the pistol fully extended, wondering if he would be able to pull the trigger, and then he notices that one of the other young men has gone around the pickup and is moving towards the American from that direction. There is nothing else for Mikal to do but fall back onto the American, to keep everything in sight, their two heads almost touching, feeling the mendicant's chains dig in his back, swinging the gun first in one direction and then the other. Shouts and glaring eyes and a spiralling pandemonium.

They have encircled the pickup, and Mikal is leaning hard against the American, for now unmindful of the broken arm, the 9 mm keeping them at bay, trembling electrically with fear and his heart hammering. A wooden pole has appeared in someone's hand and an attempt is being made to snag a loop of the chain with it.

The son has a large fixed-blade knife with a clip point and he swings it at Mikal and Mikal turns and catches him richly on the side of the head with the butt of the pistol. Some of the young men are servants or retainers of the family and although they circle and snarl they cannot go against the master's wishes. But the others are on full attack so they must be cousins within the family.

Two other elderly men have appeared from the house. They call the young men by name and those who have been called stop and look back. The master of the house is still struggling with his son, who has half climbed over the side of the pickup, breathing heavily, his face distorted and mouth slobbering as the father puts him in an armlock. He pulls him off and stands holding him, the knife flashing in the hand.

"O Allah!" says the father. "O Allah, I seek refuge in You!"

With hands raised threateningly and other displays of rage and authority, the two elderly men have subdued the cousins. The father pushes the son away from the pickup. "I want you to control yourself," he says.

"All right."

"All right *what*? All right, you dog? All right, you wretch?"

"All right, Father."

The man stands with his hands on his hips, catching his breath. Then he turns to Mikal. "Start talking, boy."

"I was hoping to spend the night here before moving on."

"You just thought I would let you do that with him sitting in the back?"

"I was about to tell you everything, but then they came and wanted to start a war."

"What did you think would happen when someone saw him?"

"I didn't know what else to do, uncle."

"What do you mean start a war?" the son shouts. "We are already at war."

"I know that."

"They killed my brother last November." The son points at the American with the knife.

"If you know we are at war," says the father, "tell me what you are doing with that man?"

"I discovered him in the desert. I would have left him there but then I saw that he had the snow leopard. The cub belonged to Akbar's sister." He gestures towards the house. "The people Aunt Fatima works for. So this man has probably been into Akbar's house in Megiddo. I need to find someone who can ask him a few things."

The man considers the information. Behind him the younger men are pacing, their jaws working with wrath.

The man turns to them. "Everyone go back to the house. Ghulam, make sure no one leaves the house. *No one.*"

Turning back to Mikal he says, "Nobody here speaks English."

"I thought one of the teachers at the school might."

The man thinks for a few moments. "You're right. One of them can."

Only now does Mikal realise that he is still leaning against the American. He pulls away and stands up and climbs off the bed.

"The English-speaking teacher lives on the other side of town. Someone could go and bring her here," the man says, "but I don't think it can be done right now."

"No." Mikal nods in agreement.

"We have to wait until morning. I'd rather not go knocking on people's doors in the middle of the night. Anyway she won't want to come at this time. Her family will want to know where we want to take her."

"If word got out she'd spoken to an American who knows what might happen to her." Mikal looks at the man. "I am sorry for involving you in this."

"If word gets out I had an American in my house who knows what will happen to me? And to the rest of my family. The whole town is full of Taliban and al-Qaeda."

"I am sorry. Maybe I should leave right now."

"Why would you think I meant that?" the man says. "You're here now. We need to work out what to do next. I think we should wait until morning, and when it's time for the school to start, the teacher will arrive and we can bring her here without anyone knowing."

"I won't be able to leave here till well into the morning?"

"It seems that way."

"I have to go back to Heer as soon as possible."

"Where is that?"

"It's the place I am from. In Punjab."

"Call them in the morning and tell them you'll be late. And what are you going to do with the American once he has answered your questions?"

"I haven't thought that far ahead." Mikal leans against the pickup door.

The man's eyes examine him closely. "When was the last time you ate?"

"I am just tired."

"I'll wake the women, if they aren't already up. Come in and they'll feed you. Just listen to those dogs."

"Uncle, his arm is broken."

The man stands looking at the American. "I'll get Ghulam to set it. You come in."

"I think we should feed him too."

"What does he eat? We don't have anything special."

"I have food for him."

He takes out the rucksack and looks at the MREs. Unzipping a small pocket in the rucksack's lining he takes out the blood chit and unfolds it. There is a phone number. He stands looking at it and then puts it back in the pocket and turns around to face the man. "I'll stay out here with him. I don't want to leave him on his own." He thinks of the son's thick steel knife, the broad six-inch blade. It must be a fighting weapon because a strip of brass is inlaid at its back to catch an opponent's blade, an upper guard that bends forward to provide protection to the owner's hand during parries.

"We'll put him in the garage at the back of the house and lock the garage door," the man says. "You come and eat and afterwards you can feed him."

"He had the cub?" Fatima asks. She and her sister are awake, preparing a meal for him. Mutton and peas are being heated in a pan. She spoons it onto a plate. He hears men's voices from the other side of the wall, raised in argument as Fatima brings him a chapatti in a chintz cloth.

"Yes."

"He must know what happened at the house."

He nods and she goes back to the stove. "His fellow soldiers are probably looking for him," she says. "Do you think they could track you here?"

"I don't know."

"The leopard's grown a little," she says.

"He has, hasn't he."

"Are you sure it's the same one?"

"I checked. The dark spot on the inside of the left ear."

As he begins to eat Fatima's sister asks, "Will you let the American go eventually?"

"There is a contact number in his rucksack," Mikal says.

"I don't want American soldiers near my home," the sister says. "They have killed one of my sons already."

"I'll call them when I am far away from here."

"I don't want you endangering my family," the woman says. "What if he brings other soldiers back here to arrest us and carry us all away?"

"It won't come to that. I'll take him far away from here, he won't be able to find his way back."

"For all we know they are following him right now," the woman says. "I'd go out there with the rifle right now if I thought his countrymen would invade my home to rescue him. They'll kill us all."

Mikal is sure that a similar discussion is taking place in the other room.

"I promise I won't involve you any further. And I am sorry about your son."

The woman suddenly hides her face behind her hands and begins to weep, her shoulders and head bowed. Mikal stops chewing. Shocked, he becomes still as he listens to her. And then—just as suddenly—she absorbs her grief back into herself and stands upright.

"How many chapattis will you eat?" she asks, her voice uneven.

"I have enough here."

Fatima looks at him and then touches her sister's back. "He'll need two more at least."

"It's not a problem."

"Thank you," Mikal says.

After he has eaten he goes out to the garage and sees that they have fitted a tarpaulin over the frame of the pickup's bed. The back is now perfectly enclosed. A box of tough taut cloth. In places it is as resistant to the touch as plywood.

He lifts the flap above the tailgate and looks in to see that a strip of black cloth has been tied over the white man's eyes. He opens the MRE with his teeth and sits down beside the soldier, mixing the chemicals in the sachets to heat up the sealed large piece of meat. Talking so he will know it's him, touching the food to the white man's lips until he opens his mouth. He tells the soldier he has eaten an American MRE in Peshawar where they were on sale for some reason, telling him how he has eaten shark meat on the edge of the Arabian Sea, a bird of prey, a butterfly.

"If you can understand what I am saying please answer me. I beg you."

The man of the house appears at the tailgate with a padlock and stands watching him.

When the MRE is finished he stands up and leaves and the man locks the garage.

"Is there another key?"

"No," the man says.

"You'll make sure no one gets out of the house during the night and informs the rest of the town?"

"It's a matter of our safety too," the man says. "We are just as concerned. Now go into the house and sleep. Fatima is making up a bed for you."

Jeo and Basie come to him while he is asleep. He wakes up sometime later unable to recall the details of the dream, lying there in the darkness of the room with his eyes open, and eventually he remembers that he had asked Jeo and Basie what it was like being dead. He struggles to recall the answer, and he is drifting back to sleep when a hand touches him in the darkness. He sits up just as a flashlight comes on in the room. It's one of the cousins, standing beside his bed.

"Would you sell him to us? I have been sent to ask you how much you'd take for him."

"He's not for sale."

"In cash."

"I said he's not for sale."

The boy looks at him and nods. "We thought we'd better ask."

"You have my answer."

"Are you sure?"

"Absolutely."

"Aunt Fatima said they had imprisoned and tortured you."

Mikal looks away.

"You should want to lick his blood. He's your enemy."

"Not like that, he's not."

"He'd do the same to you."

"Then that makes me better than him."

And with that he lies down again. "Now I want to go back to sleep. I have a long day ahead of me tomorrow."

The boy switches off the flashlight and Mikal hears him leave in the darkness. He gets up and bolts the door, looking out through the window and seeing the man of the house beside the garage door with the deer rifle. He tries to stay awake, his fear breeding images out of the dark, djinns and nightgrowths, but he falls asleep at some point. Either Jeo or Basie asks him if he is certain that he hadn't wanted to shoot the two Americans by the lake—wondering if he had killed them intentionally—but the questioner disappears before he can answer. When he wakes the sun has risen and it is six o'clock and he stands up immediately. He passes the son in the corridor. The mark of bitter thoughts is on his brow and he neither returns Mikal's greeting nor looks at him. There is a poppy bruise on the temple where Mikal's gun connected last night—it is either not serious or he has left it untreated because he doesn't wish to signal any weakness to Mikal. Almost everyone seems to be awake. Smells come from the kitchen, the women making parathas, churning lassi and frying eggs, murmuring as they work, it being too early to speak loudly, words disrupting the pure pleasure of living.

The main door of the house is still locked. The man is still there outside the garage, now with the snow leopard cub on his lap, the clear golden sunlight flickering on the pattern of the fur. The rifle leans against the chair.

Mikal walks out to him. The man puts a hand in his pocket and brings out shattered pieces of a satellite phone, large silver shards and fragments of broken plastic and torn sections of microcircuitry.

"We discovered this on him. In the shorts he wears under his shalwar."

"I didn't think to look there," Mikal says quietly.

"I thought it best to destroy it." The man throws the pieces on the ground before him and sits looking at them like a soothsayer reading the future in the pebbles he has scattered. "We have cleaned him," he says, "taken him to the bathroom."

"What?"

"Well, he soiled himself. So we had to change his clothes. He put up a great struggle."

"Give me the key."

"He's fine. Go in and eat."

"Give me the key, uncle."

"Go in and eat."

Mikal nods but doesn't move.

"I need to make a phone call," he tells the man eventually.

"I have hidden the phone in case someone tries to call out. I'll connect it for you after breakfast."

"Thank you." He imagines them at the house in Heer, the breeze and scents in the garden, the scratch of the broom as it sweeps fallen leaves from a red path. Naheed wiping the dew off the mirror above the outside sink, the flowers hanging overhead. *Before the science of botany was established just three hundred years ago,* he remembers Rohan telling him and Jeo when they were children, *flowers in their infinite variety and lack of human order were said to be proof of God's existence.*

The young men watch him from a distance, from various corners of the house, gathering in groups here and there and withdrawing, and he makes sure not to meet anyone's eye. As he eats Fatima tells him that the school will open at eight thirty and that the teachers should begin to arrive around eight.

At seven forty-five Fatima's sister puts on her burka and her husband unlocks the main door and she goes out to the school to position herself outside the gate, to wait for the arrival of the English-speaking teacher.

Mikal enters the garage and approaches the back of the pickup and lifts the tarpaulin flap. The soldier, blindfolded, senses someone's presence and moves his head. His arm is in plaster and is nestling in a triangular sling of white muslin that was once a flour sack. He is wearing a new set of shalwar kameez and there is a large saffron and black bruise on his forehead. Mikal feels he is watching him through the blindfold, perhaps through the round naked discolouration above the eyes. The street is just on the other side of the garage and from it comes the chatter of the schoolchildren arriving for a day of learning.

He hears the front door being opened and looks out of the garage to see Fatima's sister coming in with another, much slimmer figure. Her burka is tighter than the older woman's, with long clean lines, and she has a leather handbag slung over her shoulder and her feet make clicking noises he hasn't heard from the women in this house. Sturdy and purposeful, as opposed to the maternal and domestic shuffling that comes from the others. He watches them disappear towards the kitchen.

Five minutes later the man comes out to Mikal. "The girl knows English but refuses to speak to the American. She's too afraid. She says they'll cut off her tongue, or she'll be killed outright."

"Can't you persuade her?"

"We are trying."

"What happened to his forehead?"

"I told you. He struggled when we were cleaning him. Threw us around everywhere and got tangled up in the chains."

"I thought it might have something to do with what's written on his back."

"It isn't. But I'll tell you one thing. He'll pay for that piece of poetry if he is caught by someone out there."

The man goes back into the house and returns a few minutes later. "She's terrified. She is about to leave."

Mikal steps out of the garage to see the girl hurrying across the courtyard, sobbing loudly inside her black burka. He moves towards her with one arm extended and says, "Sister, listen—"

But she gives a squeal at his approach and he stops.

The father unlocks the door and just as the girl steps out two of the servants make a dash for it and leave the house, pushing the man aside. High-pitched screams and shouts come from outside as the two escaping men crash into children. The man of the house scrambles up and locks the door once again.

Everyone is stunned.

"They are afraid the Americans will raid the house and carry them off," says one of the other servants.

"They will tell everyone in the bazaar," the son says. "In half an hour every man in Allah-Vasi whose honour, faith and manhood is still intact is going to descend on this house." He comes forward and strikes Mikal hard on the face. "Get out of here. Go."

The father doesn't say anything or reprimand the boy.

"I'll take him away." Mikal nods. "I'll leave."

Taking a cigarette lighter from his pocket and flicking it alight the son begins to burn a piece of paper with it. Only too late does Mikal realise that it is the American soldier's blood chit.

"We don't want you bringing the Americans into this area," the son says, letting go as the flame creeps towards his fingertips. The last small piece of whiteness falls to the ground with the flame still attached. It is ash by the time it lands. "We are keeping the Kalashnikov and the bullet-proof vest and the dollars," he adds. "The tarpaulin isn't cheap."

"You can keep the pistol for your protection, and also his food," the father says.

"I want the snow leopard too," says the son.

"The cub is mine," Mikal says as vigorously as he can.

The father looks at the son. Then at Mikal. "You can take the cub with you."

Mikal turns to leave the room.

"You said you needed to make a phone call," says the father. He points to a door. "The phone is through there."

There is no answer from Heer. Mikal hangs up and dials a second time but again no one picks up.

Five minutes later he is easing the pickup out of the garage, the father walking beside the vehicle.

"Where will you go?" Fatima appears on the veranda.

"I don't know. I think I'll go to Megiddo. Hide him in the house and go to the school there and try to find a teacher who speaks English."

"Just leave him in the desert and move on," the man says. "Go home. Do what other young men do, watch films and apply for jobs and quarrel with your sisters."

"He knows what happened to Salomi and to Akbar's brother."

"I'll come with you," Fatima says.

"No," says her brother-in-law, raising his hand in the air.

"That's not a good idea," Mikal says gently.

"If I am in the vehicle with you, there will be less chance of you being harassed. They'll respect a woman."

"Fatima," her brother-in-law says. "If they find out who he's got tied up in the back, it's not going to matter who he has sitting with him in the front."

The leopard is curled up in his lap, yawning to show its pale pink tongue, the thick tail twitching in the air. Mikal has a large lunch tied up in a cloth on the passenger seat, along with three Nestlé bottles filled with tap water. There is a bottle of dark brown bitter-smelling oil for the American's arm, though when he is supposed to rub it on he doesn't know, since the plaster cast should stay on for days.

"Be careful," the man says with feeling, just before letting him out.

"Thank you, uncle. And I am sorry."

"I was thinking of letting them deal with him during the night. To save you from yourself."

"I know."

"Maybe I should do it right now."

"I'd better go, uncle."

"Fine. Stay off the road. Go through the desert and keep the Pahari hills on your right. It'll take longer but it's the safer way. When the road floods people often cut through the desert so it can be done. I have done it myself. And now I am beginning to think you should wait till nightfall."

"No. I need to end this as soon as possible so I can go back to Heer."

Children are walking towards the school, and at the crossroads at the end of the street he stops to let a dozen of them pass. A boy, carrying a bag of books twice the size of his torso, reacts to the sound of chains coming from the other side of the tarpaulin and thumps Mikal's door. "What's in the back?"

Mikal sits with his arm out of the window.

"Is it a calf or a goat?"

"It's my brother. It's his wedding day but he doesn't want to get married, so I have tied him up and am taking him to the bride's house."

Noon finds him in a burning plain, the bare crust of the earth enclosed by the rim of hills which the sun illuminates while blinding the onlooker. He keeps a constant watch behind him in the rearview mirror in case he is being followed. To the west of him a pall of dust travels horizontally along the ground and then curves upwards obeying some law of wind he doesn't know, and the hills are pale in the stark light, standing with cruel dignity and grandeur, and the wheels of the pickup crunch over the desert floor, the heat coming in gusts as though the rocks are breathing. It is a reminder that, in contradiction to the Koran, there are some places on earth over which man has no dominion. He drives into the terrace land of low hills eroded by the wind and drives through a pass in the blazing light, looking again and again at the temperature gauge. Soon it is displaying hot, too hot, and he imagines coolant bubbling out of the top of the radiator header tank, the vehicle overheating.

He halts in the shadowed lee of a cliff east of the pass and gets out into the searing wind, the river of heat rushing through the stone channel, and in the flow there are stinging specks of dust and mica. When he lifts the tarpaulin flap at the tailgate, the American's blindfolded head moves instantly in his direction. The man is drenched in sweat and his skin is red, which is what must happen to white people in the heat, he thinks. The red is thick as paint. The cast on the arm is perfectly dry now, a translucent white in the dimness. Mikal removes the blindfold and gives him water, dropping a purification tablet into the bottle beforehand. Afterwards he walks back to the river he drove past a few minutes ago, a precise serpentine curve of water through the landscape. At his approach, a pair of lapwings flees black white black white over the surface, and he stands with his feet in the water, watching them. The river is warm and he feels as though there are two iron hoops at his ankles. He walks into it fully clothed with the leopard on his shoulder, the simple uncomplicated gravity of the creature a relief to him. He lifts silver drops onto the fur with his hands. The sunlight floating on the surface around him in half-molten ingots. He sits down among the reeds that are dead to the root, and then he fills the plastic bottle and comes back to the American. He holds the man's head steady with one hand and begins to trickle water onto him, taking care not to wet the cast, and the man blinks and Mikal wipes the wet hair away from the bruise on the forehead and he blinks and looks up at Mikal and Mikal cups his hands under the jaw to catch the falling water and pours it back up onto the head to cool him. He expels drops from the eyebrows by running the tips of his thumbs over them. Then he stands looking at him.

The man seems fascinated by his missing fingers.

He visits the river four times and when he is finished the American is drenched, the chains and the corrugated bed of the pickup glistening. The air undulates with heat, a killing flood. He sits at the tailgate with the leopard in his lap, as motionless as a toy, feeling his clothes dry by the minute, feeling the American's eyes on him. There are clay nests of swallows high on the tilting face of the cliff. Now and then the American makes a move and there is a clink of chains and Mikal looks towards him. The white man's eyes are a doorway to another world, to a mind shaped by different rules, a different way of life. What kind of a man is he? Is he well spoken, a union of strength and delicacy? Is he in love with someone or is he oblivious? Does he, like Mikal, have a brother?

He opens a tin of food for the cub and places it in front of it and then feeds the American. Afterwards he takes a chapatti and a piece of mutton from the napkin and eats his lunch. The clothes cool his skin as they dry, the shade beginning to feel as good as a rainfall. Now and then the man looks out past Mikal into the heat as though he has heard someone or something. Or he stares fixedly at one spot on the tarpaulin as though someone is standing just on the other side. Sitting wrapped in the chains in the cross-legged position, the good arm bound to the side of him. He seems to doze and after a while so does Mikal. He rouses occasionally and looks at the tide of the cliff's shadow as it revises itself with the sun's movement. Telling himself he'll continue when the jag-line reaches that scrubby bush, that striped rock, that cleft in the earth.

Eventually he gets up and removes a hubcap and fills it from the river and puts it on the passenger seat and places the leopard cub in it.

He sets off across the valley, the sun standing perfectly motionless in the sky. There is grass here and there and it is golden in the sun and in a distant clump of it he sees a black jackal and for a second he mistakes it for the missing Airedale.

An hour later he drives out of the barren valley and begins to climb through the hills. Thin grass and sparse acacias. He lowers his speed when, ahead of him, beside boulders the colour of raw sugar striated with blue, he sees an emaciated man and woman sitting in the dust, with a thin black goat wearing the sole of a rubber slipper around its neck to ward off the evil eye. They tell him they are refugees from the fighting in Afghanistan. Their daughter has died in a bombing raid. "They are still fighting," the woman says. "Her death didn't shame any of them." And then she asks Mikal if he has any jasmine perfume. "The goat won't let us milk it unless we wear the perfume our daughter used to wear when she milked it." Mikal shares some of his food with them.

"Why have you stopped here?" he asks.

"They charge money to let the refugees pass."

"Who?"

The man waves his hand in the direction Mikal is going. "The tribal lords of this area. They have set up a toll on the road. Do you have money to pay them, to pass through?"

There were no tolls on the road when he left Megiddo yesterday. They entrust him to Allah's protecting power and he leaves. After jour-neying through the high rolling desert for half an hour he gets out and climbs to a ridge—going up an incline of thick gravel that lies like wheat escaping from a torn sack—and looks out onto the other side. A quarter-mile ahead of him is the road that he should have taken, and on it he sees a toll booth. A crudely made wooden shed. He immedi-ately drops to the ground. Raising his head thirty seconds later he sees a vehicle coming in his direction, a trail of dust connecting it to the toll booth. Change of any kind is obvious in spare terrain and they have seen him.

"Whatever you're going to do, do it fast," he tells himself.

He turns and is off the ridge in five leaps. Getting back behind the wheel he realises there is nowhere for him to hide and with the vehicle in reverse he crashes into the bushes as fast as he can go, now looking at the side-view mirror, now in front, the water sloshing out of the leopard's hubcap. He takes the pistol out of his waistband and holds it in his left hand and continues until the low-lying stand of mesquite he had seen earlier comes into view. He backs into it, the branches thrashing hectically against the side. The other vehicle comes into view and two men get out a few yards from where he was, looking up at the ridge, one of them with binoculars. After five minutes they get back in and drive off towards the toll booth.

An hour from sunset and he is in a small south-facing valley, sitting among the rocks beside a pool that has small blue flowers growing at its edges. The pickup is on a ridge ten feet directly above him, the door on the driver's side open. He has driven in several directions and met culs-de-sac again and again. He is very hungry and he sits with the leopard in his arms, the creature testing the air with its nose. He walks up to the bush five yards away, the branches full of yellow berries as though hundreds of dots have been made with a thick piece of coloured chalk. Letting their thin blood run from the corners of his mouth he begins to pick and eat them, and as he stands chewing he looks towards the pickup. In the palm of his hand he collects berries for the American and climbs up to the pickup and lifts the tarpaulin flap.

The first thing he sees is that the man is standing up. His left leg is free of the chain. Then he sees that the uninjured right arm is free as well. He sees the hand gripping the knife owned by Fatima's nephew. All that holds the man captive is the chain attached to the right leg and the one attached to the neck ring.

He stands square to Mikal, a cold reptile calculation in his eyes. The skin is raw on the ankle of the freed foot where he has pulled it out of the ring.

Mikal takes in air with great movements of his lungs, his eyes on the man. There is a notch at the bottom of the knife's blade, near the hilt, and he knows it is called the Quetta Notch, meant for stripping sinew, repairing rope nets. He raises his hand to his mouth and begins to eat the berries without taking his eyes off the American. The leopard is in his other hand and madly he wonders why the animal's heartbeat has remained steady unlike his own. He backs away from the tailgate, letting go of the flap, and sprints to the front. He can feel the American turning on the other side of the tarpaulin to keep pace with him, feeling the green and brown gaze through the cloth. He arrives at the open door a second after he hears the sound of breaking glass: the American has broken the long window behind the driver's seat, and is now looking at Mikal through it. The 9 mm is in the hollow between the two seats and Mikal is not sure if the man knows it's there, not sure if he can see it through the broken opening. Is his arm long enough to reach in and grab it?

Once again they hold each other's eyes, breathing fast. He resists the urge to measure the distance between the glass window and the pistol with a quick glance—not wanting to alert the man to the gun's presence. He reaches in just as the American swings the dagger through the window at his arm. The blade cuts through his sleeve without making contact with flesh, just as Mikal closes his fingers around the pistol.

He lifts it and brings it out and is now bending down to release the cub onto the ground. Lifting the flap at the tailgate he stands looking at him, the American with the knife raised in the air and eyes burning.

Mikal points the gun at the hand with the knife. He jabs the barrel and flicks the barrel towards the floor to indicate that the American should drop the knife. He does it three more times. Then he does it with his free hand: he has no index finger to point with, but he hopes the gesture is understood.

The man stands there.

"Do you think I am joking?" Mikal says as he climbs in, letting the flap drop behind him, and moves a step closer and pulls the trigger. The shot rings out across the desert as the bullet goes through the tarpaulin. He points at the dagger again and the man drops it at his feet. Mikal would have to move close to pick it up. "Kick it over." He makes a motion with his feet but the man watches him without obeying.

Mikal repeats the motion and jabs the air with the gun again and it's then that he hears a voice from the other side of the tarpaulin. The American too hears it and looks to his left.

The sunlight from the bullet hole is like a brilliant lance in the enclosed space, dust floating in it in coloured hints and sparks.

Out there several other voices join the first one and Mikal slowly backs away towards the tailgate, hiding the gun in his waistband as he lifts the flap and climbs out to find himself facing a group of two dozen or so men, women and children. A loose gaggle of families, all on foot, some of the children naked, a few of them on their knees beside the pickup's back wheel, talking to the leopard cub hiding under the vehicle.

"We heard a shot," says a man, curiosity playing on his face amongst the points of perspiration. He has a large birdwing moustache, and a thin vertical line is shaved under the nose to keep the two halves of the moustache separate.

"That was the pickup backfiring," Mikal tells him.

They are pilgrims from a village in the western Paharis, journeying overland to a sacred site for a blessing, and they tell him that they have been travelling for a week and that three more days lie before them, unless it rains in which case they'll have to slow down. Mikal doesn't know what to do as he listens, feeling adrift in confusion. He looks around. A man is peering in through the open front door. Mikal walks past him and gently closes the door, a quick glance towards the shattered window but there's nothing to be seen there. Just the toothed line of glass along the rim. Filled with terror, he expects the tarpaulin to be slit with the dagger anytime. "What kind of a shrine is it?" he asks the man who spoke first.

"It is the grave of a Taliban soldier," the man says. "A source of great energy in the ground."

"He was a great warrior and his grave is twenty foot long," a boy of about thirteen says. "The Americans killed him." He is carrying a basket covered with cloth on his head. The man motions towards the basket— which Mikal assumes is full of provisions—but when the man removes the cloth he sees that it contains hand grenades. "To be blessed at the shrine," the boy says. "Then we take it to Afghanistan and throw them at the invaders."

Mikal doesn't know how to extract himself from the situation. The pilgrim women seem about to set up camp beside the pickup. Preparing to make cooking fires. He wonders if he could just take his leave and drive away—but knows the American would reach in with the dagger and attack him.

"They killed two of my sons," one man says. "The Americans. They are worse than Genghis and Halagu Khan."

"I am sorry," Mikal says.

"Thank you." The man leans forward to give Mikal an embrace, a prolonged one to convey the strength of emotions. Afterwards he points to the canvas-covered back of the pickup. "Will you and your family eat with us?"

"We have already eaten."

"The shrine is near Allah-Vasi. If you are going the same way maybe our women and children could ride in the back of the pickup."

"I am going in the other direction."

Some children are stamping on the ground in the dust a few yards away. It is probably a scorpion or a snakeling.

"It's boxthorn," the man says.

Mikal nods. The despised plant. The Prophet Muhammad said, *In the Final Fight between the Muslims and Jews, when a Jew hides behind a rock or a tree, it will say, "O Muslim, O Servant of Allah, there is a Jew behind me, come and kill him." All the trees will do this except the box-thorn, because it is the tree of the Jews.*

"I saw a nest of snakes here earlier," Mikal says, at last struck by inspiration. "Kraits." And it works. The word spreads through the group and immediately everyone gets ready to move on, the children being called closer in alarm, instructions given. Mikal bends down and scoops the leopard cub out from under the pickup and watches the pilgrims gather into a tight knot again. A small wizened woman goes past him, her face carved with deep wrinkles like tree bark, her eyes rheumy and her hair dyed a deep orange with henna. She stops and looks at him and says, "The Americans can take over this entire land." She pauses for breath and her head nods gently as though she is listening to a story. "They can have complete dominion as long as they promise to exterminate every man from it." She spits in the dust and adds: "They are a curse." And then she walks on to join the group. Mikal watches them leave, watches as a man breaks away and comes partway back to him. "Is there anything you'd like us to pray for at the shrine?"

Mikal shakes his head. "Just pray for the whole world."

There wasn't a single clink of the chains during the entire time he conversed with the pilgrims but now it starts up again, loud and constant. The man is standing up, working the dagger into the link of a chain when Mikal climbs in. He stops when Mikal raises the gun. Mikal makes him drop the dagger once again and with the gun pointed he leans forward and reaches out blindly—his eyes fixed on the American's face—picks up the dagger and climbs out into the open.

He stands looking at the sunset. He goes to the front and reaches in without giving the broken window even a single glance and lifts a bottle of water and unscrews the cap and takes half a dozen deep gulps. He puts the dagger under the seat. He goes around to the back and studies the American who is standing exactly where he last saw him.

"If he was angry with you before, wait till he discovers you stole his knife," he says.

The man looks at him.

"Yes, I'm talking to you. *And* you broke the glass window in the pickup owned by his aunt's husband."

Tightening his grip on the 9 mm he climbs onto the bed and gestures for him to sit down, and then moves closer with his eye fixed on the free uninjured arm, beginning the process of securing him again, locking the ring around the free ankle. He gestures for him to put the wrist of the good arm into the ring and he obeys. Then he selects another chain loop and wraps it around the arm and the body three times so he won't be able to reach in through the broken opening, going under the sling, and around the back. He ties the two feet together, winding a length of chain up the shins, not stopping until it is just under the knees. At some point the soldier decides not to make it easy for Mikal. Refusing to move, becoming a dead weight. Energetically passive. Mikal might as well be wrestling with a rock. He knows about these soldiers, their skills in using lethal force in complex and ambiguous conditions, the years of preparation. "Let's show some care with the cast," Mikal says to him. "They'll break Ghulam's arm for putting it on yours." After he is fully bound up again, Mikal says, "We are almost there. I just need to find a way to bypass the toll booth and then we'll be back in Megiddo." And he adds, "We'd better hope Fatima's nephew isn't waiting for us there."

He can see the great helpless rage on his face, the eyes filled with detestation as he inhales long noisy draughts of air. The American soldiers are not allowed to go more than ten kilometres into Waziristan or Pakistan—so he is clearly used to doing things his own way.

"Vere iz gurl vere iz gurl vere iz gurrl," Mikal murmurs to himself as he climbs out. He is shocked that night has fallen, taken aback that he has done everything in the darkness. There is the almost electronic noise of the insects. The moon is out and its light is falling undiluted onto the pale vastness around him. It is as though snow has fallen on the desert.

It's past midnight when he concedes that there is no way to circumvent the toll booth. Leaving the pickup behind, he walks out onto the ledge above the road and squats and examines the land to the east, to the west and north, the road cutting through it. They have placed pieces of wood on the road outside the booth and set them on fire. When the wind changes he can smell the tar of the road burning.

He comes back and gets into the pickup, lowers his forehead onto the steering wheel and closes his eyes for a few seconds. Sleep overpowers him and he dreams that the American soldier has disappeared from the back of the pickup, the sloughed-off chains lying there on the bed. In the dream he panics that he will be attacked by the soldier from any direction and he stands paralysed in the darkness. Then he sees the American, sleepwalking, and he watches as the man approaches and gets into the back of the pickup and carefully begins to rechain himself.

He awakens from the dream but remains in the same position, brow touching the steering wheel, and it's a while before he realises that he can hear a melody. He raises his head. He switches on the flashlight and looks in through the broken opening to see that the soldier is singing to himself. He gets out and stands looking at him from the tailgate, listening to the song shining in the darkness, a sudden Paradise of sound. The man doesn't stop or meet Mikal's gaze, the rapt concentration on his face unchanging as he forms the English words which at one moment seem to be an ecstasy of praise for everything he knows—he, Mikal, everything all humans know in fact—and in the next moment a lament, by turns tender and bloody, a weapon forged out of the steel of woe stabbing at him from the very heart of suffering. Mikal wants to cut open the words with a razor and examine their insides, their secret colours, and he doesn't want to move for fear of breaking the spell and after a while he begins to recognise a few phrases that recur, and after a while he feels that there is nothing else at all in the wide hills and desert but that song and its careful singing and its subtle colours of permanence, the unafraid resonance connecting the two of them across the heat-thinned air.

What he decides to do. He will take the soldier off the pickup, still in chains, and hide him somewhere in the landscape. Then he himself will drive up to the toll booth—let them examine the pickup if they want. Moving on he'll park the vehicle, and return on foot through the hills to the place where he left the American. Bring him back to the pickup and drive on.

He is not sure whether he should wait till dawn to do all this, sleep for a few hours and reconsider everything freshly. He sits thinking, one hand on the leopard, the rib cage rising and falling softly with each precious breath. Tomorrow will be yet another day without him beginning his journey to Heer. He wonders whether he should tie the cub next to the American, because they might want to confiscate it.

With no warning a blazing jewel appears from the darkness, holding itself almost stationary before his eyes for a moment. A pinch of humble dust, the firefly goes by outside and he watches it making its weightless turns for as long as he can. He looks away from the miraculous sight and back at the American, wondering if there are fireflies in his country. Looking through the broken window between them he is suddenly overwhelmed, not by any emotion he knows, suddenly feeling himself unequal to so wide a chase, so remorseless a life. He is shocked to find himself close to weeping, a few initial sobs escaping. He wipes the tears but can't stop and he covers his face with his incomplete hands and weeps loudly, uncontrollably. He reaches out a hand and places it on the man's shoulder and, his mouth full of failed words, tells him about Naheed, the sidelong gold of her look, and about Jeo, and about his incarceration by the Americans and by the warlord who mutilated his hands and sold him to the Americans for $5,000. About Rohan's blindness. About the death of Basie.

"I am sorry I killed your countrymen."

The American is trying to look over his shoulder, or is looking at the hand with the missing finger on his shoulder. All these things are painful for him to know and he wonders how the man would feel about them if he understood them. And so he stops. Not wanting to hurt him more than he has to. Emotions disrupting thoughts, he withdraws his hand eventually and sits facing the front for some minutes.

He drives onto the road half a mile from the toll booth, the speed low, looking to either side of him with a flashlight in search of a location where he might leave the American and the leopard. A wind is carrying the dust from this side of the road to the other, low over the tarmac. When he rounds a curve and sees a toll booth located ten yards ahead of him, it's too late to turn back. He hadn't been able to see this booth from the ledge. A small bulb is lit outside it and the man sitting on a chair outside has risen on seeing Mikal. He is waving for him to stop.

He should have known there would be more than one booth. The entire area is a patchwork of clans, full of rivalries even though descended from a common ancestor who had met Muhammad in Arabia and had been charged by him to take Islam back to Waziristan.

The toll booth is actually a well-built square room of plywood, with a corrugated-iron roof. A gleaming black Corolla station wagon and a Pajero are parked beside it. Mikal lifts the dozing cub from his lap and places it at the base of the passenger seat as fast as he can and covers it with a rag and brings the vehicle to a stop. The man's beard is awry, his eyes blinking in the headlights. He is holding a tired-looking red rose and has an ancient .45 automatic slung at full cock on a belt at his right hip. Behind him the door to the room is open and Mikal can see a number of sleeping figures. The man's eyes take inventory of everything about Mikal.

"Get out of the vehicle. What's your name?"

"Mikal. I am on my way to Megiddo."

"Come out. What's in the back?"

"My mother and sister and my wife," Mikal says as he climbs down, closing the door behind him swiftly.

The man sniffs the petals of the rose, spinning the flower very slowly under his nostrils. "Where are you going with them at this hour?"

"We were meant to be home several hours ago but the pickup broke down."

The man nods. "How many are there? Tell them to come out."

"They're asleep."

The man swears under his breath and walks to the tailgate and kicks it several times. "Wake up." The noise certainly wakes his companions in the room, one of whom utters a curse, another a threat, a third an insult. One stumbles to the door, loosely carrying a Kalashnikov, and after looking around with eyes screwed up, and assessing that there is nothing untoward about the situation, he calls his companion a "dirty infidel" and goes back inside. The man with the rose returns to Mikal.

Mikal reaches into his pocket. "I am very sorry for having troubled you. How much do I owe you?"

"Give me a hundred and go," the man says, holding out the palm of the hand that has the blossom pinched between the tip of the thumb and first finger. He raises himself on his toes and casts a casual glance through the driver's window.

Mikal decides he'll give him 110; but the man is now leaning into the window for a closer look at something. Mikal knows it's the leopard,

and the man confirms it by opening the door and picking up the cub—
he turns and stands facing Mikal.

"Is this yours?"

"Yes. Here's one hundred and ten. I am very sorry to have troubled you."

"How much do you want for it?"

"I can't sell it."

"Why not?"

He studies the man, the cub quivering in his hands. "It's not mine to sell. It's my sister's."

"The sister in the back?" the man says. "Wake her up." He turns his head at an angle and spits on the ground without taking his eyes off Mikal.

"Actually it belongs to my father." Mikal reaches out but the man makes no move to relinquish the cub. There are sleepy murmurs from the booth, muffled protests that the transaction is taking too long, the sound of this conversation interfering with rest.

"Where is your father?" There is a note of menace in the voice now. "Why did you say it was your sister's?"

"It belongs to my whole family. I said what I said because I am tired. It's been a long day."

"They are sound sleepers," the man points to the back of the pickup.

Mikal proffers the money again, giving a quick glance to the automatic at the man's hip. "Here is what I owe."

The man looks deeply at him. "Is the necklace around your neck your sister's too?"

Mikal wasn't aware that it had revealed itself. A small section of it is lying over his collar and he covers it up, sending it below the neckline just as the man reaches into the pickup and takes out the ignition key. His eyes are full of mystery and black silence. It seems that all human relations are to be weighed anew at this site. "Wait here," he says, handing the leopard cub to Mikal. "And I want them out of the back and lined up here in thirty seconds." He turns and walks towards the room, switching on the light in there, shouting at the others to get up.

It takes Mikal five seconds to reach the door of the room and another five to pull it shut with a bang and secure the bolt. The men shout and rattle the door but he is already in the pickup, taking the spare key from the glove compartment and starting the engine. By the twentieth second there are several yards between him and the toll booth, the tyres speeding up, but he knows it won't take much to break down the door.

Ahead on the road he already sees the original toll booth he had been trying to avoid, the pile of wood burning across the road, a Pajero parked outside it. Without slowing down he tears through the flames, brilliant cinders spraying into the night. He hears a gunshot or perhaps it is something in the fire, a knot exploding in a log. Not knowing when he took it out of the waistband, he is holding his gun in his hand. The leopard is clamped between his thighs and the jangle and clatter of chains comes from the back of the pickup and the road winds through the night and it isn't long before he sees a trail of dust raised by the vehicle that is following him, perhaps a mile and a half behind him, the dust glowing faintly in the moonlight the way mist marks the path of a river, and he sees the funnels of two headlights and cannot believe the speed at which they are gaining. He hears the flat reports that long-barrelled guns give over open ground, one bullet shattering the mirror on the passenger's side. And in his own mirror he sees another set of headlights moving across the open desert floor in a pale hovering of raw dust, coming at him at a diagonal. Somewhere ahead is the Wolf River. After crossing the bridge he would be only twenty minutes away from Megiddo.

Sweat is soaking through his clothes. Rounding the corner of the second-to-last hill, he brings the pickup to a sideways halt in the middle of the road. Ahead of him the bridge over the river is burning with flames as tall as electricity poles. He gets out and stands looking at it, pieces of wood falling into the water twenty feet below. The ground seems to shake with the force of the fire, as though the dead are making room for him down there—a vision of Allah's left side on the Day of Judgement.

He takes the tarpaulin off the frame, undoing the straps that fasten it to the metal. The American, exposed, looks at the fire in astonishment. Mikal drags the tarpaulin towards where the ground slopes

towards a gravel bar at the edge of the river, and walks into the river
with the heavy cloth until he is up to his waist in the moving water,
pushing the folds of the tarpaulin under with both his hands. He looks
up towards the bridge—calculating how many of its wooden planks are
gone. The burning pieces fall and hiss as they meet the red-lit water.
By sitting down and dipping his head below the surface he drenches
himself completely, and then walks out of the river dragging the soaked
tarpaulin behind him, twice as heavy as before.

He comes up the slope and the American begins to struggle wildly
against the chains when he sees him appear with the waterlogged cloth,
fully comprehending what Mikal has in mind. The man twists with his
teeth gritted and then screams the English word Mikal does understand,
"No! No! No! No! No!" feet scrabbling against the metal bed, running
sideways. Mikal hurls the tarpaulin onto him like a fisherman's net, dripping golden drops, losing his balance from the swing for a moment, and
then climbing up after it, making sure that the man is entirely covered.
He leaps off the bed and gets in behind the steering wheel, putting the
cub under his wet shirt. Working the steering wheel as fast as he can he
aims the pickup into the mouth of the fire. *I thought of your beauty and
this arrow made of a wild thought is in my marrow.* The words Naheed
had quoted.

He enters the blind lethal power of a hundred suns and the American hasn't stopped shouting or struggling under the tarpaulin and the
tyres judder as they go over the burning planks, the thickets of flame
pressed against the vehicle, twisting in their own hot wind and the fire
has a sound too, the roar of a primordial beast, the sound of the river
fading within it, but as he progresses across the bridge it returns, the
flame suddenly silent, and the phenomenon repeats itself as he moves
forward, the blunt needles of the cub's paws digging into his skin,
the heat becoming unbearable and soon he realises that he is saying
Naheed's name, calling out to her in desperation, because he has to get
across, because the bridge is the bridge between the innermost part of
him and the American's, something that can't be consumed or rendered
meaningless even by fire, a bridge to his parents and Basie, to a world
where Jeo is still alive and where Tara never went to prison, to the white-

hot core of the fire, the flash that took away Rohan's sight. He won't let them catch the American soldier, and at that moment he loves the American soldier, and he loves the two he killed, and he loves the dead girl who wore jasmine, so much so that he feels his heart will not bear the weight of it and will kill him before the fire kills him. The pickup lurches from side to side as the planks break under it. The flames reach in when the windshield blackens before his eyes and then cracks with a shear of light, and he no longer knows if he is moving in a horizontal line or falling through the air vertically with the vehicle covered in flames. But then suddenly he is on the other side. He stops and opens the door and, dropping the cub onto the ground, struggles back onto the bed of the pickup, feeling as though he is doing it with extreme slowness. He coughs the smoke out of his lungs. Catches a glimpse of the burning tyres as he goes, the blistered paintwork.

The tarpaulin is on fire here and there in coin-sized patches and he rips it off the American, revealing him and his chains. Long fronds of steam are attached to them, taking fresh shapes with each new second, the sling and plaster cast smouldering a fevered red in one place.

The man gasping for breath. Mikal smothers the fire on the plaster and touches the chains to see if they are hot and then wipes the sweat and condensation from the American's eyes with both hands. When he climbs down he sees the group of men ten feet away from the pickup, the hostile spirits of unfamiliar places, lit by the burning bridge. More than a dozen guns are pointed at him and at the American, and one of the men is holding the cub. He is as large and strong as the American. Mikal stands watching them with his hands placed on top of his head, all the exhaustions of his life catching up with him.

The room they are put into has the odour of dust. A hood has been placed over the American's head, his chains removed. Mikal gave them the keys and several of the men climbed onto the pickup's bed. Instead of freeing the American completely from the chains they unlocked the strands that bound him to the pickup and carried him down like a metal effigy, a chainmailed knight.

He doesn't know where they are—Waziristan or Afghanistan. The wrists of both of them are tied behind their backs.

They travelled through the darkness until the modest birds of the desert had appeared in the young air, and the sun climbed in long lengths of gold, scarlet and silver, and begun to burn without diminishing, and it was midmorning by the time they arrived at a small village and drove through its central street full of rolling dust, past the mosque, the few shops, a dozen children and almost as many dogs running behind their truck. The truck stopped at the gate of the largest house on the other side of the village and one of the men from the back leapt out and opened the gate and the truck drove through into a large courtyard filled with towering she-date palms in flower.

They left them here in the room and went away. Mikal had refused to answer their questions concerning the American and had watched them puzzle over the situation. Should they release Mikal? He had after all captured the American and put him in chains. But what lay behind Mikal's ambivalence, almost tenderness, towards the soldier?

Mikal looks at him in the semidarkness. The cloth bag over the head. The singed cast on the arm. The fabric of the shalwar kameez that is minutely wrinkled from where Mikal had wound the chains about him.

It is an underground room and the floor is of large unglazed clay tiles, badly out of line, like the walls. There is a high glassless window from which a shaft of light barely reaches the floor, most of it dissolving in the darkness above their heads. He sleeps in dreamless exhaustion and wakes some time later when the door at the top of the stairs opens. An old man is climbing down very slowly. He comes and stands looking at Mikal and the American. It is obvious that he doesn't see very well. The silhouettes of several children have appeared at the door at the top of the stairs and the man walks to the lowest step and raises his antler-like hands, shouts at them and they scatter. He is small and dark and Mikal suddenly has a feeling that the smell of dust and soil is coming from him. As though in old age he has decided to slowly revert back to what humans are made of.

"Do you want something to eat?" he asks Mikal quietly.

Mikal nods. "What about the white man?"

The man's black eyes look at the cloaked head. "I'll see what I can do." He takes a step closer to Mikal.

"Did you catch him deliberately? To claim the bounty offered by that Arab guerrilla?"

"No."

"Who are you?" the man says.

It is hot in the room and he can see the drops of sweat on the man's abraded brow.

Mikal shakes his head. They remain silent.

"I am looking for some people," Mikal says. "I think they have been taken away by"—he nods towards the American—"his people."

"Westerners."

"Yes."

"Westerners," the old man says in his raspy voice.

"Yes."

"What is your name?"

"Mikal."

The old man says the name in silence to himself. "Who are your people?"

"You wouldn't know. I am not from Waziristan."

The man thinks. "You caught him yesterday? It was a day with three suns."

"There was a sun and two sundogs, one on either side, yes."

"It's mentioned in great and ancient books."

Mikal nods. He'd read about sundogs in his astronomy books. The man looks at the American. "I fought against Westerners when they were here in the 1930s." He closes his eyes and opens them again. In the weak light the eyes betray nothing. He seems to be studying the shadows in the room.

"I myself was held captive by the Americans," Mikal says. "I didn't really know what they wanted from me. I am afraid of what they might be doing to the people they have picked up."

"We can't know what the Westerners want," the old man says. "To know what they want you have to eat what they eat, wear what they wear, breathe the air they breathe. You have to be born where they are born."

"I am not sure. You mentioned books. We can learn things from books."

"No one from here can know what the Westerners know," the man says. "The Westerners are unknowable to us. The divide is too great, too final. It's like asking what the dead or the unborn know."

The man reaches out a trembling hand in the partial light and wipes the sweat off Mikal's brow. He is shocked to find it cold. Hard and bloodless.

"Is this your place?" Mikal asks. "What will happen to us, me and him?"

"I am just a servant. They will decide tonight. They have sent for all the leaders of the surrounding tribes."

The man turns to go.

"I need to make a phone call," Mikal says, realising how absurd it sounds as he says it. "I need to tell someone that I am coming back, need to tell her not to lose heart."

"Is she your love?"

"Yes, but she might have to marry someone else."

The man's nod is a reminder that certain things will persist in the world. He nods and then continues towards the stairs.

The sunlight from the high window has become dark yellow when the old man returns and reaches behind Mikal and slowly unbinds his hands. "I have been told to bring you out. They want to talk to you."

Mikal follows the old man up the stairs and they go out into the large courtyard. Somewhere nearby a cow has just been slaughtered. Several men cross their path with tubs full of glistening meat—one is holding a set of bloody knives, another is dragging an enormous rear leg, the hoof scoring a line on the packed earth of the courtyard. The singed pickup has been brought here from the riverbank and sits propped on stacks of bricks in one corner, its charred tyres taken off. Two boys appear—they must be children of servants because their clothes are dirty and their hair matted, the teeth already yellow—and they walk at a distance behind Mikal and the old man, their words coming to Mikal. "He single-handedly caught the American, who killed fifty dear Muslims and cut out their hearts . . ." "The American will be released into the hills tomorrow and hunted with dogs . . ." "The American stole his uncle's pickup and he gave chase and caught him . . ." The old man turns around and his mere glance is enough to make the boys vanish, and then Mikal and the old man go along a veranda that is being washed and wiped with a rag by three small children.

They enter a room. It is the house of a very rich family, the doors tall with great brass hinges, the ceilings four times as high as the doors. Sitting in the room on a large overstuffed sofa is the hale-looking man with the eagle's profile Mikal remembers from the burning bridge. He had made to shoot off the American's chains until Mikal gave him the keys. He is in his early thirties, a bandolier full of rifle bullets crossing his torso at a diagonal, a pistol in a holster of tooled black leather under the armpit. He is holding the dagger. On the table in front of him there is a half-eaten meal, a newspaper and a plastic vase full of plastic flowers. He glances briefly at Mikal and then goes back to contemplating the dagger.

"What is your name?" he asks without looking up. The floor at his feet is glistening in wet arcs, some small, others wide, depending on the length of the children's arms.

"I think I've told you that already," Mikal says.

The man raises his head and stares at him. Then he puts the dagger on the newspaper. Even his small gestures are expansive, referring to and taking in his entire mansion.

"Tell me about the American."

"There's nothing to tell. I found him in the desert."

"Why didn't you kill him the moment you saw him? Don't you know they are at war with us?"

"Where's the leopard cub?"

"Tell me," the man leans forward and says, "have you heard of a lady called Madeleine? No? In 1996, this lady named Albright Madeleine, the US ambassador to the United Nations, was asked on television how she felt about the fact that five hundred thousand Iraqi children had died as a result of US economic sanctions. Do you know what she said? She said that it was 'a very hard choice' but 'we think the price is worth it.' These are her exact words. How do you feel about that?"

"How do you think I feel about that? And I would take your love for children more seriously if you didn't have children cleaning your floors."

The man watches him for a while, then says, "Do you think having them clean floors is as bad as starving them to death?"

"That is not what I said."

The man waves him away. "I have decided to let you go."

"I am not leaving without the American soldier or the cub."

There is a laugh of mockery.

The old servant touches Mikal's arm but Mikal doesn't acknowledge it. "I am not leaving."

The man stands up.

"You are used to giving orders, aren't you?" Mikal says.

"It's worse than you think. I'm used to being obeyed."

Mikal stands outside the house all afternoon, the sun burning above him, hearing sounds from the other side of the tall gate, the watchman conversing with someone now and then. The gate is opened when a vehicle arrives and the watchman gives him a glance before closing the gate again.

"Is it true the American violated and then murdered the woman you love?" he asks Mikal from the other side.

"No."

Just as the sun is setting he begins to walk away from the house. He walks into the street that passes through the village, the shops selling rice and cooking oil, threads and buttons, children's sweets, gram flour, rice husk to feed horses or scrub cooking pots. He asks if there is a public telephone he might use but there is none. He buys a mango, the vendor telling him that it is the same variety that Alexander the Great had tasted, and he eats it with the skin on as he continues along the street. He encounters himself in the darkness at the back of a shop, halts, and realises it's a mirror. He sits down to rest on the other side of the street, where the fields begin, and watches a convoy of vehicles move towards the house at the other end. He sits listening to the call to prayer issuing from the minaret—the concentric circles of sound expanding in the air, making it seem that this is the very centre of the earth. The call rising from the core of the planet. But then it ends abruptly halfway through, something suddenly going wrong with the loudspeaker. He goes into the mosque and washes the dust and sweat off his face and then stands in a row with the others to say his prayers. Afterwards he sits on the mat and tries to ask questions about the owners of the large house. He walks out of the mosque and buys food from a teahouse, flies spinning around the place like marbles swirled in a jar, and he feeds the bones from his meat to a street dog, talking to it in words and whistles, much to the displeasure of the owner and the other diners. He asks them questions about the family that owns the house. At around ten in the evening, as he sits smoking a cigarette at the edge of the emptying street, listening to the music of the crickets, he sees the old man in the distance.

Mikal stands up and walks towards him.

"I have come to ask you to leave for your own good," the man says. "They have seen that you are still here and they want to bring you back to the house."

"I'll come."

"No. I am here to warn you. You should leave."

"I can't."

"If I steal the leopard for you, will you leave?"

"No. Not just the leopard."

"Go," the man says. "If they catch you they won't release you again."

He stands there, shaking his head. "Have they done anything to him?"

"I don't know. I told you I am only a servant." Just then he sees a giant in a black turban walking towards the two of them.

"He has come to fetch you," the old man says. "Run away. Go."

"No," Mikal says, walking towards the man in the distance.

He emerges from the house two hours later and walks into the hills, feeling himself to be an addition to the ghost-life of the night, the thousand desert stars above him, each of them blinking alone. The dark air is warm around him and his feet crush the scent from a fragrant hill plant as he climbs upwards. Looking back now and then at the village lights receding behind him, nothing eventually except the bulb at the tip of the mosque's minaret. And then that too disappears. An hour later in a valley sculpted of rock he lies down at the edge of a stream, the trees pale as paper around him. Sleeping close to the ground, the insulted earth, he enters a nightmare . . . Or perhaps it is a confusion of dream and memory of what he saw a few hours ago . . .

Around two he wakes and realises that a beam of light passing over his face has roused him, a shaft of gluey brightness. He rolls over on his stomach and watches the four vehicles containing Americans. They pass within yards of him. Commandos or task-force soldiers or intelligence collectors. After they are gone he gets up and begins to walk back to the village as fast as he can, breaking into a run until a stitch appears at his side, letting it dissolve and then running again. During sleep he has clenched his hands in anguish and two of his nails are bloody. He passes through the dark abandoned street, whistling when a pair of dogs begin to roar at him, and they fall silent immediately. He approaches the large house from the rear and is on the roof within five minutes, climbing onto the water tank and leaping down. He goes along the wide raw-brick expanse of the roof. Climbs a set of open banister-less stairs onto a lower roof. The courtyard below is scattered about with squares and rectangles of pale light, the date trees dark, and he crosses it weaving from shadow to shadow. He pushes open the kitchen door and reaching into the tandoor finds a lump of coal and puts it in his pocket. He turns and is about to walk out when he hears a sound.

"I knew you'd come back," the old man says. A core of light with blurred edges flicks on and reveals him standing in the far corner with the leopard cub. He comes forward and hands Mikal a key, the leopard and finally the flashlight. "The key is to the room where he is. I have also unlocked the gate. You can just walk out."

"Why are you doing this?"

"My son is in American custody. If I am kind to him maybe they'll be kind to him."

"I wonder if that's how it works."

"Where will you take him?"

"I don't know."

"He won't be able to walk very far."

"Can you get me the keys to one of the cars?"

"They'll hear the engine."

"Yes." He switches off the flashlight and walks towards the kitchen door.

"Do you feel your amputated fingers?" the man asks him through the darkness.

"Sometimes."

"Then it's a sign that Afterlife exists."

With the piece of coal Mikal begins to draw a jeep on the floor. The American watches him. On the bonnet he draws a large American flag. He points to the drawing and then upwards beyond the stairs.

Just as they leave the gate, a light comes on behind them and someone shouts. The American is leaning on him, the weight making Mikal feel like he is wearing the chains. In the darkness he keeps his eyes on the light at the minaret's tip. They enter the street and when they come to the mosque he motions for the American to sit down behind the stand of canna lilies planted along the shadowed front step. Putting his feet into alcoves and mouldings on the facade, he scales the wall, his two damaged nails leaving small red smears as he goes. He leaps into the courtyard on the other side and opens the door to let in the American. He locks the door again and bends down to unlace the American's boots and take them off. Against the wall behind them is the plank of wood on which the dead are bathed. He takes off his own shoes and then both of them enter the sacred building, the weave of the reed prayer mats shifting under their feet. Entering the main prayer hall he bolts the door behind them and walks to the cupboard beside the *mimbar* pulpit and opens it. Inside is the equipment that allows the muezzin to call the faithful to prayer—the ancient amplifier and the steel microphone shaped like the head of a golf club. He hears people gathering at the mosque's front door, someone asking for a ladder to be brought, a rope.

Mikal switches on the amplifier—several small red lights becoming illuminated—and gestures towards the microphone.

"Call out to them," he says in Pashto. "Call them. Tell them where to come and find you. Tell them to come to the mosque." Perhaps he should draw the picture of the jeep with the American flag again, but the American seems to grasp the idea immediately and nods.

There is no knowing if the Americans Mikal saw are within hearing range, but there is no alternative. When and if the Americans come there will be a fierce gunfight. The white man begins to speak but they hear nothing from the minaret, no echo of his words outside, no amplification. Mikal twists the volume button up to maximum but it makes no difference. Then he remembers how, earlier in the evening, the call to prayer had ended abruptly only partway through.

The American has stopped speaking and is bending down to examine the wire that emerges from the back of the amplifier, leaves the cupboard and climbs up to a transom window located near the ceiling, going out and connecting to the loudspeaker at the tip of the minaret. He points to a six-inch gap where the wire has melted away due to a power surge.

Mikal stands looking at it, the sounds outside the door getting louder. There are footsteps in the courtyard, that susurration of the reed prayer mats. Reaching behind his neck he undoes the clasp of the necklace. With two quick twists he splices the necklace into the gap in the amplifier's wire, completing the circuit.

The American takes up the microphone again and the room fills immediately with the sound of his breath magnified ten, twenty, thirty times. It seems to put swords in the air. The minaret, meant to invite the faithful to offer prayer and praise to the Almighty, is summoning unbelievers, to arrive and desecrate His house. The words spread through the darkness and over the clay shale and hills and flatlands, the bouldered desert that had watched the arrival of humans many centuries ago, and that has witnessed the shedding of older blood, prophets and lovers, pilgrims and warners.

· · ·

It takes fifteen minutes for the Special Forces soldiers to arrive at the mosque, and the school-bus-sized Chinook helicopter appears overhead a further ten minutes later, the blades whumping.

"American hostage!" the white man shouts through the locked door of the prayer hall. "American hostage! American hostage!" He had kept talking via the mosque's loudspeaker for a full seven minutes, summoning his countrymen, guiding them. But then the loudspeaker had stopped working. The heat of the electricity had melted the necklace.

Mikal stands beside the American with his back pressed against the wall, and the cub cheeping its distress in the crook of his elbow. He is thinking of Naheed, near whom what mattered was whether he was good or bad—not strong or weak, not favoured by God or cursed. The commandos are coming closer and closer to the prayer hall, blowing their way in with explosives through walls and doors.

"American hostage, open the door and approach me on your left with your hands in the air and lie down on the ground!"

The white man takes Mikal firmly by the wrist and unlatches the door.

Under heavy fire, the American soldier is half dragged, half carried out of the mosque by the commandos. Through the blur of English and Pashto shouts and the screams of the wounded, and the flare and smoke of explosions, he is hurried to a dimly outlined cornfield behind the building where the helicopter has landed. The commandos tell him they will go back and attempt to look for the boy with the leopard cub. When exactly in the confusion and carnage his wrist slipped out of his grip, he doesn't know. And it is too soon to know whose face it was that he saw, with a red knot on the upper part of the forehead and several lines running down from it to spread out over the features, as though someone tried to draw a branch of coral on the skin. Later he will try to bring order to the various memory fragments, slide them correctly into a sequence. For now the Chinook is rising into the air, above the blink of muzzle flashes, and some of the soldiers are leaning out and firing downwards, the mosque getting smaller and smaller, and then the helicopter swings away from the violence of war and the building disappears completely, nothing but stars shining in the final blackness, each marking a place where a soul and all the mysteries living in it might flourish, perennial with the earth.

37

It is still dark above Pakistan, and in the distances the sky and the ground can be distinguished only with difficulty. Three-quarters of an hour before sunrise, a few luminous bands of orange appear above the eastern horizon—light compressed yet breathing at the very edge of the world. Then it disappears and there is greyness, followed by moments of growing blue light. The sun when it comes up is a surprise—the world appearing once more, the usual rules seeming to apply.

Naheed stands on the dew-covered path, her face serious.

"What are you doing?" he had asked her last week, before he left for Waziristan. She was spreading paint onto the petals of a flower, making its yellow more vivid. She was using Sofia's paintbox and one of her thin brushes.

"Next year when this plant blooms again, Father will be completely blind," she had told him. "So I want to make sure he can see it today."

The brush had travelled along the outline of the petals carefully one last time, and then she had washed the yellow paint off the soft bristles and begun to add small points of red inside the flower's throat.

He had walked into Sofia's room and located another paintbox and brush and had clambered up pillars and tree trunks, painting the flowers above her, disappearing from sight now and then, using rainwater pooled in the crevices of the bark, the drops collected on the leaves, or his own saliva when no other liquid was nearby, the creases in his lips as filled with colour as the lines he drew on some of the petals, the roses and the crepe myrtle, the drab blossoms of the music tree that grow straight out of the trunk, the thorny pink cassia. He met birds in the canopies, exploding flocks of them as he leant down into the Rangoon creeper with the white-loaded brush, humming.

She breathes the dawn air, thinking of the moment he will return pale with road dust and with her necklace at his throat. Damaged and scarred, he is still perfect and she sees why the gods might wish to use human beings as instruments.

IV

Isaiah

For all the boots of the tramping warriors
and all the garments rolled in blood
shall be burned as fuel for the fire.

—*Isaiah*

38

Year by year the irises enlarge their colonies. Three erect petals with three sepals—each blossom on its hollow stem is slate blue with veins of a darker shade, and a cavity of silk at the centre. Naheed stands beside them and turns her head to see the two children playing with the toy truck. Mikal's son and that of Basie and Yasmin. They run along the paths with it, their shouts filling the clear rain-cooled air.

She enters the kitchen and begins to make chapattis, shaping them carefully so that it is pleasure as well as work. Mikal had pointed out that she rolls the ball of dough in the palm of her hand anticlockwise. Like Tara and Yasmin. He had no memory of how his own mother did it.

These years later, his child is out there on the red path with his cousin.

She counts the chapattis, knowing how many each person will eat. Yasmin teaches at the Aligarh Secondary and High School and will return home soon and they will sit down to eat together. Father Mede has never been heard from since the siege but his school is slowly being rebuilt. By the time it is ready Naheed herself will have qualified as a teacher. She knows about Galileo singing to mark time as he measured the pull of gravity, and Newton carefully inserting a needle behind his own eye to learn how light causes vibrations in the retina, and Syed Ahmed Khan saying, "There is no difference between the word of Allah and the work of Allah."

She imagines what the boys will be like as young men—reserved in manner on the whole, but with a component of laughing wildness in the personality, revealing itself occasionally.

Within the garden she has tied a cord from place to place. They refer to it as the "rope walk" and it connects all the different plants and locations Rohan likes to visit. Rohan makes his way through the garden by holding on to it, feeling his way along the red line zigzagging through the trees. Sometimes the children suggest that it should continue outside the house too, a thread connecting the house to the mosque, the bazaars, the houses of acquaintances. The rope walk takes in Sofia's study. And it leads from Baghdad House to Mecca House, from Cairo House to Cordoba House and Ottoman House, and finally to Delhi House, the banyan above it and the laden warm sway of mangoes on two-foot-long stalks.

Ardent Spirit is still there on the other side of the river, though Kyra has disappeared and is wanted by the government, according to the newspapers. Some say he is in Iraq or Waziristan. Ardent Spirit is now run by the government and for the time being Rohan and his family are allowed to remain at the house, their status and life precarious, but no worse or better than most in this heartbroken and sorrowful land.

Naheed watches the boys, Tara chewing fennel seeds for a minute to soften them and then passing them from her mouth into theirs. Tara, who had moved in here when the family prevented Sharif Sharif from marrying Naheed, and he asked Tara to leave her home. They are outside Ottoman House. Each yellow tulip that grows outside it has a dark brown pupil at the base of the cup, and to look into it is to feel that the flower is returning the gift of attention—strengthening one's existence that way. The parentage of Mikal and Naheed's son is a secret from the neighbourhood. Halfway through the pregnancies Naheed and Yasmin went away to a distant village and returned after the births, with the claim that Yasmin had had twins. It's a lie no one would rather tell but there is no alternative, and again they remind themselves that they are more fortunate than many in this country.

And so she watches the boys, engaged in their games and small conspiracies out there, the years slowly passing as she waits for Mikal who is by now more a feeling than a person, a sensation in the breast and a penumbra of associations created by separation, the days lengthening and shortening and the arrival and disappearance of seasonal fruits and vegetables in this kitchen. At night sometimes she sees him when the lightning reveals the faces of prophets and kings suspended in the bark of the surrounding trees. He had told her that the brightest planet in the sky was Jupiter and storms had raged on its surface for hundreds of *years.*

She had waited for him once before, and that time too everyone said he was no longer alive.

In the glasshouse Rohan touches the germinating seeds with his fingertips and recites a verse from the Koran. *It is God who splits the seed and the fruit stone. He brings forth the living from the dead and the dead from the living . . .*

She looks up from the page she has been reading just as the gate opens to admit Mikal. Perhaps it is his ghost, here to convince her to continue with her life without him. He raises his hand slowly and she stands up and walks towards him, her own hand held out. The insects weave a gauze of sound in the air. She moves towards him and her eyes are full of a still intensity—as though aware of the unnamed, unseen forces in the world, and attempting in her mind to name and see them.

ACKNOWLEDGEMENTS

This is a work of fiction. The characters, events and organisations depicted in it are either the author's creation or are used fictitiously. No resemblance is intended to any persons, living or dead, or to any organisations and events, past or present.

My first debt is to Candia McWilliam, from whose perfect novel *Debatable Land* I have taken the words "Ardent Spirit." The italicised lines on page 20 are from *The Temptation to Exist* by E. M. Cioran (The University of Chicago Press, 1968). The italicised passage on page 120 is from Salman Rushdie's *The Moor's Last Sigh* (Jonathan Cape, 1996). The letter quoted on page 140 is by Walt Whitman, from *Walt Whitman's Civil War*, edited by Walter Lowenfels (Da Capo Press, 1960). The line that ends the section on page 245 is the reverse of one to be found in *Mitti ki Kaan* by Afzal Ahmed Syed (Aaj Publications, Karachi, 2009). The original reads, "Love is *not* a distinguishing mark, something by which a dead body can be identified." (My italics.) The italicised words that end the chapter on page 290 are by Simone Weil. The lines Mikal remembers on page 346 are by W. B. Yeats. A book I found helpful was *The Interrogator's War* by Chris Mackey with Greg Miller (John Murray, 2004). Another was *Beslan* by Timothy Phillips (Granta Books, 2008). An early study for chapter 16 appeared in *Granta* 116: *Ten Years Later*. I am grateful to John Freeman and Ellah Allfrey for their advice and kindness.

Thank you Salman Rashid, as always. Lewis Burns. Mrs. Shamim Akram. Andrew Wylie, Sarah Chalfant and Charles Buchan. Stephen Page, Lee Brackstone and Angus Cargill in London, and Diana Coglianese and Sonny Mehta in New York.

A NOTE ON THE TYPE

This book was set in Minion, a typeface produced by the Adobe
Corporation specifically for the Macintosh personal computer, and
released in 1990. Designed by Robert Slimbach, Minion combines
the classic characteristics of old-style faces with the full complement
of weights required for modern typesetting.

TYPESET BY SCRIBE, PHILADELPHIA, PENNSYLVANIA

PRINTED AND BOUND BY BERRYVILLE GRAPHICS,
BERRYVILLE, VIRGINIA

DESIGNED BY ROBERT C. OLSSON